WESTERN

Rugged men looking for love...

The Maverick's Christmas Countdown
Heatherly Bell

A Rancher's Return
Jen Gilroy

MILLS & BOON

Heatherly Bell is acknowledged as the author of this work
THE MAVERICK'S CHRISTMAS COUNTDOWN
© 2024 by Harlequin Enterprises ULC
Philippine Copyright 2024
Australian Copyright 2024
New Zealand Copyright 2024

First Published 2024
First Australian Paperback Edition 2024
ISBN 978 1 038 93558 8

A RANCHER'S RETURN
© 2024 by Jen Gilroy
Philippine Copyright 2024
Australian Copyright 2024
New Zealand Copyright 2024

First Published 2024
First Australian Paperback Edition 2024
ISBN 978 1 038 93558 8

® and ™ (apart from those relating to FSC ®) are trademarks of Harlequin Enterprises (Australia) Pty Limited or its corporate affiliates. Trademarks indicated with ® are registered in Australia, New Zealand and in other countries.
Contact admin_legal@Harlequin.ca for details.

This is a work of fiction. Names, characters, places, and incidents are either the product of the author's imagination or are used fictitiously, and any resemblance to actual persons, living or dead, business establishments, events, or locales is entirely coincidental.

MIX
Paper | Supporting
responsible forestry
FSC® C001695
www.fsc.org

Published by
Harlequin Mills & Boon
An imprint of Harlequin Enterprises (Australia) Pty Limited
(ABN 47 001 180 918), a subsidiary of HarperCollins
Publishers Australia Pty Limited
(ABN 36 009 913 517)
Level 19, 201 Elizabeth Street
SYDNEY NSW 2000 AUSTRALIA

Cover art used by arrangement with Harlequin Books S.A.. All rights reserved.

Printed and bound in Australia by McPherson's Printing Group

The Maverick's Christmas Countdown

Heatherly Bell

MILLS & BOON

Bestselling author **Heatherly Bell** was born in Tuscaloosa, Alabama, but lost her accent by the time she was two. After leaving Alabama, Heatherly lived with her family in Puerto Rico and Maryland before being transplanted kicking and screaming to the California Bay Area. She now loves it here, she swears. Except the traffic.

Books by Heatherly Bell

Montana Mavericks: The Trail to Tenacity

The Maverick's Christmas Countdown

Charming, Texas

Winning Mr. Charming
The Charming Checklist
A Charming Christmas Arrangement
A Charming Single Dad
A Charming Doorstep Baby
Once Upon a Charming Bookshop
Her Fake Boyfriend

The Fortunes of Texas: Hitting the Jackpot

Winning Her Fortune

Montana Mavericks: The Real Cowboys of Bronco Heights

Grand-Prize Cowboy

Wildfire Ridge

More than One Night
Reluctant Hometown Hero
The Right Moment

Visit the Author Profile page
at millsandboon.com.au for more titles.

Dear Reader,

I hope you love Christmas as much as I do!

I wrote much of this book during the holidays last year. Some authors have to re-create Christmas during the summer they are writing their book, and honestly, that's not a bad idea. I was lucky enough to have Christmas going on all around me as I was writing. The tree was up in mid-November, and I happily posted a photo on social media with the words: *No, it's not too soon*.

For me, the holidays are a time for decorating with wreaths and garlands, baking, family get-togethers, big dinners, tree lighting ceremonies, parades and cookie exchanges. (Did somebody say *cookie*? No wonder I love this holiday!) These activities are some of the fun our heroine, Allison Taylor, and her friend Rowan Scott get into this season. They are forced to fake being in love, and what do you know, it happens for real. That's Christmas for you. Love is the biggest gift of all.

From my house to yours, I wish you a joyous and safe holiday season.

Happy reading—and happy holidays!

Heatherly Bell

To everyone who loves Christmas.

CHAPTER ONE

"ENGLISH WAS MY favorite subject in high school," Allison Taylor said from her stool at the kitchen counter.

On this sunny December day in Bronco, she was helping her niece, Jill Abernathy, with her homework.

"I'm more of a math and science person, and I don't know what to do with this assignment." Jill's big eyes were narrowed in confusion. "I'm supposed to pick a book and then find a parallel to something in my own life."

Allison rubbed her hands together. "Oooh, it sounds like an essay, my favorite kind of assignment!"

"I wish it were *already* Christmas break. Then I could have some fun and relax." Jill's shoulders slumped. "Would you help me figure this out? I don't know how a book is anything like real life!"

Allison had been about Jill's age when her older sister Charlotte and Billy Abernathy had first fallen in love as teenagers. His daughter was now Charlotte's stepdaughter, and reminded Allison so much of her father as a teen. Same eyes, same easygoing attitude. But, at the moment, she was clearly frustrated, as though there was so much she'd rather do than sit inside with a book. Just like Billy, who'd always preferred to spend his time running the Bonnie B ranch. According to Charlotte,

Jill had demonstrated an aptitude in math and science, but she was still finding her way as a fourteen-year-old in her first year of high school. Allison would let her sister encourage all things STEM, but she would do what she could to encourage a love of reading.

"Actually your life is probably a lot more like a Western book." Allison chuckled.

"Ugh, I'm sick of cowboys. Bronco's just a boring town full of cowboys."

"How about a Christmas theme? Then you can tie it into what you're doing right now. Looking forward to the holiday. Shopping, decorating, gift giving." Allison couldn't help but make at least one specific suggestion. "One of *my* favorite holiday stories is *The Gift of the Magi*. It's a classic. You should check it out."

"Great idea. Thanks, Aunt Allison!" Jill stood and rushed up the steps, past Charlotte, who was slowly coming down them.

Charlotte padded into the kitchen in her robe and slippers, fresh from a nap. She was due soon, a scheduled C-section next month. At thirty-eight, she'd been ordered to take it easy for the rest of the pregnancy.

"You're so good with her. The boys, too. Face it, you're good with kids."

Allison sighed. She didn't want to dwell on the envy she felt rolling through her every time she looked at Charlotte's swollen belly or felt the baby's swift kick against her palm. Her big sister deserved all this joy and happiness and more. Over twenty years ago, she'd been a pregnant teenager with Billy's child, but had had a devastating miscarriage a few weeks into the pregnancy. Even though they were still to get married, in a rather huge wedding thrown by the Taylors and Abernathys, seventeen-year-old Charlotte had had second thoughts. She'd abandoned Billy at the altar to fulfill her dream of becoming a marine biologist.

She and Billy had spent over two decades apart but were together now, and it was a beautiful thing to watch.

Allison stood to pour hot water from the kettle into a mug. "Maybe it's because your stepkids are great. Anyway, someday I'll meet the right man."

"Whatever happened to that guy you were dating a few months ago? He sounded so promising."

"Don't remind me. He was a dud dressed in prince clothing."

Allison still cringed remembering the way he'd invited her to a fancy dinner just to inform her he worried she was getting way too attached to their relationship.

"I think we might want different things," he'd said in a patronizing tone that had made her want to down her pricy cocktail as fast as possible. "I'm not ready to settle down, and I can see the eagerness in your eyes. After all, I'm only thirty-eight."

For the record, there had been no such eagerness on her part.

Charlotte made a face. "I'm sorry. You've sure had to kiss a lot of frogs."

"Look at it this way, thanks partly to him, you now have a built-in babysitter."

"Except when you're back in Seattle."

"Well, I'm here at least until the baby is born."

Fortunately, Allison had enough vacation time accrued from her job as a human resource specialist to take a month off to be with her older sister and help her family.

"I'm glad you're here." Charlotte accepted the mug of hot water and dipped her herbal cinnamon tea bag inside. "But you may have overstepped at Thanksgiving. What are you going to do if Mom and Dad ask to *meet* this fake boyfriend of yours? You've already had him out of the country once."

Charlotte had asked the question of the year.

Allison would rather not dwell on this unfortunate complication and simply enjoy all the holiday festivities with her sister's blended family. She wanted to relax and enjoy the most magical time of the year, but Charlotte was correct. She had a teeny problem.

At Thanksgiving dinner with her family last month, she'd lied about having a serious boyfriend. In her defense, her parents had been openly trying to fix her up with Frederick Lloyd Huntington III, one of her father Thaddeus Taylor's oldest friends and business partners. A man even richer than her father—and at least twenty years her senior.

"It's time you settled down, young lady," her father Thaddeus had pronounced just after the turkey had been carved and served. "Frederick is a fine man. He's expressed interest and I've decided he's worthy."

"That biological clock is ticking!" Imogen, her mother, had shaken a finger. "You don't want to wait too long. Look at Charlotte."

Zero preliminaries. Straight from slicing turkey to slicing into Allison. She hardly needed the memo about her biological clock. It ticked in her ear like a time bomb most days.

"You can all stop worrying about me. I won't be able to marry Frederick since I'm dating someone new and it's very serious."

"Can he support himself?" Thaddeus had snorted. "Or is he an *artist*?"

"He is, in fact, a *doctor*. So, yes, he can, in fact, support himself, and quite nicely. The only reason he's not here with me is because he had a previous commitment to Doctors Without Borders."

Her sisters Eloise and Charlotte had glanced up in surprise. They'd known she hadn't been dating anyone since the software engineer who hadn't worked out. No one had worked out. And, frankly, she was happy enough single. She had friends in Seattle and work that satisfied her. The problem was, in the quiet of the night she had to admit the truth to herself, even if to no one else: she wanted to have children. And she was old-fashioned enough to want it all. Marriage to a wonderful man like the ones her sisters had been lucky enough to find.

"Wonderful!" Imogen had said after a gasp of surprise. "I'm so happy to hear this."

"Doctors make lousy husbands," Thaddeus had muttered. "They're never home."

She'd apparently never make her *father* happy, so Allison had long ago stopped trying. The lie had come swiftly and effortlessly because she'd been so tired of hearing about Frederick. Her father thought he could rule her life, which was why she didn't come home to Montana often. But Charlotte needed her, and she was one person Allison would never disappoint.

"I'll think of some excuse why the doctor can't be here," Allison said now, putting away a clean dish left lying on the counter by one of the kids. "In all fairness, when I lied about my boyfriend—"

"The *doctor*," Charlotte interrupted.

"Right. The doctor. I didn't know I'd be staying with you for the holidays."

"Hey, don't blame me. This is what happens when you have a 'geriatric' pregnancy." Charlotte held up air quotes. "Now I have to stay off my feet as much as possible for the rest of the pregnancy."

"It wasn't a problem. I usually come out for a few days every Christmas anyway."

"But this is much longer than you're used to dealing with Thaddeus, and I appreciate you being here. I know it isn't easy."

Charlotte reached across the counter to pat Allison's hand. She'd had her own struggles with their father.

"Anything for you, sis."

Truthfully, she would have preferred spending the holidays in her adopted city of Seattle among her good friends and neighbors. But when Charlotte had asked Allison to come and stay a little longer this time, to get her through the end of a difficult pregnancy, Allison hadn't been able to turn her down.

She might not be able to stand her ruthless father, but her mother was okay. And Allison adored Charlotte, Billy and their family. Now there would be another little one coming along soon. Charlotte and Billy's only child. Their five-bedroom farmhouse would soon be busting at the seams. Allison was staying in the nursery now, and every morning she woke to a beautiful mural of dolphins and sea life perfect for the daughter of a marine biologist. Charlotte was on maternity leave from her position at Wonderstone Ridge Indoor Theme Park and Aquarium. Because Charlotte had had an amniocentesis, she'd decided to find out the sex of her child. A little girl, though she hadn't told Billy, who wanted to be surprised. And if Allison knew her sister, the act of keeping such monumental news a secret may have been compromised at some point. So far, Billy seemed clueless so the surprise hadn't been ruined for him.

Just the idea of a baby girl in the Abernathy household and the sister that Jill would now have thrilled Allison to bits, and all the excitement surrounding the new Abernathy baby had infected her.

"See if this imaginary boyfriend of yours can get you pregnant." Charlotte echoed Allison's thoughts. "If you're not careful, you'll be like me. A geriatric mother."

Allison made a face. "You're not a geriatric *mother*, you have a geriatric pregnancy."

"Potato, potahto," Charlotte said. "I feel so old when I hear the word *geriatric* in reference to me."

"Anyway, I don't care if I wind up like you. I *want* to be like you. Look at you, you're doing great. The most important thing is to have a partner who supports you all the way, and you have that. You couldn't do better than Billy."

"So true," Charlotte sighed, no doubt thinking of her handsome rancher husband. "He was worth waiting for. But you're going to be a great mother. My stepkids already love you probably more than they love me."

"I doubt that."

Allison was enjoying spending time with Billy's children by his first marriage, Nicky and Jill. The oldest, Branson, was away at college for the first time, getting ready to come home for holiday break after finishing his first semester at the University of Montana. He'd wanted to skip higher education and simply be a rancher like his father and hadn't seen the point of an education. Thankfully, his parents had felt differently. All three of Charlotte's stepchildren were amazing, but Allison was a little partial to Jill. She was always so clear in her thoughts, holding nothing back. If she was having a bad day, everybody knew it. And with a father like Billy, she obviously felt comfortable expressing her feelings.

Unlike Jill, growing up, Allison had never had an easy time expressing herself in a household where Thaddeus had taken away anything she'd ever cared about. She'd been shipped off to boarding school over her protests. Her punishment because her *sister* had gotten pregnant before marriage and one evening Thaddeus had overheard Allison talking about the cute new boy at school. "Best to nip that in the bud," he'd ordered. No more unmarried and pregnant daughters! When Allison had heard about their youngest sister Eloise's out-of-wedlock pregnancy, even if years later, Allison had had a good laugh.

Because of all this, she'd learned to keep her desires and private thoughts to herself. She hadn't expected the tendency to spill over into all areas of her life, but now found it second nature to be protective and secretive when she truly wanted something. She was suspicious, as if she might "jinx" something by saying the words out loud.

Even now, Allison had trouble expressing to her own sister how much she wanted a baby of her own. Someday, maybe. If it happened to her sister, it could happen to Allison, who was two years younger. But she better get on that.

"You could always adopt, if it comes to that." Charlotte stirred organic milk into her tea. "Did you hear about Baby J? He was found at the church, wrapped up in blankets, in a Moses basket. Can you imagine?"

"Have they had any luck finding the mother?"

"Not so far. His mother must have been desperate to abandon her baby, especially like that."

Allison agreed. "I hope they're reunited, and soon."

Charlotte brightened. "Hey, maybe you could adopt him! Would you ever consider adoption?"

Allison would love to adopt, but she could already see the scowl of disapproval on Thaddeus's face. If she so much as mentioned any interest, too, he'd probably find a way to intervene and make sure it didn't happen.

"Can you imagine how our parents would react to my adopting a baby without knowing anything about his background?"

Charlotte sighed. "You're right. Not that I think it matters, you understand. Hopefully, Baby J will be reunited with his mother."

"That would be the ideal situation."

Allison was still thinking about the poor baby who'd been abandoned by his mother when her phone rang with a video call.

She glanced to see the caller. "I have to take this."

Charlotte stretched her arms and yawned. "Go ahead. I think I'll go lie down. If I fall asleep, wake me when Billy gets here?"

"I would, but he's the one always running upstairs to wake you." Allison hustled up the steps to the nursery to answer her phone.

The video call displayed Rowan Scott, her friend and neighbor at her apartment complex in Seattle. She'd asked him to water her plants and bring in the mail while she was gone.

"Hey," Allison said. "Everything okay? Please don't tell me I've had a flood or some other disaster."

"Nothing like that." Rowan turned the screen to show a lineup of her three ferns sitting side by side. "Just checking in. Larry, Mo and Curly are doing fine, as you can see. And, yeah, I've named your plants. Hey, also don't forget that I'm hosting casino night in your apartment every night. Going well so far. I'll deal you in on the action, not to worry. We're going to make some serious coin. Sixty/forty, right? It's your apartment, but I'm doing all the work."

"Ha, ha. You better not be having fun like that without me."

She and Rowan had been buddies since the day she'd moved in across the hallway from his apartment and he'd helped carry the heaviest of her boxes. He was just that kind of a guy; always helpful, always seeming to have a smile on his face when she saw him.

"Sorry, I have to joke to mask my true feelings." He turned the image back on himself and for the first time she noticed the tightness in his mouth, the bags under his eyes.

Rowan was forever cracking jokes and rarely serious. She couldn't imagine why he'd be sad.

"What's wrong?"

He worked as a data analyst for a major software firm, a well-paying tech job he did from home and could do from almost anywhere. This made him convenient for plant watering and mail gathering, and she certainly hoped he hadn't been laid off. Not right before the holidays. As the director of human resources at another software giant, she'd told her HR colleagues before she'd left for her vacation, "Tell all managers: absolutely no layoffs while I'm gone. It's Christmas!"

"Perri. We broke up again. And without you here to help me drown my sorrows in Pinot Grigio, I've had to resort to Three Stooges' and casino night jokes."

"Oh, I'm sorry. Not again. Who broke things off this time?"

Rowan and his girlfriend broke up every few months and, by Allison's calculations, this was right on schedule. If it wasn't her breaking up with him, it was Rowan breaking up with

Perri, tired of her drama. Then one or the other would decide to give it another try and the madness would start all over again. It was getting to where Allison could practically set a clock by their breakups.

"She broke up with me this time. Via text message. Classy, right?"

Allison groaned. "That's a new low."

"This is it. I can't keep doing this to myself. I'm moving on. Perri and I are not right for each other. I've known it for a while."

So had Allison, and all of their mutual friends, but even now she refused to say anything. He'd said those very same words to her in the past. She couldn't trust those two wouldn't get back together again, especially during the holidays when nostalgia deepened. Take it from her, being single at Christmas was not an ideal situation. She ached for Rowan as the timing couldn't be much worse.

"What was her reasoning?"

"I'm not *serious* enough for her."

"What? You're a jokester. Fun. That's your personality."

"Yeah, well, obviously she doesn't like my personality." He shrugged.

"That's ridiculous. You've got a great personality."

Allison's mind briefly went to those old lame fix-up jokes. "Let me fix you two up. He's got a *great* personality." This usually implied looks weren't optimal, which certainly didn't apply to Rowan. He actually didn't *need* a personality with looks like his, but God had thrown it in anyway. Rowan was classic matinee-idol handsome with dark wavy hair, blue eyes and a jaw that could cut glass. His looks and good character were wasted on Perri. Though the woman was beautiful, she had zero personality.

"So, who are you spending the holidays with?"

Rowan held up one of Allison's plants and winked. "Nothing until Christmas Day with the fam at my brother's. For now, I'm hanging with my new best friend here and cleaning up at casino night."

Allison didn't like the idea of Rowan alone until Christmas. If he were here, she could keep him busy and take his thoughts off Perri. It was what she'd do if she were back home in Seattle. Take him out for a drink, let him unload.

Now that she'd thought of it, having him come to Bronco might not be a bad thing. There was always so much going on in a full household like the Abernathys that even Allison didn't have time to dwell on her troubles. The fact that she was still single and now faking a relationship was something she could ignore for entire stretches of time between laundry and picking up kids from school. If she were to put him in charge of some of these tasks, he'd soon be too busy to be upset about his breakup.

Allison tipped her head. "Hmm. I have an idea. Can you get Mrs. Havisham in 2C to water my plants?"

Her name wasn't actually Mrs. Havisham but Allison and Rowan nicknamed her after the Dickens character for fun. Twice, she'd answered her door with only one shoe on, so she'd "walked" right into that one.

"Why?" He glanced sideways at her ferns, still mercifully alive. "Does one of them look sick? I thought green was the only requirement."

"No, silly! I can't stand you being alone and feeling sad, and I want you to come to Montana. Spend some time here with me and my family. We'd love to have you."

"Are you serious?"

"There's plenty of room at my sister's place and I could use the help. I'm doing all the cooking, cleaning, decorating and shuttling around of two teenagers."

"What a nice offer. I look forward to you turning me into Cinderella for the holidays."

"I promise you'll have fun. We have so many small-town holiday festivities around here. Have you ever had a down-home Christmas, Montana-style?" Allison happened to know Rowan was born and bred in Washington state.

"You *know* I haven't."

"Then I say it's time."

In fact, he'd never visited Allison's hometown even if she talked about it frequently enough. No one had ever met him. Wait.

No one in her family had ever *met* Rowan.

Perfect.

This idea was so crazy that it might actually work.

"I take it back. You don't have to help me with any of the cooking and cleaning. What if you help me in another far more important way? In return, I have one favor to ask of you."

"What's that?"

"Pretend to be my boyfriend while you're here?" She winced. "I'm in trouble. Remember when I lied to my parents at Thanksgiving, said I was dating someone, and it was serious? Well, now that I'm here for a month, they're bound to press me about my boyfriend. You know, the one that doesn't exist? And if I tell them some other lie about how he can't be here, *again*, they're definitely never going to believe he exists."

"Well, so what? He *doesn't* exist. You don't have a boyfriend. It's not the end of the world."

"Um, remember Frederick III? He's conveniently still single. Shocker. And if I'm here, all alone, they're going to hoist him on me. They won't stop. It won't work, of course, which will only make the holidays awkward and difficult to get through. I wanted them to give up trying."

"I knew you'd get yourself into trouble by lying. But…didn't you tell them your boyfriend is a doctor?"

"Um, yes. That's right. It sounded impressive. My father made some snarky remark about a starving artist, and it was the perfect comeback."

"Not so perfect. I can't pretend to be a doctor! I can't even spell Naproxen."

"You can fake it."

"Oh sure. I'll see if I can sign up for an online course some-where. 'How to be a doctor in thirty minutes or less.'"

"You're a data analyst. Do an analysis of doctor personalities and assume one of those identities."

"That's…not how this works." He shook his head and fought a smile.

"Pretty please?" Allison batted her eyelashes. "I miss you. It will be like having a little piece of Seattle with me through the holidays. Best of both worlds for me."

"All right, *fine*. I'll come for a few days, but you owe me for this. *Big* time. In fact, you might have to put me in your will."

"Thank you, thank you!" Allison said. "I can't wait."

When her parents, especially her *mother*, got one look at Rowan, they'd know in an instant that Frederick III didn't stand a chance.

Faking would be easy for her, too, since she already had a wee but harmless crush on Rowan. She would never truly pur-sue him. Given his history with Perri, it was highly likely the two would be back together before Christmas. He'd go back home to Perri, having done his duty as her fake boyfriend and no one would ever be the wiser.

CHAPTER TWO

USING THE BUSINESS airline miles he'd accumulated over the years of traveling, Rowan was able to score a ticket to Montana the next day.

"Toto, we're not in Kansas anymore," he muttered as he buckled up in the rideshare he'd ordered.

From the airport, the driver took him to a winter fairyland, Western-style. They passed through the main street covered with festive green garlands hanging from every post and fence. A sign near a park proclaimed Christmas Tree Lighting Here Tonight. The tree was a mammoth pine that wouldn't look out of place in the forest.

"Yeah, we go all out here in Bronco," the driver said, waving an arm in one direction. "This is downtown. The tree lighting tonight is at the park between Bronco Heights and Bronco Valley, the two sides of town. We've got plenty of holiday shopping and also touristy stuff. Bronco Ghost Tours is in Bronco Heights, and it's always really popular at Halloween."

Rowan laughed, not realizing he would get a personal guided tour. "Bronco has *ghosts*?"

"Depends on who you believe. Run by Evan Cruise, and there's a history of psychics in his family, so, yeah, I think he believes."

"I'm visiting a good friend, so I'm sure she'll show me around."

Rowan spotted a store with some Western gear in the display window. He would get a pair of boots soon so he his entire look didn't scream "big city tourist."

Rowan was flattered when Allison said she'd missed him. She'd only asked him here to get out of a jam with her parents, but he would enjoy himself and her company. He refused to think of anything other than friendship between them as Allison had never expressed any interest, even during the times he and Perri were broken up. After this latest breakup, he thought he'd be more disappointed. It was Perri who'd talked him into giving them another chance two months ago and he'd caved.

Now, he'd come to a startling revelation. He'd always believed he didn't have much luck with relationships. But the truth was he always seemed to choose the wrong woman. He excelled at decisions elsewhere in his life, but when it came to romance, he made the wrong choice time and again. Whether it was his college girlfriend or any of the women he'd dated since then, it was almost as if he believed he couldn't do any better. He now doubted himself when it came to these decisions. His job for the next few months was to reevaluate everything. He'd stay single and figure out why he was continually drawn to women who felt that a relationship would complete their lives. Or who wanted him as an accessory, rather than a true partner. He tried but failed to find emotional satisfaction in those relationships.

No, he longed for a relationship with a woman who was fully independent. Someone who wanted a partner, but didn't need a man to feel complete. Someone like…

Allison.

This trip would be the distraction he needed and it was the only reason he'd accepted Allison's invitation. This time, he was a little surprised by Perri's timing. During the holidays, she'd always loved their romantic celebrations—and it never hurt when he'd tried to go overboard with an expensive gift or two. He always delivered, because he'd also liked their holidays together. This year, though, something was different. After two years of dating on and off, he suspected she might think it was time for a ring, but he couldn't bring himself to get there.

Maybe Perri had sensed a ring wouldn't be forthcoming this Christmas and broken it off before he could disappoint her.

As he glanced out the window, he realized he was curious about the town where Allison had grown up. She'd told him a lot about this place, sometimes over happy hour cocktails with friends, or at a neighborhood Super Bowl party here and there over the time he'd known her. Once, they'd even double dated with whatever guy she'd been seeing at the time.

Rowan had noticed her memories of the town were equally intermixed with happiness and frustration. He understood it went all the way back to her father, Thaddeus Taylor, a wealthy rancher who tried to control every aspect of his six children's lives. Especially his three daughters. But that was a common enough occurrence among fathers of daughters, and he figured she'd exaggerated the situation.

Curiosity had driven him to look up the man's financial status. Thaddeus Taylor's Triple T ranch was quite a successful venture, and the man was co-owner, along with his brothers, of Taylor Beef, which supplied beef to all of the west and even farther. The man was worth millions. Rowan couldn't help but be shocked. Allison herself was so down to earth and likeable. He'd never seen her splurge on the latest fashions, shoes and bags the way Perri had. Allison could be found most of the time in a sweater and jeans, her chestnut-brown hair often up in a casual ponytail. It was her smile that drew most people in. Him, too, were he being honest. Her smile leaned a little toward the wicked, as did her laugh.

When he'd first met Allison, he was certain she had a husband or fiancé. No way would she be single with those looks and her friendly personality. And then later that day, not surprisingly, the boyfriend showed up to help. Rowan had made himself scarce, but that same night Allison knocked on his door to deliver a six-pack of beer as her thanks for his help.

Over the next few days, Rowan made jokes every time he'd run into her in the hallway, issuing himself a personal challenge to give her at least one belly laugh a day. By the time he realized she was once again free and single a few weeks after moving in, he'd already cemented his relationship with her as friend and neighbor. Friend-zoned.

Growing up with an older brother whose good looks were often compared to Henry Cavill's, Rowan had learned to rely on his personality. If he stood next to his brother, he became invisible. When he spinned his jokes, at least women would then notice and gravitate to him. He made a lot of friends that way, but been shocked when someone as outwardly gorgeous as Perri expressed her interest and gone after *him* for a change. And she'd come after him hard. It was flattering. Perri told him he was actually better looking than his brother and, much as he hated to admit it, she'd hit a tender spot with that compliment.

The driver had taken him miles out of town, into ranch country, and now they passed under a sign that announced the Bonnie B ranch. Some minutes later, he pulled over in front of a two-story farmhouse.

"This is it. The Bonnie B ranch."

It looked like something out of a movie. The exterior of the main house, covered in gray stone and brick, had a wraparound covered porch. The view of shady, leafy trees surrounding the house, rolling hills, and cattle grazing in the distance gave way to images of the old time Westerns he'd watched with his father as a kid. He had officially arrived in cattle country.

Rowan tipped the man, grabbed his bags and then slowly made his way up the stone-paved walkway. He took a moment to breathe in a whiff of fresh air. What people said was true. The oxygen had a better quality in the countryside.

Suddenly the front door flew open and Allison came rushing outside.

"You're here!"

"Hello, ma'am. I heard you're looking for extras for a Hallmark movie. All I need is a hot meal and I'll stand around wherever you need me."

"You would make a handsome cowboy and you can stand anywhere you like." She laughed and threaded her arm through his as they walked together up a slight incline toward the home.

"This place is amazing," he said, surveying the acreage surrounding them.

"This is all Abernathy land, and the entire family lives on some part of this huge property. My brother-in-law is devoted to the Bonnie B."

"A real cowboy, huh?"

"You could say that. Come inside and meet everyone. We've been waiting for you."

She went ahead of him and swung open a dark wood door layered with textured glass inserts.

"Rowan is here!"

She said this with the same enthusiasm a child might say Santa Claus had arrived. He followed her down the hall to a living room with gleaming wood floors, a wide leather sofa and several oversize chairs. A huge flat-screen dominated one wall, and another wall displayed a magnificent floor-to-ceiling fireplace.

A hugely pregnant woman with a passing resemblance to Allison waved to him from the couch. "Hello, Rowan. It's nice to finally meet you."

He set down his suitcase and walked toward her, bending to offer his hand. "You must be Charlotte. I've heard a lot about you."

"Same." She reached up to hug him instead. "Oh my goodness, you smell so *good*!"

Both Allison and the kids in the room burst out laughing.

Rowan bit on his lower lip to keep from making a joke.

"Take it easy, there." A tall, broad-shouldered man wearing a tan Stetson chuckled from nearby. "Don't forget you're married. I'm Billy Abernathy, Charlotte's husband."

He offered his hand and Rowan shook it. "Good to meet you."

"You always smell good, babe," Charlotte said, patting a space beside her on the couch. "Come sit with me."

"This is Nicky, Billy's son." Allison tapped the shoulder of a teenaged boy who looked a lot like his father. "And Jill, Billy's daughter."

Both kids respectfully shook his hand.

"You have a full house," Rowan said, tipping back on his heels.

"Our son Branson is away at university until winter break, or it would be even fuller," Billy said. "You're right, with a baby on the way, we're busting at the seams."

"You'll take Branson's room until he gets back," Allison said. "Let me get you settled."

"Nice to meet you all. Thanks so much for inviting me for the holidays." Rowan waved and followed Allison up the staircase to a second-floor landing with a cathedral ceiling that gave a nice view of the cozy room below.

Rowan had checked the forecast and temps had dipped into the midthirties today, so he wasn't surprised to see Billy starting a fire in the hearth. Honestly, were the home not infused with touches of family photos and cozy knickknacks everywhere, he'd feel like a visitor at a rustic B and B in the countryside.

He dropped his suitcase inside a room that belonged to a teenage boy who clearly loved ranch life. There were 4-H ribbons hanging all over one wall, along with photos of horses and cattle. Otherwise, the room was spotless, meaning he hadn't been living there for a while.

Jill waved her hand toward the trophies. "Needless to say, Branson wants to be a rancher just like his dad."

"Obviously."

"But he got sent off to college anyway. I talked to him the other night when he called, and he can't wait to come home for an entire month."

"And the other kids? Do they also want to be ranchers like their father?"

"The gene may have bypassed them, but the Bonnie B will always be part of their lives in one way or another. Still, I doubt Billy will force any of his kids to take on ranching life. He's made it okay for them to follow their own path. Nicky loves music and he plays drums in the marching band. And Jill is still finding her way, though she and Charlotte bonded over marine biology. She's just a freshman this year and I'm helping her with an English assignment."

She plopped down on the twin bed without the slightest hint of awkwardness. Rowan, on the other hand, now realized he'd never been alone in a bedroom with her. Funny how his thoughts immediately ran to a fantasy-dream scenario. He told himself it didn't help that she'd been the one to suggest he play her devoted boyfriend on this trip.

How far did she intend this farce to go and would fake kissing also be involved?

"So...do *they* think we're dating?" He hooked a thumb toward the door.

"Oh no, I've already told Charlotte all about you. She knows you're my neighbor and good friend. You can't be the random doctor I'm dating. At least, you won't have to pretend around them."

She took his hand and pulled him down beside her on the bed.

Obviously, this situation did not affect her in the same way it did him.

"I'm *so* glad you're here."

"Yeah." Rowan swallowed hard. "Me, too."

For a second, she simply stared in his eyes, her own eyes shimmering, and he wondered if…but no.

He filled the silent pause. "So, Mrs. Havisham is watering the Three Stooges and checking our mail. She came to the door with *two* shoes. We might need a new nickname."

"Oh! I almost forgot." She stood and clapped her hands. "It's the first Saturday of the month! Do you know what that means?"

"Free steak tonight at the OK Corral?"

"Close, but no cigar. Tonight is the *tree lighting* ceremony downtown. We have to go. It's a huge tradition and you don't want to miss it."

"I would rather die than miss that."

"Okay, smart aleck. Why don't you unpack and relax for a bit before we go? I'll get changed and let you get dressed. Nothing fancy, just jeans and a sweater. But it will be cold, so layer up under your jacket. Gloves, too."

"Yes, ma'am. One second, though, before you go."

She stopped in the open doorframe and turned to him. "Yeah?"

"How's this going to work, since we're going to be out in public together tonight? I assume this is opening night of our three-act play."

"Oh…right." She tipped her head, wincing. "I'll need to introduce you as a doctor. Hope you don't mind?"

"Rowan Scott, MD. Kind of like the sound of that. Boy, those eight years went by in a flash. I feel smarter somehow." He straightened and touched the glasses he occasionally wore.

"You *are* smart."

"Nobody ever called me stupid, that's for sure." He hesitated. "But you know, maybe you haven't thought this all the way through."

"What did I forget? Nothing important, I don't think."

Either she did not want to discuss this with him, or the

thought was completely foreign. She'd never thought of the physical part of this fake relationship, obviously, or at least not the way he had been since the moment she brought it up.

He was almost afraid to ask, but if she wanted him to pretend...

"Only something huge." He cocked his head. "Can I kiss you?"

Her hand flew over her mouth and her cheeks pinked. "I... I guess I did forget something."

"I'm a thirty-six-year-old man and I usually kiss my girlfriends."

"It would be weird not to. I agree." She cleared her throat. "Well... I mean, is that okay with you?"

"Is it *okay* with me?"

"I've already asked so much. I don't want you doing anything you're not comfortable doing."

Was she *kidding?*

"I suggest in public we hold hands, and light PDA." He cleared his throat. "Like kissing."

"Yes, one hundred percent on board with that plan." She gave him a thumbs-up.

"Be sure not to slap me if I kiss you." Rowan winked. "Out of instinct."

"No, because *that* would be weird."

Then she smiled and was out the door, leaving him alone to decide what to wear so he'd at least *look* like a doctor.

CHAPTER THREE

TWINKLING LIGHTS HUNG from the boughs of every tree, lamp-post and shrub in downtown Bronco. Lit garlands with accentuated red bells were strung from one side of the street across other. Poinsettias and small potted trees adorned every spare inch of space. All the local storefronts from those located in Bronco Heights to Bronco Valley participated with kiosks, local brick and mortars displaying window decorations, outdoor and indoor trees, wreaths and lights. They'd turned the entirety of downtown into a winter wonderland. Bronco at Christmas was a little like being trapped inside a snow globe. In a good way.

Allisson turned to Rowan and stretched her arms wide. "What do you think? Do we go all out or what?"

"You definitely do," Rowan said. "There's no denying it."

Charlotte and Billy had chosen to stay home, cozy and cuddling in front of their fireplace like a couple of lovesick teenagers. The kids were meeting friends, which left Allison and Rowan to wander the streets alone together. Ever since they'd discussed their first public event as a couple while sitting side by side on a bed, alone, her skin prickled with heat despite the freezing temperatures. Leave it to Rowan to *ask* if he could kiss her. She noted he hadn't asked if he "should" kiss her, just taken it on himself to ask if he "could."

On the spot, she'd agreed. He had a point. No one would believe them unless they put on a show. But Rowan had been through a breakup recently, one Allison wasn't even sure would stick. By all indications, though, he was serious about remaining free and clear of Perri, so Allison didn't feel guilty. They were pretending, but she could kiss Rowan anyway because neither one of them was cheating. If they had to kiss... well, sacrifices would have to be made. She was up to the task. It wasn't like she hadn't ever pictured kissing Rowan before.

Once, they were sharing takeout from the Chinese food place down the street from their apartment complex when he and Perri were on a break, and she'd almost opened up to him. She'd been on the verge of telling him that she wasn't happy in her current relationship and wanted to break up with her boyfriend. The reason? Well, she hadn't wanted to tell Rowan that the *real* reason was she didn't think she should be dating someone and picturing herself kissing Rowan. But she'd chickened out and thought it best to wait and see what happened between him and Perri. The following month, they got back together, and Allison was glad she hadn't said anything.

She'd ended her relationship anyway because despite his reconnection with Perri, Allison continued to fight her feelings for him.

She and Rowan walked toward the enormous tree in the center of the park for the ceremony that would start soon. Outdoor speakers were piping in music from *The Nutcracker*. They stopped at the Bean & Biscotti kiosk to order a hot cider for him and a hot chocolate for her.

"To us," Rowan said, holding up his cider cup.

"To our friendship," Allison said, to make sure he felt no pressure.

"Man, this is *good*." He then pointed to a makeshift stand.

"Holy cow, are those roasted chestnuts? I didn't know that was an actual thing."

"Yes, let's go get some." Allison grabbed his hand and tugged him toward the street vendor.

She almost didn't see the man coming at her until she nearly collided with him. *Frederick.* He looked as he always did, his upper lip curled as if he smelled something rotten.

"Allison." He nodded by way of greeting, as warm and fuzzy as a colicky horse.

"Hello, Frederick." She must have squeezed Rowan's hand instinctively because he squeezed back. "I want to introduce you to my, um, my boyfriend. Dr. Rowan Scott. Rowan, this is Frederick. He's a good friend of my father's."

Rowan stuck out his hand. "Great to meet you, sir."

Frederick dutifully shook hands, but with his typical sour look. "I trust you are both enjoying the festivities."

"I certainly am." Rowan didn't let go of her hand but, with his free one, he went hand to chest. "I live in Seattle, so I've never seen anything quite like this."

Frederick, arms tucked behind him, tipped back on his heels. "As a doctor, you must be quite busy. Are you here for long?"

"I wasn't planning on it, but I'm having such a fantastic time. And I sure hate to be away from Allison for long. Maybe I'll cancel all my surgeries." He tugged her close. "I think I'll stay until New Year's Day, babe. I can't have you ringing in the year without me. That's bad luck. What do you say?"

Not for the first time, her sister had been one hundred percent on point. The man smelled divine.

"Oh, that sounds great. Yes. Uh-huh."

Wow, he was really turning on the charm and he'd apparently just called himself a *surgeon.* Oh dear. But, judging by Frederick's demeanor, he believed him. Every word, she'd say. Then Rowan bent low, tipped her mouth up to meet his lips, and kissed her.

Just when she thought she'd managed to quash that attraction to Rowan it came rushing back with a white hot fury. She lost her footing during the kiss, holding on to the lapels of his jacket to steady her equilibrium. A tingle thrummed through her body from head to toe. Holy Christmas!

He'd prepared her for this moment, but opportunity did not intersect with expectation. The part of the Venn diagram where reality met fantasy was stunning, and electricity hummed through her legs.

"Well! I guess I will leave you two alone then," Frederick said, forcing them both to come up for air.

"That's it?" Rowan stared after him as he walked away. "He doesn't seem that disappointed. Or jealous."

It took Allison a moment to regain the power of speech, so she simply blinked at Rowan, the *world's best kisser*.

Who knew? That was nothing like she'd imagined it would be. She'd expected Rowan would put in the least amount of effort required, a simple peck on the lips. And quite honestly she'd hoped for a little less passion so as not to tease her too much with what she couldn't have. He might not belong to Perri at the moment, but given their history that was temporary.

"Um…"

"I mean I guess he must not like you much," Rowan said with a shrug.

"Me? He doesn't like *me*. My money? That's a different story. I'm a Taylor, so someday I'll come into a massive fortune. I bet he doesn't even know what color my eyes are. I think Frederick looks at me and sees dollar signs in my eyes."

"So, he sees green eyes instead of blue? He wants to whisper sweet stock dividends into your ear?"

Allison laughed. "Something like that."

"Not very romantic. What a chump. I can't even imagine basing a marriage on financial assets. My parents have been married for over forty years and they're still in love. When they met, neither one of them had much of anything."

"You're lucky. You had great role models. That must be

what makes you such a great boyfriend." She waved her hand dismissively. "I mean for Perri."

"She doesn't seem to think so."

"Then she's missing a sensitivity gene."

"You're just saying that because you and I are friends."

"I'm saying it because it's true. And, thank you. After that kiss, I'm sure word will spread through town and get back to my parents. That's the main idea."

"You're welcome, but kissing you was not exactly a hardship." He winked.

She was saved from a response when people began to move in small groups around them. Clearly, they were about to light the town tree. Rowan held her hand as, together, they walked toward the event. A few minutes later, everyone clapped when the bright, colorful, blinking lights went up the length of the tree, and the small crowd oohed and aahed into the night. "All I Want for Christmas Is You" by Mariah Carey rang through the speakers and this year's Santa Claus went around handing out candy canes to the children.

"Should we walk around?" Allison said. "I'll be your tour guide. If you have any Christmas shopping left to do, I'll have to take you to Sadie's Holiday House in Bronco Valley because that's the place to start."

"I still need to get something for my mother. She's picky. With my dad, buy him a tie and he's happy. My mother expects a much more heartfelt gift from her sons."

"Smart woman." Allison pointed to the Bronco Ghost Tours kiosk owned by Evan Cruise as they walked by. "My cousin Daphne is married to the proprietor. Want to stop by and sign up for a tour?"

"A ghost tour? How could I say no to that?"

"It's such a touristy thing to do, but what the heck? You are a tourist." She spotted Evan immediately and made the introductions.

She hated lying to Evan, but she presented Dr. Rowan Scott again. "We'd like to sign up for a tour."

"I'm a doctor, so I'm a science guy," Rowan said in full character. "But Allison is trying to keep me open-minded."

"Everyone should be. I believe in science, too, but that doesn't negate believing in some things we can't yet see or fully understand. Remember when we split the atom? Who knew, right?" Evan pulled out the schedule and flipped through it. "How've you been, Allison? Still living in the rainy city?"

"Yes, that's where Rowan and I met."

Rowan nodded. "I have my medical practice in Seattle."

"What kind of a doctor are you?" Evan said.

"A surgeon." Rowan straightened.

"What kind of surgeon?"

Rowan cleared his throat. "Um, a little bit of this, a little bit of that."

"So, a general surgeon," Evan said.

"Exactly."

"How did you two meet?" Evan asked.

Allison had never known her cousin's husband to be so talkative. She wished he would stop asking questions already. Rowan was digging himself in deep and, pretty soon, he'd announce he'd won the Nobel Prize.

"Well, it wasn't because she was my patient, because that would be illegal." Rowan chuckled.

Evan quirked a brow. "And also scary. I hope you never need a surgeon, Allison."

"Oh, me, too. Me, too." Allison laughed, wishing she hadn't thought to stop by. "Actually, we met when I moved into the same apartment building."

The truth. Always so much easier.

"Cool," Evan said. "Well, there's room on a tour next month. We're already pretty booked up."

"Oh dear. I might not be here by then," Allison said. "I'm glad business is still good."

Evan gave her a small smile. "Thanks. It's a bit hard to celebrate this year, though, with my great-grandmother gone."

"My condolences," Rowan said.

"No, she didn't *die*." Evan frowned. "Winona just kind of... disappeared. On her wedding day. She and Stanley Sanchez were getting married."

"She still hasn't been heard from?" Allison asked.

She'd heard the news of Winona Cobbs's disappearance from Charlotte, but assumed the nonagenarian had simply wandered off and would be located soon. Winona was known to be a free spirit and it would not surprise anyone if she'd decided to chase a butterfly just before her wedding.

Evan shook his head. "Everyone says she got cold feet and changed her mind about getting married. They say she must be off on her next adventure."

"But you don't think so?" Allison asked.

Evan shook his head firmly. "No way. She loved Stanley, and she wouldn't just leave our family like this, especially after finally reconnecting with her daughter."

"But... I heard she left you all a message saying she was fine," Allison said, remembering the latest gossip.

"That's true, but I can't help but believe something is terribly wrong. I sense it. And, yesterday, I got another message."

Allison gasped. "What did the message say? Did you tell the police?"

Evan sighed. "No. Not that kind of a message. Lately I've been having strange dreams. One was of a locked room, a pen and paper. A note on the paper read, 'Don't believe them.' I can't prove anything. But I think somehow she's trying to send me a message."

"Did you tell anyone?" Allison asked. "The police work with psychics all the time, don't they? Maybe they would listen to you."

"If I get more details, maybe I will." Evan shook his head. "I wanted to tell Stanley, at least, so he wouldn't worry too much, but his family talked me out of it. They don't believe me, of course, and, anyway, it would probably upset Stanley."

There was little worse than not having the support of your family. She should know. But Allison believed in the unexplainable even if she wasn't sure what it all meant. She wished Stanley's family was more open to the idea because it could give him some comfort.

Allison patted Evan's shoulder. "I believe you. And I hope you find her soon."

Allison and Rowan said their goodbyes to Evan and continued their walk through downtown.

"Do you believe in that sort of thing?" Rowan said. "I don't know. Sounds like a lot of smoke and mirrors to me. Pretty far out there."

"I know how it sounds, but weird things happen in Bronco. Stuff that's sometimes hard to explain. Many years ago, when she was living in Whitehorn, apparently Winona had a column she called 'Wisdom by Winona' and she seemed to be able to predict the future. Strange, right?"

"That *is* weird."

"If Evan has even a little bit of Winona's talent for predicting the future, his dream might be trying to tell him something."

"Damn, I hope they find the poor lady." He elbowed Allison. "Hey, what would you do if you could predict the future?"

"I'm not sure I'd like it. Knowing me, I'd get the kind of vague messages that are open to interpretation and spend most of my days trying to figure out what they meant. Then worrying whether or not I got it right."

"I wouldn't like it either. Half the fun is watching the future unfold and imagining all the possibilities."

"Hey, good job on deciding what kind of surgeon you are on the spot." Allison laughed and threaded her arm through his. "I was worried there for a second. 'A little bit of this and a little bit of that'?"

"Evan sort of saved me there. I walked right into that opening he so kindly handed me."

"Maybe you should have kept your medical career more low-key than surgery. You could have been a family practice physician. Flu shots and annual exams."

"Boring. I think I kind of like being a surgeon."

"No wonder. In the medical field, I've heard surgeons are considered as close to God as you can get."

"So, every time you say 'thank God,' I'll know you're talking about me, and I'll say 'you're welcome.'"

Allison laughed and shoulder-checked him. "I think we should keep everything as close to the truth as possible from this point on, like where and how we met."

Allison stopped in her tracks because walking not far from them were her mother and father. They almost never came out to these events. Just her luck.

She would now have to pretend with the two people who'd known her for her entire life. They'd seen her lie before and fail before. They'd seen how she behaved with someone she liked, like a boyfriend. They were now going to watch her put on the performance of a lifetime. If anyone noticed a crack in the truth, it would be her mother.

"This is it. Are you ready, Dr. Scott?"

"For…?"

"You had a trial run and now you're going to meet my parents. It's showtime." She flashed jazz hands.

"Put me in, coach." He pulled on the lapels of his coat. "I'm ready to play."

"All right. Let's see if you can score!"

She would just have to hope they didn't strike out.

CHAPTER FOUR

"ALLISON!"

A woman Rowan thought could pass for Martha Stewart's fraternal twin rushed up to them and embraced Allison in a hug.

"Hi, Mom. Dad." Allison turned to Rowan. "I'd like to introduce you to my boyfriend, Dr. Rowan Scott."

"Nice to meet you, Mrs. Taylor. I've heard so much about you."

Rowan stuck out his hand and the much more self-possessed and apparently restrained Mrs. Imogen Taylor did not switch to a hug the way Charlotte had upon meeting him. She also did not remark on how good he smelled. That was fine. This whole pretend-doctor thing was messing with his head. Pretending to be in love with Allison came way too easily, however.

And that kiss! For a second, he'd forgotten where he was. The depth and intensity of his automatic reaction slapped him with surprise. He'd always found her attractive, and assumed she didn't feel the same way about him. But Allison wouldn't have reacted and kissed him the way she had if there weren't *any* attraction there. He wondered if it was possible for her to fake that kind of chemistry.

He caught himself alternating between guilt and relief. Relief that at least this part of their charade would be easy if nothing else. He'd nearly made a fool out of himself with Evan. Maybe he wasn't all that psychic since he couldn't tell Rowan wasn't a surgeon. Allison was right. He should have picked something more familiar and relatable, like family physician.

He hoped he was acting aloof enough, too, like a real doctor might. And he had to stop cracking jokes because the real doctors he knew didn't have a sense of humor. Too much death and sickness in their field probably. There was a lot to consider in a lie this large, but he was up to the task.

Mrs. Taylor gave him a smile. "I'm sorry we missed you at Thanksgiving."

"I'm sorry, too, but I had that trip scheduled months in advance."

"To Europe, was it?" Mrs. Taylor said. "It's very philanthropic of you to give so freely of your time."

Except her snooty tone of voice and pursed lips made it sound as though she didn't approve. He understood. Only a horrible boyfriend would leave his best girl alone during the holidays. Were Allison really his girlfriend, he'd never stand her up for any holiday or family function.

Though slightly distracting, he continued to ignore the buzzing in his pocket. Earlier tonight, he'd been shocked to get a series of texts from Perri. She'd claimed to be worried about him, wanted to make sure he hadn't taken the breakup too hard. Wanted to know if he'd made any plans and where he'd be for Christmas. He had not responded. Let her wonder where he was. Tonight, there was nowhere else he'd rather be.

Until the moment Allison's father strode up to him.

"Thaddeus Taylor." He stuck out his hand and shook Rowan's with surprising strength. "So. You're a doctor."

"Yes, sir."

Rowan broke out in a cold sweat. Regardless of his age, this man's eyes were sharp and intelligent. He would be difficult to fool.

"I wonder if I could get your advice with a medical condition." He rolled up his sleeve. "My doctor said I might have early skin cancer. I'd like a second opinion. What do you think?"

"Oh my gawd." Allison clapped a hand over her eyes. "Please."

"What?" Thaddeus barked.

Mrs. Taylor tapped his shoulder. "He's on vacation, Thad. Why not let the doctor enjoy the little time he gets off?" She turned to Rowan. "I'm so sorry, dear. He just can't help himself. I'm Imogen, by the way. Allison's mother."

"Don't they teach you this in medical school?" Thaddeus roared. "It's just a *freckle*! Why waste my money on a biopsy?"

Rowan tipped back on his heels. He so had this. Recently, he'd picked up a little freelance work on data analysis of skin cancer in the US and surrounding countries. Skin cancer, especially basal cell carcinoma, was a bit of an epidemic. But on the other hand, if he said too much, there might be further questions he couldn't answer. Or shouldn't. The last thing he wanted to do was give someone bad medical advice. He had to sleep at night, after all.

Rowan cleared his throat. "Unfortunately, I have made it a policy not to treat friends or family. I would definitely get the biopsy, however. Can't ever be too careful. Skin cancer is a bit of an epidemic in our country but it's not my field of expertise."

There. He sounded very smart.

Mr. Taylor pointed. "All you doctors do is *specialize*. In my day, you went to one doctor and he cured everything from the flu to a broken leg."

"Yes, dear. We know. We know." Mrs. Taylor patted his back.

"I almost went into family practice," Rowan said, giving Allison a pointed look. "Might have enjoyed that."

She bit her lower lip as if she were biting back a smile.

"You're coming to our big Christmas dinner, right?" Mrs. Taylor turned to Allison.

"Yes, of course, but I'm not sure Rowan will be able to."

"I'm staying until New Year's, remember?" He pulled Allison close. "Things slow down during the holidays."

"What? Nobody gets *sick*?" Thaddeus said, voice dripping with suspicion.

"Not many elective surgeries are scheduled, and for emergencies, I have my partners on call."

"That's wonderful," Mrs. Taylor said. "All of our family will be together this year."

"Family and *friends*," Mr. Taylor corrected. "I think Frederick will attend. He's invited."

Family and work colleagues. It didn't sound like a family Christmas to Rowan. Thaddeus probably made it some big corporate event, mixing business and pleasure.

If Rowan stayed until Christmas, he'd miss his first one with his family in years. His mother wouldn't be happy, but when he told her he would not be spending it with Perri but instead with his friend Allison, she'd cheer up. She'd met Allison once while visiting him from Whidbey Island, where she and Dad had retired. Not surprisingly, she'd adored Allison and pointedly asked Rowan whether she was single.

He'd quietly reminded her he was dating Perri so *he* wasn't single.

"Oh, that's right," his mother had said, as if she'd forgotten.

"Well, we should go," Allison said, taking Rowan's hand. "I have to get up in the morning and take the kids to school."

"Yes, and I have to check in with my answering service. Just to make sure everything is fine and no one needs any emergency doctoring."

Allison squeezed his hand and gave him a tight "Are you for real?" smile.

Thaddeus's eyes narrowed to slits. "A doctor's work is never done."

But he may as well have said, *I know you're lying and somehow I'll prove it.*

MONDAY MORNING, ROWAN woke to his phone buzzing. Again. Groaning, because he'd slept on a twin bed when he was used to his king-size mattress, he located his phone. Perri once again, with no less than seven text messages, all expressing regret they would be apart during the holidays for the first time, hoping that he was okay. She missed him. On one text, she'd sent a photo of them in happier times. His heart still bruised over the breakup, he didn't want to talk to her. But if he didn't respond, she would keep texting until he did.

I'm fine. Wish you the best. No hard feelings. Have a good holiday and don't worry about me.

Her response was immediate: a smiley face, a kiss face, and a Christmas tree. It reminded him of the sweet side of Perri, and he already missed her in a lot of ways, but he was also tired of their ups and downs. She needed to make up her mind about what she wanted, and so did he. He was done with the drama.

He shut his eyes and tried to get a little more sleep but, after a few minutes, gave up. He rose, showered, dressed and powered up his laptop to do a little work. He'd have to log in a few hours every day as he hadn't taken the entire week off work. One hour into replying to work emails, he realized he needed coffee. He'd never been a big fan before moving to Seattle, but with a shop on every corner, he quickly became a convert. The moment he opened his bedroom door, the smell of brewed coffee assaulted him all the way upstairs and down the hallway. He went like a bear to his honey.

"Good morning," said Charlotte from the kitchen table. "If

you're looking for Allison, she took the kids to school. Help yourself to coffee."

"Thanks, I will." He found the automatic coffeemaker and poured himself some in the ceramic cups lined up nearby.

"I've got cream if you want it." Charlotte pointed to the tray of sugar and cream she had near her.

"Thanks. By the way, if I haven't said so yet, you have a lovely home."

Rowan admired the kitchen's cream-white cabinets and stainless-steel appliances. Someone had decorated tastefully with dark brown accents here and there, giving it all a cozy but modern look.

"Billy used to live here with his first wife, Jane, but I've added my touches since then. This is actually our first Christmas as a married couple, and I want to make it special for Billy and the kids. The kids have had a lot to adjust to in a short time. They deserve a special holiday with all the traditional touches, but time is getting away from me. I thought I'd have a lot more done by now. Billy helps where he can, but the Bonnie B keeps him busy all day."

"I'm happy to help in any way I can."

"Was it easy to just drop everything and come to Bronco for the holidays?"

Ah, so she was probably making sure Rowan had a solid career and wasn't some kind of gold digger after the Taylor money.

"I'm a data analyst, so I work from home. I'll actually be logging in every day until my vacation starts next week."

"Are you an only child?"

"No, I have an older brother."

"Are your parents still married?"

"Yes, happily so, for over forty years."

"And where did you go to school?"

Charlotte proceeded to ask him so many questions, he felt a bit like a goalie, keeping each one out of the net. Yet he answered them all. It made sense that she'd want to get to know the perfect stranger currently residing in her home with her husband and stepchildren. Besides, he had nothing to hide.

"And how did you meet Allison? I've heard her side of the story, now I think I'd like yours."

The questions continued. And he was ready for anything.

"We're neighbors, of course, but I've been living in the apartment complex for longer. I moved back home to Seattle when I got my first job just out of college. When she moved in, I introduced myself and tried to be a good neighbor. We've been friends ever since."

"You're underestimating yourself. Allison said you practically helped her move in."

"It was just a few boxes," he lied. "I think her boyfriend at the time ran late."

"Yes, and by the time he got there you were all conveniently done." Charlotte made a face. "I remember Tony. He didn't last long, did he?"

"I'm not sure." Actually, Rowan knew the day and time because Allison had come over to cry on his shoulder. "But, yeah, she deserves better."

It was the first time he'd seen such vulnerability in Allison, who always seemed so strong and upbeat. It awakened an unexpected tenderness in him.

"I agree." Charlotte took a sip of her tea. "I'm sorry if I've sounded like the inquisitor, but both Billy and I feel protective over Allison. My father has given all his daughters a difficult time. He seems to judge us in a different way than he does my brothers. But for Allison, who was closest in age to me, it was tough. I blame myself for what she had to go through as a teenager."

Rowan was about to ask why it would be her fault when Allison came bustling through the side door into the kitchen.

"Brr! It's freezing out there." She slowly unwrapped herself. Scarf, hat, gloves and, finally, her jacket.

Allison's cheeks were red and Rowan had no trouble believing her. Were her *teeth* chattering? He resisted the urge to pull her in and share his warmth, but they didn't have to pretend here. She'd think it odd, and he didn't want to overstep and indulge his recent fantasies about her.

"You're both spoiled with Seattle weather," Charlotte joked. "It's probably going to snow soon. I bet we'll have a white Christmas this year."

Allison turned to give him her full attention. "So! How are you this morning, Dr. Scott? Did you find anyone that needed *doctoring*?"

He snorted. "Yeah, I'm sorry about that."

"I take it you ran into some people last night and had to put on a performance," Charlotte said.

"Both Frederick *and* Mom and Dad." Allison poured herself a cup of coffee and wrapped her hands around it. "But Rowan pulled it off. Like a boss."

"Barely. Somehow, I got the bright idea that it might be fun to be a surgeon. I should have kept it simple."

"Oh no! A surgeon?" Charlotte laughed. "You've got your work cut out for you now. If you're not careful, our father will figure this out."

"I like a challenge," Rowan said. But, yes, he was worried.

"Dad already asked him for medical advice!" Allison said. "He rolled up his sleeve and asked him about a mole!"

Charlotte covered her face. "Oh my gawd."

"That's what I said."

"I think I recovered quite nicely," Rowan said. "At least they believe we're dating, and that's the important thing."

"You two look so good together, anyone would believe you're dating," Charlotte said.

"Mmm," Allison said.

Rowan bit on his lower lip and wouldn't look at Allison. He happened to agree, but that was beside the point. Even with that kiss, and her enthusiasm, she didn't seem inclined to take him out of the friend zone anytime soon. It made sense, and this was probably him again on the verge of making bad decisions. Even if Allison seemed perfect for him. It had been a long time since he took a risk with a woman.

For the past few years, he'd been inclined for a sure thing, which was one of the reasons he'd made such a mistake with Perri. Sometimes a risk was in order. In business, risk was related to reward. The bigger the risk, the bigger the reward. He was beginning to think it might be similar in his personal life.

"Why don't you take Rowan out for a ride on one of the horses?" Charlotte said.

"Once it warms up, maybe." Allison shrugged. "What do you think, Rowan?"

"Sure, I'm up for a ride."

It had been years since he'd been on a horse, city boy and all, but he welcomed new adventures. Why not, if it meant spending part of his day with Allison? He wouldn't say no.

"Well, you two have fun. I have a few things to do." Charlotte rose, walked over into the attached laundry room, and dragged an enormous laundry bag into the middle of the living room.

It took Rowan a second, but he interceded as fast as he could. "Let me help."

"Charlotte! What on earth are you doing?" Allison rushed to help. "I'll do the laundry, you have to rest."

"It isn't laundry. This is how I hide the kids' presents. It's the only place they're never going to look."

"Brilliant," said Rowan. "You realize you already have first-rate mothering skills."

Charlotte turned to Rowan. "Wrapping presents is an example of one of those things I planned to do but haven't gotten around to yet."

Allison frowned. "I thought you were going to let me help."

"You're already doing so much around here. The least I can

do is wrap presents. It should be simple enough, but my energy level is so low lately."

"That's because the doctor said your iron is low. You're supposed to be resting." Allison yanked the bag out of her sister's reach. "I'll take care of this."

"And I'll help," Rowan said.

Charlotte gathered scissors, tape and gift tags and set them on the coffee table in front of the leather couch. The room was toasty warm with a fire going.

"It's a good time, while the kids are in school." Allison dug through the bag. "Let's hurry. Then we'll go for a ride, and I'll make lunch before I go pick up the kids."

Charlotte sat on the couch. "Don't worry about Nicky. He gets a ride home since he has band practice. But you will need to get Jill."

"I don't know how you keep track of these schedules," Allison muttered.

"The life of a singleton is much simpler." Charlotte laughed. "I remember it well."

Rowan exchanged a look with Allison. He didn't know about her, but he was ready for a family and all this wonderful chaos. More than ready. Two people who loved each other and loved their children. Love multiplied. If only he could find the right woman for him.

He now painfully realized that he'd wasted two years with the wrong one.

CHAPTER FIVE

"HEY, FOR A DOCTOR, you're pretty good on a horse," Allison said.

"I should have been a veterinarian," Rowan joked. "But what can I say? Mother always wanted a doctor in the family."

Allison was impressed with the way Rowan took to Nicky's horse, Thor. Because Rowan was so tall, she hadn't thought it appropriate for him to ride one of their smaller geldings. Thor was a seventeen-hand black quarter horse who'd been well trained by Billy's crew. Allison rode Jill's horse, Sugar Bean, who was an unusually sweet mare. Hence the name. Though Allison used to ride, life in Seattle did not afford many opportunities and it had been a while.

All morning, she and Rowan wrapped presents in front of a fire while Rowan made Charlotte laugh. She found it was colder in Montana than she remembered. It might rain in Seattle a great deal of the year, but at least they were spared these freezing temperatures. She'd bundled up for the ride, because even the bright sunshine wasn't enough to quell the chill lingering in the air.

What she'd really like to do was fold herself into Rowan's warm embrace. She'd discovered he was solid and strong.

Stop thinking about him.

Just because that kiss had rocked her world didn't mean it had done the same for him. He certainly hadn't said anything about their kiss. She'd noticed, too, when he'd pulled out his cell a few times at the tree lighting ceremony. Someone had been pinging him. He'd put the phone away without responding, which made her think it hadn't been work or family. It was none of her business but she couldn't help worry those texts had been from Perri, trying to get him back. Heaven knew it had happened before. But she'd decided not to pry and simply pretended it wasn't happening.

She hoped this time he'd stand his ground and realize he could do much better than a woman who didn't appreciate him. Allison hoped he'd learn from the demonstration of a spectacular example of healthy love between Billy and Charlotte. Those two were utterly devoted to each other. Even with a blended family, they were making their union work. This example of romantic love was what Allison wanted, too. Everyone should hold out for true love and a real partnership. Her sister had been through a lot of turmoil early in her life and deserved every little pinch of joy coming her way now.

Their horses trotted through the hills and valleys of the Bonnie B, a gorgeous green carpet below them. When they came to the top of a hill filled with lush evergreens, she stopped to look below at the sight spread before them. A bird rustled in the trees and a cow lowed in the distance. She felt happier and more content than she'd been in years. Coming home was turning out better than she'd imagined.

"I don't know if I would have ever left here," Rowan said quietly. "It's not that I don't want you in Seattle, because I do, but I mean, why did you ever leave this place?"

She wondered how she could explain her love/hate relationship with Bronco. With her parents.

"Bronco might be better for me if my father wasn't so strong-willed. I never got along with my parents. Especially not him. When Charlotte got pregnant the first time, as a teenager with Billy's kid, *I'm* the one who got sent away to boarding school."

"I don't think you've ever told me this. *You* got sent away?"

"Yes." She sighed. "I mean, looking back, I understand his reasoning, not that I agree with what he did. He's a very controlling person and when he realized he couldn't control Charlotte, he worried with good reason that he couldn't control me either. So, best to send me to a school that would monitor my activities all day before I got pregnant as a teenager, too. He did the same with Eloise, my younger sister. But I was never a bad kid. Just curious. The funny thing is, all my life I've been afraid to express what I want because as a kid I knew the moment I did my father would take it away from me. So now, even though I know better, I'm still afraid to say what I want out loud."

"You realize that doesn't make sense." Rowan's smile slid easily across his face.

"Yes, but I guess some things are ingrained so deeply in us as children that we have to work hard to get past them. In answer to your question, why did I leave? Well, the first time, I was forced to leave, and I didn't come back for a few years. I wound up following Charlotte to Seattle, and then when she left there, I stayed. Not coming back to Bronco was my choice. I didn't feel like I belonged here anymore after so many years. And now? This is home, but it doesn't always feel that way. Know what I mean?"

He nodded. "And Billy's kids? I take it they're from his first marriage."

"Yes, he was married for eighteen years to their mother."

Rowan whistled. "Whoa. Big investment."

"Billy has custody, but she sees them every other weekend and one day a week. Charlotte and Billy were high school sweethearts and they reconnected last year when she came home. Her dream was to be a marine biologist and she made it happen. She has a great job at the new aquarium in Wonderstone Ridge, though she's on leave now. It was hard being from a small town with the weight of everyone's expectations. Our dad never took it easy on her either."

"I know about weighty expectations. My older brother was the first to play football at our high school and he dominated on the field. It didn't matter how good *I* got. He was there first. I had to find my place somewhere else. It didn't help that he's extremely good-looking and good with the ladies. So, I became the jokester."

"That explains…a lot." Allison made a valiant effort at biting back a laugh without much luck.

"Okay, stop laughing." Rowan grinned.

"You mean that you developed a personality, don't you?"

"If you want to put it that way. I worked hard to be accepted for who I am."

"Well, now I have to see your brother, because I think *you're* extremely good-looking. Show me a photo of him." She held her hand out for his phone, which he'd been carrying with him presumably so work could always get in touch.

Reluctantly, he pulled out his cell and swiped a few times then handed it over. "Meet my brother, Grayson, but don't get any ideas. He's happily engaged."

Allison snorted, as if she'd be insensitive enough to ask for Rowan's brother's contact information. She didn't care what he looked like, but viewing the photo, she was amazed at what she saw. A man who might pass as Rowan's twin looked into the camera with a wise and confident grin. The grin said, *You'd be* lucky *to be with me.* She knew the type. Had dated the type. Hence her single status.

She handed Rowan back the phone.

"Well?" Rowan said.

"It's amazing."

"I know." He shrugged.

"I mean it's amazing how differently we see ourselves than the rest of the world sees us." She hesitated only a beat. "He looks just like you, Rowan. Or you look like him. Either way. But looks are only one part of the equation."

He put the phone away. "Maybe you're right. I guess I got set in my role as second."

Rowan was that rare man who didn't realize how attractive he was. He'd enticed the likes of Perri, an indisputably beautiful woman. But she'd toyed with his emotions, perhaps realizing that on some level he hadn't believed he could do any better than her.

Well, if Allison did nothing else this Christmas, she would show Rowan he deserved so much more than he'd ever realized.

By the time they rode back, brushed and put away the horses, it was lunchtime.

Allison found Billy by the stove, heating up some chili. Beside him were sandwich fixings and condiments. This wasn't good. She was late to make her sister lunch, so busy showing Rowan the Bonnie B. She'd been caught up in talking about their pasts and getting to know each other on a deeper level.

"Hey," Billy said. "Caught her trying to make herself lunch."

"I'm not an invalid, babe!" Charlotte said from a stool in the kitchen.

"No, but the doctor told you to stay off your feet." He plated the sandwich then reached for a bowl from the cabinet.

"I told you I'd be back to make you lunch!" Allison went hands-on-hips.

"Sorry," Rowan said from beside her. "I guess I kept her away too long."

"Forget about it," Billy said. "We want you to enjoy your stay here, too, and I can help here and there."

"But he really wants to check on that heifer in labor," Charlotte said. "Which I find...ironic."

Billy laughed and ladled some chili into a bowl. "I may not be able to pull my own baby out, but I can help with that heifer. She's having a tough time."

"I hope this isn't an omen." Charlotte made a sad face.

Charlotte was worried about going into labor early or something bad happening to her or the baby. They were the concerns of a later-in-life pregnancy such as hers. That, plus high blood pressure, high blood sugar and any number of dangers Allison didn't even want to know about.

Billy set the plate and bowl in front of Charlotte and tenderly kissed her temple. "It's not an omen. The baby is healthy, and we just need to keep you healthy, too. Remember, I can't do life without you."

Allison observed the love and tenderness before her as Billy and Charlotte had a moment, quietly whispering to each other. She glanced at Rowan to make sure he was also noticing this sweet display, but instead he was looking at her. Her cheeks blazed with heat.

Self-consciously, she tucked a loose strand of hair behind her ear. "Now that I missed making you lunch, tell me how I can make it up to you."

"Since you mentioned it," Charlotte said, "I wanted to bake holiday cookies for the kids and I bought everything I would need."

Christmas cookies? Allison watched the Great British Bake Off on occasion and realized that she'd never be able to make it into the big leagues. She could do standard baking, like basic cakes and chocolate chip cookies, but anything that had to look like you could display it at the Louvre instead of eating it was not in her wheelhouse.

"You walked right into that one, Allison," Billy said with a big grin.

"Cookies? Well, I'm willing to try!"

"And I'll help." Rowan rubbed his hands together. "As long as I get to sample the product."

"Well, that's a given. You're the taste tester." Charlotte pointed to him and chuckled.

"And if you need quality control, leave some for me."

Billy pointed a thumb to his chest. "I need to get back out there now."

"Go ahead, Billy. Do your cowboy thing." Allison shooed him with both hands and gave him a thumbs-up. "I've got this!"

Oh dear. She did not have this.

CHAPTER SIX

"CONFESSION TIME. I'VE never baked Christmas cookies before," Allison stage-whispered. "But how hard can this be?"

After lunch, Billy had headed back outside, and Charlotte had gone upstairs to lie down. Now, it was just her and Rowan.

"Right? And I've actually *seen* people bake them before, like my mom," Rowan said. "So, I feel like I already have a general understanding of the process."

Before she'd gone upstairs, Charlotte made it known she wanted those cut-out sugar cookies in different shapes and sizes. She'd bought all the cookie cutters. There were snowflakes, gingerbread men, trees and stars. Allison lined them and all the ingredients in a row on the counter. Rowan, bless his heart, pulled up a video on his phone and together they watched someone roll, cut out, decorate and bake cookies. The baker made it look so easy.

At the end of the video, they exchanged a look. While he looked confident, she was pretty sure her general appearance said, *I'm in trouble here.*

"Don't worry." Rowan fist-bumped her. "We've got this."

But as they mixed and rolled and cut the cookies out, nothing went smoothly. They'd forgotten to turn the oven on and then realized, after their first attempt, that the instructions said the dough was to sit in the fridge and chill for at least an hour before being rolled. Allison sent Rowan upstairs so he could get some work done while they waited for the dough to chill. She busied herself emptying the dishwasher for the five hundredth time and shuttling a load of laundry from the washer to the dryer.

When she returned to the kitchen, Rowan's phone pinged with an alert, and she found it under a dishtowel where he'd forgotten it. Allison couldn't help but notice Perri's name flash across the screen. An annoying insecurity flashed through Allison. It was entirely possible that Rowan and Perri were communicating again, trying to work things out. And here Allison was, drawing closer to Rowan each day. If they were thinking of getting back together, it was none of her business. She had to give herself a reality check.

"Are we ready yet?" Rowan hurried into the kitchen. "I was looking some stuff up, and the rolling is a *technique*."

Allison nodded toward his cell. "You forgot your phone and it pinged while you were gone. I didn't want to disturb you."

Rowan picked it up, looked at it, made no comment, and slipped it back into his pants' pocket.

Allison held her breath. "Anything important?"

"Nah. Perri is texting that she misses me." Rowan pulled the bowl of dough out of the refrigerator. "This is our first Christmas apart since we got together so it's kind of rough for us both."

"I knew she would regret breaking up with you."

Her heart had no right to take the nosedive it did. Rowan was getting back together with Perri. It was just a matter of time.

"That does seem to be her pattern."

"Rowan, I don't want you to feel obligated to me. Feel free to call her back and I'll take care of these cookies on my own."

"Don't worry, we're baking cookies. I'll call her back later."

This was classic Perri. She was already regretting her decision to break up. They had such an unhealthy dynamic, but it wasn't Allison's place to say anything. Let him figure it out for himself.

This time, the dough rolled out much easier after being chilled.

"It's because of my newfound rolling technique," Rowan said.

"Riiiight."

She didn't know about his technique, except it was messy. The kitchen looked like a flour tornado had swept through, the dark wood floor dusted with white as were the granite countertops. They each also had a white dusting on their clothes.

After the cookies baked and cooled, it was finally time to decorate them. Allison had looked forward to this part. Charlotte had bought the icing, too, and Allison mixed some with green food coloring in a bowl while Rowan mixed red in another.

"This is going to be great," he said.

She wasn't so sure about that.

"I'm glad you're optimistic. The shapes don't look perfect to me, but maybe that's not the important part."

"How they *taste* is the important part."

Well, he'd obviously never watched competitive baking.

She iced the trees green and he gave the gingerbread men red bow ties.

"We're terrible at this," she said, thinking her tree looked like a four-year-old had decorated it.

"Speak for yourself. I'm rocking these bow ties."

Suddenly, he looked at her and broke out in a big grin. Clearly, she had something on her face. She'd been so careful, but baking cookies had turned out to be a messy ordeal. Already she dreaded the cleanup.

She rubbed her chin. "What?"

"You've got something…right there."

He moved close and reached with a finger to carefully touch

the tip of her nose. Then his hand lowered to cup her cheek and stayed there, his eyes blazing with heat. The buzzing that went through her body surprised her because it meant the other night hadn't been a one-off. There was something between them and it thrilled her at the same time that it made her palms sweaty. Rowan was too soon off a breakup, and she didn't want to be his rebound. She didn't want to be someone temporary between his breakups with Perri. Their friendship was too important. And Perri was not going to give up until she got Rowan back.

But then Rowan leaned forward even closer and kissed her, and she forgot all her reservations. The pads of her fingers grazed against his rough beard stubble. The kiss was even better than the first one, tinged with more heat, maybe because they were alone. He pressed into her, putting his entire body into the kiss, but then suddenly broke it off.

"I'm sorry—"

There was nothing to do but kiss him back, and show him how *not sorry* she was, so Allison grabbed him by the shirt lapels and pulled him back to her lips. This kiss was hers and hers alone, an exploration of Rowan's gorgeous mouth. He did not disappoint.

When they came up for air, he brought her hand to his lips. "What are we doing?"

"I'm not sure, but I don't want to stop."

"This is bananas, but it also feels so...perfect. Why is that?"

She didn't want to say it out loud, but maybe because they were trapped in the small-town holiday festivities and the warmth and love of the Abernathy household. Maybe Charlotte and Billy had infected them. If so, she didn't want any medicine.

"It smells delicious down here!"

Charlotte's bright voice startled Allison and she stepped back. Only then did she realize how close she and Rowan had been standing.

"Thanks," Rowan said. "Our first time baking and I think we nailed it."

Charlotte muffled a laugh. "Your first time *baking*?"

"Christmas cookies, anyway," Rowan explained. "I baked a cake once, but that was easy. It came out of a box."

Allison spread her hands out to indicate the tray of stars, trees and gingerbread shapes. "Our best effort."

"I bet they taste great," Charlotte said. "The kids will be pleased."

"I better get upstairs and log into work for a few more hours. Don't clean up the kitchen without me." Rowan grabbed a tree cookie and took a bite.

As he left, he brushed his fingers against Allison's. She nearly swooned.

"Wow," Charlotte said after Rowan left the room.

"What?" Allison got busy wiping the countertops. "I'm sorry we made such a mess, but I'll start cleaning now. Soon it will be time to pick up the kids. And what are you doing down here, anyway? Didn't Billy tell you to rest?"

"I had enough rest, and I wanted some tea." Charlotte grabbed a mug and a tea bag. "So, you and Rowan? You didn't tell me you two were a thing. When did that happen?"

Allison sighed. "It *didn't* happen."

"Liar. You can't fool me. You two were standing awfully close. Why do you think I spoke so loudly when I walked in? I had to announce myself because you two were really into it."

Allison shrugged. "It's just one of those things. I blame you and Billy. You're lovesick and it's spreading."

Charlotte laughed. "Rowan's very good-looking and so funny. I wouldn't blame you for crushing on him."

"Right? But the thing is, we're friends, and he's just out of a long-term relationship. Granted, it's an unhealthy one and apparently they just broke up, again, but—"

"But *what*? It sounds like he's free and clear."

"You don't understand. He's said that before, but they always get back together."

Still, they'd never been free at the same time...except for now.

"Sometimes it's all about timing," Charlotte said. "When someone is worth waiting for, you do it."

"It's just physical. And there's no way I'm having a fling with him."

"Yeah, you don't want a *fling*. You and me?" She waved a finger between them. "We're too old for flings."

"Speak for yourself," Allison snorted. "And you're not too old, you're too *pregnant*!"

"I'm too in love." She smiled with obvious satisfaction.

"I'd be lying to say that I'm not ready to settle down and have kids before it's too late for me. But it has to be right. At this point, I don't want to waste any time chasing someone who isn't serious."

"And how does Rowan feel about settling down? Isn't he about your age?"

"Yes, and we haven't really talked about that. I always got the feeling he was far more invested in a relationship with his ex than she was. She's someone who sees how good and kind he is, and takes full advantage of his forgiving nature."

"I see." Charlotte smirked from behind her mug of tea. "It sounds like you need to *save* him from her."

Thankfully, Allison had a good reason to avoid the rest of this conversation. "Oh my goodness, look at the time! It's time for me to make you a snack."

"Way to avoid the subject."

"I'm just busy, busy, busy. Not avoiding you or anything." She pulled out the cutting board and sliced some cheese to have with crackers. "Have y'all decided on a name for the baby yet?"

"Honestly Allison, you can't avoid your feelings about this forever. This is what you always do."

And it's exactly what she was doing. "I'm going to take that as a no. I sincerely hope you're not going to be dillydallying on the name for much longer. You'll wind up with Beyoncé if Jill has her way."

"Okay, c'mon, Allison. Let's talk about this."

"Talk about what?" She looked up and waved the knife in the air. "My shocking inability to settle down, or the mean way I can slice this Havarti with my eyes closed?"

"Door number one, and it's not your inability to settle down. It's your fear."

"Ha! I laugh in the face of fear." She laughed maniacally.

Charlotte sighed. "I blame myself, actually. And Billy."

"Why would you do that?"

"We were stupid teenagers, and we weren't careful, so I got pregnant." She lowered a hand to her belly, no doubt remembering their first baby, the one she'd miscarried.

"Right, you were the wild one."

"I'm sorry that Dad sent you and Eloise to boarding school because of me. It wasn't fair. At the time, I didn't think much of it. I was so caught up in the fact that I didn't want to get married so young. But when I ran off, which was so cowardly of me, I left you and Eloise to deal with the legacy I'd left."

"Oh, don't be so dramatic. If I hadn't been so obvious and head over heels for Jimmy Lee, our father wouldn't have worried. But you know how it is. He just assumed I'd follow in your footsteps and forget the birth control."

"It just wasn't fair to send you all the way to New England, so far from home and family. I left but it was my choice. You didn't get one."

"I admit it was lonely for a while, but I got a first-class education and friends I still have to this day. It helped me get into a good university, where I made even more friends. It all worked out."

"Your education worked out, but what about your love life?"

"The search continues. I haven't found 'the one' yet." Allison shrugged.

"But maybe that's because you've shut down. You won't put yourself out there and tell a guy what you want. Marriage and children. The whole kit and caboodle."

"First, I would scare any guy off if I said that. And, second, *maybe* that's what I want."

"That *is* what you want, and you can't fool me."

"Admitting that I want to get married someday isn't going to do a thing but light a fire under our father to find me the right billionaire."

"He's the real reason you're afraid to admit what you want. You think he's somehow going to be able to take whatever you want away from you again."

Allison hated there was truth to that statement. Letting Rowan this close to her father was dangerous. Thaddeus could ruin this before it ever got started.

"Remember that guy I was dating a year ago? All it took was meeting our darling father *once* and he broke up with me. It didn't help that our father interrogated him over dinner and nearly asked to see his bank statements. He just couldn't hack the pressure."

She was only fake dating Rowan, and her father was already wreaking havoc and trying his best to make any normal man regret being a part of his family. If they were ever truly involved, maybe Thaddeus wouldn't stop until he'd scared Rowan away for good.

"It takes a special kind of man to handle our dad, that's for certain."

"Hey."

Billy's baritone voice behind Allison caused her to startle. Then she turned, saw the ax in his hands, and may have jumped a little.

"What in the—"

Billy grinned. "Char, your sister forgot what an ax looks like."

"She's been living in the city far too long." Charlotte

chuckled. "I hope you're about to do what I think you are with that ax."

"Exactly." He leaned his shoulder against the wall. "I'm going to cut down a Christmas tree. Have I got any takers?"

"No, thanks." Allison held up both palms. "Not me."

"The kids aren't much interested these days either." Billy shrugged. "Jilly Bean is head of the decorating committee, but she's no longer as excited about hiking out to find the perfect tree."

"Did someone say something about cutting down a tree?" Rowan appeared in the doorframe of the kitchen. "Because I'm in."

"All right! I got a live one. That's all I need." Billy turned. "Jacket, hat and gloves, city boy. Let's go."

CHAPTER SEVEN

ROWAN TRUDGED THROUGH the hills and valleys of the Bonnie B following Billy. They seemed to be headed into the outermost regions of the property. Rowan had pictured Allison coming along with them, which was pretty much why he'd volunteered. That would have been half the fun of the excursion.

Because, damn, that kiss in the kitchen. It was electric. He'd had to force himself to go upstairs to regroup, throw himself back into work, and ignore the fact that Allison waited downstairs. Ignore the fact she'd kissed him like she'd meant it. She'd held him tight, pressed her body into his, sending him the clear message this was what she wanted, too.

He'd like to think that you couldn't fake that kind of chemistry.

Don't make another bad decision. You're done with that.

He kept reminding himself that, somehow, when it came to women, he always made the wrong choice. Perri was simply the latest exhibit in the sad latest entry of his love life. He'd been asked to Montana for a respite so he could relax and have a small-town Christmas. That's what he would do. No get caught up in kisses with his beautiful neighbor and friend. They were not in a real relationship, and he had to remember this. Allison possessed the ability to truly mess with his heart if, when they went back to Seattle, she ghosted him. If she suddenly disappeared out of his life, she wouldn't leave a hole. She'd leave a crater.

It was a risk he wasn't willing to take. Couldn't.

"I didn't know you had Douglas fir trees in Montana," Rowan said to make polite conversation.

"We don't have many of them."

With an ax over his shoulder, jeans and a plaid shirt, Billy bared a passing resemblance to Paul Bunyan.

"The Alpine fir grow at high elevations and are similar to Douglas fir. Many years ago, my mother forced my father to plant seedlings for our annual tree, so now we have our pick."

Billy seemed like a good guy, but Rowan barely knew him. Allison had said a few things in the past about her brother-in-law. Now that he'd met the man, Billy seemed so down-to-earth, it was difficult to believe that all this land made him and his family multimillionaires.

They finally crested a hill and, in the distance, Rowan viewed a crop of narrow trees with layered branches, all growing close together.

"So. You and my sister-in-law. What's that all about?"

Far be it from Rowan to be anything less than honest with a man wielding an ax. Still, it just didn't seem appropriate to reveal their kiss-bonding over cookies when even Rowan didn't know what it all meant. Allison had been worried and skittish with him, but she'd also told him she hadn't wanted to stop. He was hanging on to that.

"Ah, she asked me out here to spend a real country Christmas. I work from home, so it makes it easy to pick up and go."

Billy narrowed his eyes and Rowan got the distinct feeling he was about to be put through the big brother interrogation.

"My wife said something about pretend dating?"

Rowan cleared his throat. "Yeah, that part sort of hit me by surprise. Especially the fact I'm supposed to be masquerading as a doctor."

Billy quirked a brow. "A *doctor*?"

"Yeah." Rowan sighed. "You can't make this stuff up."

"Or, you know, you *can*."

"Ha. Yeah, exactly. I'll be making it up as I go. I'm going to do my best but, quite honestly, your father-in-law will not be easy to fool. I think he already suspects something is off. It doesn't help that I'm a terrible liar."

"Being a terrible liar is actually a point in your favor as far as I'm concerned. Don't let Thaddeus intimidate you. You don't look like the kind of man who scares easily. That's good."

"I suspect it's a requirement to hang out with this family."

"You would be right. My father-in-law tries to ramrod over anyone who gives him a little room." Billy stopped in front of what easily had to be a ten-foot tree. "I never give him the room."

"That's good advice." Rowan eyed the tree. "This is the one?"

"Yeah." Billy dropped the ax and set his hands on his hips. "I'll need your help dragging the beast back."

Rowan slipped on the work gloves that Billy had handed him earlier.

"You can probably figure out by now that I'm a little protective about Allison. I've known her and Char for most of my life. They've always been close. I remember Allison always wanted to do everything Charlotte did, especially when it came to the first wedding. All the decorations, party favors, cake, bridesmaid dresses. Very exciting for her."

"First wedding?"

"The one where Charlotte ran out on me." He grinned.

Funny, he didn't seem bitter. "I'm sorry to hear that."

"Don't be. It was painful at the time, but we've grown up. Getting married as teenagers wouldn't have worked out for us. Charlotte needed to achieve her goals first. Last year she came home to stay."

"You're a lucky man."

"Tell me about it. It's like getting a second chance at my entire life. The one I always wanted. There's nothing like falling in love and doing life with your best friend."

It sounded like the impossible dream to Rowan.

"I can only imagine."

"Look, let me be brutally honest. Allison is very special to all of us. My wife would never tell you this, but I will. She appears like this completely-put-together professional businesswoman, and she is. But at the heart of her is a young girl who got sent away from her home and her family for no damn good reason. Just…whatever you do, don't hurt her."

Billy stuffed his hands in his pockets and studied the ground.

And somehow that was a far more powerful statement than holding an ax. There was simply no need to ask Rowan not to hurt Allison. If anything, he stood the risk of having his own heart broken when they went home and resumed life as neighbors.

"You have my word. I won't ever hurt her."

ALLISON TURNED UP the volume in the SUV. She had *The Nutcracker* playing through her Spotify playlist, and Jill hadn't complained once the entire drive. Good thing, because the music always put Allison in the mood for the festivities.

"How's your English assignment going?"

"I liked the story, but it's kind of sad."

"How so?"

"I mean, they're poor, so she cuts off all her hair and sells it to get enough money to buy him a pocket watch chain, and then he sells the pocket watch to buy her jeweled combs for her long hair. Dude! That's sad. She doesn't need the gift anymore. Neither does he."

Allison bit back a laugh. "The story is about sacrificial love. Selling what you own to give someone you love what they treasure the most, even if it means giving up your own treasure."

"I don't know how I can apply this to my life. Those people were poor and they lived in the olden times."

"Find a way to modernize it. But I'm not telling you to sell or give up something you love to give someone else a gift. I'm just thinking maybe you can use it as an example. A special and heartfelt gift, in other words."

Speaking of gifts, Allison still had a lot of shopping to do. Maybe she could talk Rowan into going into town with her while the kids were in school tomorrow. She wanted to get Charlotte and Billy a special gift and had no idea where to start.

In the past, she and Rowan had exchanged silly gift cards the way neighbors might. He'd give her a gift card to the coffee shop she haunted and she'd give him one to a department store so he could choose whatever he wanted. Too impersonal for this year. What did you give a man you wished you could get to know a whole lot better? She didn't want to overstep bounds, but this attraction to him actually wasn't entirely new for her.

She'd noticed him from the start. He was ridiculously handsome and so relatable. Always willing to help, expecting nothing in return. The men she'd met in the city who had Rowan's looks had always been on the make and had zero personality. Unfortunately, those were the guys who'd expressed an interest and usually asked her out. No wonder she was still single.

"Why don't you write about giving someone a gift but expecting nothing in return? That's sacrificial and goes with the idea."

Jill sat up straighter. "One time I gave Branson a belt buckle I found because I knew he'd like it."

"I'll bet your dad was proud of you."

"Yeah. He told me I'm his best girl."

"You definitely are. That's what I've heard, too." Allison slowed as they approached the Bonnie B. "That's the story you write for your assignment. How you expected nothing in return but gave your brother a gift anyway."

Outside the house as they pulled up was Billy, sawing away at the base of a huge pine tree. Rowan was right behind him, helping hold the tree down.

Jill jumped out of the passenger seat. "Hey, you got a tree!"

"Yep. Time is getting away from us and Charlotte really wants to get the tree up. We want everything ready for when Branson comes home. I picked the one I knew you'd like the best."

"For real?" Jill jumped up and down. "Yay! So, I did pick it."

"Yes, you did." Billy went back to sawing.

Allison walked up to him, shivering from the cold. "Um, need some help? I don't see how you're going to get that huge tree inside. How much are you going to cut off?"

"It's the same size we usually get. It looks bigger than you think. It's only about ten feet tall. I'm just trimming some of the lower branches."

"I don't know about this." Allison shook her head.

"You sound like your sister. Trust me. Thanks for your help, Rowan."

"No problem."

His hair was adorably mussed, falling down over one eye as it did whenever he didn't have it slicked back, which she'd noticed was often when lounging around the house. Today he had on his hipster glasses, the ones she only rarely saw him wear. He claimed he only slipped them on when his eyes were tired from staring at the screen all day.

Oh my gosh, she was so attracted to this man. To...everything about him. Even the way he bent to assist Billy, and then a few minutes later when he barely broke a sweat hauling in the tree.

This intense pull of physical longing was so...unexpected.

Allison followed them inside, watching as pine needles sprayed all over the ground outside, through the threshold, and trailed a path to where they propped it. There was a perfect cove by the staircase where the cathedral ceiling gave plenty of room. The tree was not only tall, but bushy.

This would be a wonderful Christmas, if only Allison could stop thinking about how she'd like to get Rowan alone and kiss the stuffing out of him. That wouldn't be smart.

Best to keep it friendly and forget that kiss.

Forget that it rocked her world.

Allison clapped her hands. "Who would like some hot chocolate and cookies?"

CHAPTER EIGHT

THREE DAYS LATER, they finally got around to decorating the tree. Allison watered it every day, but the trimmings were in the attic and she didn't want to bother Rowan much while he was working during the day. Billy had been busy with that heifer and Nicky and Jill kept forgetting she'd asked.

Finally, after Billy hauled every decoration down from their attic, the living room Allison had straightened earlier was in utter chaos. Boxes of ornaments, wreaths and garlands covered the wood floor. But it was a good kind of mess. She sat between Charlotte and Rowan and they munched on cookies and hot chocolate while Jill sorted through the ornaments and Billy went outside to talk to his brother Theo, who'd come looking for him.

Then it was almost time for dinner and Allison didn't know what to make. It seemed like all she did lately was cook, clean, do laundry and eat. Oh, and kiss Rowan. But that was only twice and, as she glanced sideways at him, she found herself picturing a third time.

"It's almost time to get Nicky from band practice," Allison said. "Then we'll figure something out for dinner."

"I'll be grateful when Branson is back. He used to do some of the driving for us," Charlotte said. "We were so worried about having a teenage driver in the house, but it came in handy."

"I'll get him," Rowan said. "I just need to borrow a vehicle."

It was almost too much. He could have disappeared into the guest room to work, or relax, but instead he was finding other ways to help her. Besides pretending to be her boyfriend, that is.

"Thank you!" Charlotte said before Allison could protest that he was their guest. "My keys are right in the bowl by the front door. The ones with the dolphin tags."

"And I'll bring back dinner, too." Rowan grabbed the keys.

"That's fine," Allison said. "We could always have chicken potpies for dinner."

Jill groaned. "Not again."

"How does pizza sound?" Rowan suggested.

"Yes!" Jill raised a fist in triumph. "Pepperoni for me."

"The best pizza is from Bronco Brick Oven," Charlotte said.

"Let me give you my card," Allison said, reaching for her purse.

"Nope, this one is on me." Rowan grabbed his coat. "Just ping me the address."

With that, he was out the door.

"Holy cow, too bad they didn't make two of him," Charlotte mused, gaping after him.

"Why do we need two of him?" Jill asked from beside the tree where she'd started to put up ornaments.

Charlotte smirked. "It's just an expression."

"Oh look." Jill held up an ornament with a photo of her and her adorable toothless smile in the center. "Here's one I made in first grade."

Allison joined Jill, taking a trip down the Abernathy family memory lane. She was surprised to see that Billy had wound up with all the sentimental ornaments the children made over the years. But then again, this was the home their family had lived in. It made sense for everything to be there.

"You'll be making new memories soon," Allison said, thinking of the new baby. "Charlotte and I were talking earlier about the name for the baby."

"I think we should name her Beyoncé. Dad said it's a girl and he didn't need the amnio to tell him that," Jill said.

"He just has a sense about these things?" Allison quipped, keeping it quiet that he'd guessed correctly.

Jill shrugged. "He knew I was going to be a girl."

"Or maybe he just hoped." Charlotte smiled. "It would be nice for you to have a sister. I know how much I love mine."

Allison's heart squeezed with love. She had missed hanging out with Charlotte. Their younger sister was busy with her new baby, Merry, but Allison would see Eloise soon. Even the idea of seeing her brothers Seth, Ryan and Daniel again was exciting. She hadn't realized how much she'd missed everyone.

"I've never seen my sister so happy," Allison said to Jill as she handed her a candy cane ornament.

"That's because she's in love with my dad."

Charlotte snorted. "She speaks the truth."

"And, also, he knocked her up, which no one thought was going to be this easy." Jill reached to put an ornament on a higher branch. "He's really good at making babies."

"Please, Jill," Charlotte said, and tears were coming out of her eyes as she gave in to a belly laugh. "You're going to make me pee."

"You don't think I know how this *happened*?" She turned, hand on hip, looking outraged that anyone would think her stupid. "I'm in Honors Biology and at the head of the class."

Allison was trying not to look at Charlotte because, if she did, she'd start laughing so hard she wouldn't catch her breath. Been there, done that.

"Yes, and do me a favor and don't *forget* how this happens," Allison said, biting her lower lip.

"No worries," Jill said. "No glove, no love."

"I'm so glad your dad isn't here right now," Charlotte said, starting to wheeze with laughter. "But good talk."

Half an hour later, Rowan and Nicky returned with the pizza and they all dug in. Billy joined them, calling it a day at last.

"This is delicious," Rowan said. "The best pizza I've ever tasted."

Allison had to agree. There was just the right amount of cheese and sauce on it. Rowan brought them three large pizzas and one of them was a specialty chicken with white sauce that should win a culinary award.

But tree trimming wasn't over until, after dinner, Billy lifted Jill on his shoulders to place the star on top of the tree.

The rest of the evening, they all sat around admiring their handiwork by a roaring fire. More than once, she caught Rowan's gaze on her from across the room. And whenever a space beside her on the couch was empty, Rowan found a way to be right next to her. She told herself this was good because they should be familiar with each other if they were going to fake being in love around other people. He was simply doing his due diligence in playing his part.

But she was enjoying it far too much.

BY THE TIME he finished his shift on Friday and was officially on vacation time, everything was going so well, Rowan didn't want this time with the Abernathy family to end. He loved Allison's family. Nicky was another good Abernathy kid, as it turned out, and on the day he'd picked him up at band practice, they'd talked music and favorite bands all the way home. Then, after eating pizza, they'd sat around admiring the colorful lights on the trimmed tree, Allison cuddled next to him.

She seemed to do that quite a bit these days, whether they were watching a movie with the family in the evenings or simply sitting around talking. Of course, he engineered it by making sure to always find a seat next to her.

Today, after work, he'd gone for a horseback ride with Jill, then come in to help Allison with dinner.

"All right. What are we making tonight?" He rubbed his hands together.

"Nothing fancy. Lasagna."

He noticed she had the noodles boiling and the meat sauce simmering.

"Looks like all I get to do is the layering."

"And that's a big help."

"You're not letting me do any real cooking. And you're not asking for my help around the house enough. What happened to turning me into Cinderella?"

"You had work, so I haven't wanted to bother you too much."

"Well, today is officially my last day until after Christmas." He raised his arms triumphantly. "I'm free."

"Time flies. I can't believe you've already been here a week. Want to go Christmas shopping tomorrow?"

"Try and stop me."

They worked in perfect harmony together, him layering the strained pasta, Allison ladling spoonfuls of hearty meat sauce, then they both sprinkled on the shredded mozzarella cheese. He did so far more generously than she did.

"Don't be stingy with that cheese." He popped her hand lightly and she dropped a handful in one spot.

"Hey, now see what you did. There's too much in one spot."

"Au contraire. Easy fix for that." He then dropped a handful in the remaining spots. "Can't really ever have too much cheese."

"I see you like lasagna with your cheese casserole." Allison smirked.

But the entire Abernathy family seemed to love plenty of cheese, because at the dinner table, it went faster than Seahawks' tickets during the playoffs.

After a dessert of ambrosia salad, they all filed into the living room to enjoy another one of Billy's roaring fires. This time, it was Allison who grabbed a seat next to him and cuddled in close. If he had it his way, he wouldn't move from this position all night.

Fair to say he was in heaven, so, when the doorbell rang, he automatically wondered whether one more person would change this relaxing family dynamic.

And he wasn't wrong.

Billy went to answer the door and came back with his inlaws in tow.

"Mom! Dad! What are you doing here?" Charlotte said. "It's late."

"Not that late! I can still drive after dark. I'm not completely helpless yet," Thaddeus barked.

Oh boy. This man was positively delightful.

"Of course, you can." Billy motioned to the couch. "Have a seat. I just made a fire."

"Oh, you're tree looks just lovely," Mrs. Taylor said, bending to kiss Charlotte's cheek. "What a great job you did."

"Thanks. Dad picked out the tree I liked," Jill said, patting her chest. "And I did most of the work."

"She's the head of the decorating committee," Billy said.

"Hey!" Nicky exclaimed from his perch on an oversize chair where he was playing a video game. "I helped."

"We just ate dinner and finished off every last piece, or I'd offer you some lasagna," Allison said.

"A doctor eating *lasagna*?" Mr. Taylor said. "Isn't that bad for your heart? It's filled with cheese and red meat."

Well, he just wasn't going to let up, was he? "I allow myself to indulge every now and then."

He supposed Thaddeus wouldn't be satisfied until Rowan walked around wearing a lab coat with a stethoscope hung around his neck. Then again, he *wasn't* a doctor, he reminded himself, so Thaddeus was right to doubt. The man had a razor-sharp wit, which he would respect if Thaddeus wasn't so mean.

Jill's eyes widened. "You're a doctor?"

"Anyway, guys," Charlotte quickly interrupted, "we do have some frozen chicken potpies. If I have any takers, we can heat them up. It's Billy's mom's recipe, and I know how much you love your grandma Bonnie's cooking! Right, Jill?"

"Sure, I'll have a chicken pot pie." Nicky looked up from his game.

"You just ate half a casserole of lasagna," Allison said.

"*So?*" the gangly teen said.

"No thank you, dear," Imogen said. "We've already eaten."

"I'm glad to see you two," Charlotte said. "How've you been?"

"More importantly, how are *you* feeling, dear?" Imogen took her daughter's hand and put her other on the large baby bump. "Oh! The baby just kicked. I felt it."

"She or he is saying hello," Billy said.

"Any names yet?" Imogen said.

"Don't pick anything stupid or trendy like Eleven or Twelve, or name your child after a fruit." Thaddeus shook his head in disgust.

"We won't," said Charlotte with what appeared to be a stiff smile. "But Billy and I haven't decided on a name yet."

"And the C-section is still scheduled in January? We want to be there," Imogen said.

Thaddeus was eyeing Rowan suspiciously, as if expecting him to add something to the conversation since he was a surgeon and all. He should know about C-sections and, of course, he knew what they were. Everyone did. A C-section meant avoiding hours of hard labor. He'd heard people talk about it as "the easy way."

"Good thing she's having a C-section," Rowan said with an intellectual nod. "The recovery should be faster and smoother."

Dead silence.

Allison was looking at him with an expression he recognized. Shock.

What? It wasn't faster? If so, why did people call it the "easy way"?

"Actually, dear," Imogen said, not unkindly, "the recovery is even longer with a C-section. Natural is always best, but not everyone can do that. Don't worry, most people don't know this."

"But a doctor would!" Thaddeus said. "Especially a *surgeon.*"

Why, why, why had Allison asked him to pretend to be a doctor? Rowan thought his best response at this point was utter silence. He became a vault. Decided to take a vow of silence. Pretended to be a mime.

"Tell the truth! You're not a doctor." Thaddeus shook a finger at him.

"Thad," Imogen said. "Your blood pressure."

Thaddeus ignored his wife. "He's lying. Do you know about this, Allison, or has he fooled you, too?"

"No, I—" Allison said.

"You're always so gullible, that's your problem," Thaddeus said.

"Dad, *please,*" Charlotte said. "Don't do this now."

"Thaddeus, calm the hell down. I can't have you upsetting my wife," Billy said between gritted teeth.

"Your wife is my daughter and I have three of them. *Three* daughters! You're lucky you only have one. At least Charlotte is fine now, finally, but we need to help Allison come to her senses. Even Eloise is starting to wise up. It's Allison who's still making mistakes."

Rowan cleared his throat, and stood, abandoning his brief mime career.

"Let me help clear this up. You're right, I'm not a doctor."

"Aha!" Thaddeus held up a pointed index finger like Hercule Poirot in an Agatha Christie mystery. "I *knew* it."

"And so did I." Allison held Rowan's hand and squeezed it. "*I'm* the one who asked Rowan to pretend to be a doctor. It's because nothing I ever do is good enough for you and whatever I want is deemed stupid and inconsequential. And you know what? You proved it when you even found fault with a doctor! I'm sick of it all. I make my own decisions and I don't need your approval."

"All I want is for my daughters to be happy and content, but you need help," Thaddeus said. "You make *terrible* decisions."

The words hit Rowan hard. He was the one who made bad decisions, up until the moment he'd agreed to visit Montana. Best decision he'd ever made, despite this humiliation.

Thaddeus wasn't done, even if his wife was pulling on his shoulder, trying to get him to stop talking.

"You need a man like Frederick. If I talk to him, I bet he'll still give you a chance. He has money and can take of any of your little whims, whatever they might be. You'll never have to work a day in your life."

Now, Rowan was annoyed.

"Excuse me, sir, but I have a fine career in the tech industry and can fully support myself and a wife, too."

"But you don't have *real* money. Legacy money. The kind that changes lives."

No, he did not. But he knew that didn't matter to Allison, it clearly only mattered to her father. Rowan couldn't take it anymore. Whether or not he was a doctor was not the problem. Whether or not he was rich was also not the issue here. Not to him. One other little matter presented itself front and center: they still thought Allison was dating him and, right in front of him, were trying to take her away. The lack of respect to someone who wasn't *legacy*-money wealthy astounded him. This was insulting and nonsense.

He understood now even better what Allison had told him on the ride. Her father took everything she wanted away because he didn't think her capable of making her own decisions. So, as she'd told him, she'd stopped sharing her ultimate desires. This was deeply ingrained in her because this man couldn't respect his daughter's choices. They would never be good enough as long as they were hers.

Rowan straightened to his full height, happy to press his advantage in this case.

"See, the thing is, Allison can't date Frederick because she's engaged to me."

Dead silence again, this time accompanied by a small gasp from Allison's mother.

He didn't dare look at Allison, but if she looked anything like Charlotte right now, her jaw was about to come off its hinges.

Billy sat next to his wife, holding her hand, a wide grin on his face.

"What? Engaged?" Thaddeus roared. "Is that *true*, Allison?"

"Y-yes," she said, and Rowan finally dared to glance at her, still sitting on the couch. "We…we're engaged. There's no ring yet, but we're thinking maybe after New Year's we'll pick a date. I…wasn't going to tell anyone because…well, because—"

"Because we didn't want to take the attention away from Charlotte and the new baby. So, we kept it quiet," Rowan said. "I'm sorry. My fault, I convinced Allison that we should keep it a secret."

There. That made sense.

Truthfully, Rowan had shocked himself, too. It wasn't just the idea of Allison dating Frederick or his wanting to protect her from an overbearing father. For two years of dating the same woman, he'd hardly been able to think the word *marriage* in her presence, much less say the word out loud. That should have been a clue. Only now did he fully realize his mistake. He'd wanted to settle down so much, he'd lost sight of the big picture. But his heart spoke for him now.

Thaddeus was still scowling but, thank God, he'd been rendered temporarily speechless.

"That's wonderful!" Imogen reached over and hugged Allison. "Looking at the two of you together, I just *knew* this was going to be the one. Welcome to the family, Rowan."

"Thank you," he said, wishing it were real.

A few days with Allison and there was no doubt in his mind what he wanted was her. It was that simple and that complicated. He wanted her any way he could have her. Things would never be the same after this.

Not for him.

But she had no idea how he felt. He feared that he was falling in love with Allison and had no idea what to do about it.

CHAPTER NINE

"THAT'S ONE WAY to clear a room," Billy said a few minutes later, chuckling. "Thank you."

"You're welcome. What can I say?" Rowan shrugged. "It's a gift."

Allison's parents left shortly after the engagement announcement. Mrs. Taylor and Charlotte certainly seemed happy enough about it. So did Jill, who'd already asked if she could be a bridesmaid when the time came. Did he feel terrible lying to everyone? Yes, he did. But the kindergartener in him wanted to shout, *Allison, you started this!*

Allison left for the kitchen with some excuse and hadn't looked at him since her parents' leaving. Rowan was in trouble, but he couldn't help himself. The reaction had been automatic, and he was already in survival mode. The lies just kept coming. He'd started to grow real feelings and the engagement lie had come far too easily. The problem: he feared he was no longer faking. Obviously, Allison didn't quite feel the same.

It was one thing to feel a magnetic attraction and pull toward someone, quite another to become invested in a real relationship. Eventually, they'd both have to go back home to Seattle and face their real lives. He had no doubt they could work as a couple if she gave them half a chance. Just because he'd arrive at this point first didn't mean she couldn't get there, too. He was a patient man.

"You really didn't have to keep the engagement to yourself," Charlotte said with a wink. "We would have understood."

"I'm confused," Billy said. "I thought you were fake dating."

"Keep up," Charlotte said. "They went from fake dating to fake engaged. It's like a reality show I can't stop watching."

"She's right," Rowan said. "I was in survival mode after admitting I wasn't a doctor. Then it occurred to me that as far as Thaddeus knew, Allison and I were still *dating*, even if I wasn't a doctor. He was trying to fix her up with someone else right in front of me."

"Rude," Charlotte said.

"I guess I lost my head for a minute."

"Rowan, can I talk to you in here for a minute?" Allison popped her head in the living room and beckoned him down the hall.

"Uh-oh," Billy said with a smirk.

"Hang in there, Rowan!" Charlotte lifted her hands in the sign of triumph. "I believe in you."

"Thanks." Her encouragement might be a little premature, but he followed Allison into the kitchen. "What's up?"

She stood by the stove, hand on hip. "Are you bananas? Why did you *do* that?"

"He was tearing into you, Allison. It was hard to just stand there and let him attack you like that. He doesn't have any faith in your decisions, or in your ability to make your own choices. I had to do something. I told you I shouldn't have pretended to be a doctor!"

"Fine, that was my mistake and I'm sorry I dragged you into this mess. But…geez, now everything is so much more complicated. You heard Jill! She wants to be a bridesmaid." Allison covered her eyes.

Rowan felt terrible about lying to the kids. "Maybe we can explain later."

"*We?*" She crossed her arms.

He touched his chest. "I... I will explain."

"I'm going to have to give you a pass, I suppose, because you don't know how things work in Bronco. By morning, the news of our engagement will be everywhere. If not for the fact it's Christmas, someone would already be happily arranging our engagement party. And that someone is my *mother.*"

"I'm sorry. But I just couldn't let him try to set you up with Frederick. Is that what you wanted? Should I have let it happen?"

His heart seemed to skip a beat waiting for the answer. If she'd changed her mind and wanted to hang with the old guy, Rowan would step aside. But he couldn't see that happening.

Not after the way she'd kissed him.

"No, of course not. But I'm used to dealing with my father. I can handle him."

"You shouldn't have to take that from him."

She nodded, acknowledging the truth. "It's true the fake engagement certainly saved me from Frederick. And that was the point of all this."

"You have to admit, Thaddeus is really going to give up on you two now. Nothing says 'off the market' like an engagement."

"I suppose that's true." Her fire seemed to lower from a boil to a simmer. "Not that I would know. I've never been engaged before."

"Me either. But I've been told by—" He resisted completing that sentence because he didn't want to mention Perri's name.

"By whom?" Allison narrowed her eyes.

"Um, Perri. She let it drop that one way to keep a woman is to 'put a ring on it.'" He held up air quotes. "And it drives all the other men away."

"I see. And are you doing all this with me to make *her* jealous?"

"Am I here with you in Montana to make Perri jealous? Hell, no. She doesn't even know where I am or that I'm with you."

"Because if she knew we'd just announced our *engagement*, I have a feeling she'd be at the door right now, trying to reconcile. Pulling out all the stops. She obviously still wants you, Rowan, given the fact she keeps texting you. And she'd be an idiot not to try to get you back."

He let those last words encourage him and put his hands on Allison's shoulders, drawing her closer.

"Listen carefully. I would have never kissed you the way I did if I was still thinking about my ex. Fact is, I haven't thought of her once."

She gave him a little smile. "Well, we have a choice now. We can either ride it out at the Bonnie B for the rest of your visit, where we don't have to answer anyone's probing questions about our wedding plans. Pretend we're hermits."

"Or?"

"Or you go home and we tell everyone we had a big fight."

That was his least favorite option. "Try again. *Or...*?"

She studied him from underneath lowered lashes. "Or we go all in."

"I'm all in. This is my fault, after all. I'm here for you. Plus, I have some shopping left to do."

"Me, too. I don't have anything for the new baby or a Christmas gift for my sister Eloise's baby."

Shopping wasn't the only reason he voted for going all in, but it was better than mentioning the truth. He wasn't done living this fantasy. The way he felt, he would never be done. They'd go back to Seattle engaged for real if he had anything to do with it. But he couldn't scare her off with the idea. It was going to be difficult to know exactly what Allison wanted since she tended to keep her real feelings inside. She'd already told him that. The question was whether she was afraid to say it out loud, or whether she didn't feel that way at all about him.

"Good. Then we'll go shopping as a team," Allison said.

"And we'll handle the questions together."

"This also means we'll have to make an appearance on Christmas at the Triple T," Allison said.

"Your mother likes me, and I can handle Thaddeus. He's done his worst tonight. Everything else from here is uphill."

WHILE HE'D BEEN working the past week, Allison gave Rowan the entire day to himself for work and only saw him when he came down for coffee, wearing those adorable glasses. But now it was Saturday and next week he'd be officially on vacation, so they had plans after lunch to head into town for their shopping excursion.

On her stool at the kitchen counter, Charlotte stirred her soup. "Are you sure this is all fake between you two? It looks so real."

Every time Allison recalled the expression on her father's face when Rowan announced their engagement, she smiled. She'd never seen Rowan so fired up and it was a side of him she liked. His was a righteous anger and he had a point. They were trying to fix her up with Frederick right in front of him. A lesser man would have simply pouted, but Rowan made his point with her father. He hadn't been intimidated.

"I assure you. I'm not engaged." She held out her ring finger. "See?"

"Maybe that part isn't true, but I thought you two were just friends and neighbors."

"We are."

"You could have fooled me. I know what love looks like. And unless he's a Screen Actors Guild member, Rowan behaves like a man in love."

"He's not. Rowan is a friend, and he was simply trying to protect me the other night."

"It was inspiring the way he went after Dad. Not many men stand up to him the way Rowan did. There's Billy and, well... Dante."

Yes, Eloise's husband deserved to be in that select group.

"You're both lucky. A strong man is required to stand up to our father and put him in his place."

"And I think you may have found that man."

Allison shook her head. "I'm not getting my hopes up. His ex is still texting him and I don't like that at all."

"Hasn't he made himself clear with her?"

"He *says* he has. He says he's done with her."

But it bared repeating: he'd said that before.

"Then I think you should listen to him. Just keep pretending you're engaged, have some fun, and maybe when you go back to Seattle it will turn into something real."

"You know me, I don't want to get my hopes up and be disappointed again. Men have a history of doing that to me every time I start to get invested."

"Maybe he'll be different. You know what you could do?"

"What?"

Advice from her big sister was always welcome. For someone who was a marine biologist, so career driven she'd almost bypassed her childbearing years, Charlotte was living the dream now with her true love.

"You could tell him how you feel. Tell him what you want. A home. A family and children."

"How do *you* know that's what I want?"

Allison thought she'd done a fairly good job of hiding her desperate need to become a mom. She didn't talk about it because she might jinx it ever happening for her.

"Because you're my sister. I know you, and I see the way you look at me." She planted her hands on her huge belly. "This, too, could someday be yours. Well, not *this* one, but you know what I mean. I didn't know I'd have this chance again, but I hoped."

"And there was also Winona's special stone."

It was a rhodonite, a pink stone marbled with gray, on a silver chain. Winona said it helped the wearer achieve "emotional balance, cleared away emotional wounds from the past and nurtured love in the present."

"Which you could always borrow, by the way." Charlotte said, then sighed. "When and if they ever find her again."

"I don't know if I believe in that kind of thing."

"The point is, I let Billy *know* how I felt, and that I wanted to have a child. That I still loved him, and never stopped."

"Look at you, making it sound so easy."

Allison could never be so open and honest. She realized that didn't make sense. It wasn't logical, but her heart had a mind of its own. It seemed to believe the moment she expressed what she wanted it would be ripped from her. It wasn't true, of course. Thaddeus couldn't take her desire for a baby away from her. No one could.

"Are you ready?"

She turned to find Rowan behind her, wearing those sexy hipster glasses, his hair flopping down over one side of his brow. Holy Christmas! How did he manage to be more attractive to her each day? Of course she'd always found him attractive but her heart had never fluttered before when he walked in the room.

"Yes, let me just get my coat."

"How are you feeling, Charlotte?" Rowan said. "Can I get you something before we take off?"

"Nothing for me, thanks. And, by the way, the kids won't be home for dinner. It's their night with Jane. So, if you two want to stay out, that's fine with me. Billy will reheat chicken potpies for us. You two deserve a break."

"Is this your way of telling me you want some alone time with Billy?" Allison said.

"Well…" Charlotte answered with a silly lovesick smile. "Before long, we'll be parents and it's going to be about our baby twenty-four-seven. I'm counting the days I have left with him all to myself."

"Say no more." Rowan held up a palm. "I'll keep Allison

out as long as possible. I'd like to have dinner with my affi-anced anyway."

"And take a coat and gloves, city boy!" Charlotte said. "It might actually snow today."

Allison finger-waved goodbye from the front door as she grabbed the keys to Charlotte's SUV from the bowl. Rowan joined her at the door and she quickly led him outside. Slid-ing into the driver's seat, she smiled at him as he buckled in, started the engine, and then drove them into town.

"We'll start in Bronco Heights, and then later we can drive over to Bronco Valley. First stop. The Hey, Baby store." She pulled over. "I need something for my nieces."

"Okay, and while you're in there, mind if I get myself a pair of boots over there?" He pointed down the street to the artsy window display of cowboy boots with elves popping out of them, straw hats covered in red and green bandannas, and sparkly belt buckles.

"Okay, see you back here when you're done."

Inside Hey, Baby, the adorable displays of baby clothes overwhelmed Allison. She would like to say it was due to the embarrassment of riches. So many choices. The truth was, her empty womb leapt with joy at the possibilities. Just walking in here gave her uterus false hope.

"Hi, there! Can I help you find something?" the clerk, Lisa, someone Allison vaguely recognized as being a friend to her cousin Daphne, asked. "Oh, Allison. How've you been?"

"Good. Absolutely great!" Allison said with false bravado. *Fake it 'til you make it.*

"Oh my goodness!" Lisa said. "Are you expecting, too?"

Why? Do I look pregnant? She bit back her sassy remark. "No, I'm here to get gifts for Charlotte's baby, and for my niece, Merry."

The clerk led her to an array of little holiday dresses, each one more precious than the last. Allison had no idea they made them this small. She could already picture little Merry in the frilly pink-and-white one with little ribbons. So precious.

She loaded up on dresses in all the growing sizes. "I'll take one of each."

At the register, Lisa rang Allison up. "You're such a great aunt. I'm sure someday you'll be in here shopping for your own little one."

It felt like pity talking and Allison bristled. Nothing worse than someone feeling sorry for her.

"I'm not sure I want children," she lied. "I've got a demanding career in the city."

"Hey, babe."

Allison had no idea how much he'd heard of their conversation, but Rowan strode right up to Allison, planting a kiss on her lips.

"Are you about done?"

Well, he apparently had trouble acting like a doctor but no trouble pretending to be her fiancé. He was quite gifted at this, actually. Almost like he'd done it before.

"Just paying right now."

"I'm Rowan Scott, Allison's fiancé." Rowan offered his hand. "Nice to meet you."

"You're engaged? I hadn't heard! Congratulations."

"Thank you," Allison said, handing over her credit card.

Lisa accepted it, then practically bent over backward, presumably to catch a glimpse of her ring. Allison took pity on her acrobatics. If she kept twisting and turning like that, she might injure herself. This was so irritating.

"We don't have a ring yet," Allison said.

"It's very new," Rowan said. "In fact, we should do something about that today."

"Sure." Allison gathered her purchases. "Very nice seeing you again. Merry Christmas."

"Merry Christmas!" Lisa called out.

Rowan held open the door for her. "Where to next?"

His enthusiasm was infectious, she'd give him that.

"I just realized something. You really love Christmas, don't you?"

"What's not to love?" Rowan grinned. "Parties, gifts, food. Candy canes. Hot chocolate. Santa Claus."

"Santa Claus?"

Hand to his chest, he feigned shock. "Don't tell me you don't believe in the man."

"Okay, I won't tell you," she deadpanned. "But my older brother once told me that our parents were Santa Claus. I think I was eight."

"He ruined it for you."

"It would have happened sooner or later."

"Some people tell their kids straight off that they're Santa Claus because they don't like lying to them. But I think there's something really magical about the myth. Good for the imagination. I'm going to tell my children about Santa Claus. The minute they ask Santa for a car, I figure that's time to fess up."

Allison was a bit stunned at how easily he talked about having children, as if he never doubted the possibility.

"Seems like a reasonable compromise."

"Hey, is everything okay?" Rowan took her hand. "You seem a little off. Irritated, maybe."

"It's just…" She blew out a breath, trying to find a way to put her feelings into words. "The store clerk. She tried to make me feel better about not having a baby. As if because my sisters are having babies, that means I should rush to do the same."

"Right. It's not a race."

"Well, not for you men it isn't."

"Do you want to have kids?"

They'd never talked about this before, but why would they? It was the type of conversation one had with a boyfriend or significant other. And that meant that if they were playing at being engaged, they should talk about it.

"Kids?" Allison cleared her throat. "I'm not sure. I mean… yeah, probably."

"Is this one of those things you're afraid to admit out loud?" He cocked his head.

Bingo! How did he know this when most of her ex-boyfriends had been eternally clueless about Allison? She blamed herself because she hadn't been exactly open with them, unwilling to risk too much. Rowan made it easy to admit the truth. Whether it was because they were just playing at this or because it was just the ease she felt around him, she didn't know.

A safe answer involved changing the subject.

"Since you love Christmas, I know exactly where to take you next."

CHAPTER TEN

"SADIE'S HOLIDAY HOUSE is always a favorite." She pointed in the direction of the shop. "It's Christmas year-round in there. Charlotte and I used to love that place. An old friend took over and I haven't been in there for a while."

"Sounds like the place I need."

They'd finished their shopping in Bronco Heights, and Allison was eager to introduce Rowan to her favorite stores in Bronco Valley, not to mention some of her favorite places to grab a bite. But even she was shocked at the speed of the town gossip mill! They were offered congratulations by no less than three couples on their way to the shop a few feet next door.

"See what I mean?" Allison said. "You can't keep a secret around here."

"You're right. Word gets around fast. But everyone is being so nice, don't you think?"

"You won't find too many mean folks in Bronco, that's for sure."

The display window at Sadie's Holiday House was themed on "The Twelve Days of Christmas," with twelve wreaths decorated in the gift of each day. There were little drummer figurines and instruments in one, another decorated with five large golden rings, and so on. A chalkboard hanging on the door denoted the countdown to Christmas.

Rowan held the door open, chimes sounding like sleigh bells ringing out. Allison walked inside, immediately assaulted with the aromatic smells of cinnamon and pine, two of her favorite scents. "White Christmas" piped through the store's speakers. Surrounding them were ornaments, artificial trees, wreaths, snow globes and even some jewelry under a clear display case. The store of her youth was now even better than her memory served.

Last year, Charlotte had informed Allison that the new owner, who happened to be her old grade school classmate, Sadie Chamberlin, had married Sullivan Grainger on Christmas Day. She was the same bubbly girl Allison remembered, all grown up, with wavy blond hair and dark eyes. Sadie Grainger now.

"Allison! I haven't seen you in ages! Welcome back to Sadie's Holiday House, and Merry Christmas!"

"Merry Christmas. I've been wanting to congratulate you in person on your wedding. Charlotte told me all about it."

"I got your gift all the way from Seattle right after the holidays. That was kind of you. Had I known you were in town, you would have also been invited."

Just like Sadie, who never wanted to leave anyone out of the fun.

"I didn't stay long last year," Allison said.

"How do you like city life?"

"Love it." She hooked a thumb at Rowan and the lie slid out of her mouth easily. "This is my fiancé, Rowan Scott."

The problem with all this pretend was how much she wished it were true. Lying had become as effortless as breathing.

Sadie smiled at Rowan. "Nice to meet you. You're both visiting?"

"I'm also from Seattle," Rowan said. "And I left my shopping to the last minute, as usual."

"Let's see the ring!" Sadie said cheerfully.

Allison sighed. "Oh, we haven't—"

Rowan piped up. "Actually, that's sort of what I'm here about. I got so excited, I asked her to marry me without a ring! Can you believe it? I'm *lucky* she said yes!"

"I can't see anyone saying no to you," Sadie said with a laugh, an obvious glint of male appreciation in her eyes.

Her thoughts echoed Allison's own. *How in the world is this guy still single?*

Allison would unwrap this mystery tonight. After all, Perri had been in the picture for only two years.

"Do you by chance have any rings we could see?" Rowan took Allison's hand and squeezed it.

"Rowan, I—" Allison said.

Sadie interrupted. "No diamonds in here, I'm sorry to say. But we have some beautiful vintage pieces, if you're interested in taking a look."

"I'll buy you a diamond when we get back to Seattle. I have contacts with some conflict-free diamond jewelers back home. But you need something for now." He followed Sadie to the glassed-in display case.

Allison stared at the case, dumbfounded. Was this really happening? No. It was all pretend. A show. But, seriously, Rowan was taking this farther than she'd imagined. It wasn't necessary to buy her a ring, for goodness' sake. She didn't want to think how much this would set him back. What was she supposed to do after the holidays? Give the ring back? Sell it and pay him back?

"Rowan." She pulled on his sleeve. "Maybe we could borrow one—"

"It's fine."

She should have considered asking to borrow one of Charlotte's rings. Allison had plenty of her own that, while not diamonds, would do the job when put on the left hand, but she'd left all those home.

Rowan seemed caught up in his shopping spree.

"Can I see that one?" Rowan pointed and Sadie brought out a beautiful ring, strands of roped gold with a yellow stone in the center. "What do you think?"

"Um, too *Game of Thrones*." Allison laughed and shook her head.

"That's what I think!" Sadie said. "Here are a few more that I think are more Allison's style."

Rowan reached for one ring after another until he held up a sapphire, a beautiful diamond-shaped stone set in a simple gold band. "This one. Don't you think? It reminds me of your eyes. So blue."

He reached for her left hand and slid it on her ring finger. "Hey, it fits."

Allison admired the ring then locked eyes with Rowan. Speaking of blue…his eyes were a deep indigo shade that reminded her of twilight. The dark piercing blue before it blended into the night. The kind of blue that—

Stop right there. This is bananas. Nuts.

But she couldn't stop. And now she knew why. She was in love with this man. He was more wonderful than she'd ever imagined. To think, all this time, he'd been across the hall from her.

"It's…beautiful." She stuck out her ring finger, staring like she'd never seen anything so sparkly in her life.

A thousand real diamonds could never replace this ring. It was one of a kind, sort of like Rowan. Just like that, a tear rolled down her cheek before she could wipe it away.

"Hey, what's wrong?" Rowan tipped her chin to meet his gaze. "Is this not the one?"

"Those are tears of joy," Sadie said.

"Yeah? Is that joy?" Rowan whispered, holding her gaze.

Allison quickly nodded, not trusting herself to speak.

In his eyes, she saw his concern for her, and her heart tugged almost painfully. The truth was, she didn't want to pretend anymore, but telling him the truth was another story. He wasn't ready for this, just off a breakup. He was just playing a part. Having fun. Because it *was* fun to put on a show if you weren't too invested in the outcome.

But she was far too invested. She didn't know how she could go back to Seattle and resume her normal life after having someone this wonderful in her life. Even for such a short time, sad to say it was the best relationship she'd ever had.

And it wasn't even real.

Rowan paid, thanked Sadie, held Allison's hand and, together, they walked outside. Only then did Allison realize, in her stupor, that she'd forgotten to do some of her own shopping. Good grief. She was practically in a trance, walking as if in a fluffy cloud, barely feeling her feet touch the ground.

"Hey, everybody! We're getting married," Rowan shouted.

"Rowan—"

He winked. "Got to make this look real. All in, remember?"

The next thing she knew, Rowan picked her up in the air like she was made of straw, lifting her feet off the floor, his smile wide.

Bystanders stopped to congratulate them.

"Good luck!"

"Invite me to the wedding!"

"Never go to bed angry with each other!"

Rowan set her down, took it all in stride, and waved. "Thanks for the advice!"

A truck passed by, driven by none other than Billy's own brother, Jace Abernathy. He slowed and leaned out the window. "Kiss her, you fool!"

"I think I will!"

Hand clasped on the nape of her neck, Rowan drew her close and kissed her in his spine-melting, brain-cell-dissolving way. He kissed her with such fierceness that Allison began to feel down to the marrow of her bone that something very real was happening. To both of them.

With his hands low on her hips, hers clinging to his shoulders, she was in another world. His lips were hot and insistent on hers, and she gave in completely.

Then the second most amazing thing happened in a smattering of days filled with incredible and welcome surprises.

It began to snow.

CHAPTER ELEVEN

THE FIRST SNOWFLAKE fell on her nose. When Allison pulled back, Rowan's dark jacket was dusted by white. Flakes of snow were settling in his thick dark hair. She reached to brush them off.

He grinned. "I guess your sister was right about the snow."

Fortunately, Bean & Biscotti was across the way. Rowan pulled her into the establishment.

Two crossed candy canes clung to the glass window display and inside was a small, brightly lit Christmas tree. Ornamental red bulbs that almost looked like glossy red apples were strung along the counter between the register and coffee machines. The clerk wore a "Santa, I Can Explain" sweatshirt decorated with red-and-green bows and complemented by her elf hat.

Then the patron she'd been serving turned and Allison recognized her cousin Brandon's wife, Cassidy Taylor.

"Hey, cuz!" Cassidy said. "Brandon told me you were visiting."

Rowan blinked. "Are you related to everyone in town?"

"It just seems that way some days. But Cassidy is married to my cousin Brandon."

She introduced Rowan to Cassidy.

"What are you doing in here?" Allison asked.

Cassidy owned Bronco Java & Juice on the other side of town.

"Just checking out the competition." She smiled. "Now, can I see the ring?"

No doubt she'd witnessed the Oscar-worthy performance outside the window.

"That's gorgeous," Cassidy said. "Congratulations to you both. Rowan, you really got a good one, I hope you know. We're only related by marriage, but she's still my favorite cousin. I claimed her."

"I know," Rowan said quietly, almost privately, to Allison. "I'm very lucky."

"I'm sure I'll see you on Christmas Day at the Taylors!" Cassidy sang out, holding her coffee in one hand and waving goodbye with the other.

They ordered their drinks and the clerk served them in short order.

"Should we bring the kids home some of these cookies?" She pointed to the display case with decorative cookies, piped with icing in bright colors.

They were down to only a few of the cookies she and Rowan had baked together. No one had cared what they'd looked like. Nicky and Jill ate them with gusto and saved only a few for Branson.

"The kids will love you forever if you bring more cookies," Rowan said.

"You mean *you'll* love me forever," Allison chuckled before she fully realized what she'd said.

It took on an entirely different significance now and she wished she could take it back.

"Well, that's a given." Rowan brought her hand to his mouth and brushed a kiss across her knuckles.

Rowan found a table for them and they settled in, facing the snow as it fell. To Allison, snow was always so much better from the inside looking out. Warmer, for one. Drier.

"Beautiful view," Allison said, cupping her mocha latte for the heat.

"Agreed."

But when she glanced at Rowan, he was looking at her.

She cleared her throat. "So, Rowan, I was thinking that I don't actually know my fiancé quite as well as I thought I did."

"You know everything that matters."

"I'm not so sure about that."

"What do you want to know? Ask away."

"This is a tough one, but…why in the *world* are you still single?"

Rowan laughed. "You sound like my mother."

"It's just… I know about you and Perri, but that's only two years. You're thirty-six, so I know you have a longer dating history than that. And I wondered…was there ever someone special? Someone that you *almost* married?"

"Ah…you're asking about the one that got away. That kind of thing?" He took a sip of his coffee. "I could ask the same about you. Why are you still single?"

"I asked first."

"Fine. I'm definitely a one-woman kind of man and I've mostly had long-term relationships. Not a lot of casual dating, except for a little while in college. Yes, there was a girl or two who broke my heart, but I never asked anyone to marry me. I always felt when it came to that point, I'd know it, you know? I wouldn't be able to live without her. I kept hoping I'd get there with Perri, but if I'm being honest with myself, it was never meant to be."

"I understand. I asked because…well, sometimes you seem almost too good to be true."

"Obviously, I have my faults. I'd rather not list them for you right now, but I can be messy and…" At this, he scowled a little. "I pout when I'm mad. And I stop talking...well, I'm working on that."

"That's very honest. And if that's all you can come up with, you're a prince among men. *No* guy likes to talk about feelings."

"I don't know everything about you either. You told me about boarding school, and I've met some of your family. But was there ever someone special? Someone here in Bronco?"

"No," Allison admitted. "When I was a teenager, I used to envy Charlotte so much for what she had with Billy. It all seemed so romantic to me at the time, that young first love. It didn't work out for me with Jimmy Lee, but I even tried to... now this is going to make you laugh, but I thought if it worked for Charlotte... I tried to get together with Billy's brother Theo. My father would have probably loved that. Theo had zero interest in me, however. He and Bethany are very happy together."

His phone buzzed with a text and he pulled it out then quickly replied, thumbs flying.

Allison couldn't help but worry it was Perri again. "Any problems? Work?"

"No, work is good. I've been working at nights after dinner, so I have more time free during the day. Then I had the catch-up day yesterday. Plus, it is always slower this time of year. That's why I took some time off, even before I realized I'd be staying until the New Year."

"You really don't have to stay that long. I feel so bad dragging you into all this."

"Hey, it was my idea to be engaged." He squeezed her hand.

"What about the plans you had to see your family?"

"Actually that text was from my mother."

"Oh no, is she upset?"

"She might be, a little, when I tell her I'm not going to be seeing her on Christmas Day."

"Rowan!" Allison lightly slugged his shoulder. "You haven't *told* her?"

"Don't worry. I'm phoning her tonight when we get back. She'll understand."

"She's going to hate me for keeping you away from your family."

"Are you kidding? She loves you. And this year Christmas dinner is going to be at my brother's house in Everett, just a short ferry ride for my parents. So, it's not like I'm missing my *mother's* Christmas."

"Do you get along with your brother?"

"I do now. We're just surprisingly different. He tends to show off all the money he earns at his marketing job while I live more frugally and sock it away."

"Like me."

"Got to admit, I was surprised to find out about your family. You struck me as a very down-to-earth, middle-class girl when we met. You're so unassuming, no one would guess the kind of wealth you come from."

"Money has never been important to me. Of course, I realize I can say that since I've been privileged enough to always have my basic financial needs provided for."

"Emphasis on financial."

"You know me so well." Feeling a strong pull of melancholy, Allison watched the softly falling snow outside. "I'm closer to my mother because at least she tries. She understands how difficult my father can be and tries her best to even out the playing field by playing good cop to his bad cop. But, unfortunately, he overrules her far too often."

"My dad tries to do the same, but I have to tell you, they have the best marriage. A lot of compromise. Marriage is work."

"I never thought of it that way, but you're right. Charlotte and Billy are so in love, but there's no doubt they've done a lot of work to blend their family. His kids were not thrilled with her in the beginning. Even though their mother had moved on, with a new partner, they must have wanted their father to stay single forever."

"Yet she won them over."

"Yes, as you can plainly see, but my sister is the best. There's no way you can't love her. Just no possible way."

Rowan smiled. "I believe you and I think it runs in the family."

This was all so confusing. Yes, they were now putting on a show and doing a great job. But he didn't have to say such sweet words when only she could hear him. He could have also just given her a peck on the cheek instead of kissed the breath out of her.

"It's still snowing," Rowan said. "Good thing I bought these boots. You know, I still have a little shopping to do. Why don't we each go our separate ways and then meet back at the truck?"

"Okay. Then we'll have dinner at Bronco Burgers."

Rowan went in one direction, saying he wanted to find something for his mother, and Allison went in the other. Once she saw him go around the bend, she headed toward Cimarron Rose. She still needed a gift for Rowan, and she wanted something special. He'd bought her a beautiful ring, completely unexpected. No, it wasn't truly an engagement ring, but he was right in that the stone matched her eyes. It was such a sweet and sentimental gift, and she wanted something similar for him. But she had no idea where to begin and hoped maybe the proprietor would have some advice.

"Hi, Allison!" Everlee Abernathy, formerly Roberts, greeted her at the door. As usual, she was adorably dressed; this time in a cream white dress cinched with a dark brown leather belt. Brown leather cowboy boots completed the outfit.

"Hi Evy! You look amazing, as usual. I need something special for my fiancé."

"Congratulations. I heard all about your engagement."

Good grief. Allison rolled her eyes. "I'm sure my mother

had it broadcast on the evening news, but I must have missed the announcement."

Evy laughed. "What did you have in mind?"

"I have no idea, but in the past, I've given him gift cards."

This year she needed something a lot more personal. But what? They weren't intimate—unfortunately—so it would be very inappropriate to give him the gift of her lingerie. She always thought that was a strange gift anyway, although ex-boyfriends swore to her it really was a gift to *them*. Cologne would be nice, but face it, he already smelled so good. She didn't know what he wore but she definitely didn't want to change it.

"I put some things together that we carry and might make good gifts for men." Evy led her to a gift section, but she didn't see anything that struck her as quite right.

Allison finished the rest of her shopping while she gave some thought to what might work for Rowan. A beautiful silk scarf for her mother, and a money clip for her father. Sort of a gag gift on her part, though he wouldn't get the joke.

He could never have too many of those.

And then she saw the gift. It seemed as though a neon arrow pointed at it. Perfect.

"Wrap that one up! I'll take it."

CHAPTER TWELVE

ROWAN CIRCLED BACK to Sadie's Holiday House once he and Allison separated because he'd seen the perfect gift for Allison. The ring felt like a gift of necessity, and she might think he'd done it to play the game. Far from it, but he saw why she might think so. But this gift would remove all doubt about his feelings when she opened it on Christmas morning. He was only waiting to see some kind of acknowledgment from her, a revelation and spoken words that this was no longer a performance. It was real, down to the snowflakes that fell on them like they were trapped in a real-life snow globe.

Allison was special to him and reliving his romantic history with her earlier had only put a fine point on it. He'd never felt this way about any woman he'd dated and yet, in other ways, she made him feel like a teenager all over again with his first crush. He couldn't stop touching her, couldn't stop kissing her, and he wanted so much more. Her mouth, those mile-long legs, her beautiful eyes. He was out of his mind with lust.

"You're back!" Sadie said when he opened the shop door and the chimes sounded.

"I saw something while we were here before, but I want this gift to be a surprise." He pointed to the gold chain with a locket in the shape of an envelope. Perfect.

A way for her to remember the time she'd asked him to pick up her mail but instead he'd visited her in Montana and fallen in love with her. He hoped when they both returned to Seattle everything between them would be different. The locket was beautiful and perfect, but as he held it, one side slid open and revealed a message engraved inside: *I love you.*

Was it too much? He understood that Allison was hesitant to express her feelings, so he couldn't play that game, too. Instead, it was time to reveal what he wanted, what he now knew he'd wanted since the day he'd first laid eyes on her. But beyond just having a good time as he'd initially fantasized, he wanted an entire future with her.

He was going to tell her before Christmas.

It didn't take him long to finish his shopping after buying the locket, so he took a minute and stepped outside to phone his mother. The call was long overdue.

"Hey, Mom. I have some bad news. Don't be too upset with me, okay?"

"Oh no. What has she done now?"

Yikes. She thought this was about Perri, no doubt. Mom was not a fan.

"I'm not going to be able to make it home for Christmas."

"But you spent it with Perri's family last year. It's our turn!"

Rowan winced. She was right. "I promise to make it up to you next year."

Next year, maybe he and Allison would spend Christmas in Washington with his family. They would all love her.

"Don't tell me you're working."

"No, not working."

"Going to *Perri's family* again?" The tone in her voice said she might consider cutting him out of the will.

"No, actually, Perri and I broke up."

A beat of silence and then she said in a cheerful voice, "Well, that's too bad."

"It was time. We're really done."

"Are you sad? You don't sound sad."

"Maybe at first because I feel like I've invested so much in her. But now I'm happier than I've ever been."

He considered how much he should reveal. The whole pretend-engagement thing sounded a little farfetched. His mother wouldn't appreciate the farce and might worry too much.

"Remember my neighbor, Allison Taylor? She needed my help, so I'm in Bronco, Montana, literally having a white Christmas."

"You're with Allison? That's…why, that's wonderful."

"Yeah, so I won't be able to make dinner at Grayson's. Should I call him, or will you tell him?"

"I'll let him know, don't worry. His fiancée is a bit nervous about hosting this year, so at least this will ease some of her tension."

"Why? It's just one less person."

"She wants every little detail to be perfect. You know she tries so hard to impress you. They both do."

Wait. *What?* In Rowan's mind, they tried hard to one-up him. Whatever Rowan did, they did it bigger. Last year, Rowan had sprung for a new water-efficient dishwasher in his kitchen. They'd renovated their entire kitchen with energy-saving appliances. When Rowan bought a Tesla to save on gasoline they'd purchased his-and-her matching ones.

"I don't know why she's worried about impressing me. You know me. I'll eat just about anything."

She chuckled. "It must be because she knows how important you are to the family. You're the lifeblood of the Scotts. Our comic relief when something goes wrong. Our cheerleader and protector. But we'll try to be fine without you this year. Just promise me one thing."

"Of course. Anything."

"Don't leave Montana without telling Allison how you feel about her."

Rowan coughed and hit his chest. It was as if she could read his mind, or the tea leaves, or some such thing.

Maybe Evan Cruise wasn't the only psychic he'd met.

"Um, *what*?"

"Honey, it's so obvious. The entire time you've dated Perri, you've talked about Allison instead. 'Allison thinks this' and 'Allison said that.' You did things with Perri, you *dated* her, but you talked about Allison. She was in your heart from the moment she moved into that building. Am I wrong?"

She wasn't wrong and Rowan didn't know how he'd never realized it before this trip. Maybe because she seemed like a far-away impossibility. Like someone who'd never think of him as more than a friend. He didn't know if this pretend relationship had been the clincher to make her see him in a new way, or if maybe this had been a possibility all along.

Either way, he'd take it.

BY THE TIME dinner rolled around, Rowan had walked from one end of town to the other, appreciating everything he saw. The snow was sticking to every available surface. People were scurrying by on their way to a shop or their vehicle. The air had a bite to it, a slight wind occasionally breaking through the barrier of his jacket.

After a few minutes, he saw Allison by the truck, loading some of her bags, and ran to join her. Throwing some of his own shopping into the back seat, he kept the locket in his pocket and close to him. He didn't want her catching even a glimpse of it a moment before Christmas. Timing was everything and this time he'd get it right.

"I hope you're hungry," Allison said. "Bronco Burgers has some juicy burgers but a little bit of everything."

Not surprisingly, the establishment was busy with many people seeking shelter from the falling snow. They were able to snag a seat in a booth, however, and, rather than sit across from Allison, he slid in next to her.

"I'll be right back for your order," the server said.

Rowan reached for Allison's hand. "I missed you."

She laughed. "We were separated for two hours, if that."

She thought he was simply pretending for the crowd around them. And of course she would assume that, since he hadn't made any effort to tell her the truth. None of this was fake anymore. Not for him.

"What are you having?" She flipped through the menu. "The burgers are flame-broiled and exceptional. I haven't had one of those in ages. And they're really known for the shakes."

He would like to have Allison on a platter, both for appetizer, dinner and dessert. But that wasn't likely to happen at her sister's house.

Behave yourself, Rowan.

"I'll have the same." He hovered over her shoulder, glancing at the menu even though he had his own. "You know what I was thinking?"

"That you want dessert?" She smiled and winked.

The way she'd said the words, it was almost as if her thoughts were running parallel to his own.

"And maybe even before you have a burger?" She completed the thought.

Yeah. He wasn't *that* lucky. "What I was thinking is that, for an engaged couple, we haven't had a lot of privacy."

"Shh. Don't tell anybody, but we're not actually engaged," she whispered.

"That doesn't mean I wouldn't like a little privacy."

"For…?" Her eyes were dilated and shimmering.

"To kiss you the way I really want to. The way I'd do it when it isn't a public display."

She bit her lower lip. "Given the way you kissed me, if it gets any hotter, I might explode."

"Yes, exactly. I *want* you to explode."

"Rowan. What are we doing?" She cupped the side of his face.

"Whatever you want. For as long as you want." He rested his hand on her leg, their knees bumping against each other. "Tell me you don't feel something real happening between us."

"I do, but I don't know what to do about that."

"Let me help you. Had I known you felt even a small amount of interest in me, I would have asked you out a long time ago. I thought you'd relegated me to the friend zone from the start."

"I never did, and I've always been attracted to you. It's just the timing was always off for us."

"I know, and I feel like I've wasted so much time. I don't want to waste any more."

"I understand wasted time. I'm thirty-six years old and I want…so many things."

"Are you willing to tell me what you want? Because I need to hear it from you. You've told me how hard it is to express your feelings and that's why I'm telling you first. I like you a lot and everything we've been doing since I got here is like a fantasy come to life for me."

This was exactly the moment the server came to take their orders, making Rowan wonder if their timing was still off. They both ordered burgers and when the server finally left, Allison turned her entire body to his.

"You asked me what I want. I'm going to be honest. Maybe… I don't know, but *maybe* I want a baby someday soon because I'm running out of time. So, if you're not interested in a family, that's a deal-breaker for me, even though, yes, I'm kind of crazy about you, too."

He did not hesitate. With the right woman, he was ready for everything.

"Sign me up. I love kids. For sure I want at least one, maybe two, but you know I'm a conservationist." Rowan wanted more even if he realized he might be pushing her too far. "And what else do you want?"

"I'd like to be married first, to the right man, of course. Not necessarily for me, but mostly for my mother. And as much as my father annoys me, I would rather not give him a coronary. He already had two daughters pregnant before marriage."

"And what else?"

"I've already said enough. What if none of this happens just because I want it too much?"

"You know in your heart that doesn't make any sense, babe." It was the first time he'd called her by the name privately. "I want to give you everything you want."

"I swear, you're too good to be true." She rested her hand on his knee.

"Nope. Far from it. Just wait until the Seahawks lose their chance at the Super Bowl again."

"Oh, I do remember. Wasn't that the time you didn't come out of your apartment for days? I'd usually see you in the hallway every morning when you were on your way back from grabbing a coffee and I was on my way to work. That week I was so worried about you I knocked on your door for a welfare check." She seemed to fight a smile.

He was flattered she remembered. Almost as much as he'd been when she'd knocked on his door to check on him all those months ago. The next day she'd had a condolence fruit basket delivered with a card that said, "Maybe next year! Go, Seahawks!"

He'd smiled for days.

"I hope you know a girl doesn't just ask *anyone* to come out and visit her hometown and stay with her family. She doesn't ask a random guy to pretend to be her boyfriend. I asked you because I trust you. Because for me, you're...special."

"You're special to me, too."

The server arrived with their plates, and it was difficult to eat when they were touching each other every few seconds. She fed him a French fry and he kissed her, wanting a taste of her meal. They didn't have dessert, after all, because suddenly it seemed they both wanted to get out of there fast. He wanted to find that privacy he'd mentioned earlier and hoped she was thinking along the same lines. If their timing was good, Charlotte and Billy would be asleep since they were both early risers. As for the kids, he wasn't sure if they'd be back right after dinner at their mother's. They were sort of the wild card. But for Rowan, hope sprang eternal.

They pulled up to the ranch house a few minutes later. Almost every light in the house appeared to be off.

"Maybe everyone's gone to bed," Allison said, and they walked hand in hand to the porch.

Rowan mentally crossed everything. When they got to the porch, he couldn't wait another minute and turned her to him, bringing her in for a hot kiss. She responded and, before long, he'd moved her against the porch rail, lifting her leg up and kissing her hard and deep. She moaned and threaded her fingers through his hair. They were both wearing too many clothes, making this all difficult. Inside, he'd like to peel every piece of her clothing off. Slowly.

She pulled away with a gasp. "Let's go to my room."

Rowan would have torn the front door off its hinges to get there but it seemed her key worked fine. He was right behind her, hand on her butt as she swung open the door.

"Hey, Aunt Allison."

The light was dim, but he spied two teenage boys lying in juxtaposing positions on the big couch, each holding a handheld device. He would bet everything he had that the two were online gaming in the same world, a few feet away, speaking to each other only through the game. Obstacle number one and number two. The boys.

This was probably Rowan's punishment for having once been a teenage boy with only one thing on his mind.

Similar to tonight, in fact.

He'd never seen one of the boys before today but the minute he turned to face them, Rowan knew he'd have recognized him anywhere. He was the teenage version of Billy Abernathy. The lanky kid stood and did the obligatory nephew hug with Allison, an awkward sort of half hug.

"Welcome home, stranger." Allison patted Branson's back, giving Rowan a frozen smile over the young man's shoulder. "We sure missed you around here. Rowan, this is Branson, Billy's oldest. He's going to bunk with his brother while you're here."

Rowan offered his hand. "Rowan Scott. Thanks for sharing your room."

He was stuck on whether he should refer to himself as Allison's fiancé, boyfriend, or simply friend. Friend who was in love with her. But TMI for the kid who, Rowan knew, did *not* want to know what Rowan had pictured doing to their aunt only seconds ago.

"Oh, you're the one who pretended to be a doctor," Branson chuckled. "Dude, that was awesome. Nicky told me all about it."

"Not so awesome. I screwed up because I didn't know anything about a C-section." Rowan shook his head. "Turns out I'm a terrible surgeon."

"All I know is you stood up to Mr. Taylor and my dad was wicked impressed."

"Good to know." Rowan faked a yawn. "Well, I'm going to bed. We spent all day shopping."

"Yes, me, too. I'll see you two in the morning," Allison said and gave Rowan a small conspiratorial and wicked smile.

They were halfway up the stairs, him right behind Allison again, when Jill came down the steps.

"Could you help me with the essay for my assignment? I got an extra day, but I said I'd email it to my teacher tonight. I just want another set of eyes before I hit Send."

Obstacle number three: the brilliant niece. Rowan saw his hopes evaporating.

"Oh. Sure, honey."

And with those words, Rowan kissed away all hope of spending the night in Allison's arms.

It had probably been a bad idea anyway.

CHAPTER THIRTEEN

FOR THE NEXT WEEK, Allison tried to stay away from Rowan, which wasn't easy living in the same crowded ranch house. She'd watched him slowly disappear into Branson's bedroom on the night they almost let their raging hormones get the best of them. Then she'd followed Jill into her bedroom and helped her with the assignment until it was time for bed. She'd wanted desperately to go to Rowan, coming so close she had her fist hovering against the door of his bedroom ready to knock.

Saturday morning, Allison woke to the alarm she'd set on her phone. She picked it up and, for a moment, simply stared at the words in confusion: food drive at the high school.

The commitments around here never stopped. She groaned and rolled out of bed, reminded of how busy the holiday season could be in Bronco. Everyone contributed in some way, and when she'd first arrived, Allison had been approached to volunteer her time at the food drive. It meant she'd spend at least part of the day at her old high school where it was being held this year.

It would be another way to avoid Rowan for at least part of the day. She'd been doing a fine job of it since the night they'd almost made a huge mistake and slipped into her bedroom together for a little adult fun. The moment had seemed so right, so perfect, but divine intervention had come in the form of three teenagers. At first, she'd been annoyed and disappointed, but it didn't take long before Allison realized what a huge mistake she'd almost made.

Maybe it was time to overcorrect the situation. She'd let herself get carried away with a fantasy that only had to exist outside this ranch house. Allison became used to sitting next to him on the couch in the evenings by the fire, but now she always chose a seat on the other side of the room. She tried not to look at him, but every time she did, she'd catch him looking at her. He'd quickly glance away, apparently as self-conscious as she'd been about their "almost" hook-up a week ago. Possibly also a bit embarrassed by how caught up they'd been in the moment.

Whenever his phone would buzz and he'd glance at it, then put it away without responding, she wondered if it was Perri again. She wondered if he'd already talked to her privately as he'd said he would. For all she knew, last week they were texting and making plans to get back together again when he returned to Seattle. Maybe he viewed that night as a wakeup call they were letting this fantasy get out of hand. They'd been close to making a choice from which there would be no coming back.

It would be so easy to fall into bed with Rowan, but it might also be a mistake.

Their friendship would not survive a casual fling. Last week, they'd allowed their hormones to rule the day and she could not have that happen again. Rowan always said the right things and she found that she believed him. But he was still very much on the rebound even if he didn't realize it. There was every possibility he'd come to regret a hookup with her. She didn't want him to have any misgivings when they went home to Seattle. She didn't want him left wondering whether he'd jumped too quickly into another relationship. He should not have any doubts. Hadn't he said that he tended to make bad decisions when it came to women?

She did not want to be one of those bad choices.

What if she'd been about to become another disappointment? A rash hookup best relegated to a vacation-style fling. Besides, their passion for each other didn't mean they had to rush into sleeping together. This relationship of theirs was a lot more than physical. She'd revealed so much to him, but not the most important thing: she'd fallen *in love* with him.

She had to talk to him, of course, and she could tell he wanted to talk, too. In the evenings, when they were all sitting around the fireplace with the family watching holiday shows, she'd catch him staring at her then quickly looking away. Privacy in the Abernathy household was not a thing and she'd been able to avoid a deep conversation.

Rowan, meanwhile, excelled at making the kids laugh. Often, she'd catch him playing video games with the boys. Jill always grabbed him whenever she wanted something too high to reach. Allison could tell Charlotte already adored him and Billy, too, was a fan.

Maybe later today, when she got back from the food drive, she'd find a private moment and explain why this couldn't happen. She'd list all the reasons why sleeping together would be a bad idea. He'd probably already decided the same thing and the conversation would be short.

After showering and dressing, Allison made it downstairs to find she wasn't the only one up. Jill was already dressed and eating from a box of sugary cereal.

"*That* doesn't look healthy. I'll make you a solid breakfast." Allison pulled out the cast-iron skillet.

"No worries, I don't have time. Mom's picking me and Nicky up in a few."

"What about the career fair? You're not doing it again this year?"

Last year, apparently Billy had dragged Jill to career day

only to run into Charlotte, who'd been recruited to talk about careers in marine biology. And the rest was history.

As for Allison, she wasn't looking forward to revisiting old memories of the high school she'd just become used to when she'd been pulled out and hauled away to boarding school. She still remembered the expressions on her friends' faces when she'd announced she was leaving. But, funny thing, they'd all moved on fine without her. She couldn't fault them for that, but it had still stung to realize how easily she'd been forgotten.

"I did that last year. Maybe I'll drop in later. Depends on if Mom has anything special planned for us this weekend."

"What about Branson? What's he doing today?"

"Who knows?" Jill looked up with a conspiratorial smile. "Maybe hanging out with his girlfriend. Mom said he could meet us later."

Probably the same one he'd had for the past year. Allison hoped history wouldn't repeat itself.

"Oh! There she is!" Jill stood up, carrying her bowl of pink milk and depositing it in the sink. "Nicky! Mom's here!"

"See you la—" Allison called out.

The front door slammed shut. Two minutes later, the door opened and closed again. Looking out the kitchen window, she saw Nicky hop in the back seat of the dark luxury sedan and they all drove off.

"Good morning," Charlotte said. "Was that the kids taking off with Jane?"

Allison turned to her, spatula in hand. "Yes, and Nicky didn't even eat breakfast!"

"You are taking your role of breakfast dispenser seriously." Charlotte laughed. "She did come early, I got to admit."

"Well, I'll happily make a healthy breakfast for you. Have a seat and take a load off."

"Didn't you volunteer for the food drive? You better get going." Charlotte grabbed a mug from the cupboard. "Don't worry about me. I'll eat my overnight blueberry oats in the fridge."

"All right, if you're sure. But would you mind entertaining Rowan today?"

"Why don't you take him with you?"

"I thought I'd let him…you know, hang out at the ranch. Take a breather."

"You two haven't been anywhere in a week. What happened to letting everyone in town know you two are engaged?"

"I think we accomplished that perfectly." Allison held up her ring. "We actually may have…you know, overdone it."

"I know. You have a *ring*."

"Safe to say pretty much everyone in Bronco believes we're engaged."

"It's no wonder. I half believe it myself."

That makes two of us.

This was dangerous because she wanted it all to be real and Rowan was doing his best to indulge her greatest fantasies about him. No wonder she'd been about to hop into bed with him.

"And, last week, after that performance…we almost…we…" Allison spoke in a hushed tone. "Almost went upstairs together."

Charlotte grinned. "Why didn't you?"

"Because it's not *real*." Allison crossed her arms.

"But you could change that. You want this to be real."

"I'm afraid to even say it out loud, but yes. I do."

"While I understand not wanting to hook up in a baby nursery with nosy teenagers in rooms on either side of you, I encourage you to go for it. At some point. You'd be a fool not to. I mean he's…you know…wow." Charlotte made a motion with her hands like that of a minor explosion.

"Who's wow?" a deep male voice said from the entrance to the kitchen.

Rowan. Oh dear. How much had he overheard? Allison felt her cheeks blaze with heat.

Charlotte's cheeks were as pinked as Allison's probably were. "Oh, the…um, the new high school biology teacher. One of the kids said something."

"Ah," Rowan said, grabbing a mug from the cupboard. "How's everyone this morning? What are the plans this weekend?"

"Well, Allison was just saying how she'd love to take you with her to the food drive," Charlotte said. "I know they always could use the extra help."

Allison shot her sister a warning look.

"Count me in," Rowan said. "You didn't mention it."

Allison brushed by him. "You've been busy and I didn't want to disturb you."

"I admit I got called into a Zoom meeting a couple of days ago but it turns out even grinches like me deserve a few days off around Christmas."

Grinches like him? What was he even talking about? Rowan was like a hot Santa and an elf rolled up into one juicy male package.

"Okay, great. I'll just go get my jacket and gloves and meet you outside."

CHAPTER FOURTEEN

THE SUN SHONE brightly but Rowan felt the chill even inside Charlotte's SUV. Allison had mostly been avoiding him. He'd been waiting for the right moment to apologize for pushing too hard and too soon, but it had proved tough to catch her alone. A couple of times he'd thought of knocking on her door after bedtime, but he hadn't wanted to send the wrong message.

Hello, I'm here for a booty call.

Nope. Plus, both of their rooms were near nosy teenagers. So, it had been an entire week of dancing around each other, trying not to get into each other's space.

This was finally the moment he'd been waiting for and if it took an afternoon at the local high school, he didn't mind a bit.

"Hey, I'm sorry."

Allison started. "Why? What did you do?"

"I'm sorry if I put too much pressure on you. I got caught up in the moment and scared you off."

She snorted. "You didn't scare me. I scared myself. All these feelings I have. They're so intense and I'm confused."

"And then I came in guns blazing. My fault."

"I wanted to be with you that night, and without the kids' interruption, it would have happened."

"But...?" He sensed her thought wasn't complete.

"Maybe that would have been a mistake." She gripped the steering wheel. "Our friendship is too precious to me, and we wouldn't survive a fling."

"Good, because I don't want a fling."

But he cursed his lousy timing since he didn't want to wait an appropriate amount of time before he could seriously date Allison. What was the arbitrary number of days a man should wait before he went after the woman he'd wanted to be with all along? The thought of dating someone else, anyone else, did not even slightly appeal to him. He didn't want to waste any time when he already knew who he wanted. When he already understood who would be perfect for him, and he for her.

"We're agreed then. No fling."

"Absolutely *not*." He waited a beat. "I mean we're engaged. Would we even qualify as a fling?" Yeah, that was a reach on his part, and he had to force his lips to keep from quirking into a smile.

Allison gave him a sideways smirk. "Nice try."

After a few minutes, Allison pulled into a parking space at the high school near the auditorium entrance and, together, they followed the signs pointing toward the food drive. The building looked like an ordinary secondary school with well-manicured lawns and the appropriate school spirit signs stating, "Go Mustangs!"

"So, this is where you went to high school."

"For about a year, until my parents shipped me off to boarding school."

It hadn't occurred to him how difficult this might be for Allison. He mostly had fond memories of his high school days, but he'd excelled at football. If not for that, he might have hated every second of those insecure years. One of his best friends had been mercilessly teased for his acne-pockmarked face and Rowan had appointed himself his personal bodyguard. High school could be hell for some kids and with social media, he'd heard it was even worse now.

"What was that year like for you?"

"Good if not perfect, because you know…high school. I went with some of my best friends. Kids I'd grown up with all through grade school. I was the kind of student filled with school spirit. Tried out for the cheerleading team and made it for my sophomore year. Unfortunately, I never even had a chance to order the uniform."

Rowan reached for Allison's hand and squeezed it. The hint of regret in her words pierced him in the heart. *Ouch.*

"Well, honestly, you probably didn't miss much."

He was lying. She'd missed going to high school with the friends she'd known her entire life. All those connections and relationships. She'd been torn out of the world she'd loved and understood.

"Right. High school is just four years of a kid's life. College was better and, bonus, I was already accustomed to being away from home. I could have taught the graduate course."

Somehow, that didn't make him feel any better. He continued to hold her hand, only letting go to swing open the double doors. There were more signs pointing one way to the career fair and in the other direction for the food drive. He followed Allison, hanging behind, giving her space.

By a large sign indicating they'd reached the food drive, conveniently across from the cafeteria, a group of people had gathered around lunch tables and cardboard boxes. The student body president introduced herself.

"We've already got barrels and barrels of nonperishable food and more coming in all day," she said. "I'm pairing all the couples up, so you two can come over this way and start putting family boxes together. One of each item. Later on, we're going to be making the deliveries so everyone can have a Christmas dinner."

Working with Allison was easy, because as he'd already noticed they seemed to be in tune with each other. It was as if he could anticipate her next move and she could do the same for him. As activity buzzed all around them, the students accepted donations then placed them in one area. One couple was making up the boxes and two other couples were helping to put together the boxes. Two gravy packets, a box of premade stuffing, canned green beans, and all the typical items.

While other couples were bumping into each other, at times putting in the same items, he and Allison had a system. There was a reason they were friends. They had a natural cohesiveness. A way they simply fit together.

They'd been working in sync for an hour when a teacher ran up to Allison.

"One of our presenters had car trouble and isn't going to make it to career day. Do you think I could pull you away from here to present? Could you talk about careers in IT?"

Allison blinked. "Sorry."

"Oh, you're from Seattle, so I just assumed."

"A common assumption," Allison deadpanned.

"I don't know what I'm going to do! I have a classroom full of teenagers and if I don't provide a speaker, there's no telling what will happen."

Rowan lightly touched the younger woman's shoulder. "I can talk about careers in IT."

She whipped her head around. "Who are you? Do I know you?"

"This is my fiancé, Rowan Scott."

"Oh, you're from Seattle, too?"

"I am." Rowan nodded. "I've worked in IT since I graduated from college. I've been employed by Microsoft and others."

"Rowan," Allison interrupted, "they've put you on the spot, and that's not fair."

"But it would really help. Just sayin'." The teacher tossed her hair and swiped through her tablet.

Allison took his hand and pulled him aside. "Listen, you

don't have to do this. It's *my* old high school and if anyone should be obligated, it's me."

"But what will they do with a classroom full of students and no speaker?"

"Well, that's not your problem, is it?"

"Don't look now, but you sound like the Grinch." He tapped her chin.

"I would do it, honestly, but—"

Ah, she felt guilty about not doing this herself and throwing him to the wolves. But this was his wheelhouse.

"Yeah, I know. You prefer to be better prepared, and I understand that. But here's one thing you don't know about me: I'm gifted with the rare ability to actually enjoy public speaking."

Allison gasped. "You're a unicorn."

"A professor once taught me the secret of a twenty-minute speech on any given subject. You want to hear it?"

"Of course."

"First, you start with an acronym regarding your subject. Shorter words are for shorter speeches. For this talk, I'll probably use TECHNOLOGY. Starting with the letter T, I'll mention a few basics about technology. Then I'll move on to the letter E, possibly educational requirements. With C, I'll go to careers in tech. And so on, letter by letter. No matter the subject, it's an easy way to do a last-minute speech."

"Great way to organize the talk in your head. I'll have to remember that. Unlike you, I'm not a huge fan of public speaking. I'm okay in small groups."

The teacher rejoined them. "I'm sorry, but if you're doing this, I need to know. Otherwise, I have to go run and ask every adult here today and I better get going. Please?"

Rowan held out his arm. "Just lead the way."

"Thank you!"

He squeezed Allison's hand one last time and followed the teacher down the hallways into a classroom filled with students.

* * *

"Allison!"

When she turned a few minutes later, Allison recognized her friend and former classmate, Zuri.

"Hey, how are you?"

A strange feeling had gripped Allison as she'd walked down the old hallways and wound up straight across from the cafeteria where, for an entire year, she'd sat to eat lunch and gossip with friends. She hadn't expected to see any of those friends here today. Zuri looked almost exactly like Allison remembered her, with black corkscrew curls and flawless latte skin.

"I'm great, but not as good as you!" She turned in the direction Rowan had walked. "Who was *that* with you?"

Allison wasn't going to lie. It gave her great satisfaction to say, "That's my fiancé, Rowan Scott."

Zuri waved her hand in a "too hot to handle" motion. "Girl! Congratulations."

"Thanks."

Zuri had been the one in high school with so many interested boys chasing after her that Allison lost count. She remembered how envious she'd been of Zuri's easy popularity but also incredibly grateful of how kind and generous she'd been. A year older than Allison, she'd suggested Allison try out for the cheerleading squad. Zuri had sensed Allison's insecurities and encouraged her to "wear the coat." When Allison asked what she meant, she'd borrowed her jacket, shrugged it on and strutted back and forth. Allison's plain sheepskin suddenly looked like the sharp coat of a movie star on the red carpet when Zuri wore it. And she swore it wasn't the jacket. It was the way she *wore* it.

"How've you been?"

"I'm a new teacher here. I just started teaching biology."

Allison bit her lower lip. So, this was the "wow" teacher Charlotte had mentioned. Funny, she'd pictured a man, and definitely not one of her old high school chums.

"That's you? I've already heard all kinds of good things about the new biology teacher. Billy's kids are apparently impressed."

"It's been a whirlwind." She smiled and cocked her head. "Hey, you look fantastic. I always wondered what happened to you after high school."

Allison wondered if everyone in town had come to their own conclusions. Personally, she'd never bothered to ask. Charlotte had moved on, and Allison tried to be equally as resilient, even if it hadn't been her choice to leave Bronco.

"After college, I wasn't sure what I wanted to do with my liberal arts degree, so I followed my sister Charlotte to Seattle. When she wound up leaving to do her marine biology thing in the Bahamas, I stayed. I love living in the city and I have a nice career there in human resources."

"Well, it's so good to see you," Zuri said, turning in the direction of an approaching student. "And we'll catch up some more at the cookie exchange."

"Cookie exchange?"

And in the next moment, Allison groaned when she remembered. When she'd first arrived in Bronco, Eloise had invited her to a cookie exchange on Christmas Eve. There'd been so much going on since Rowan arrived that she hadn't spoken to Eloise recently and the whole event had slipped her mind.

"At your sister Eloise's."

"Right, I remember now."

"You've been busy, I take it, with your dreamboat fiancé." She winked.

"Yes, uh-huh, but I'll—we'll—be there." Allison gave her old friend a smile.

"See you then." Zuri waved and walked away, curls bouncing. No less than four students and two adult volunteers followed her with their eyes as she *strutted* off.

A few minutes later, unable to resist the temptation any longer, Allison excused herself from the food drive. Trying her hand at "wearing the coat" she strut-walked toward the class-rooms, following the Career Fair signs. While she thought it might be difficult to find the exact classroom, all she had to do was peek inside an open door with standing room only.

Rowan stood at the front of the class, commanding the room. Though she'd always found him attractive, and even if she'd already realized something very real was happening between them, now something unnamed slid into place. And, like a key finding its lock, it clicked. She found nothing quite as alluring as watching a man thrive in his element. Whether it was on the range, in the boardroom or in a classroom.

She listened, spellbound, for the next several minutes as Rowan spoke effortlessly and after a while took questions from the students. He was dressed simply in jeans and a flannel shirt but might as well be wearing a pin-striped, tailor-made suit. Someone had once showed Rowan had to "wear the coat," or it simply came naturally to him. He oozed self-confidence and, seriously, was there anything more attractive than a self-assured and intelligent man?

When he was done speaking, he received a standing ovation. And Allison even noticed a number of students gazing, dreamy-eyed, at Rowan.

Get in line, kids.

CHAPTER FIFTEEN

AFTER THE CAREER FAIR, Allison took Rowan to lunch to thank him. He'd come through for the students, and people were already talking about how Allison Taylor's "fiancé from Seattle" saved the day. They wound up at Bronco Burgers again, site of the place where afterward they'd gone home and almost slept together. After a juicy burger and fries, Allison was ready to tackle the rest of the day.

Last night, Jill had begged for help wrapping her presents, since she'd be gone all this weekend with her mother. The boys wanted help, too, claiming to be "all thumbs," even if Branson was practically an expert roper. He wasn't fooling her. She guessed she and Rowan would be wrapping their presents for the next two days. Nothing like leaving it till the last minute.

On the drive home, she caught him up on the talk she'd had with Zuri.

"I was reminded there's a cookie exchange at my sister Eloise's place on Christmas Eve. There will be plenty of people there, some that might know my parents. So, I'll have to call on you once more to play the part of devoted fiancé."

"Great. I was wondering when I would have a chance to reprise my award-winning performance." Rowan winked.

"Eloise had a baby last December, but at least Charlotte's

baby will be born well after the holidays. It's a tough time to have a birthday."

"Are you going to stay in Montana until after Charlotte's baby is born?"

"That was the plan."

"Then I guess I won't see you for another month once I go back."

"Yes."

A silence settled between them.

By the time she got home, he and Perri might already be reunited, leaving any opportunity for the two of them gone. Oh, he'd be kind and give Allison a gentle brush-off because he'd want to stay friends and good neighbors. But despite the fact she'd tried to reign in her feelings, Allison would be heartbroken.

"By the way, you don't really have to stay until New Year's Eve. I think we only told that *particular* lie to Frederick, and we can always make up some excuse as to why you had to go home early."

Rowan stayed quiet, his gaze on the beautiful Montana wintry day outside.

The forecast called for snow in the next few days and, with any luck, a white Christmas.

"Is it okay with you if I stay?"

She was a bit taken aback by the words, which sounded almost wistful.

"You're enjoying Montana that much?"

"I guess I'd have to say that I'm enjoying hanging out with *you*. The location doesn't really matter."

She was glad to be driving, so she could avoid meeting his eyes. Because she knew that in hers, he'd be able to see all the longing for him she'd been trying to tamp down.

Raw emotion stirred through her. "Me, too. I'm never going to forget this time. Promise me something. No matter what happens when you get back, we'll always be friends."

"I promise."

It felt like her heart hung on the edge of a precipice, waiting for a shove into the abyss.

She had wanted to avoid heartache, but it was too late now.

ON CHRISTMAS EVE as planned, they headed to the Heights Hotel in Bronco Heights for Eloise's cookie exchange.

Rowan, for his part, seemed ecstatic about the thought of more cookies.

"Honestly, we had two days to bake the cookies. Why didn't we?" Rowan said.

"Are you forgetting the presents we've been wrapping non-stop?"

There had been no time to bake. She'd fed the family no-frills lunches and dinners, and a couple of times Rowan had run out for more of that pizza.

The guilty plastic-wrapped plate of store-bought cookies sat in her lap as Rowan drove them to the cookie exchange. She could have carried the cookies in the cute pink box from the store, but they were trying to pass them off as their own.

"Don't worry." Rowan squeezed her leg now. "Our cookie secret is safe. No one will ever know the difference."

Earlier today, while Allison had been helping Charlotte sort, fold and stack baby clothes in the nursery, he'd driven into town to place an order of snickerdoodles and gingerbread men. They'd planned to pass them off as their own, and considering this was a gathering with more than just Eloise and Dante, they would continue the engagement ruse, too.

"Let's leave as soon as we can," Allison said. "I still have a few presents to wrap before tomorrow morning and I don't want to stay up too late."

"Mine?" he said.

"What makes you think I got you anything?" she teased.

"Your reaction on the day we went shopping, when I offered to bring in your packages. You said, and I quote, 'Keep your paws off my shopping bags, Scott!' I'd like to think you wouldn't say that if you weren't hiding something from me."

"Okay, maybe I did get you something." She smiled and shifted in her seat. "And you never told me. Is your mother terribly unhappy about you spending Christmas away from home?"

"No," Rowan said simply. "She's absolutely fine with it. I said I'd make it up to her next year. I also discovered something fairly surprising. Apparently, Grayson's fiancée is stressed about hosting at their home this year. She will have one less thing to worry about without me there."

"What does that mean? Do you have any food allergies I'm not aware of?"

He shrugged. "Apparently, they both try hard to impress me, which is ironic."

"Is it though?" She laughed, realizing once more how differently people saw themselves. "You don't seem to realize how much people rely on you. At our complex, whenever something is broken or not working, we all ask you. That time the WiFi was out, remember? It was as if you could magically fix it for all of us."

He shrugged. "Everyone thinks when you're in tech that you know more than you actually do."

"You know a lot more than you want to admit. And you help everyone who asks, so it's no wonder people appreciate you. Let's start with you helping me move in because my lame boyfriend didn't show up until later."

"I wasn't raised to stand by and watch a woman carry a TV upstairs. I let you take the little stuff, didn't I?"

"Yes, you did. How kind of you."

He was a born helper and had grown up in the shadow of a flashier brother. And she'd been stuck in old patterns, thinking that her father still had some control over her when he didn't. He hadn't controlled her for years. Even though she worked hard to keep the family peace, it was more for her mother's sake. Hence the lie about being engaged so she didn't have to be rude and tell her father to go jump off a bridge.

"Tell me more about your sister Eloise."

"She's the youngest in our family, and yet the first to have a baby. You'll meet her little girl Merry, who's a year old now. Even though I'm closest in age to Charlotte, I guess you could say Eloise and I bonded over the fact that in a way we were both punished for Charlotte's mistake."

"She went to boarding school, too?"

"Yes, and she also didn't come back to Bronco for many years. She lived in New York City and had a highly successful marketing business. The funny thing is, even as a grown woman, she still had a baby before being married."

"Bet good old Thaddeus wasn't too jazzed about that."

"Lighting striking twice? Not at all. But once the baby was born, all was forgiven. Merry's their first grandchild, and quite adorable. I didn't get to hang out with her much last year, so I'm excited to see her today."

They parked in the hotel's visitor parking area and took the elevator to the fifth floor. Allison knocked and the door swung open to Eloise, wearing a red-and-white sweater exactly like Allison's.

"Hey, great taste in sweaters." Allison pointed.

"We're twinning!" Eloise took the cookie plate from Allison and led them both inside the hotel suite. She leaned in to whisper, "Hey, and great taste in men."

"Eloise, this is Rowan Scott, my...my fiancé." Allison made the introductions for the others in the room to hear. "He came out from Seattle to help me with Charlotte and her family."

"And, I heard from Charlotte, to run interference with our blowhard of a father," Eloise said in a hushed tone. "Don't worry, your secret is safe with me."

"I'm surprised to find you all still at the hotel," Allison said. "Why aren't you in the house yet?"

Eloise and her husband Dante started renovating the fixer-upper they'd bought nearly a year ago. She'd sent Allison photos via text of the modest, three bedroom house with a basketball hoop in the driveway. If it were Allison, with a one-year-old, she'd be more than ready to give up hotel life.

"Everything took far longer than we expected. I'm sick of contractors. But it should be ready to move into any day now. Probably right before Dante goes back to school after the holiday break. We've already moved some of our stuff, and it's sitting in boxes in the finished garage."

"Where's my adorable niece?" Allison said. "Must get my baby fix."

"Fair warning, Merry has the sniffles and we've been mostly staying in. I don't want to take her around Charlotte, either, since she's so close to her due date."

Eloise and Dante's apartment was decorated with a Douglas Fir, dozens of brightly colored wrapped presents under it. Allison always felt that Christmas was mostly for young children. *It must be wonderful to have your own little family*, she mused, wondering how many of those presents under the tree were for Merry.

Dante came over, holding the baby. She wore a dress similar to the one Allison had picked out at Hey, Baby: a frilly green-and-white dress with a matching hairband. She was still mostly bald, only a few blond hairs sticking up, and she was adorable.

Dante must have sensed her baby fever, so he handed Merry over. She didn't cry or scream but simply checked Allison out like she was a new, bright and shiny object.

Allison hadn't expected tears to well in her eyes, but they did. As if he sensed it, somehow, Rowan was right behind her, one hand steady on her lower back. She had come to rely on his solid presence.

"Hi, Merry," Allison said. "I'm your Aunt Allison. I'll be the one sending you US savings bonds over the years. It will be tough, but just wait until they mature."

Dante chuckled. He probably appreciated that low-key financial lesson for his daughter.

"Goo," Merry said, and stretched her chubby little arms out for her mother.

Eloise took the baby back, far too soon for Allison, but she wasn't there for a baby fix. She was there to make an appearance and bring a big tray of cookies back to the Abernathy house, following which, the children would nominate her for sainthood.

After Dante introduced a few of his colleagues from the local school where he worked as a third-grade teacher, they were led into the suite's small but modern kitchen where the tiny gray-granite countertop was filled with plates of cookies. Eloise put their offering with the rest.

The event turned out to be like an open house. Friends were coming and going for hours. Zuri eventually arrived with a tall, well-dressed and really gorgeous man by her side.

"Hey, good to see you." She hugged Allison. "Please meet my date, Marcus."

"Hi, Marcus." Allison settled her hand on Rowan's chest. "This is my fiancé, Rowan Scott."

"Please to meet you both." Rowan offered his hand, but Zuri circumvented and grabbed a hug instead.

Smart girl.

"You're the one who saved the day at the career fair," she said.

"Ah, it was nothing. My pleasure."

After a while, Allison noticed people loading up on cookies. A few from each of the trays, making a potpourri of scrumptious Christmas confections.

Allison moved to the counters, in awe at the many choices. "And to think I've never been to a cookie exchange before."

"The Sanchez family does this every year and so we figured we'd start our own tradition," Eloise piped up.

"Any word on Winona?" Allison asked. The thought of poor

Stanley, alone at this time of the year and missing his fiancée was disheartening.

"No," Eloise said. "The Sanchez family is just trying to get through the holidays. It's tough."

"I can only imagine," Rowan said. "Just the thought of Allison taking off on me on our wedding day makes me sick. It would break my heart. I have no idea what I'd do."

There was such sincerity in his voice, Allison wanted to believe desperately that this wasn't an act. Rowan took the lead and started loading up their plate with a few of each cookie. There were chocolate-chip cookies, butter cookies, Russian teacakes, caramel sea salt cookies, brownies, almond biscotti, and lemon cookies.

"Sampling is allowed," Eloise chuckled.

She didn't have to tell Allison twice. After some sampling, she decided the lemon cookies were her favorite. By the time they were done, the plate was about three levels high.

"This ought to keep the Abernathy kids happy," Allison said.

"What? These cookies are for you," Eloise said. "Take another plate for the kids."

Allison and Rowan exchanged a look.

"If you insist."

Sampling did take place, but in the end, the gathering seemed to be more of a cocktail party than a cookie exchange. Most everyone imbibed from the spiked punch and one of the teachers took orders at a makeshift bar.

"Can I make you a drink?" she said. "Just name it. Anything! I bartended my way all through college."

"How about a Cosmo?" Allison said.

She pointed. "You're trying to trip me up, but I know how to make it! Just give me a second."

Allison finished the drink and, damn, if everybody here didn't suddenly look extremely pretty. But she'd always been a lightweight. She noted Rowan had been whisked away by a few females who now seemed to be hanging on his every word. She'd lay money down that Rowan had not noticed the women were licking their lips and tossing their hair for his benefit. But Allison had. It made her a little sick to her stomach. If she didn't step up her game, she was going to lose Rowan. Not tonight, but soon, to someone who had the nerve to tell him how she felt. To someone willing to tell him she loved him and wanted a future with him.

She joined Rowan just in time for someone to ask about his fiancée.

"Here she is." He put an arm around Allison, drawing her close. "The one I was telling you about."

"You were talking about me?" Allison said. "I'm sorry I missed this."

"He was just telling us how you met," one of the women said. "Adorable meet cute."

"So, what are you guys going to do now that you're engaged? Keep one apartment or move into a house together?" another woman asked.

The question stumped her as much as it did Rowan. Real estate prices in Seattle were astronomical. She hadn't thought about any of this.

"Well... I think we will probably move into one apartment and save for the wedding," Rowan said.

"Yeah, that makes sense," Allison said. "I like my apartment."

Rowan squeezed her shoulder. He probably liked his apartment, too. She couldn't be so set in her ways not to at least consider his apartment. It was slightly bigger than hers but didn't have a view. Oh wait. This wasn't even happening. It didn't matter because they weren't engaged. Right.

The truth was he'd go back to Seattle first and maybe this time around when he reconciled with Perri, she would actually move in with him.

"Would you ever move back to Bronco?" someone else asked.

"I don't think so," Allison said, even while she realized she would miss seeing Merry grow up. She'd miss watching Charlotte and Billy's baby grow up, too.

"But we will come back to visit often," Rowan said.

"I would like that," Allison said. "The truth is, Rowan can work from anywhere."

"Definitely a perk."

Allison turned to see Eloise beckoning her, so she excused herself and followed her sister to her bedroom.

"What's up?" Allison said.

"I thought we could talk privately in here."

"About what?"

"For starters...um, tell me about this ring!" Eloise reached for Allison's ring finger and held it up to inspect. "It's gorgeous. Where did you get it?"

"Rowan gave it to me. We were shopping at Sadie's Holiday House and he thought it would be a good idea for me to have a ring. If we were really going to sell this engagement thing to the town."

She thought of how he'd given it to her and then lifted her up and spun her around to "make it look good." Even now, the memory made her heart tug with a powerful emotion. What had been the game they intended it to be was still real to him, but her feelings were real.

"That seems over the top for a game you two are playing."

"I'm not sure it's a game anymore. At least, not for me."

"How long have you been crushing on this man? Isn't this the guy you told me was simply your neighbor?"

Allison opened her mouth to object but there was hardly a point anymore. She was, apparently, obvious to the people who knew her well.

"It's been a while that I've been having stronger feelings for him, but, honestly, we were just friends."

"*Were* being the operative word."

"I don't know what's going to happen. We'll just have to see when we get back to Seattle. He's going to go home before I do, and I think that's when he and his ex will reconcile. She still wants him and who can blame her."

"He seems really into you. And the ring just proves it. He didn't have to do that, I'm sure you know."

"Yes, we could have just said the ring was being sized. I guess he wanted to. Honestly, I'm…a little crazy about him."

"I can see that. Have you told him?"

"We've been very…affectionate, even in private when we don't need to pretend."

"'Fake it 'til you make it' takes on a whole new meaning." Eloise smiled then sobered as Allison didn't share the humor. "Why do I sense a hesitation from you?"

"Because he's too good to be true? Mostly, because he's just off a breakup with a woman he dated for two years."

"Great. So, he's not a commitment-phobe. He really hangs in there."

Leave it to Eloise to spin this in a positive light.

"Yes, true, but he might also not be completely over his ex. And, more to the point, I doubt she's going to leave him alone. She's been texting him almost the whole time he's been in Bronco."

Eloise groaned. "Not good. You're worried they're not really done with each other. But what does he say? You have asked him."

It wasn't a question. Allison would have been silly not to bring it up.

"He says it's over, but he's said that before. Their pattern involves going back and forth with each other. I just don't want to be a casualty in their on-again, off-again dysfunction."

"You might not be. If they're not right for each other, and you can see it, just give it some time. He'll come to the same conclusion when he can compare his old relationship to a high-functioning one. Be patient."

Allison wanted to be patient. She wanted to believe with

all her heart things would work out this time. But for her, the things she desperately wanted usually did not work out.

"You know what? For a little sister, you give great advice."

CHAPTER SIXTEEN

ALLISON LEFT THE girl-talk moment with Eloise reassured. No matter what happened, Rowan would have this time they'd had together to measure against any possible future he may or may not have with Perri. Even though they'd broken up before, maybe this time was different. He'd said so, for one thing. She should take him at his word. And, more to the point, she didn't think Rowan had ever dated anyone else between breakups, definitely not seriously. Plus, there was the fact he'd been attracted to her from the start of their relationship and simply not acted on his feelings. Add the additional fact that they'd never both been free and single at the same time before now.

When she and Eloise rejoined the others in the living room, Allison caught a sight that took her breath away.

"Oh. My." She brought a hand to her chest.

Rowan sat on the couch, Merry in his lap. She was turned to him, her little chubby, and likely sticky, fingers reaching for his chin. Just the way he held her, so gently and tenderly, while at the same time seeming completely enthralled with her, sent a strong jolt of awareness through Allison. He'd been so good with the Abernathy kids all this time, too, joking around with Nicky and Branson. More than once, they'd asked for his advice on a video game world they were both trying to conquer.

Apparently, Rowan had long ago reached the highest level, so he'd become a demigod to them.

And the day after the first snow, she had caught him in the front yard with Jill, helping her build a snowman. It must have been freezing, and he didn't exactly own a winter wardrobe, but that hadn't stopped him when she'd asked him to help her.

He would be a good father. No. An amazing father.

Allison came to sit beside him. "Hey."

He turned to her, grinning. "I think she likes me. She hasn't spit up on me or screamed once."

"Well, don't jinx it." Allison smiled and tugged gently on Merry's shiny patent-leather shoe.

Just sitting here, next to him, she pretended for a little slice of time. For this moment, and only this moment, Merry was their daughter. Rowan was her husband. She told herself it wasn't any different than pretending she was engaged to this man, but somehow this felt much more intimate. Real. She and Rowan fit together, and she couldn't deny any longer that she wanted this. *All* of this. A family, but not just any family.

A family with him.

The thought scared her since it came ripe with possible heartache, but for the first time in her life, there was less a sense of fear than excitement that filled her. She had to stop thinking of all the ways this could go wrong, and start imagining all the ways this could go right.

On the way home, it began to snow again. Allison had to admit the soft white flakes cast the town in an almost ethereal glow.

"Something about the snow makes me feel like it's truly Christmas," she said. "My sisters and I used to pray every year for a white Christmas. Then again, we were spared the shoveling."

"My brother and I also had a tradition. We used to sleep by the fireplace hoping we'd catch Santa in the act. I had a notepad nearby so I could keep track of clues left behind."

"Aw, how sweet." Just the memory of a young Rowan made her heart squeeze.

"So, tell me. What's your favorite Christmas movie?" Rowan asked.

"That's a tough one. I love all the Hallmark holiday movies, but my ageless favorite classic is *It's a Wonderful Life*."

"Good choice, sweetheart," Rowan said in a pretty amazing imitation of the classic Jimmy Stewart drawl. "Why, you've got good taste. Shall I lasso the moon for you?"

"That's not bad." Allison laughed. "And what's your favorite Christmas movie?"

"Die Hard," they both said at once.

Allison laughed again. "Okay, tough guy, somehow I knew that was your answer. I'll allow it."

"Sorry, but your favorite classic makes me cry."

She narrowed her eyes. "Really?"

"A tear came down my cheek one time when my mother insisted we all watch it as a family."

"A *single* tear."

"What? That's considered *crying*."

She nudged his elbow. "And what about favorite Christmas song?"

"Definitely 'I Saw Mommy Kissing Santa Claus.' There's something about knowing mom and dad are still getting it on that's enormously appealing to me."

"That makes sense. I agree." Allison cleared her throat. "But I'd have to say my favorite is 'Silent Night.' Charlotte and Billy are fans of *The Nutcracker*, and I do like Tchaikovsky."

They were halfway home when the snow really started to come down.

"Are you sure you can handle this?" Allison asked. "Maybe I should drive."

He squinted, his eyes never leaving the road. "Should I be offended? You know, I've definitely driven in the snow before. Maybe you forget it snows in Washington, too."

"But not like this. I think we'll have at least three inches by morning."

"Hey, maybe we'll get snowed in." The thought seemed to cheer him.

She hoped so, because the idea of having an excuse not to go to her parents' big holiday party and instead stay home in front of a fire, cuddling with Rowan, held enormous appeal.

"You *want* to get snowed in?"

"With you, the idea has appeal."

He never seemed to give up on finding a moment with her, even if it seemed unlikely with the lack of privacy. She'd started to give up on the idea, thinking it best not to take that risk with her heart. If he was serious about ending things with Perri, it would become evident once he went home and might run into her again.

"Um, about that…" she said. "I'm sorry we haven't found much privacy. I do want to be alone with you. You know that, right?"

"I'd hoped so, but it's good to hear it out loud."

"The moment hasn't been right."

She saw him nod in the light of the dash.

"My friends who are married say that's what happens when the kids become teenagers," he said. "It's back to when they were two, but worse, because they have a key to the house and the car. So, it's no surprise with a household of teens that there's little privacy for anyone."

"But we'll have all the privacy we want when we go home."

It was the first time she'd spoken her thoughts out loud. When they went home, she wanted to continue where'd they left off. If that's what he wanted, too. She waited to hear him agree and the silence seemed to stretch between them. She'd expressed clearly that this was what she wanted.

He was what she wanted.

"Is…is that what you want, too?" she asked him finally.

His head jerked in surprise. "Are you kidding? I thought I made myself pretty clear. I'm crazy about you."

Hearing the words said out loud was like someone had inflated her chest like a balloon. She was...full. It was like getting what she'd always wanted for Christmas. The best, most impossible gift.

"I really like you, Rowan. I always have. But you've been..." She didn't even want to say her name. "Dating someone for the past two years."

"Not anymore," he said. "I keep telling you—that's over."

He'd said that before, and she didn't want to argue with him anymore. Maybe it *would* be different this time. She hoped.

"But I understand how you must feel. Let's just...take it slow." He skimmed his warm hands down her arms.

"That's...that's a good idea." She framed his face, mesmerized by his gorgeous mouth.

"Here's the thing... If I'm being honest, I was checking you out the day I helped you move into the building. And then your boyfriend at the time showed up. So, this isn't really new. Not for me."

She sighed. "It's not new for me either."

The snow was still falling when they pulled up to Billy and Charlotte's house. It looked cold enough to be an unpleasant walk the few yards to the main house. She reluctantly unhooked her seat belt and went for the car door, but Rowan stilled her hand.

"Hang on."

"It's okay. I'll make a run for it. We'll thaw in front of the fireplace."

"I have an idea." He threaded her fingers through hers. "This, right here, is a private space."

"You have a point." She glanced outside. "It's also quite warm in here, at least for now."

"And we'll make it hot."

She slid across the bench seat until she was so close she

could smell his delightful scent. He smelled like sandalwood and one hundred percent Rowan. Her hands went against his strong, firm chest. She wanted to see him naked. Wanted to see him at least without his shirt.

"Hey, stranger," he said, brushing a kiss across her knuckles. "Have I ever told you how much you intrigue me?"

She traced along his jawline. "Me?"

Of all the sisters, she may have been the least interesting. She'd followed Charlotte to Seattle after college, when her older sister moved. After she'd had to move for her marine biology work, Allison stayed in the city. She couldn't picture herself living in the Bahamas where Charlotte had relocated. While her job in human resources didn't exactly make Allison an adrenaline junkie, she liked her work just fine. Every once in a while, there was a bit of employee drama or juicy gossip that proved to be just enough for her. She'd had a childhood filled with drama and she hadn't wanted any more of it. So, *interesting* was never a word associated with herself.

"Yeah, you're intriguing," he said. "Because you come from such wealth, but you're such a simple girl. So down to earth. And gorgeous. You really slay me with your smile."

How nice for him to mention her smile. Not her legs or her behind, which most men seemed to zero in on. Rowan liked her *smile*.

The strong beat of his heart thumped under the pads of her fingers as she pressed her mouth to his. He kissed her with purpose, as if she was the most precious thing he'd ever touched. His tough beard stubble scraped against her sensitive flesh as he kissed down the column of her neck. She moaned, fisting his shirt, practically climbing into his lap. This wasn't going to work. She wanted more of him. More than she would get in the cab of this truck.

"You make me feel like a teenager with his first crush," Rowan said, his talented fingers roaming under her sweater, making her tingle and squirm for more.

"I wish we'd met a long time ago. I've wanted someone like you. I've looked for someone like you."

This was the time to tell him. *Tell him. Tell him.*

Tell him you love him.

But the words felt too big. Life-changing. She'd never say those words to him without knowing the impact they might have. Good or bad. She could scare him away, or she might get everything she'd ever wanted.

"This is going so fast," she said, breathless.

"Too fast for you?" he whispered, his warm breath fanning against her neck.

"Too fast and yet not fast enough."

She kissed him again, threading her fingers through his thick hair, tugging him close. And it wasn't close enough. Out of the corner of her eye, she noticed they were fogging up the windows. "I think we need something to cool us down." Allison laughed.

"You might be correct. Much more of this and I'll be tearing off your clothes."

"Or tearing off *your* clothes." She smirked. "I have an idea." She swung open her door. "Come with me."

"Where are we going now?"

She reached for his hand and tugged him along the freshly fallen snow to the perfect spot.

"I haven't done this since I was a kid."

Then she dropped to her back and lay down in the powdery snow.

"Allison? What are you—"

The moment after she began to flail her arms and legs in half circles, he dropped down a couple feet next to her to do the same.

"Snow angels," he said. "Yeah, I remember this."

Delight pulsed through Allison and she didn't care she was cold and would soon also be wet. Memories came back of some of the best days she'd spent in Bronco as a child with her sisters and brothers. The first snow of the season meant running outside to catch snowflakes on her tongue, making a snowman, sledding down the hill in the back of their property, and snow angels.

Those were the better days, before she'd ever disappointed her parents enough to be sent away from home.

She got a kick out of watching Rowan beside her, laughing and smiling with her. The last boyfriend she'd had would have never wanted to mess up his precious hair enough to cut loose like this. He would have called her a nutcase. But Rowan was so playful right along with her, so fun and open to just about anything.

Allison stood to admire her snow angel on the ground, and so did Rowan.

"Yours is bigger," she said.

"But yours is better." He took two steps toward her and took her hand. "Now that we're both cold and damp, I have to tell you something."

"Yeah? What's that?" She wiped a damp strand of hair from her face.

"This isn't working." He gave her as slow smile, which moved from his crinkly eyes to eventually take over his whole face. "I'm still picturing you naked."

"Same. And I have to say, you look fantastic."

He laughed, a deep and hearty sound, took her hand and led her back to the truck to get the plate of cookies.

"We can't forget these."

"Absolutely not. That's my ticket into sainthood with the kids." She took the plate of cookies from him and hugged them to her chest.

"Just please make sure I get one of those snickerdoodles." Rowan steered her inside, hand low on her back. "Whomever baked those is the one who should be canonized."

"Rowan, you can have all the snickerdoodles."

"Score," he said, and then gave her a sweet kiss.

And later that night after prep time for the morning breakfast and another warm kiss in the hallway with Rowan, Allison barely slept. It was a bit like being a little girl again, anticipation thrumming through her on what she might find under the tree in the morning. Whether or not Santa had listened and brought what she'd asked for.

This time, the dreams and hopes were bigger. They were wishes for a future with the man of her dreams. He was only two doors down from her right now, not all that differently than he had been for the past few years when he'd simply been her neighbor across the hall. Handsome, smart and funny. Unavailable.

But now, possibilities shimmered like stars in an evening sky.

CHAPTER SEVENTEEN

ON CHRISTMAS MORNING, Allison woke with a deep sense of happiness and excitement such as she hadn't experienced since being a small child. She'd always loved Christmas Day when she and her siblings would wake before sunrise. Their parents would force them to stay in their bedrooms until the sun came up, but after that, it was fair game. As they grew into teenagers there was less excitement early in the morning, everyone sleeping in. Allison expected this would be the case in the Abernathy household. But in a few years, there would be a little one ready to rush downstairs and find what Santa brought.

Before anyone else woke, Allison showered and dressed, planning to start a big breakfast for the family. She'd peeled potatoes and mixed pancake batter the night before. It would be a down-home, big-country breakfast, the way her mother's cook used to make.

It's a Wonderful Life played softly on the TV screen in the background while Allison brewed coffee and cooked. She couldn't wait to see how everyone liked their gifts. A great deal of thought had gone into each one.

As she bent to put a tray of biscuits in the oven, Rowan's arms wrapped around her from behind. The now-familiar rush of adrenaline hit her along with the heady scent of his spicy cologne. When he leaned in closer to place a kiss on the column of her neck, her body buzzed with desire. Oh, this man; there was something about him that thrilled and excited her. It wasn't just one thing about him, but everything. The way he touched, the way he kissed, the way he fit right into her family. The way they fit together.

"Good morning." She turned in his arms to press a kiss against his lips. "And Merry Christmas."

"Merry Christmas." Then he said words that would have her fall in love with him if she wasn't already. "Do you need some help?"

"Yes, please. I told my sister I'd make them all this wonderful Christmas breakfast just like our family cook used to make."

"You won't have to do it by yourself. That's why you have me."

They worked together, which made it all go so much faster, and before long they had the table set, complete with a big hearty plate of bacon, eggs, potatoes and flapjacks.

"Don't forget this." In the center of the table, Rowan placed the platter of cookies from last night, still wrapped. "Probably shouldn't unwrap these until after the kids are finished eating."

"Sure, but I'm a grown-up." Allison fished under the plastic and grabbed a tea cookie, taking a bite.

"You little sneak." Rowan made as if to grab it from her hand, but she offered him a taste. "Hmm. At least you're generous."

From behind them, someone cleared their throat and when she turned, Billy stood there, one teenage son on either side of him. Rowan made no move to put space between them. Instead, his fingers slid down her arm to hold her hand.

"Merry Christmas," Billy said, and Branson and Nicky did the same.

"Wow, look at this!" Nicky gravitated toward the table.

"Did you cook all this, Aunt Allison?" Branson said.

"Yes, with Rowan's help." She brushed a hint of powdered sugar from the side of his mouth.

"Charlotte will be thrilled," Billy said. "I was just going to bring her up some oatmeal."

"I'm sick of oatmeal!"

Charlotte appeared in the doorway, looking bedraggled and wiped out. There were bags under her poor sister's eyes.

"Babe, I was bringing you breakfast in bed, remember?" Billy draped his arm around her.

"My back hurts and I can't lie down anymore."

"Look at this," Billy said, pointing to the table. "Allison and Rowan went all out. We're having a countrified breakfast."

"Thank you, sissy." Charlotte waddled up to Allison and hugged her then embraced Rowan. "And, Rowan, if I haven't said so before, you're a prince among men."

Jill ran into the kitchen so fast, she partially slid across the floor in her socks. "What did I miss? Are we opening presents yet?"

"First, breakfast!" Allison spread her arms and ushered everyone to the table.

They descended on the food like a pack of wolves, or perhaps more like bears who'd come out of hibernation.

"Stop!" Charlotte said and everyone turned to her. "We have to say the blessing first."

"Right," Billy said, and they all held hands as they gave thanks.

For the next few minutes, conversation was light as everyone seemed too busy chewing. A good sign.

Then Nicky pointed to the cookie tray. "Where did those cookies come from?"

"Your Aunt Allison got them for you," Rowan said with a grin.

Allison sat up straighter, ready for her medal. "Rowan and I went to Aunt Eloise and Uncle Dante's cookie exchange, and this is what we brought home."

"You mean you just show up to this exchange and they *give* you cookies? Why didn't I ever know about this?" Branson said, sneaking his hand under the plastic wrap to take one.

"No, dummy," Jill said. "You have to *bring* cookies, too. That's the exchange part."

"It's official," Charlotte said. "Allison, you win Christmas!"

"Why, thank you." Allison went hand to chest.

"Speech! Speech!" Nicky said.

"Thank you all so very much. I would like to thank the Academy..." Allison said. "Sorry, I have always wanted to say that."

Everyone laughed, but none harder than Rowan.

"It's Christmas Day, so I have one important and possibly life-changing question." Rowan spread his hands to indicate everyone at the table. "You don't have to answer if you're not comfortable, but is *Die Hard* a Christmas movie, yes or no?"

"Totally a Christmas movie," Branson said, and he and Nicky fist-bumped.

"Wait," Allison said. "Is this going to be split down male and female lines?"

"No way," Jill said. "It's totally a Christmas movie. Bruce Willis attends a Christmas party! There's music, and a tree, and presents. I mean, c'mon!"

"And a lot of violence," Charlotte said with a wince.

"Well, in *It's a Wonderful Life*, there's a war!" Nicky said. "You don't get any more violent than that."

"Okay, okay, point taken," Billy said.

Never mind the "war" wasn't showed in the movie, Allison had to agree to a point.

"What side do you fall on in this?" Rowan nudged her.

"Fine!" Allison raised her palms in an "I give up" motion. "It's a Christmas movie."

She received a round of applause.

A few minutes later, the kids announced it was time for presents. Though there'd been a gift name exchange so the kids wouldn't break their banks, Branson had a gift for everyone. Of course, all of it was University of Montana gear.

Rowan immediately put on his U of M silver-and-maroon beanie cap and looked adorable.

Then he opened the present she'd bought him.

"I get it," he said as he held up the gift. "For casino night!"

It was all she could find with special meaning. A set of chips and cards to commemorate his joke about how he'd been managing her apartment while she'd been gone.

"Casino night?" Charlotte asked.

"Private joke," they both said at once.

They had one other private joke: their neighbor, Mrs. Havisham.

Charlotte opened a gift from Billy, a pair of diamond earrings that had to have set him back.

"Oh my God, Billy. I love these!" She kissed her husband sweetly.

Once again, Allison was reminded of how every love story happened in its own time. Charlotte and Billy had been apart for years and, for her part, Allison never dreamed they'd ever be back together again. And yet she could see so clearly how well they belonged together, like they were made for each other.

Jill, who'd appointed herself the dispenser of presents from under the tree, gave Allison a small package. "This one says it's for you."

To Allison.

From Rowan.

She immediately recognized the brightly colored wrapping paper and stickers from Sadie's Holiday House that meant he must have gone back later without her. The box was small, which usually meant jewelry, but she didn't want to get ahead of herself. She already had a beautiful ring from him. Tearing into the wrapping paper, she gently lifted the lid. Inside was a golden locket in the shape of an envelope. The front was engraved with the words *Air Mail*. Taking it out of the box, she held it by the long chain.

She'd asked him to pick up her mail while she was gone. The gift was sentimental, special, and showed her a great deal of thought. Rowan had actually picked out a far more heartfelt gift than she'd managed to do. As she traced each letter, the locket suddenly slid open like an actual envelope to reveal another message inside. This one said *I love you*.

I love you. He'd said it first, with a gift she'd never forget. This present held far more meaning for her than anything he could have given her, including a ring. It was his heart, given open and freely to her, when she'd been keeping hers locked up tight.

She wanted to cry with relief that she hadn't imagined anything. These emotions between them were all as real as she'd hoped.

She stood and walked toward him. "Thank you."

He put his arms around her, tightly, pulling her close. "You're welcome."

The entire Abernathy clan stopped what they were doing to watch. Allison could feel their gazes boring into her. When she hugged Rowan, she looked over her shoulder and caught Charlotte and Billy exchanging confused looks. Were she and Rowan together for real? Or still pretending? No wonder they were confused. Allison wanted to shout to the world that she was in love, and it had all started with a little white lie.

She was about to say those very words when the doorbell rang.

"Who could that be?" Billy said, getting up to answer the door.

"Whoever it is, I'm sorry, but I'm not in the mood for company," Charlotte said, rubbing her back. "I need some more Tylenol."

"I'll get it." Jill ran out of the room.

"Are you feeling okay, Charlotte?" Allison said. "You don't look too well rested."

Her whole demeanor seemed different this morning and now distracted Allison. The pregnancy had been rough on her sister and Allison wasn't sure how she'd make it to her scheduled C-section. She'd tried her best to lighten her sister's load, but maybe everything she'd done hadn't been enough.

Charlotte clapped a hand to her forehead. "Actually, I think I'm going to skip out on the big holiday celebration today at Mom and Dad's."

"No one will blame you. We'll figure something out. I'll stay with you and Billy can take the kids."

"I'll be fine," Charlotte said, pulling up her blanket. "You go and bring me back some of Mom's apple cranberry crunch. And some cranberry walnut cake. Oh, and don't forget the apple cinnamon."

The kids laughed.

"What?" asked Charlotte. "It's the only time of the year Mom actually bakes anything, and her stuff is so good I wish she'd do it more often. I crave it all year!"

"We'll bring you one of each," Branson said.

"We have company." Billy reappeared in the living room carrying a large, wrapped present.

Allison's eyes widened when she saw Perri standing next to Billy, carrying a large gift bag brimming with even more presents.

Allison didn't think it was her imagination when Rowan took a step back from her. The shock of seeing Perri in her sister's home, in this scenario, rendered Allison speechless. Her stomach dropped. She almost felt as if she'd done something wrong and had been caught in the act, when nothing could be further from the truth. Rowan was a single man. At least, according to him.

"Hey, everyone! Hi, Allison." Perri dropped her bag of gifts. "Rowan. Hello."

"What are you *doing* here?" he asked her.

"I called your mother to wish her a Merry Christmas and she told me you were visiting Allison and her family in Montana. I couldn't stay away." Perri turned to Allison's family, most of whom were giving her curious gazes. "Please excuse me for intruding. But Christmas is a time of reconciliation, don't you think? It makes you realize who and what you love. Perspective. I know I sure needed some."

Yes, she usually did. And it was just as Allison suspected. Perri was going to try to slide back into Rowan's life as if a breakup had never happened.

Jill walked into the room with the bottle of Tylenol. "Hello. Who are you?"

"I'm Perri. Rowan's girlfriend." She smiled, bright as the evening star.

Allison noticed Billy cringe and Charlotte cover her face in obvious sympathy.

"*Ex*-girlfriend," Rowan said a moment too late for Allison.

"Oh, we just had a little fight." Perri waved her hands dismissively. "We do that a lot but then we can never stay away from each other for long."

Allison's heart jerked and spasmed with anticipated pain. This was her worst fear come to life. Perri had officially changed her mind, wanted Rowan back, and was already here to claim him. On Christmas Day of all things. Worse, how was Rowan supposed to let her down gently? Assuming he *wanted* to, that was. She didn't have any doubts the feelings he'd expressed for Allison recently were real, but this was a living, breathing reminder of his past. Of home. Seattle, where they'd be going back after this brief interlude. He saw before him his past and his possible future.

They might both be Perri.

Maybe they, and all this, had simply been a wonderful little dream.

"Um, Perri," Rowan said, "we were just celebrating Christmas with the Abernathy family."

"Yes, and I do apologize, but I brought gifts for everyone." The kids' faces brightened, as if they needed any more presents after their haul.

"And I got a room for us at the Heights Hotel because I know it must be cramped here with all of you!" Perri said this as if she were doing them all a great big favor.

"That's kind, but…well…let's go outside and talk for a minute." Rowan led her, hand on the small of her back, toward the front door. "Folks, I'll be right back."

The door shut and the quiet seemed suddenly deafening. All eyes were on Allison, waiting for her to…do what? Fall apart? Cry? Throw herself at Rowan and beg him not to go back to his ex?

"Somebody *say* something." Allison flopped back on the couch.

"I don't think this is my size," Jill said, holding up a sweater.

"You can return it," Charlotte said. "Allison, what's going on? I thought you and Rowan—"

"I don't want to talk about it."

"Don't worry, Aunt Allison," Branson said. "A lot of guys don't go for women like her. They prefer a good personality."

Oh joy.

Billy gave his son the parental stare-down and poor Branson wilted under it.

"I think you're beautiful," Jill said softly. "And smart, which is more important anyway."

Allison appreciated Jill now more than ever.

"You are beautiful in *every* way," Charlotte said. "And if Rowan can't see it, that's *his* problem."

"You guys… I mean, he's just *talking* to her," Nicky said. "Geez."

But the "talking" became louder as they were right outside the front door on the porch.

"Are you *cheating* on me? With *Allison*?" Perri could be heard saying.

"I thought that was his ex," said Branson.

"It is," Allison said. "I guess she's having a difficult time letting go."

Outside, Rowan and Perri moved farther away from the door and couldn't be heard any longer.

Thank you, God.

"Let's talk about something else, okay?" Charlotte said. "Like how huge I am. And how tired of being pregnant I am."

"But we talk about that every day." Billy smirked.

"Did you decide on a name yet?" Jill said.

"No," Charlotte and Billy said at once.

"But there are lots of heavy contenders," Billy said. "I think we've narrowed down the list. Especially on a boy's name. Eric."

The kids started shouting out more names, for a boy and a girl, some of them ridiculous, and it was almost enough to take her attention away from what was obviously happening outside.

Finally, after several minutes, Rowan walked inside. Alone.

He grabbed his coat. "Allison, can I talk to you for a minute?"

Feeling a ball of needles settling in her throat, Allison led him into the kitchen. The same kitchen where they'd bonded over baking cookies. The place where they'd first kissed. The place where this morning he'd wrapped his arms around her like he would never let her go. They'd been so domestic. Comfortable. Like a real couple.

She almost didn't want to hear what he had to say next. He was going to shatter this little bubble of hers with a few words.

"First, I had no idea she was coming here," he whispered.

"I figured." She lowered her head, not wanting to meet his gaze and see the regret in them.

He would no doubt hate the idea of hurting her, but Allison

should have known better than to get in the middle of this on-again, off-again dance. It was her own damn fault for taking a risk. Her damn fault for not keeping what was pretend right where it should be.

And above all else, her own fault for letting her heart get involved.

"It was incredibly rude of her to just barge in like this and I apologize on her behalf. Sometimes, she...well, her insecurities cause her to make rash decisions."

And there it was. It sounded as though he were defending her.

"I understand."

"I'm going to have to talk to her. I think I should take her back to the hotel."

"Oh."

Back to the hotel. That didn't sound like a good idea to Allison. It didn't sound like a good idea at all.

"She says she wants us to get *married.* The breakup made her realize that I'm her end game."

For a moment, Allison was speechless. This moment was turning into her worst nightmare. Previously her worst thought was that when she'd return to Seattle she'd find Perri had moved in with him. Now she wanted to *marry* Rowan?

"Allison?" Rowan said. "Did you *hear* me?"

"I heard you. She wants to marry you. That's...well, I gotta say, that's pretty shocking." Allison stood back, trying not to touch him.

It seemed particularly dangerous to touch him now. If she reached for him, she might take him by the shoulders and shake him, remind him that not long ago they had tentative plans to be together.

Remind him that just a few minutes ago he'd given her a locket with the words "I love you" on it!

"Tell me about it. I don't know who or what gave her the idea. She said she's frustrated that I never asked her to marry me even after two years of dating. She hoped it would be this year and when I didn't show any indication I was shopping for rings, she gave up."

"And now that she thinks you've moved on, she can't stand it."

"I swear that I didn't encourage her in any way."

She tipped her chin. "Not in a way you were aware of anyway."

"What's that supposed to mean?"

Unless Perri was unhinged, maybe Rowan had inadvertently said something to encourage her. Or maybe, just by being a good guy again, he was sending her mixed signals. Either way, Allison didn't want to be a part of this.

"It means I don't see how she got to the point of believing she could just show up here and you'd take her back. There's a reason. You've somehow…allowed this."

"No way. I'm not allowing it."

"Maybe you should."

The words were bitter, and she didn't mean them for a second. It was as if her brain was making decisions without her.

Constructing a barricade around her heart.

Rowan blinked. "What? *Why?*"

"I think deep down this is what you want. How will you know you can move on otherwise?"

"Allison, is that what *you* really want?" Rowan shook his head, scowling.

"Well, I don't think she should stay here. It's my sister's house, and—"

"That's…not what I meant."

She didn't know what he wanted from her. If she had a temper tantrum like a child, insisting he call Perri an Uber instead of driving her himself, she'd be childish. She'd sound unreasonable. Insisting she go with them would be awkward and smack of jealousy, doubt and insecurity. But the truth was she didn't *want* him to take Perri back to the hotel. Allison could see how Perri would manipulate the situation further once she was alone with Rowan.

And because Allison was in love with him, everything had changed. All her old insecurities had come home to roost.

She couldn't tell him she loved him…not now. He had a choice to make. If he was truly done with his ex, this was the moment of truth.

"I… I don't know what you want me to say. If you want to take her back to the hotel to talk, I guess I understand. You have a lot to discuss."

"Not that much. She's *not* going to interfere with everything we have planned for today."

This was kind of him, as he understood they'd be going to her family's holiday party and he should be in attendance. It was an important appearance in their charade.

"Okay. You take her back to the hotel and explain everything. Tell her we were just having fun. You were trying to help me out with my controlling parents. I'm sure she'll understand."

"Is that what you want me to say?"

No! I want you to say, "Goodbye, Perri. I've fallen deeply in love with Allison and we're going to be together from now on. I'm never going to marry you. I didn't mean to hurt you."

She couldn't say the words out loud. She couldn't beg.

Taylor women didn't beg.

Allison crossed her arms over her heart. "I think you should do what you want to do. What you feel is right to deescalate the situation."

"Right." Rowan sighed and dragged a hand through his hair. "Well, I'm going to the family party with you. I won't let you down."

"Okay."

She waited a beat to see if he'd hug her or kiss her goodbye. It felt like a wall stood between them now when just hours ago they'd been all over each other. But when he didn't make a move, she didn't either.

He turned and walked out of the kitchen.

Allison wasn't certain she should hope or even expect him to come back.

And she wasn't sure she wanted him to either.

CHAPTER EIGHTEEN

ROWAN COULDN'T BELIEVE THIS.

First, Perri's timing.

Second, her proposal! *Seriously?*

Third, Allison.

Allison.

His heart had crashed and burned when she suggested he do whatever he wanted to do, as if it didn't matter to her one way or another.

He'd whisked Perri away from the Abernathy house as fast as he could. Rowan hadn't even looked at Billy and Charlotte. What must they think of him? They probably thought he was playing two women against each other, and one of them was their sister. He'd be lucky if they allowed him back in the house. Both Billy and Charlotte were protective of Allison and he didn't blame them. He also felt protective over her, and the look of confusion and hurt on her face had killed him.

But he was hurt, too. Hurt and disappointed. He'd given Allison plenty of opportunities to tell him she loved him. She hadn't taken a single one. The gift he'd given her *said* he loved her. He couldn't have been clearer. But she obviously still had doubts. At this point, he didn't know if they were about Perri anymore.

Maybe the person she really doubted was him.

One of the things he loved and admired most about Allison was her sense of security in herself. She understood who she was and wouldn't try to be anyone else or play games. When she'd sent him away, it was tough to believe insecurity had anything to do with it. And then he remembered the old relationships she'd told him about. How just as she was ready to let her guard down, she learned a boyfriend had lost patience and moved on to find someone with less defenses. He had to find a way to prove to her that would never be him. He'd have all the patience in the world for her to get to where he was with her.

At least he had one thing going for him. The gift. She'd seen it. It wasn't just a simple necklace. It had a message. There could be no doubt as to his feelings. He told himself this would all blow over when he got back to the Abernathy ranch.

Snow was still falling as he drove Perri to town in the truck he'd borrowed from Billy. He didn't even dart a look over at Perri when he said, "We need to talk."

"Look, I'm sorry I ruined their Christmas, but now we can take the entire afternoon to discuss our future." She turned a bit to face him. "Please, please, *please* give me another chance. I know I blew it. But everyone deserves a second chance."

"And you've had plenty of second chances. Look, I don't want to get married."

Not to Perri. No matter how hard he'd tried to talk himself into the idea, he'd known for a while they had issues that would never be overcome. They wanted different things. He had no idea how they'd stayed together so long. The shocking truth that hit him now was that he hadn't thought he deserved any better. He'd been so wrong.

"You won't even think about it?" From the sound of her voice, Perri was beyond frustrated and halfway to angry. "How is that fair to me? At least consider it! Are you telling me I wasted two years of my life with you?"

"I'm sorry, but I don't love you. It's over, Perri. We went over this. We're not even together anymore. That was your decision."

"I wasn't serious about that, and I regret it. You know me. I get frustrated by your lack of commitment. We're both not getting any younger, you know, and I thought at thirty-six you'd be ready to settle down. It's confusing. You send me mixed messages. I thought I'd have a ring by now. We've been dating two years. Two *years*!"

"I wonder if we put all of our breakups together if we'd even average an entire year."

She dismissed his comment. "You're exaggerating."

"I'm not. Either way, it doesn't matter. We're done. This isn't going to work, no matter what we do, because we're not right for each other. I don't think we ever were."

"I think we *are* right for each other!" she rebuked. Then her tone softened. "Maybe we should try premarital counseling."

Rowan could just see that. The counselor would laugh them out of the office.

He should have been better prepared for this. Allison had warned him, and he hadn't listened. He hadn't believed Perri could be this desperate to hang on to him. At the very least, he'd thought she'd wait until he'd returned home to try to get him back. It was his fault, he realized, for being far too nice. He saw in Perri a desperate kind of insecurity he recognized from his own past. But it wasn't his job to heal her. He would have to let go of his need to help people, including people who didn't want to be helped.

He drew a deep breath then said, "I've made up my mind and I'm moving on. I'm sorry."

"So, how long have you been attracted to Allison? Why didn't you tell me?" Perri swung right into bitterness and jealousy.

He could tell her the truth, but it was also none of her business. This was the time to establish boundaries. His love life, what might be left of it after this, was not Perri's concern. She couldn't understand if he told her that, for the first time in his life, he understood what it was like to be in love. He now had firsthand experience with the inability to stop thinking about someone, day or night. He now understood what it was like to wake up with someone on your mind, and to fall asleep with them still there, too. It was true what people said: falling in love was basically like being a sixteen-year-old again.

These were all things he'd never once experienced with Perri, not even in those early days of romance.

His feelings toward Allison were best kept to himself. So, he simply said, "We're not talking about her."

"Oh, so that's how it is!" Perri crossed her arms and turned away from him. "I can't believe you!"

They didn't speak the rest of the way.

Ever the gentleman, when they reached Heights Hotel, Rowan carried Perri's suitcase inside the lobby of the hotel. The brightly decorated lobby didn't look cheerful through his eyes. The mood for him now was heavily *The Nightmare Before Christmas.*

He walked her to the elevator and waited for the doors to open. He wheeled her suitcase in and she stepped inside. As the doors began to slide closed, Perri stuck her arm between them.

"Aren't you coming up?" Her eyes were shimmering, her lower lip quivering.

"No. I'm not. I think you'll be fine from here."

"Rowan, the truth is I was only insecure because of the way you always talked about Allison. She seemed to be on your mind, and it seemed sometimes that you valued her opinions more than mine. Even though I know you loved me, and you were with me, it didn't feel that way. Just think of how that made me feel."

"I did love you, and I really tried." He lowered his head then gave her one last look filled with regret. "I'm sorry, Perri. I hope we can be friends because I care about you."

She let the elevator doors close without saying another word.

He turned and walked back outside into the heavily falling snow.

There was still a way to salvage this day. Glancing at his phone, he calculated that he'd been gone well over thirty minutes, a result of his driving while distracted by his encounter with Perri. With this snowfall, it would take him even longer to get back. But he'd get back, talk to Allison, and get ready for the Taylor party tonight. It all seemed within reach. He'd actually tell Allison he loved her instead of letting a necklace pendant do it for him. After all, what if she hadn't slid the locket open to see the inscription inside? She might have thought he'd simply given her an envelope locket. Well, either way, he'd tell her tonight that he couldn't live without her.

Rowan didn't know if he'd been driving two minutes or two hours because, in this snowfall, he'd begun to lose perspective. But somewhere around mile marker five, the truck slid off the road.

He cursed a blue streak. Unbelievable. He was having a run of bad luck after an incredible one of good fortune. So, by his calculations, he was now midway between the Heights Hotel and the Abernathy ranch.

He pulled out his phone and texted Allison.

On my way back and will explain all when I get there. I had a little mishap. Truck slid off the road.

He waited a few seconds for her reply, either via words or exclamation emojis. She'd have someone on the way to get him immediately, he was certain. Either that, or he was going to have to walk to the ranch.

He sent another text.

I'm going to push the truck out of this ditch. Should work. Right? What could go wrong?

A full five minutes later, Allison still had not responded. There were not even the bubbles indicating she was composing a reply. But she was probably too angry and disappointed with him to find words. It wasn't his fault Perri had showed up, but Allison had been right all along. Perri still wanted him. But, after today, he had a feeling she'd finally received the message. Now, he'd seen what a healthy relationship looked like, and a future with Allison was what he craved. What he wanted more than anything.

If he had still loved Perri, he would not have let this attraction to Allison grow the way it had. More to the point, it shouldn't have had a chance to even take a foothold.

Now, if only he could know for certain that Allison felt the same way about him.

He sent one last text.

Don't give up on me. I'll be there to take you to the party or die trying.

CHAPTER NINETEEN

So, ROWAN HAD left with Perri. Oh sure, he'd said it was to take her to the hotel, but Perri wanted to get *married*. Married! Allison didn't have any doubts that she'd do her best to get Rowan back. If Rowan's mind could be swayed that easily, then she didn't want him.

Unfortunately, this wasn't the truth. She very much wanted him. Forever.

And the idea petrified her.

This wouldn't end well. She felt it in the marrow of her bones.

Allison ran up the steps to her bedroom where she could cry in private. She was terribly embarrassed by all of this. The kids had heard Perri claim to be Rowan's girlfriend. He'd corrected her, sure, but somewhat half-heartedly, in Allison's opinion. Seeing Perri again might have been the only thing he'd needed to realize he still had feelings for her. He should, and probably would, let Allison down easily, once he returned to the house.

If he returned.

Allison couldn't fault him for doing the right thing and taking Perri to the hotel. It was classic Rowan. A good guy. He was still doing his best to help Allison, too, and they had the

Taylor party tonight. He would not let her down. She had to remember that.

Wiping away her tears, she sat on the bed and fingered the locket again. Was it possible he hadn't even realized the message was inside the locket? Maybe he'd been in such a hurry that he'd bought and paid for it without realizing he'd accidentally told her he loved her? The point being, he hadn't said the words out loud. Neither had she, for that matter, though she'd been about to. And she would be forever grateful for the timing of that doorbell saving her from further humiliation.

She'd been alone in her room all of ten minutes when there was a knock on her door.

Charlotte entered the room, her face puffy and pink with exertion.

"What are you doing?" Allison said. "Why did you come up here? I could have come downstairs. Can I get you something?"

"I need the exercise. Believe it or not, I suddenly have all this energy. Sure, I'm carrying a lot more weight around than normal, but I'm tired of sitting on my behind all day." Either way, she waddled right to the twin bed and sat down with a little gasp. "My back is the problem now, not my energy level. So…what's going on with you? It's not like you to hide away like this."

"I'm feeling sorry for myself when I have no business doing that. I had a bad sense this was coming." Allison sniffed and wiped away a tear. "I should have been prepared."

"You knew his ex would show up uninvited to someone's private family celebration?" Charlotte spoke through a tight jaw and gritted teeth.

She was clearly very angry on Allison's behalf.

"I *told* you she wasn't going to let him go."

"Yes, you did. But he has something to do with all this. What makes you think *he's* going to give her another chance?"

"History?"

"Yes, but he's never been with you before. That has given him new perspective."

It sounded very optimistic, and exactly the encouraging words Allison would expect from her big sister.

"I'd like to think so, but who knows?"

"You'll find out when he comes back in a few minutes and explains everything. He really cares about you, and I can see you've developed some real feelings for him."

"I fell in love with him." Allison choked back a sob. "I never thought it could be like this, not this overwhelming feeling that suddenly I can't live without him. It's scary."

"Oh, I remember. Terrifying. When you can't live without someone, you have to wonder what happens if they have no trouble living without *you*."

"Exactly."

"It happened fast for you two, but that's how it is sometimes. I still remember the first time I laid eyes on Billy. Though I didn't even know what to call it at the time because I was so young, now I think it was definitely love. That hot, kablammy, fireworks feeling that your life has changed forever because of one person."

"I've always wanted what you and Billy have."

"And you will have it, Allison." Charlotte patted her sister's leg.

"Probably not with Rowan."

"Don't be so sure." Charlotte bent over. "Oh, my back. I've never had back *pain* like this. I... I think...oh, God. No."

"Charlotte? What is it? Talk to me!"

"It...can't be." Her face was frozen, her eyes bulging, her forehead breaking out in a sweat. "But I think my water just broke."

Everything happened fast after that.

Allison frantically called for Billy, who came running upstairs as if the house were on fire. "Charlotte!"

"I'm sorry. I feel so dumb. I was probably in labor this whole time, but it was pain wrapping around my back, not cramps, like I expected. I didn't even recognize I'm in labor. I don't want to have a baby on Christmas Day! Think of the pressure on the poor kid."

"It's a great day to be born. Hey, look at it this way. Everyone is already celebrating," Allison said, emphasizing the positive as her sister had just done for her.

Charlotte half moaned, half groaned.

Billy raked his fingers through his hair. "I should have called the doctor. I've been worried about you for days." He leaned out the door and yelled, "Branson! Go fire up Charlotte's truck. Hurry up! We're going to the hospital. Now!"

Jill squealed and came running upstairs. "Oh my gawd! It's *happening*? Hang on, I need my phone."

"No phone!" Billy and Charlotte said at once.

"What's happening?" Nicky said from behind Jill.

"She's having the baby!" Jill threw her hands up.

"Like, *now*?" Nicky said. "On *Christmas*?"

Billy managed to carry Charlotte down the steps in his arms. She was still in her pajamas and robe, so Allison grabbed her coat and boots. The kids quickly dressed in winter gear because the snow was now coming down harder. It would take longer to get to the hospital.

But they had to get there, and soon.

Allison and Billy sat in the middle row seat of the SUV, one on either side of Charlotte.

"Drive carefully, Branson," Billy barked. "We don't want to slide off the road."

"Why did you say that? I'm already nervous," Branson said.

"You're not going to slide off," Allison said, trying to give their driver some comfort. "Don't worry."

"You better not. I don't want to get out in this snow and dig," Nicky said from the back.

As if this was their biggest problem. Digging. Allison could hear the sounds of his video game. Oh to be so unconcerned and blasé about a woman in labor! He must not have heard the news of babies sometimes being delivered in cars en route to the hospital. At the moment, Allison was trying to vanquish each of those stories from her mind by shutting her eyes tightly.

"You're not going to have the baby in the car, are you?" Jill turned from the passenger front seat with a look of sheer terror on her face. "I don't want my baby sister born in a car on the side of the road!"

"Jilly Bean, I am equally invested in that scenario. Believe me," Charlotte huffed.

"Wait," Billy said softly. "We're having a *girl*?"

"Oops!" Jill laughed. "I'm sorry, Dad."

"Look at this way. You were going to find out in a few hours anyway," Branson said. "And there's a fifty-fifty chance it's either one. I don't see what the big deal is."

"I've known the whole time and kept it quiet," Jill said. "Charlotte only told *me* since Dad wanted to be surprised and she knows I can keep a secret."

Charlotte groaned. "Please get me to the hospital."

"Everyone shut up back there! I'm trying to concentrate!" Branson yelled.

Quiet ensued, punctuated only by Charlotte's groans and Billy's soft whispers of encouragement.

A FEW MINUTES LATER, Allison sat in the Labor and Delivery waiting room with the kids.

She was going to text Rowan that the party was off tonight, which would suddenly release him from at least that obligation. But she realized in all the chaos that she'd forgotten her phone at the house. It could wait, she told herself. He'd go back to the house, which in their haste they'd left unlocked, and make himself at home.

"Allison!" Her mother rushed over to them. "We ran right over when Billy phoned."

Both Imogen and her father were still decked out in the formal wear they'd donned for the party before the baby news.

"What timing." Thaddeus shook his head. "Now our party is ruined."

"Thad! The most important thing is Charlotte," Imogen chastised him. "She's early and I just hope the baby is okay."

"I'm sure she and the baby will both be fine," Allison said, though she wasn't sure of any such thing.

They'd called the doctor, who'd said he might now have to deliver naturally. And that would be difficult, considering the baby had been in a breach position at Charlotte's last couple of appointments. Allison wasn't sure how all this worked, and she didn't want to ask to borrow a phone and do an online search to get a fast medical degree. Sometimes ignorance was bliss.

"I don't have any information for you," Allison told her parents. "She and Billy are back there. That's all I know."

"Have a seat, Thad." Her mother pointed to an empty seat near Branson. "We might be here for a while."

"Where's that fiancé of yours, Allison?" her father said, taking a seat and straightening his jacket. "I don't see him around. Did he already take off on you?"

The words were like a poison-tipped arrow, since she worried her father might be right this time. But, as God was her witness, she would not admit defeat in front of her father!

"Absolutely not! He—"

"He had to go take his girlfriend to her hotel," Nicky said with the emotional intelligence of a six-year-old.

Branson elbowed him hard in the gut.

"What?" Nicky said as if waking up from a dream.

"*Ex*-girlfriend!" Jill said.

"Allison sure can pick 'em." Thaddeus snorted and shook his head.

"I'm right here, Dad!" Allison held her arms open.

"Maybe now you'll give a good man another chance. Frederick is still available and has plenty of his own money. You don't seem to realize that some of these men you pick might just want you for your money."

"Why? Because I have nothing *else* to offer?"

"No, no, of course you have so much to offer the right man," her mother said. "Thad. Shut. Up."

"I'm only trying to help. She only comes home once a year and this is my chance to straighten her out," her father said.

"Don't you mean marry me off to one of your friends?"

"He's a fine man," Thaddeus said.

Allison didn't know how much more of her father she could take. "Maybe it's best if I don't come home again next year. Would that be better?"

"No, of course not!" Her mother stepped between them and shot her father a glare. "We always want you home."

Thankfully, Billy's parents, Bonnie and Asa, showed up then and put an end to the Taylor argument.

"How's the baby?" Bonnie Abernathy wanted to know.

"We're waiting to hear," Allison's mother explained.

"What a terrible night to have to rush to the hospital." Bonnie wrung her hands together.

Before much longer, they were fielding calls from the rest of the Taylor and Abernathy clans who wanted to brave the snow and come to support Charlotte and Billy and see the baby when it was born. They now had a full house, both the Taylors and the Abernathys taking over the entire waiting room.

"We could be here for a while, you know," Bonnie said. "I'd say the kids should go back home but the snow is awfully bad out there. Best to stay off the road."

This was true, and Allison wondered whether the snow would force Rowan to stick it out at the Heights Hotel with Perri. Snowbound together. How romantic. The idea sickened her.

But if he'd truly dropped Perri off, he should have been on his way back at least an hour ago. However, if he'd engaged in even a little bit of conversation with Perri, he might have been caught in the storm. Allison had to put an end to these thoughts. There was no point in turning this over and over in her mind, but as she paced the floor, she couldn't stop. She wandered the hospital, going to the closed gift shop and doing a little window-shopping. Finding the coffee machine, she brought coffees to everyone, and hot chocolate for the kids.

Outside, the grounds had been transformed into a blanket of white. Car hoods were covered with a thick layer of snow. It was truly a white Christmas, just not the way they'd all pictured it. She'd pictured being cozy inside by the fireplace, roasting marshmallows, not walking the halls of a badly lit hospital corridor.

Finally, Billy appeared in the waiting room, grinning from ear to ear.

"It's a girl," he announced. "And she's healthy. Small, about six pounds, but healthy, the doctor says."

"And Charlotte?" Imogen said.

"She's great. A real champ. She didn't think she'd have a chance to deliver naturally, but apparently the baby turned sometime during the night."

"Wonderful!" Bonnie said. "It will be a faster recovery for Charlotte."

Just like that, Allison's thoughts were back to Rowan and how he'd screwed up with his lack of knowledge on C-sections. She couldn't blame him. Now, she could laugh, remembering Rowan's earnest but slightly confused expression. And then, more importantly, the way he'd claimed her. Or so it had seemed to her at the time. But maybe it had been less of a romantic claiming than a way to salvage his own bruised ego. Funny how she was seeing everything in a different light now. What she wanted versus what was *real*. They were often not one and the same. At least, not for her.

"When can we see her?" Imogen asked.

"What's her name?" Jill demanded. "Do you have one? You never told us what you decided! Beyoncé is still a great name."

"You'll name my grandchild after a celebrity over my dead body," Thaddeus said.

"That could be arranged," Jill said softly where possibly only Allison could hear.

It made her smile and want to kiss Jill. Thankfully, Billy was her father, but *this* girl was never going to let any man tell her what to do.

Branson chuckled. "Or what about Taylor? Her name could be *Taylor* Abernathy."

"Now you're talking!" Thaddeus pointed, not realizing the boy wanted to name her after the beautiful singer and not the family's name.

"Oh, what a perfect marriage of both family names," Bonnie said.

"Nah. It should be a Christmas kind of name," Asa Abernathy said. "Like Eve. Or Holly."

"Well, it's just like you to want to leave my name out. But we already have a Christmastime grandchild and Merry is taken," Thaddeus grumbled.

"Charlotte and I still haven't decided." Billy held up his palms.

"Oh my gawd, what are you waiting for? For her to start *kindergarten*?" Jill scowled and crossed her arms.

Billy rolled his eyes. "Okay, well, who would like to go back and see them? They're in a private room. Only one at a time."

What ensued was similar to the mad old days of the after–Thanksgiving Day sales that had resulted in injury and mayhem. Everyone rushed Billy, but Allison literally elbowed her way to the front.

"I think we can all agree I should be first."

"But what about me?" Her mother went hand to chest. "I'm the *grandmother*."

"And so am *I*," Bonnie said.

Allison held her ground, ready to prevent the Battle of the Grandmas. "Too bad, only one at a time, and I'd hate for Billy to have to decide between you. I'm the *auntie* and at the moment there's only one here, so I win."

Fortunately, Eloise, or Billy's sister, Robin, hadn't yet arrived so that made Allison the reigning Aunt. Allison squared her shoulders and followed a smirking Billy toward Charlotte's room.

Billy held out his arm at the doorway for Allison to go through first.

Then he announced, "Here's the winner."

Allison took one step inside the room, and everything else stilled. This place felt holy on Christmas night. A streetlight from the parking lot below shone through the window, giving an almost ethereal glow, the snow gently falling outside.

Charlotte wore the smile of the Madonna, holding a tightly wrapped bundle in her arms. She didn't speak. She didn't have to because two sisters could communicate without words.

Charlotte silently revealed to Allison that she was finally holding the baby she'd dreamed about for years. In her eyes, Allison felt the gaze of a woman who now knew that a great loss could later result in a special kind of joy.

From her position, Allison could only see the top of the baby's head, so she stepped closer to her sister's side. A little dark curl of hair softened the baby's pink face. Her eyes were shut tightly, her mouth pursed as if she wasn't ready for all this commotion.

"Welcome to the world, little one." Allison reached to briefly touch the blanket.

"We don't have a name yet, but I'm leaning toward something appropriate," Charlotte said.

"Something sweet, like Eve?"

"Maybe," Charlotte said. "I'm too happy right now to worry about a name. All I know is she's mine. Do you want to hold her?"

Billy came around to help gently move his baby from Charlotte's arms to Allison's.

"She's absolutely gorgeous," Allison said, her voice thick with emotion. "I can't believe only a few hours ago she was safely inside your womb."

The baby girl was wrapped burrito-style, her little arms pinned to her sides, and she continued to sleep as if she meant serious business.

Allison turned to see both parents were watching their baby with adoration in their eyes. Billy had his arm around Charlotte, and she leaned into him. But she didn't look exhausted anymore.

Billy, on the other hand, looked like he'd been dragged through the mud.

"This was a long time coming," Billy said with a sigh.

It was a gentle reminder that even when things didn't work out the first time, that didn't mean they wouldn't eventually. Allison had to remember that.

When she walked back to the waiting room, a line had formed. Somehow, the two grandmothers had come to an agreement because Charlotte's mother was at the head of it, Bonnie behind her.

"You know what? I'm going back to the house now that I know Charlotte and the baby are okay," Allison said.

"In this snow?" Thaddeus challenged. "Eloise and Dante aren't coming because of the snow. That's smart. You're not a good driver. Sit tight and wait."

But she didn't want to sit. Also, she drove fabulously in the snow, thank you very much. Not that her father would ever admit it. She'd done everything she could for her sister, and Charlotte now couldn't be in a safer place. Everything would be all right. She'd been gone for hours and, in the meantime, Rowan was God knew where. Maybe she was a glutton for punishment, but she wanted to know whether or not he'd made his way back to the ranch. If so, he'd be wondering where they'd all gone.

He'd have questions and, after everything he'd done, and how he'd hung in there with her family, she owed him answers.

CHAPTER TWENTY

WHEN AFTER TWO HOURS, he still couldn't get any wheel traction to get the truck out of the ditch, Rowan decided to walk. In the snow. It took two minutes before he realized how dangerous this could be, and he went back to the truck. He sat there in the warmth for the next hour, trying to get a cell signal. Then salvation in the form of a truck rolled up next to him.

The driver rolled down his window. "You look like you could use some help, partner."

"I couldn't get traction to get out of the ditch."

"Good on you to wait it out for help. It's too dangerous out there right now. I'd help you pull the truck out, but we don't have the right equipment with us." The back passenger door slid open. "Hop in. Where you headed?"

"The Bonnie B Ranch." Once inside, the welcome heat began to thaw his poor raw hands. The gloves were going in the fire. They were useless.

"I'm Jesse Bandman," the driver said. "These are my brothers, Sam and Harrison."

"Rowan Scott. What brings you guys out in this weather? Heading to a party?"

"You could say that. We're driving to Star, Idaho, for our family's Hanukah celebration."

"I told you we should have left yesterday," the one named Sam grumbled.

"Aw, those forecasters are never right," Jesse said.

"They were this time," the brother named Harrison said.

Jesse shrugged it off. "So what, we'll be driving in the snow part of the way. It's an adventure!"

Thirty minutes later, Rowan had learned all about the brothers and their family. They happened to know both the Abernathys and the Taylors, too. When they pulled up to the Bonnie B, Rowan was so grateful, he wanted to give them some gas money for their troubles. But Jesse and his brothers refused, telling him it had been done clearly out of the goodness of their hearts.

"Thanks, guys," Rowan said. "You probably saved my life."

"You're welcome. The next chance you get, just pass on the good deed. That's all I ask," Jesse said.

"You got it."

"Have a Merry Christmas," the brothers chorused as he exited the vehicle.

"Happy Hanukah!" Rowan waved and watched the truck drive off, the red taillights winking once.

He turned to the house, noticing one of the trucks gone. Hopefully, Allison hadn't gone to the Taylor party without him. Either way, he needed a shower and a chance to freshen up to be presentable enough for a gathering.

The door was unlocked, and the lights were on inside, but the fire was dying out.

First thing, he removed his useless jacket, gloves, and his sad, defeated boots.

"Allison?" Rowan called out. "Hello? Charlotte? Billy?"

Rowan wandered through the house. Everyone seemed to be gone, which meant they'd all gone to the party without him. As for Charlotte and Billy, maybe they were taking a nap in the bedroom. He certainly wasn't going to knock on *their* door.

Surely, one of them would have come out when he'd called to let him know where everyone had gone.

He knocked once on the nursery room door where Allison was staying and let himself inside. There, he found the reason she hadn't responded to any of his text messages. Her phone sat on the twin bed where she'd left it, all of his messages unread.

Fine, he'd catch up with them at the Taylor party.

He hopped in the shower and let the hot water run over him, washing away the chill. His hands and feet went from white to pink as the blood began to flow again. After he thawed, he dressed. It was warm and toasty in the house and he wandered downstairs and restarted the fire. Charlotte and Billy would probably appreciate it once they finished their nap.

The phone rang and Rowan hesitated to answer it, but went ahead when no one in the upstairs bedroom picked up after three rings.

"Abernathy residence, Rowan Scott speaking."

"Hello. It's Eloise. I was wondering if you'd heard anything. No one is answering their phone now. I think possibly the storm is affecting some cell reception."

"Heard anything about what? I just got back from an errand, and no one is here."

Eloise laughed. "Oh, you poor thing. At last, someone who knows even less than I do. It's snowing so badly, we decided not to attempt the drive to the hospital. But apparently Charlotte went into labor earlier."

Words failed him. "She…went into *labor*? When?"

It had to have been soon after he'd left.

"I'm not sure. My mother called and said they were canceling the party and driving to the hospital. I just wondered if the baby has been born yet and thought someone at the house might know."

"Allison forgot her phone at the house. They must have had to leave quickly. I'll have someone call you as soon as I hear anything. Right now, I'm the only one here, but thanks for telling me the party is canceled. I was going to head over there."

"Don't. At least you're both spared the Taylor party."

Good thing because he and Allison had to talk. The way she'd let him go tonight with Perri, encouraging him to work things out with her, made him wonder if she'd changed her mind about them. It confused him, because he hadn't seen that kind of change of heart coming—not from her. He'd need to have a talk with her tonight when she got home from the hospital. Surely she'd opened the locket to see the message inside.

He loved her and now he'd prove it to her if she'd only let him.

Rowan hung up with Eloise and straightened the living room of all the detritus of wrapping paper and boxes, throwing some into the fireplace. He made himself useful, and stacked presents on one end of the couch. He rinsed dishes and loaded the dishwasher.

An hour later, the front door opened.

Allison.

She stopped short when she saw him. "You're back. I didn't think... I wasn't sure..."

"Of course I'm here. Where did you think I'd be?"

"With Perri. You left with her." Her chin trembled.

He heard the hurt and pain in her tone and winced.

"Do you *want* me here, Allison? I need to know. Because I sent Perri back home to Seattle. I could go back, too, and maybe I should."

She flinched. "Do you want to go back with her?"

"No. I'll go home, if that's what you want. But it wouldn't be to be with her. I'd have to start trying to get over you somehow." He took a step toward her. "If you want me to go, just say the word. I will. I don't want to overstay my welcome."

"No, I... I don't want you to go." Her voice shook.

"Okay." He needed more than that, but he would take it slow. "How's Charlotte? Is she okay?"

"Yes. She had a baby girl. Name to be determined."

"Congratulations. That's amazing. Eloise called, but I didn't know what to tell her. She's the one who told me you'd all left for the hospital."

"Almost right after you left with Perri, in fact. It was very sudden. Charlotte's water broke and we were all in a panic. That's when the snow started coming down heavy."

"I'm sorry, honey. That must have been so scary for you." His hands slid up and down her arms. "I've been waiting here by myself for a while."

"You have? For how long?"

So, yeah, he'd been gone for hours, but that was because he'd driven off the road, tried to get out of a ditch, and had to walk part of the way back. He could see what it might look like to Allison. As if maybe he'd spent the afternoon in a hotel room with Perri instead of nearly becoming Frosty the Snowman.

"Actually I've been gone for hours."

"I see." She took off her jacket and hung it on the rack nearby.

"No, you don't see." He strode up to her, planting himself in front of Allison. "I left with Perri, but I was waiting for some kind of signal from you. I expected you to tell me that you didn't want me to go. But you didn't. You actually *encouraged* me to leave."

He tensed, his pulse kicking up a notch or two. If she wanted him to go, he'd have to listen. But first she'd need to say those words to his face.

"I'm sorry, but I didn't want to pressure you any more than I already have. I didn't want to ask for anything more. From the beginning, you've been doing everything for me. To make my life easier."

His body suddenly lighter, he pressed his advantage. Now his heart raced but for an entirely different reason. It was finally time to tell her everything. A sense of contentment flooded his nerve endings because it could never be wrong to love someone the way he loved Allison.

"What is it going to take for you to realize I'm not a Boy Scout? Maybe I'm a nice guy, and a great neighbor, but I didn't just do this for you. I did it for me. So I could be close to you, so that I might sneak in a kiss or two. Because, you know, I'm a goner for you. I think I've made myself pretty clear."

Her eyes sparkled and her shoulders visibly untensed.

"Oh. Rowan. I wanted to believe it, but I couldn't let myself. It's just too much of what I wanted."

"And you're always afraid that will be taken from you. Well not this time." He pulled her to him, and she didn't resist. "For the first time in my life I feel like I deserve the best and for me, that's you, Allison."

He took a deep breath. "I dropped Perri off and that's it. We said goodbye. For good."

"Really?" She smiled, her voice bubbly as she reached for him, closing the small distance between them.

"You want to know the reason I kept going back with her? Because I didn't really think I deserved any better. When you and I started spending so much time together, I realized that my feelings for you went a lot deeper than a simple and harmless crush on my pretty neighbor. When Perri showed up, I just wanted to let her down easy without hurting her any more than I already would by telling her the truth. I'm in love with you. It's been you since the moment we kissed. I can't think of anyone else. I don't want anyone else. There could never be anyone else for me. Am I clear enough?"

"They're the words I've wanted to hear but how do you *know*? How do you know you're making the right choice this time?"

"The certainty. I've never had this sense of peace before. There have always been seeds of doubts in the past. The suspicion that the relationship I was in at the time was okay, yeah, but not great. Because maybe someone else would be better. Now, I know. This is it for me. Forever."

She nodded with a small smile and his heart soared with hope because he'd noticed something.

She was wearing the necklace.

He touched and fingered it gently, let the envelope slide off, revealing the interior message. "You're wearing my gift."

"Thank you for this." Her hand went up to the necklace, too, touching his own hand. "It's beautiful and I love it."

"This was my way of showing you I love *you*, Allison. With all my heart."

"Really?" She smiled through watery eyes. "Because I love you, too, Rowan. I fell in love with you this Christmas."

Finally. The words he'd needed to hear from her.

"The best present I've ever had." He brought her hand to his lips and kissed each finger. "What I want to know is why you couldn't tell me how you feel."

"You know why. I wanted to tell you, but I was afraid. Remember I told you I've been afraid to voice what I want because some part of me thinks the universe will take it away? And I didn't know if our timing was right because you're just off a breakup and—"

"I know exactly what I want. *Who* I want. You're my person. You were right in front of me for the longest time. But I wish I'd seen it sooner."

"Me, too." She threaded her fingers through his hair. "I don't want to waste any more time. When you know, you know. And you're the one for me."

"Can I have the ring?" He held out his hand.

"Y-you want it back?"

Her brow wrinkled and he realized he better hurry this up. "Just for a second."

He didn't want to wait another minute to start the rest of his life, and this had to be done. There were no doubts. Zero hesitation.

She slipped off the ring with shaking fingers and set it in his open palm.

"Here."

The minute the ring was back in his hand, he dropped to one knee.

Allison's hand flew over her mouth. He didn't know if this was a good thing, or a bad one. She was either happy and shocked, or unsure about this next step coming so quickly. He could have planned this better, but the moment felt right. It was his way of assuring her that he was in all the way. He didn't want to marry Perri, but not because he wasn't *ready* to get married. He wanted to marry the woman he loved.

Allison Taylor.

"I love you. Please marry me. I know it's quick. But it was that way for my parents, too, and this is right. I should probably wait until we go back home, date a while, move in together and all that stuff. The usual way. But why wait another second when I already know. I want to marry you, if you'll have me."

"Yes!" She fell to her knees. "A thousand times yes."

He kissed her, a fierce kiss that promised her an entire future of his devotion. She met his kiss, returning it with a passion mirroring his own. Breathless, he broke away and simply studied her beautiful face. He couldn't believe she loved him back. For a moment they simply smiled at each other without words, giddy, and overjoyed.

"Okay." He slipped the ring back on her finger. "*Now* this is all very real."

"No more make-believe."

"I have to admit my brief career as a doctor was incredibly stressful, but I had fun pretending to be engaged." He took her ring finger to his lips and kissed the tip. "Nothing but the engagement itself was actually pretend."

"And, bonus, I already know what a great fiancé you're going to be."

"You haven't seen anything yet." He sent her a slow smile. "I'm going for my personal best. In *every* way."

Her mouth formed an almost perfect circle of surprise. "Do you know what I just realized?"

He hoped her thoughts were going right along with this because he'd also become fully aware of something fairly significant to them both.

Huge.

Life-changing.

"We're alone."

She gave him a wicked smile. "Should we take advantage of this empty household?"

"With no teenagers nearby, listening, hoping perhaps to get tips? I vote a resounding yes."

"I have waited so long to be alone with you." Her fingers glided down his shirt to his abs, eager. "All those times in the past, wanting you, trying not to want you. Now I can show you."

CHAPTER TWENTY-ONE

ALLISON TAYLOR WAS ENGAGED, and she hadn't even slept with her fiancé.

That seemed like something she should remedy. Immediately.

She wasn't sure when everyone would be back, but she thought they at least had a couple of hours. Billy had given her every indication he would stay the night at the hospital, and the kids wouldn't want to leave until they'd had their turn and seen the baby. With both set of grandparents there, the likelihood was high that the kids also wouldn't come home tonight but instead would go spend the night with one set of them, if not at their mother's.

"We might have the house to ourselves all night. At least we have a few hours," Allison said.

"It's really coming down out there. Seems like people should stay where they are."

"I agree."

She went into his arms, which tightened around her waist and pulled her closer. He lowered his mouth to meet hers in a sensual kiss. It was so good, so perfect, that her body buzzed in anticipation. Rowan made love when he kissed. Hot. Intense. Intimate. She could say with certainty that she'd never been kissed with such passion.

"Let's go upstairs," Allison said, tugging on his hand. "Hurry."

Her anticipation and rush were heightened by the fact she'd waited so long to be with him. They'd had few opportunities and a couple of interruptions, but finally, it was their time.

When Allison closed the door to her room, Rowan's hard body pressed her up against it. Pinning her there, one strong arm braced on either side of her, he seared her with open-mouthed kisses down the column of her neck all the way to her shoulder. Said shoulder tingled and heat spread along her spine, sliding down to the back of her knees. He could probably kiss her *nose* and set her entire body on fire.

As if to prove it, he branded her shoulder with a hot, searing kiss. "I've fantasized this moment for so long."

"Me, too."

She struggled to unbutton his shirt while he pressed kisses everywhere. Her chin, her lips, her nose, her neck, her shoulders. When he shrugged out of his shirt, she got an eyeful of hard planes and brawny muscles. Her fingertips trailed up his beefy forearms to his biceps, luxuriating in their sinewy strength.

"I can't stop touching you," Allison breathed. "I never want to."

"Then don't."

She didn't want to disobey an order from the sexiest man alive, so she didn't.

His hands slid under her sweater and pulled it off, pure heat shimmering in his eyes as his thumb traced the lace of her red push-up bra, then followed the path with his tongue.

Allison moaned. "Rowan."

He slid her down the long length of his body, and she stayed close, wanting to feel him like a second skin. While he bent to kiss and lick her neck and made his way to the tender spot behind her ear, she slowly tugged him toward her bed. When the back of her knees hit the mattress, she fell onto it and he followed her, covering her body. A warm surge of pure desire spiked through her, and she trailed the pads of her fingers down the long and lean muscles of his chest to his abs. He groaned with pleasure.

He was so gorgeous, a light smattering of dark hairs on his brawny chest. Perfect. Speechless for a moment at his utter male beauty, she let her fingers do the talking. Then, when she could, she confessed, "I want you so much."

She managed to wriggle out of her jeans with him braced above her and assisting, smiling as though he was enjoying the show.

He stood to unbutton and slowly remove his slacks. As he did so, he turned slightly and she got an eyeful of what she'd pictured for so long in her fantasies. He didn't disappoint. He had strong muscular thighs and an incredible butt. He was hard all over, too, which became obvious the moment he was down to his tight boxers, ready to spring out of them.

Rowan took the lead and reached behind to unsnap her bra. Her breasts spilled out and he almost-reverently grazed a thumb over a nipple then drew one gently into his mouth. He sucked softly and tugged until she moaned, going from a light touch to something a little harder and wilder. When he stopped, her nipples were hard pink peaks. He continued kissing and licking his way to her waist and then her thighs.

He removed a shiny packet from his wallet and ripped it open with his teeth. She could have come just watching him slip it onto his hard length. Her body vibrated and thrummed with heat. She didn't think in all her life she'd ever needed anyone this badly. Rowan was so attuned to her, he knew her every need. Wasting no time, he braced himself above her and entered her in one long and deep thrust that made her moan deep in her throat. He moved inside her with slow and steady strokes that had waves of pleasure pulsating through her.

They moved together in a rhythm that gave her more pleasure than she'd ever had. She was slick with sweat, both his
and hers. Their bodies were sliding against each other, con-
necting, and strangely this felt even more intimate than what
they were doing. She closed her eyes at the onslaught of intense pleasure as another wave built and crested. It was going
to happen. She couldn't stop it now, almost as if her body was
no longer under her control at all.

"Look at me," Rowan said. "I love you."

She opened her eyes to see him finally lose his tight control.
His eyes bore deep into hers, and he began to pump harder
and faster as if he, too, couldn't hold back any longer. Couldn't
slow down. And she didn't want him to. She was ready for
him. Gripping his shoulders, she met him thrust for thrust as
he went even deeper. She wanted to prolong the pleasure, to
remain joined like this forever, but her climax hit with a fierceness that shocked her. And Rowan followed her.

Both of them out of breath and panting, Rowan rolled onto
his back and tucked her in beside him.

"Damn." He kissed her temple. "I knew this would be amazing, but even I'm surprised by how great it was."

"We're amazing together, aren't we?"

"I'm shocked at how good."

"We simply have a lot of catching up to do."

"And we'll have so much fun doing it."

"We have so much to talk about and decide." Allison went
up one elbow. "What are we doing to do when we get back
to Seattle?"

"Well, we're engaged, so we should probably move in together."

"My place?" They both spoke at once.

Rowan chuckled. "Babe, anything you want."

"It will be nice to save on our crazy Seattle hyped-up-for-
all-those-techy-people rent," she teased.

He was one of those techy people, but she knew he'd take

no offense. She was worried about something else, though she was sure that Rowan could handle it given the way he'd handled her family this Christmas.

"You do realize my parents are going to be a little pushy about the wedding."

"How pushy?" He quirked a brow.

"You've met my parents, what do you think?"

"Do *you* want a big wedding? Because I'm okay with that. I only intend to do this once in my life, so if it's one big party, all the better."

"We could always elope."

"If that's what you want."

At one time, Allison would have said yes. Running away to get married was romantic. Impulsive. She could do what she wanted, even get married in a hot-pink dress if that was her choice. But as she'd gotten older, she'd grown to appreciate family more, especially her mother. Imogen would love to plan a big wedding for at least one of her daughters. She'd had one huge wedding planned that had never taken place, Charlotte and Billy's second wedding was a small affair, and Eloise hadn't wanted a big wedding with Dante. It was a small thing Allison could give her for accepting Rowan and paving the way for her father to accept him. Maybe this wasn't a merger of two powerful Bronco families, but it was a joining of two hearts meant for each other.

"I might want a big wedding," she finally said. "You're going to make such a handsome groom."

She framed his face. "I love you."

"And I love you. Do you think your family is going to be happy about this, or confused?"

"Are you kidding? My mother adores you. I think she was secretly hoping this would happen all along. As usual, mother knows best."

"I'm not so sure she'll be that happy about us. This all happened so fast. I mean... I get it. She'll have questions. Maybe even worries, which makes sense from a parent's perspective."

He shook his head. "Not at all."

"But how do you know?"

"Hold on." Rowan sat up and reached for his phone. "We can take care of this right now."

"What are you doing?"

Rowan had already pressed a button and brought the cell to his ear with a smile. "Hi, Mom. Merry Christmas."

"Rowan!" Allison hissed, bringing the covers up to her neck as if his mother might see her naked through the power of WiFi waves.

"Great, great. Glad to hear it. Yeah, nothing much here. Oh, except I'm getting married." He chuckled. *"Hello?* Are you there? I'm engaged. To Allison."

Rowan pulled the phone from his ear with a wince and Allison heard the loud but clearly happy and excited squeal.

Allison covered her smile. He wasn't lying or exaggerating. His mother really liked her. She'd met her only once, and she'd been a darling sweet woman who had Rowan's eyes. Now, she could so easily picture Mrs. Scott as her mother-in-law. She bet she'd also like a big wedding for her youngest son.

"Yeah, she's right here." Rowan handed Allison the phone and pulled her into his arms. "She wants to talk to you."

Oh boy. Her first conversation as an engaged woman. She hadn't even spoken to her sisters yet. But Rowan's strong embrace, his arms holding her tight, were the only reassurance she needed.

"Hi, Mrs. Scott," Allison said. "Merry Christmas."

"Congratulations, honey! I can't tell you how thrilled I am. Welcome to the Scott family."

"Thank you. I know it happened so fast, and I just want you to know that I—we—know what we're doing. I really love your son. Very much."

"Oh, I know. Sometimes it happens like this. Rowan's father and I were a quick courtship. Two weeks and we were engaged to be married!"

Allison laughed and talked for a few more minutes with Rowan's mother about possible wedding venues—Seattle or Bronco—until she was passed around to the rest of the family. She spoke to Rowan's father, and then his brother, who sounded just like Rowan. His brother's fiancée sounded very sweet and welcoming. What a great family.

Finally, Rowan grabbed the phone. "Okay, great. We have to go. Talk soon."

"You were right." Allison smiled after he hung up, satisfied that his family wouldn't think they were too impetuous. "But you didn't tell me your parents were engaged after only two weeks."

"Honestly, I forgot about that. They were friends first, and they've been in love for decades. Some people are simply lucky in love." He kissed her bare shoulder.

"That will be us, too," she whispered. "I can feel it. We're lucky in love."

"I'm the lucky one." He rolled on top of her, seemingly ready for more of that catching up they had to do.

She circled her arms around his neck, studying his kissable mouth. "When I first asked you to come here it was mostly to cheer you up. And because I couldn't stand the thought of you alone at Christmas."

"Ah, well, even if it was pity that got me here I'm glad you asked."

Allison felt weightless and untethered, her heart forever changed. All her life she'd dreamed of this kind of love and even if it took a while, she'd found him.

"No, not pity. I should have known then my feelings for you were so much deeper than a crush. You're my person and I can't believe you were down the hall all this time."

Then she kissed him, sealing their love with a promise of forever.

EPILOGUE

Five days after Christmas

"SHE'S SO CUTE," Allison said of her newest baby niece.

Swaddled in layers of pink-and-white blankets, she moved her little mouth in a sleepy suckling motion as she snoozed in her mother's arms. Finally, a name had been chosen after much gnashing of teeth. She'd been named Clara, inspired by *The Nutcracker* ballet. Even Jill was okay with the name, thanking Charlotte and Billy for at least not naming her baby sister something "obvious" like Eve or Holly.

"Want to hold her?" Charlotte said.

"Are you sure?" Since coming home from the hospital a couple of days after Christmas, Charlotte hadn't really let go of her baby.

To be fair, Charlotte was nursing, and Clara didn't seem to want anyone but her mother either. Her little face would get all red and scrunched up right before an ear-splitting wail and she'd only calm down in Charlotte's arms.

"She's sleeping, so she should be fine. Anyway, I don't know when I'm going to see you again after you and Rowan go back to Seattle."

"You don't have to ask me twice. Fill my arms." Allison gently took the baby from Charlotte as she'd been taught.

"Don't worry. She sleeps soundly—"

"Oh, that's lucky," Allison said.

"—during the day," Charlotte finished. "Nights are another story. I need to take advantage of your willing arms while I can."

"We'll be back before you know it for the wedding this summer. Both Mom and Rowan's mother decided Bronco would make the most sense."

"Fast-track wedding," Charlotte chuckled.

"Well, I can't wait to have one of my own," Allison said, holding her baby niece's hand.

These days it was easier to be honest about her feelings and hold nothing back.

Charlotte quirked a brow. "And is Rowan ready to be a father?"

"Almost more than I am. He knows I'll be doing the tough part. But we've both waited so long that we're really ready."

The wedding would happen first, however, and as Allison had expected, it would be a big affair. Her father had accepted the inevitable and had apparently told his friends his daughter was marrying a Seattle "techie tycoon." Whatever. Her mother was beyond excited, already making lists. Rowan was fine having it in Bronco, which he now referred to as his "second home." He kept joking one day they'd have a cabin in Montana for vacations, where he'd eventually learn how to be a cowboy.

The first time he'd said that, she'd laughed and said she loved him just the way he was, even if he didn't own a pair of spurs.

"Where do you think you'll have the wedding?"

"It's looking more and more like a church wedding with a huge reception at the Heights Hotel. That's fine with me."

"That will be so sweet. The same church where Billy and I

almost got married. I hope you're ready for the five-tier cake designed by a Parisian pastry chef and the couture gown from Italy."

"I don't mind. Mom is so excited."

Memories of Charlotte's almost-first wedding flooded Allison. She'd been a teenager at the time and, quite frankly, had found the whole thing so romantic. Now she would be the bride and it was all a bit surreal somedays.

"It's nice that you're letting her have this. You know this is probably going to get out of control. She'll easily be inviting a thousand guests to the reception."

"That's okay. On the honeymoon, it will just be the two of us."

"Two weeks in Paris?" Charlotte said.

"Yes and I can't wait."

Once Charlotte and Billy had come home with Clara, Allison moved out of the nursery and she and Rowan booked a room at the Heights Hotel.

A loud ruckus came from the kitchen side entrance as Billy, Rowan and the kids strolled inside.

"You're getting better, Uncle Rowan," Jill said. "I'll give you that." Allison loved that the kids had already started calling him uncle.

"We'll make a cowboy out of you yet," Branson joked.

"How was the ride?" Allison asked when Rowan made his way to the living room and the roaring fire.

He and the kids had gone horseback riding through the trails. Rowan's cheeks were ruddy and windswept, his hair wild and unruly under his black hat. He wore new boots, since he'd trashed the first ones he'd bought in town. When she'd later heard all about what he'd been through on Christmas Day, and how hard he'd tried to get to her, her heart had shimmered with joy. If possible, she'd fallen more in love with him in that moment.

"Nearly all the snow has melted, but it's still freezing,"

Rowan said, taking a seat by Allison. "I see you're getting today's baby fix."

"You bet."

"My turn." Rowan opened his arms and Allison handed him the baby carefully.

They hadn't seen her for a few days. They'd wanted the Abernathy family to settle into their rightful rooms. Getting their own hotel room had also given her and Rowan the privacy they'd wanted as a new couple and now she was thoroughly enjoying her nights wrapped in Rowan's arms. They planned to go back to Seattle after the New Year and move in together, but in the meantime, they were enjoying their days in Bronco. And their nights.

"By the way, we saw Baby J at the hospital," Charlotte said. "He was there for a regular checkup."

"Who's taking care of him?" Allison asked.

"Dottie Saunders," Billy said. "But she's only fostering him, no plans to adopt."

Charlotte shook her head. "Dotty is getting older, and I don't think she has the bandwidth to adopt Baby J. Poor little baby boy."

"What about the mother?" Allison said. "Any luck in finding *her*?"

"None whatsoever," Billy said.

Allison couldn't imagine abandoning the baby she hoped to have one day. Baby J's mother had to have been in a desperate situation to have done so. It sounded awful and heartbreaking.

"You look good holding her," Allison told Rowan as she leaned in and pressed her cheek against his shoulder.

He was going to be such a wonderful father someday soon. She'd already seen it in the way he related to Billy's kids, Merry, and now little Clara. He loved children.

"I can't wait to have our own," Rowan whispered softly.

"Why do you think I'm pushing to have the wedding this summer? I can't wait either. I want to get pregnant and huge."

"I hope the baby is lucky enough to look like you," Rowan said. "Just please do me a favor?"

"Anything."

"Don't give birth on Christmas Day."

MEANWHILE, ONE HUNDRED miles away, a gray-haired elderly woman is served a cup of tea.

"Thank you, Victor."

"You're welcome, darling. I love taking care of my bride."

The woman shook her head. "I can't believe I don't remember our wedding."

"Well, darling, you fell and hit your head and that's why your memories are still so fuzzy."

"So, I've lived in Tenacity all my life?"

"That's right," Victor said.

He picked up the newspaper that had just been delivered.

There was an article on the front page with the headline, Winona Cobbs Still Missing Five Months After Disappearing From Bronco Wedding.

Victor quickly took the paper and threw it in the trash can.

* * * * *

Don't miss the stories in this mini series!

MONTANA MAVERICKS: THE TRAIL TO TENACITY

Welcome to Big Sky Country! Where spirited men and women discover love on the range.

The Maverick's Christmas Countdown
HEATHERLY BELL
November 2024

The Maverick's Resolution
BRENDA HARLEN
December 2024

MILLS & BOON

A Rancher's Return

Jen Gilroy

MILLS & BOON

Jen Gilroy writes sweet romance and uplifting women's fiction—warm feel-good stories to bring readers' hearts home. A Romance Writers of America Golden Heart® Award finalist and short-listed for the Romantic Novelists' Association Joan Hessayon Award, she lives in small-town Ontario, Canada, with her husband, teenage daughter and floppy-eared rescue hound. She loves reading, ice cream, ballet and paddling her purple kayak. Visit her at jengilroy.com.

Books by Jen Gilroy

Montana Reunion
A Family for the Rodeo Cowboy
The Cowgirl Nanny

Visit the Author Profile page at millsandboon.com.au.

Dear Reader,

A Rancher's Return is the final book in my The Montana Carters miniseries. Although each book stands alone, if it's your first visit to the Carter family's Tall Grass Ranch and close-knit town of High Valley, Montana, I hope you'll check out the other three books, each featuring another Carter sibling. There's also a Montana Carters short story, "Reunion at the Bluebunch Café," to read for free on Harlequin's website.

This book is Molly Carter's story. She always wanted to be a big-city nurse, and she's home in Montana on vacation, not to stay. But when she bumps into her teenage love, Troy Clayton, a onetime ranch hand turned technology entrepreneur and now ranch owner, things get complicated.

Like Molly, I once focused on having the career and life I thought I wanted without letting myself consider other options. But, also like Molly, when I learned to open my life and heart to unexpected possibilities, I found my own happily-ever-after.

I enjoy hearing from readers, so please visit my website, jengilroy.com, and message me there, where you'll also find my social media links and newsletter and blog signups.

Happy reading!

Jen Gilroy

In memory of my first literary agent, Dawn Dowdle,
founder of Blue Ridge Literary Agency,
who died suddenly, November 13, 2023.

I'm grateful to Dawn for launching my author career,
and for her support and friendship in life and writing.

CHAPTER ONE

NOWADAYS, MOLLY CARTER didn't belong in High Valley, Montana. Maybe she didn't belong anywhere else either, but she couldn't hide out in one of the community center's restrooms all evening. As her late dad would have said, she had to put on her game face and "fake it till you make it." With a smile on her face, if not a spring in her step, she straightened her shoulders, opened the door and made herself return to the party room.

Decorated with orange pumpkins, yellow squash, colorful fall garlands and twinkling white lights, the venue was festive. And while she'd lingered in the restroom, the spacious area had filled with people here to celebrate Molly's mom's engagement and upcoming marriage to rancher Shane Gallagher. Her mom and Shane were having a double Thanksgiving wedding with Molly's brother Bryce, the sibling nearest her in age, and his fiancée, champion barrel racer Carrie Rizzo. Although this party hadn't initially been planned for Bryce and Carrie, when they'd decided to get married at Thanksgiving as well, it, like the weddings, became a joint celebration.

Country music echoed from the sound system, and the caterer directed staff setting up buffet tables. Her mom's friends, members of a local women's group called the Sunflower Sisterhood, darted here and there, lending a hand where needed.

And beneath yellow-and-white bunting festooned with hearts and their intertwined initials, the engaged couples greeted their guests.

"Hey, stranger." Molly's eldest living brother, Zach, found her at the edge of the crowd and wrapped her in a hug. "When did you get in?"

"Late this afternoon. I only had time to shower and change before coming here with Mom and Shane." Molly returned Zach's hug, breathing in frosty late-October air mixed with the crisp scent of his aftershave—one their late dad had also worn. The backs of her eyes smarted. She liked Shane and he made her mom happy, but she missed her dad and thought of him daily.

"It's good to have you back, but you look tired." As Zach studied her, Molly's cheeks warmed. Of all her family, Zach was the one who was most likely to see behind her happy facade. But since his wife, Beth, was expecting their first baby soon, Molly counted on him being too preoccupied to notice much of anything else.

Molly brushed away his concern with a light laugh. "Even though I took my time, it was a long drive." She'd packed up her studio apartment and handed over the place she'd called home for the last three years to a medical student from Kentucky, as wide-eyed and eager as Molly had once been. Then she'd made the cross-country trek from Georgia, hauling a rented trailer filled with boxes behind her old but reliable SUV. For now, she'd left the trailer by the barn at her family's ranch, but it only held her visible baggage. The rest she planned to keep hidden and pretend she was the same Molly she'd always been.

"I still wish you'd let one of us fly to Atlanta and drive back here with you. Dad would have—"

"I'm an adult." Molly stopped Zach. "I know you worry but there's no need. I hardly saw any people, and no animals bigger than a desert cottontail." But those five days alone had given her too much time to think about things she usually buried deep.

"There she is." The women of the Sunflower Sisterhood came over in a group to greet her, and Molly was enveloped in more hugs. Questions quickly followed.

"Atlanta's nice but it's great to be home. I'm taking an extended vacation to be here for the holidays, the weddings and, of course, Zach and Beth's baby." Molly gave Zach a brief smile before turning back to Rosa Cardinal, her mom's best friend who owned the local craft center. "Between graduate school and contract work, the past few years have been busy. I'm glad to have a break before starting a permanent job." That job, a clinical research position in pediatric nursing, would be waiting for her in early January and she should be thrilled about it. She *was* thrilled. Molly smiled harder as she answered more of Rosa's questions.

"Where are Beth and Ellie?" As Rosa and the others dispersed, Molly glanced at Zach before scanning the crowd for her sister-in-law and teenage niece.

"They're here somewhere." Zach's grin was resigned. "I dropped them at the door and went to park the truck, but they probably got waylaid by folks. You know how it is."

"Yeah." That was small-town life. You stopped and chatted with people even if you'd seen them the day before. "There they are." Molly waved and moved toward Beth, who was with Molly's middle brother, Cole, his wife, Melissa, and several excited kids.

There were more hugs and greetings, and Molly embraced Zach's adopted daughter, Ellie, Bryce's kids, Paisley and Cam, and Melissa's daughter, Skylar.

Although neither of them had grown up in High Valley, Beth and Melissa seemed at home here, whereas Molly was now the outsider. She'd wanted city life and she'd gotten it, but at what cost? She pushed the thought away. She was here to spend time with her family, and then she'd go back to Atlanta. She'd ignore those prickles of unease that had become increasingly insistent on her cross-country drive. She was living the life she wanted. The life she'd been planning from the time she was eight years old, the same age as her niece, Paisley.

Cole grinned and said, "Look at you, Jellybean. I hardly recognized you in that fancy dress and shoes." He picked Molly up and swung her around like he'd done when she was a kid.

"Put me down!" Molly squealed in protest. "And don't call me Jellybean either."

"Sorry, Mol." Cole lowered her gently to the ground. "I'm teasing. Even grown up, you'll always be my baby sister." His tone was apologetic. "I love you, and I'm glad you're home is all."

Molly smoothed her blond hair away from her face. "I love you too." Like their dad, her brothers were good men who set a high standard. Although she'd dated a few guys in Atlanta, they hadn't matched the ones she'd grown up with.

As Molly turned around, she stilled, and her heart gave a painful thud. *It couldn't be.* She blinked, and heat rushed to her face.

"Molly?" His voice was deeper, but she'd have recognized that rich timbre anywhere.

"Yeah. Hi, Troy." She'd also have recognized him anywhere. Troy was older, they both were, but if anything, he looked even better than he had at twenty. Tall, broad-shouldered and with the same dark brown hair and vivid blue eyes, he was also somehow bigger, with a new air of confidence and leadership. "I didn't know you were in High Valley." The last Molly had heard, he'd left the area when she'd gone to college and, unlike her, he'd never come back.

"You two already know each other?" Cole glanced between them.

"I was still living at home the summer Troy worked for us as a hand," Molly said through numb lips.

"That's great." Cole beamed, oblivious to any undercurrents. "Troy and I didn't cross paths then, but I met him a month ago at a livestock auction. He's on board as an investor for my stock contracting business. He's back in town because he bought the Bitterroot Ranch." Cole looped an arm around Molly's shoulders and gave her an affectionate squeeze before turning to Troy. "While she's here, Molly's giving me a hand with the business."

As Cole's words washed over her, Molly could barely take in what her brother was saying. Troy here? It should be impossible. But, as Cole talked on, a quick glance at Troy assured here he was all too real. So many ranch hands passed through the area, and he was just one more. At least, that was what she'd tried to make herself believe. She'd put her memories of that summer before she left for college out of her mind and heart and thought she'd succeeded.

"Good to see you again, Troy." *Liar*. He was the last person she wanted to see. "I should get going. I told my mom I'd help set out the…food." Another lie, but it was the first thing she thought of. Although she'd offered, the food and everything else tonight was taken care of. All Molly had to do was have fun—which had suddenly become a lot more complicated.

"I should head out." Troy's beard-shadowed cheeks reddened. "I only came by to drop off a set of keys. My Realtor forgot them in my car earlier. He said he'd be here tonight, and since I was coming to town I offered to drop them off. I didn't know it was a party for your mom and brother."

"No worries. Stay." Cole clapped Troy's shoulder. "There's plenty of food, and some folks will remember you and be glad to catch up."

"You'd sure be welcome." Zach echoed Cole's invitation. Like all the Carters, her brothers were hospitable. Molly usually appreciated having a welcoming family but not now.

She made her way toward her mom on shaky legs. She'd only be here a few months. She'd avoid Troy when she could, but even when they happened to cross paths, they were both adults. It would be fine.

It didn't matter how a guy like Troy had managed to buy a ranch like the Bitterroot or what he'd been up to in the past nine years. Although, her stomach churned at the memory of his stricken expression as she'd left him in the barn that night.

Back then, after that brief and secret summer romance, she'd thought pursuing anything more with Troy would be the biggest mistake of her life. But now she was older and wiser. Maybe he was the best thing that had ever happened to her. Except, she couldn't admit it because if she did, she'd have to admit other things as well.

She'd made a life in Atlanta, and it was her real life—one Troy Clayton wasn't part of.

MOLLY CARTER. Troy had been back in High Valley less than twenty-four hours. It figured that the one person he didn't want to see was who he'd bump into. From everything he'd heard, Molly was long gone and only returned to High Valley for occasional visits. He'd planned to slip into the community center, return the keys to his Realtor and slip out again. Instead, he'd ended up at a Carter family party with a glass of fruit punch in one hand and a plate of food in the other, being welcomed by folks he hardly remembered like he was a long-lost friend.

He ate a cheese puff and tried to pay attention to Mr. Kuntz, a white-haired man who'd owned the town's feed store before he retired.

"You hit the jackpot buying the Bitterroot Ranch." Mr. Kuntz nodded approval. "Apart from the Carters' spread, you won't find better land between here and the Canadian border. The barns are in good repair, and there's excellent breeding stock to build on."

"That's the idea." Although Troy had dreamed of owning the Bitterroot Ranch since he and his dad had milked cows there one winter, he'd only made an offer on it because the place was profitable and could become even more so. Along with investing in Cole Carter's stock contracting venture, buying the ranch was part of Troy's strategy to diversify his business interests. As a kid on those cold early mornings in the Bitterroot's milking barn, he'd vowed that he'd take care of his family when he grew up. He'd make sure he and his folks and younger sister would never have to worry about losing their home or where their next meal came from. He'd kept that vow and more, achieving his goals even earlier than he'd planned.

Mr. Kuntz gestured to the crowd, where Molly was crouched among a group of children, her back to Troy. "Molly Carter's sure grown up into a fine-looking woman. She reminds me of my Theresa. My late wife was a nurse." Mr. Kuntz's eyes got misty. "You'll need a wife and family at the Bitterroot. How many bedrooms does that house have? At least five, right?"

"Yeah." It had been built when most people had large families. However, Troy wouldn't let himself think about having a wife and family. While he'd gotten the ranch he wanted, he'd set the rest of his dreams aside to focus on work. Once, he'd imagined sharing that ranch house with Molly, and them having a family to fill those bedrooms, but that was in the past. "I'm happy as I am. I like my own company." The ranch house, and the acres of land it sat on, were an investment. He'd use the primary bedroom, kitchen and living room and a smaller bedroom as an office. Or maybe he'd rent the house out and move into the bungalow that used to be grandparent accommodation.

Troy stepped aside to let a family group reach the buffet table and got a better view of Molly. Still with her back to him, she now stood in the center of a circle as the children ran around her playing some game. Her honey-blond hair fell in soft waves to her shoulders. In a navy blue dress that skimmed her knees, her outfit was simple, conservative even, but it had gauzy sleeves and a tailored look that drew his attention to her soft curves. It wasn't the clothes, though. She'd look as good in jeans and a T-shirt mucking out barn stalls. Despite time and the sting of hurt that Troy had buried deep, no other woman matched her and maybe never would.

"You can manage on your own, but why would you want to?" Mr. Kuntz's voice was wistful. "I used to joke with Theresa and the kids about my 'man cave' in the basement. But Theresa passed way too soon, only in her late thirties, and now with our kids grown and gone, having the whole house to myself gets lonely. I cook for myself and have a cleaner, but love and companionship are important." He patted Troy's arm. "I hear Molly's sticking around for a few months. You should make a move before some other fellow does."

Troy had made his move long ago. Although at first Molly had seemed as keen on him as he was about her, she'd sent him packing at the end of the summer. Wounded, Troy had made sure that kind of rejection would never happen again. Apart from his family and business partner, Pete, he didn't give his trust easily or depend on others, and kept his relationships casual. Money talked, as the saying went, and he was never sure if people liked him for himself or his bank account. And although his heartbreak over Molly had almost destroyed him, it had also made him more determined to reach his goals.

As several men drew Mr. Kuntz into a conversation about golf, Troy glanced toward the hall's exit. The speeches were over, and dancing had started. He'd already congratulated the happy couples. If he slipped out now, nobody would notice. He made it as far as the buffet table to set his plate of almost untouched food down when he heard Mr. Kuntz's booming voice.

"I appreciate the compliment, but you should ask one of the young fellows to dance, not an old geezer like me. What about Troy over there?"

Troy turned and saw Molly standing by the man's side. Her cheeks went pink when Troy caught her gaze.

"Come here, lad." Mr. Kuntz waved. "Don't be shy."

Except for Molly, Troy had never been shy with women or anyone else. "I'm sure Molly has lots of guys wanting to dance with her." The color on her cheeks deepened to red. "Besides, I'm leaving."

"You see?" Molly's voice was choked.

"Nonsense." A gray-haired woman came around the table and looked between Molly and Troy. "The party's only just gotten started." She extended a hand to Mr. Kuntz. "Let's show the young folks how it's done, shall we, Werner?"

"But, Mrs. Shevchenko, I… You…" Molly looked around as if searching for someone to rescue her.

"I'd be delighted." Mr. Kuntz gave the woman a courtly bow and smiled at Troy. "Nina and I went to school together. We used to compete for who'd get the highest marks in math."

"I usually won." Although Nina Shevchenko's voice was smug, she gave Mr. Kuntz a warm smile. "Welcome back, Troy." She turned the full wattage of her smile on him. "I'll drop by this week with a few meals so you don't have to cook while you're getting settled. How does lasagna and chicken potpie with a batch of my sunflower cookies and chocolate brownies sound?"

"That would be great, but you don't need to—"

"It's no trouble." She waved away Troy's protest. "If you're not home, I'll leave the food in a cooler on the porch."

She and Mr. Kuntz joined the dancers, leaving Troy and Molly alone. If he was smart, he'd make his apologies and head right over to that exit. However, when it came to Molly, he'd never been smart. He held out a hand. "Shall we?"

She took it, and her smooth skin against his palm sent shivers up his spine.

"I'll only dance with you because folks are staring. I don't want to cause a scene." As they moved onto the floor with other couples, Molly kept her head bowed.

"I don't either but…" He swallowed. Of course, it was a slow dance. The romantic waltz, "Harvest Moon Heart" by Rob Georg, with lyrics about true love, was like a knife to Troy's heart.

"Congratulations on buying the Bitterroot." As she moved to the music, Molly kept a careful distance between them. "I remember you liked that ranch."

"I did." And buying it proved to himself and everyone else that Troy Clayton had made it. He wasn't the kid whose folks lost the family ranch because of two years of crop failure and his mom being laid off from her town job. He wasn't a ranch hand any longer either, with most of his meager paycheck going to help his family, or a student juggling school, loans and multiple jobs. He'd worked hard, put himself through college, paid off those loans, sacrificed to be a success and never questioned his choices. "Cole said you live in Atlanta."

"Yes." She finally raised her head, and looking into her blue eyes still about winded him. "It's a great city."

Although she didn't say it, there was a "but" there. Maybe what she hadn't said was even more important.

He nodded. "Before moving here, I was based in California, Silicon Valley, but I've been to Atlanta a few times on business."

"What kind of work do you do?" Her voice was cool, almost as if they were strangers.

"I'm a technology entrepreneur. I start companies and then, after a few years, I sell them." There was a lot more to it than that, including creativity, a savvy strategy and luck, but Troy loved building something from nothing and seeing it flourish.

"That's...great." Molly's voice hitched. "You were always interested in technical stuff. How are your folks doing? They must be really proud of you."

"They're fine. They live in San Francisco." In a condo Troy bought for them after he sold his first company. Although his folks *were* proud, sometimes he caught them looking at him with matching concerned expressions. Maybe no matter how much he achieved in business, they worried about him the same as ever, as if he'd somehow failed in life. "My parents are done with Montana winters, but they want to spend their summers here with me. When the Bitterroot came on the market, it was good timing. Real estate's an excellent investment." Maybe he'd buy his folks a house in town where they'd have a better chance to make friends and be part of things than out on his ranch.

His gaze caught Molly's again before he made himself look away. His focus was on the ranch and the climate change start-up he and his business partner had launched a few months ago. He couldn't let himself be distracted by Molly's blue eyes or looking for her sweet smile. Even if she hadn't directed that smile toward him tonight.

"A ranch is more than an 'excellent investment.' It's a place to put down roots from one generation to the next, to care for that land for the future." As Molly exhaled, her warm breath brushed Troy's cheek. "You grew up living and working on ranches. I thought… It doesn't matter. It's none of my business…" Her voice trailed away.

"It *does* matter." Guilt curled in the pit of Troy's stomach. Had he moved too far away from those roots he'd once cherished and forgotten what land and environmental stewardship meant in reality, as opposed to theory? Even at eighteen, Molly was passionate about what she believed in, and that was one of the things Troy had loved about her. If, at twenty, he'd even known what love was.

The song ended, and Molly dropped his hand. "I promised Cole I'd pitch in with his stock contracting business, and I'd never let him down. But since you've invested in his venture, I don't want it to be awkward." She hesitated. "I'd rather people didn't know…about us." She fiddled with a silver bracelet on her right wrist.

"Of course." Troy wasn't about to blab to folks that the only woman he'd ever loved had dumped him.

"Great." She slid the bangle bracelet up and down her forearm. "We can be colleagues and friends."

"No, we can't." Molly was still way too appealing, and Troy

had to keep his distance. "Since I'm the biggest investor in Cole's business, as well as his partner, technically, that means I'm his boss. Yours too." He flinched. Even to his own ears, he sounded pompous.

"Oh. Of course." She backed away.

Troy mentally berated himself. He'd never been a heavy-handed boss and he wouldn't start now. However, Molly still had a way of breaking down the walls he'd put up and reaching the hurt kid deep inside. The one who was scared, vulnerable and wanted to make his mark in the world but hadn't yet figured out how. "I'm sorry. That came out wrong. I didn't mean—"

"It's fine." Her voice was brittle and her smile artificially bright. "I'm going back to Atlanta in a few months anyway. Until then, you'll do your job, and I'll do mine. For Cole, right?"

"Yeah." Troy stuffed his hands into his pockets so he wouldn't reach out to touch her, to hold her like he once had. Back then it had felt as if, with her in his arms and by his side, he could take on the world. "Cole needed extra capital. In a year or so, I'll have my investment back and more, and he'll be on his own again. I believe in him and that he'll succeed." Like he'd once believed in Molly, although it wasn't really the same thing. "I won't be the kind of boss who breathes down your neck."

"I never thought you would be. Anyway, I should...mingle." Molly's smile was so tight it was more like a grimace.

"Go on, then." Before she turned away, Troy made himself give what he hoped was a neutral, professional smile while trying to ignore the powerful rush of attraction that drew him to her.

Maybe coming back to this part of Montana was a bad idea. But it was too late now, and Troy wasn't a quitter. He'd just have to avoid Molly for the next eight or nine weeks. How hard could it be?

CHAPTER TWO

THE NEXT MORNING, Molly slid her empty suitcase under the bed, where the white-frilled bed skirt hid it from view, and grabbed a sweatshirt from the chest of drawers. Except for the colorful Welcome Home, Auntie Molly banner her nieces and nephew had made and hung on one wall, her bedroom at the ranch house looked the same as it always had. The view from the old casement window hadn't changed either, with land that belonged to the Tall Grass Ranch stretching as far as she could see.

Today the fields were etched with silver frost, and mist hung over the white-painted fence that encircled the horse paddock near the house. She shivered and shrugged into the sweatshirt. It was an old High Valley High School one she'd left behind when she'd gone to college and wanted everything shiny and new. Now the worn blue fleece embraced her like an old friend.

"Molly? You up?" Her mom's voice reached her from the bottom of the stairs, as it had in those school days.

"Yeah. Coming." Not bothering to brush her hair, she pulled it into a high ponytail, left the phone that held her Atlanta life on the bedside table and took the familiar stairs with their worn runner two at a time.

From what she'd seen yesterday, the ranch house was as

unchanged as her bedroom. Although her folks had simple tastes, even before her dad passed, money was tight. Apart from an occasional coat of fresh paint, her mom had "made do," as she put it. Molly's stomach lurched as she rounded the corner into the front hall with its gallery of framed family photos, where her master's degree graduation picture was front and center. Although Molly had worked part-time to pay her own way as much as she could, her mom and brothers had helped fund her education. That was likely why the stair runner and other things hadn't been replaced. Were her college costs also the reason Cole needed an investor for his stock contracting business?

"Morning, honey." From the stove, her mom greeted her with a cheery smile. Her blue eyes shone as she gave Molly a one-armed hug. "I'd have let you sleep in, but once they're done their chores the hands are reshingling the henhouse roof. I didn't want you waking up to that racket."

"I've been up for a few hours." She'd hardly slept but she couldn't tell her mom that without also telling her why. *Troy Clayton.* She turned to the coffeepot and poured herself a cup of the fragrant brew. "I unpacked my clothes, and except for a few boxes, the rest of the stuff in the trailer I rented can go in the main barn. I talked to Bryce and Cole last night. They can unload it with me later." If the biggest reminders of her Atlanta life were out of sight, maybe she could stop thinking about it.

"You don't have to store your things in a barn. I cleared space in the basement or—"

"It's fine." Molly swallowed a mouthful of the full-bodied coffee without tasting it. "With Zach, Beth and Ellie moving in here, and you moving into Carrie's place on her farm while you and Shane are building your house, you don't need my belongings taking up space."

"You're family, Molly. It'll be a pleasure having you take up whatever space you want and need." Her mom popped a plate of pancakes in the oven to warm and then came over to cup Molly's chin in her hands. "Is everything okay, sweetheart?"

"Sure. I'm tired, that's all." She manufactured a smile.

"It's no wonder. Between work, school and that long drive across the country, you need a good rest."

Except, no amount of "rest" would soothe the turmoil in Molly's heart. "I'm fine, Mom, really. What can I do?" If she kept busy, she wouldn't think about Troy or anything else. She usually grabbed breakfast on her way out the door, stuffing containers of yogurt and trail mix, a piece of fruit and maybe a muffin into a lunch bag. Here, though, her family and the ranch hands came in for breakfast, and the meal was a time to talk and get ready for the rest of the day.

"No need for you to do anything." Her mom gestured with a spatula before putting it in the dishwasher. "The table's set. Eggs, pancakes and sausages are cooked, so get some food and set yourself down in your usual place and dig in. The hands and your brothers will be in shortly."

"Are you sure? I always help. I'm not a guest." She took a plate from the stack at one end of the long farmhouse table and served herself the food her mom indicated.

"Let me spoil you a bit, all right? At least for the weekend, you're on vacation." Her mom put several slices of bread into the toaster and then filled a glass jug that had belonged to Molly's grandma with maple syrup. "Besides, I've got ranch breakfasts down to a science. After the wedding, I'll be sharing this routine with the others. It's right Zach and his family live here, but I'll miss this house and everything that comes with it."

"That's understandable but think of the wonderful new house you'll have with Shane." Her soon-to-be stepfather had emailed Molly the architect's plans and asked for her input on the bedroom with attached bath that would be hers whenever she visited.

"I know. I'm thrilled to have everything fresh and modern,

but it's hard to let go of the memories." Her mom put toast on a plate and joined Molly at the table. "I remind myself that Zach, Beth, Ellie and the baby will make new memories here. Besides, this house will still be part of my life, only in a different way."

Like it would still be part of Molly's life. She took a piece of toast and buttered it. She'd certainly changed over the years, and it made sense others had as well. But it was still strange to think of coming here and having Zach and his family living in the only true home she'd ever known.

"I almost forgot to tell you. I have an appointment at the wedding dress shop for a final fitting this afternoon. You need to try on the maid of honor dresses I picked out for you, and I thought we could look at shoes."

"Fine with me." Molly picked up her fork. "I'm happy to wear whatever dress you want. It's your wedding and—" Male voices echoed outside the back door and boots stamped on the mat.

"Look who I ran into outside." Cole came into the kitchen, and his face was ruddy with cold. "Troy and I have a meeting, but chores took longer so I invited him to join us for breakfast. We can all talk together."

"We?" Molly put a hand to her unbrushed hair.

"Yeah, you, me and Troy." In his sock feet, Cole came across the kitchen and gave her a teasing grin. "Don't worry, I'll give you a few days to settle back in before hauling you out of bed at the crack of dawn to come out to the barns." He turned to Troy. "Molly's never been a morning person. Back in the day, she always tried to get assigned the late chores instead of the early ones."

"I did not. I never asked for special favors." Molly bit back the rest of her protest. She'd never wanted to be treated differently because her folks owned the ranch, but now she didn't want to sound like a teenager arguing with her brother.

"Molly always worked as hard as the rest of us." Peace-maker Zach took his seat at the head of the table in the place that had once been their dad's.

"She sure did." Cole's expression sobered as he and Troy sat across from her, and Bryce took the chair on Molly's right. "Mom says things work out in unexpected ways, and I guess they do. I'm a lucky man having the two of you on board with my business for the next while." He raised his glass of orange juice in a toast.

After a career-ending rodeo injury that could have killed him, Cole *was* lucky, and Molly didn't begrudge him the good things that had come his way. Her once footloose and fancy-free brother was settled in life, as well as work, and content in a way she'd never imagined he could be. But why, out of all the possible investors at that livestock auction, did he have to meet Troy?

As she picked up a small bowl of strawberry jam, her gaze caught Troy's. Her mouth went dry, and she got the same fluttery feeling in her stomach as the night before when they'd danced together.

"Earth to Molly. Jam, please." Bryce touched her arm.

"Of course." She fumbled with the bowl and almost dropped it. "Oops."

Bryce took the container from her. "Remember when you put jam in your hair, and it stuck up in spikes like along a dinosaur's back."

Laughter broke out around the table, and Molly gritted her teeth. "I was five. Mom said I was too little to use her strawberry shampoo so I thought her homemade strawberry jam would work."

"We all did stuff like that when we were kids." Troy's voice broke through the laughter. "My dad said he wanted to get his grandpa's watch cleaned so I decided to surprise him by taking it into the shower with me." He shook his head. "Luckily I didn't ruin it. My dad wasn't even mad. He said kids are curious and that's a good thing, although it might not always work out the right way."

"I agree," Molly's mom added, and the conversation moved on.

Molly turned to Troy, and her heart pounded. "Thanks." As the youngest in a big family and the only girl, she was used to her brothers teasing her and telling embarrassing childhood stories. However, Troy had stuck up for her, defended her even.

Warmth suffused her chest, and she tucked a loose strand of hair behind one ear. Letting herself fall for him again would be a bad idea. But right now, all she could think of was how good it felt to have him in her corner—and the attraction that still hummed between them, no matter how much she wanted to deny it.

AFTER ZACH AND Bryce returned to work with the ranch hands, Troy poured himself another cup of Joy Carter's excellent coffee and went back to the farmhouse table, where he unpacked his laptop. Nowadays, he held meetings in boardrooms, but when he and Pete had started their first company in college, it had been at a kitchen table. Sitting at the table at the Tall Grass Ranch where he'd often eaten as a hand was comfortable and reassuring, just as with buying the Bitterroot, he'd gone back to his roots.

"Sorry, what did you say?" He turned to Cole beside him with Molly still across the table, intent on a printed copy of Cole's business plan.

"I asked if you wanted to use our office in the barn or stay here." Cole shifted in his chair and worried his bottom lip.

"I'm fine talking in the kitchen as long as you are." Troy gave the other man an encouraging smile. Entrepreneurs whose companies he invested in were often nervous, but Cole seemed unusually on edge.

"Great. All this..." Cole waved at the business plan. "It's new to me. I know about animals and the basics of cash flow, profit margins and the rest, but not at this level. I never went beyond high school so…" He shrugged and flicked through his copy of the plan as if he didn't know what to do with it.

"But you're smart, and college isn't everything." Molly looked up and touched Cole's hand. "Plus nobody's as good with horses and cattle as you. Troy wouldn't have invested in your business if he didn't believe you'd be successful. Right?" Molly's tone and expression were positive, her blue eyes determined. Troy knew that despite how things had ended between them, she was counting on him not to let her brother down.

"Absolutely," he said. "With your rodeo experience, your business has a great chance of success. Apart from the money, think of me as both a mentor and an extra pair of hands." Troy shut his mouth fast. As an investor, he often mentored budding entrepreneurs, and it was a win for both of them. He protected his investment, and the business owner benefited from Troy's expertise and contacts. But offering to be an extra pair of hands went beyond giving advice. "I mean, I won't be involved on a daily basis, but you can always call me if you need to."

"Really?" Some of the tension in Cole's expression eased, and he rubbed the back of his neck.

"Of course. I'm here for you." Troy cleared his throat and fiddled with a pen. *Never mix business with personal relationships.* He'd made that vow soon after he started out, and it had served him well. Except now, with Molly beaming at him like she was still the girl he remembered, as if he hung the moon and stars, he wanted to be more involved in Cole's venture— personally involved—than he could ever have imagined.

"Thanks, Troy. That's fantastic." Cole's voice was gruff.

"It sure is. So where do we start?" Molly looked at him expectantly.

Troy caught his breath. She and Cole had given him their trust, and he wouldn't let them down. "I want to go over a few things in the plan. I also have some suggestions for cutting costs, which should pay off in future years."

"We're all ears, aren't we, Cole?" Molly leaned toward her brother, and her eyes glowed with sisterly pride.

What would it be like to have Molly's love and support directed at him? Troy's throat went dry, and he took a mouthful of coffee.

"Sure. Whatever you say, Troy." Cole's laugh was awkward. "Boss."

Boss. He was the guy in charge. As Troy took Cole and Molly through the plan, highlighting strengths, weaknesses and opportunities, her steady gaze made him sweat more than the most demanding CEO ever had. "See here?" He gestured to her to come around the table to look at the chart on his laptop screen. "These are my income projections."

As she leaned in to study the screen, Molly's ponytail brushed Troy's cheek and he breathed in a scent of vanilla and some soft flower. Jasmine maybe? Jasmine used to be her favorite flower, and he'd bought her a plant for their one-month anniversary. Back then, each day with her had been a celebration. He'd fallen fast and hard—which was how it had ended between them too.

"You think by adding more fall-calving cows Cole could generate that much extra money?" Molly's blue eyes went wide.

"I do." His breath quickened. Pay attention to business, not memories, and definitely not that sweet, enticing scent that made him want things he couldn't have. As Troy explained his reasoning behind the income figures, Molly reached around him to point out other things on the chart to Cole. Her arm skimmed the top of Troy's shoulders, and his skin tingled through the thin cotton of his shirt.

"Why don't you two sit next to each other to look at the chart together?" He pushed his chair back and stood so Molly could take his seat. Troy hadn't been able to stop thinking about her since yesterday's party, and at least this way he could put some physical distance between them.

"Thanks." She gave him a brief smile before studying the screen again.

"But what about buying that bull? I also need a stallion and bucking mare." There was a worried furrow between Cole's eyebrows. "Even with upping fall calving, money will still be tight. Big Red, the bull we bought a few years ago, is for ranching. My plan is to develop a breeding program for rodeo. I want to have animals that are as skilled athletes as the cowboys and cowgirls who ride them."

"That's why you need to take a long-term view. On the next slide..." Troy reached for the keyboard at the same time as Molly did, and their fingers brushed. He took his hand away as quickly as if he'd touched something hot. "Go ahead. I suggest you lease a different bull and stallion to start. That's more cost-effective. Then you'll have enough money to buy a really good bucking mare." As Troy outlined the pros and cons of leasing versus buying stock, Cole and Molly listened intently.

"That makes sense." Cole's smile was approving. "I'm starting with a small herd, and we'd save feed if we were only using the animals for a few months of the year." Cole's smile was wry. "Beth says Big Red cost us more than he earned last winter. She already suggested renting him out to a friend for a month or so to make Big Red pay for his keep. Dad never did anything like that, but when Beth came on board she said the ranch had to change to survive."

"She's right." Molly folded her hands in her lap. Had she been as affected by that brief touch as Troy? "Because of Beth, this ranch is doing better than it has in years. And Troy's leasing idea is a good one."

"But can we find a stallion and bull to lease that are in the budget and have the right genetic makeup?" Cole rubbed a hand across his forehead. "I have contacts, sure, but they're for buying, not leasing stock."

"Between your contacts and mine, we should be able to get exactly what we need. Shane likely knows some good folks too." Troy hesitated. From the little he knew of him, Cole was independent and didn't like asking for help. A lot like him. However, there were times when people were stronger together.

His stomach rolled as he studied the back of Molly's head, her ponytail bobbing as she pointed out information on the laptop screen to Cole. She'd looked great last night dressed up for the party, but somehow she was even more attractive now. Maybe it was because in that old sweatshirt, with no makeup and tousled hair, she was more real.

"Okay, let's do it," Cole agreed, and held out his hand for Troy to shake. "You think Shane will be okay getting involved? He's a great guy, but he's marrying Mom. I don't want to take advantage. He's got money and contacts, sure, but he earned those, and he's got his own family."

"That family now includes you." Wearing outdoor clothes, Joy came back into the kitchen with a basket of eggs. "Shane wants to let you build your own operation like he did, but he also had help. You say the word and whether it's contacts, money or anything else, he'll be there for you like your own dad would have been."

Molly's breath stuttered audibly, and she got up and went to stare out the kitchen window.

"You okay?" Troy joined her as Joy and Cole talked about ranchers who might have stock available for lease.

"Sure, fine." Molly's voice was tight, and her shoulders were hunched. "It's all good. Thanks to you, Cole's bound to be a big success."

"Thanks to you too. You're great...at explaining things." Troy's stomach lurched. He'd almost said *she* was great, period. "He's lucky to have you on board." The vulnerability in her face touched a place he'd buried deep.

"It's only for a month or so." Was that relief or regret in Molly's voice?

"Yeah." Troy heard the regret in his own voice and took a

step back. "Cole and I are heading out to the barns to take a look at the usable space. Are you joining us?"

"No, I'm going to town with my mom for her wedding dress fitting." As Molly turned to face him, that vulnerability was nowhere in sight, and Troy wondered if he'd imagined it.

"Of course. Have fun." Troy swallowed a lump of emotion.

He respected Cole and wanted him to succeed. Yet, as he dealt with Cole's business, being around Molly, and the unfinished business between them, was stirring up all sorts of things—and feelings—he'd trained himself to forget.

Since no good could come of any of those feelings, he'd have to try harder to keep their relationship professional.

CHAPTER THREE

"WHAT DO YOU THINK?" Joy stood in the middle of the dress shop's private fitting area as Donna, the owner and primary seamstress, took some final measurements. In a pale blush pink that fell in soft folds to her ankles, the dress had long sleeves, a high back and a scoop neckline embellished with vintage lace. And as Joy caught a glimpse of herself in one of the long mirrors, her hands tingled, and warmth spread through her chest.

"You look beautiful, Mom." Molly moved from her seat on one of the gray velvet chairs and gave Joy a careful hug, mindful of Donna. "That dress is simple, elegant and chic. Like you."

Joy got misty-eyed. "Thanks, honey. I hardly recognize myself. It's sure a change from barn clothes."

"You also look great in barn clothes. I hope I look even half as good when I'm your age. What's your secret?" Although Molly's expression was teasing, it held a hint of sadness that put Joy's maternal radar on alert.

"No secret." Joy held pins for Donna, a woman near her age who attended the Carter family's church, and studied her daughter's bent head. "Some good genes, maybe, but if so, that's luck. Fresh country air and mostly homegrown food. The love of family and friends. I've had a simple life but mostly a happy one. No big excitement." Joy lifted an arm so Donna could snip a loose thread. "Not like you with your adventures at college and now in Atlanta." She nodded her thanks to Donna who excused herself as a bell rang in the main part of the store.

"I guess." Molly's voice was flat. "Sometimes I wonder... do you ever have regrets?" Molly sat on the chair again, and Joy perched on a matching sofa.

"About my life?" Joy kept her tone casual. Before Molly left for college, their relationship had been tense. It was natural, Joy supposed, and part of Molly's need to separate from her family, but since then, she hadn't seen her daughter often. And they'd never regained the closeness they'd shared before those years of teenage angst.

"Life, choices, you know?"

"Of course, I have regrets. I wouldn't be human if I didn't." Joy forced a light laugh. One day, she hoped she could be truly open with her daughter, but they weren't there yet. She could, however, open the door to a closer adult relationship by telling Molly a bit of what was in her heart. "Although I don't regret marrying your dad, looking back I wish I'd waited and gone to college first."

She stared at her reflection in another mirror. Now in her sixties, she was a lifetime away from the teenage bride who'd married Dennis. She barely remembered that starry-eyed girl in the enormous veil and billowy dress she'd chosen with her mom a few weeks after senior prom.

"That's why you wanted me to go to college. But you and Dad were happy, weren't you?" Molly's voice trembled.

"So happy." The backs of Joy's eyes burned. "My folks tried to talk me out of marrying so young, but I insisted." She exhaled. "Since I wanted to have a family right away, I grew up fast." At least in some ways. "If I'd known then what I know now..." She stopped. There was no use looking back.

"I never imagined being a bride again at my age." She made her voice bright.

"You're a gorgeous bride, and Shane's a lucky man." Molly's smile was strained. "It's going to be a wonderful wedding. Weddings. Bryce and Carrie too."

"I didn't expect to remarry but being with Shane feels right." And they fit together in a different way than Joy had with Dennis. "You never know where life will take you. It sounds trite but it's true." Joy studied her daughter. Something was wrong but what? "Is there anyone special in your life? That ER doctor I met when I visited you seemed nice." And he'd shown unmistakable signs of being interested in Molly.

"No, I'm happily single." Despite her words, Molly's voice had a bitter note. "I went out with that ER doctor a few times, but he's not for me. For a start, his job is his life."

Wasn't Molly's job her life too? *Don't interfere.* Zach, Cole and, most recently, Bryce, had all said that to Joy, but wanting your children to find happiness with a loving partner was caring, not interference. "I'm sure the right man will come along."

Molly shrugged. "Maybe I don't want to marry. I like an independent life. I can travel, join a softball team and buy a horse."

"But what about…" Joy stopped herself from saying something that might provoke an argument. Molly was a born mother. She didn't want to forgo having a family, did she? "You can do all those things as a married woman and—"

"Yes, but I'd have to consider what my husband wanted." Another shrug. "I'm fine on my own."

Zach, Cole and Bryce had all said the same thing not so long ago. Joy put a hand to her mouth to hide a smile. Was Molly protesting too much? Had she already met the right man? There'd been something about her interactions with Troy Clayton, first at the party and then at breakfast, that had also pinged Joy's maternal radar.

"You've made a good life for yourself, sweetheart. I'm so proud of you." Joy leaned over to pat Molly's hand and tried to mask her unease. She'd sensed something between Molly and Troy the summer before Molly left for college but had convinced herself she was wrong. Molly couldn't wait to leave home and start her new city life. She'd never have considered settling down with a ranch hand. "You've achieved everything you wanted, and your future is bright."

So why didn't Molly look happier? Was she upset about Joy remarrying? She'd said she was okay with it and she seemed to like Shane, but was Molly only putting a brave face on for a situation she couldn't change?

"Don't forget my new home with Shane will be yours. I know it will seem strange at first visiting somewhere else, but you'll still be welcome with Zach and Beth at the ranch house and—"

"It's fine. Here's Donna coming back. I can't wait to try on the dresses you picked out for me. They look great in the pictures you sent. I like all the styles, but in terms of color, either the soft gray or burgundy would complement your pink. What's Rosa wearing?"

Like all Joy's kids, Molly shut down and deflected things she didn't want to talk about. However, that behavior told Joy her intuition was correct. Even if she was truly okay with Shane, Molly *was* upset about the wedding. That wasn't surprising. She'd always been a "daddy's girl," and Dennis's sudden death in a farm accident when Molly was a young teen had devastated her.

"Rosa chose burgundy for her matron of honor dress, but the two of you don't have to match." For the simple wedding she wanted, Joy had chosen both a matron and maid of honor, her best friend and her daughter, to stand up with her.

Joy manufactured a smile for Donna. While her conversation with Molly was over for now, Joy had only gotten started.

"THERE YOU GO, GIRL." In a stall at one end of the horse barn, Molly checked on Daisy-May and rubbed the Appaloosa's ears. Two days after her mom's dress fitting, and with her own silvery-gray maid of honor dress chosen and with Donna to be altered, Molly had finished unpacking and was settled back here on the ranch. It was temporary, though, and she couldn't let herself get too comfortable. "I missed you." She rested her head against Daisy-May's neck and breathed in her familiar scent. "You're my best buddy, aren't you?"

Daisy-May nickered and nosed Molly's jacket pocket.

"I already gave you a treat. Did you forget about that carrot?" Molly shook her head and left the horse's stall, closing the door behind her. She'd also missed this barn and the other horses, although none was so dear to her as gentle Daisy-May.

She glanced around the high-raftered space divided in half by a wide central aisle lined with stalls. The barn looked almost the same as before she'd left for college, but there were still subtle differences. Even since she was last home, the lighting had been upgraded and several of the stall doors had been replaced.

There were new horses as well, including Christabel, a white pony with brown spots who belonged to Cole's stepdaughter, Skylar. "You're a pretty girl." Molly admired the pony who wore a dark blue blanket personalized with her name.

"A pretty expensive girl. Cole told me about her pedigree."

At Troy's voice, Molly turned to greet him. "Skylar's dad is big in the horse world, and money isn't an issue." These days, money likely wasn't an issue for Troy either. "I didn't see you." How long had he been here? He hadn't heard her talking to Daisy-May, had he? Her face heated as she tried to remember if she'd said anything embarrassing.

"I was outside in the yard with Cole. I came in to take another look at the tack room. We've got a contractor coming later to measure for an addition."

In jeans, a dark felt cowboy hat, fleece-lined denim jacket

and boots, Troy looked like a ranch hand, and Molly had to remind herself he wasn't. He was her boss. She rubbed Christabel between her ears. "It's great for Cole to have your help in expanding."

"Although you don't *always* have to spend money to make money, in Cole's case, and to get his business to the next level, he needs to invest in stock, equipment and barn space. That's where I come in."

Troy leaned against the stall and patted Christabel. His hands were well-shaped, and a faint white scar bisected his right knuckle. That summer they were together, he'd cut his hand on a rake, and Molly had bandaged it before driving him to the hospital to get stitches. She'd teased him about being her "first patient" who wasn't family.

"Cole's grateful to you. We all are. It was hard for him to leave rodeo, and now with his business he has a new and positive goal." Molly made herself focus on the present, not the past. And definitely not on how holding Troy's hand had once given her a sense of comfort, safety and steadfast love.

"You're a sweetheart, Chrissie. Not stuck up at all despite those fancy horses in your family tree."

As Troy spoke to the pony, Christabel nudged his face, and Molly busied herself with putting away an empty feed bucket. He'd always been good with horses, and they responded to his kindness and calm, gentle nature. The same things that had once drawn Molly to him. They still did. She stuck her hands in the pockets of the brown barn jacket she'd grabbed from a hook in the mudroom. "Do you have horses at the Bitterroot?"

"Two came with the property, but I want to buy a few more along with heritage breed cattle. I kept the ranch foreman on, along with any hands who wanted to stay. They're managing the place for me, but in time I want to get more involved." He chuckled as Christabel headbutted an old beach ball suspended from a hay net. "Homemade toys are the best, aren't they, honey?"

His voice was low, and its sweetness rubbed at a wound in Molly's heart that had never truly healed. Troy was talking to Christabel, not her, and she'd given up the chance to hear him call her honey. "You should talk to Bryce. He and his kids are raising Hereford pigs. His fiancée, Carrie, is big on sustainable agriculture. She says raising traditional breeds is good for both the climate and ranch business."

"For sure." Troy rolled his shoulders, and butterflies took flight in Molly's stomach. She remembered holding on to those same shoulders as Troy lifted her like she weighed nothing. "I need more hours in the day. It's good to be busy, but I'm already pulled between ranch work and my day job. Still, I'm lucky. Not a lot of people, let alone a guy my age, have their dreams come true."

Molly's own dreams had come true too, at least in terms of work. So why did she feel so off balance? "You're busy. I should get back to the house and let you get on with your day." She shivered as a gust of wind buffeted her from the open barn door.

"Wait." Troy's blue gaze caught Molly's and held. "Look, I just wanted to say… I hope life's been good. I only ever wanted the best for you. Back then and now."

"My life's great." She hugged herself in the bulky jacket. "I've got an amazing job lined up in Atlanta starting in January, and I'm sharing a condo with a nursing friend while I save to buy a place of my own. Like you, I'm lucky. I had a dream, and I went for it like I planned."

Still Troy didn't look away. "No regrets, then?"

The same question Molly had asked her mom but was afraid to examine for herself. "Everybody has regrets. Like my last haircut." She tried to joke and tugged at the choppy ends of her hair. "It's been a few months but I'm still growing out these layers."

"Your hair is…it's fine." Troy hesitated and something that

might have been admiration sparked in his eyes. "If you have time, Cole could use your input."

"Sure. On what?" If Cole needed something, why hadn't he asked her himself?

"It's a bit…awkward." Troy walked beside Molly to the barn door. "Cole's fantastic with livestock and everybody likes him, but when it comes to keeping track of details, he's…" He shook his head.

"Organizationally challenged?" Molly laughed, and what had briefly felt akin to intimacy between them vanished like morning mist. "That's my brother. He says everything he needs to know is in his head, but that would be a problem in business."

"Exactly." Troy's deep laugh blended with her higher-pitched one. "I don't want Cole to think I'm checking up on him, but if you could help him get on top of paperwork and scheduling, it would make things easier for all of us. I remember you worked closely with your mom to manage the ranch business, and you were good at it. So now, with Cole, if you could get a few things back on track by saying you want to lighten his load, I'd appreciate it."

"No problem." Although Molly had never wanted to stay on the ranch, she'd loved the business part of agricultural life. After her dad's death, Molly and her mom had shared a lot of that work, so she understood how to help Cole. And since she also understood her brother, she knew how to offer that help without overstepping and annoying him. Although she'd offered to support Cole with the business, so far he'd been the one asking her to pitch in with specific tasks. She didn't want him to think she was interfering or taking over. "Leave it with me. I'll get things sorted out, and Cole won't ever know you talked to me."

"Great." As they reached the barnyard, Troy rubbed a hand across the back of his neck. "I want Cole to succeed, and he's learning he needs to ask for help but…"

"Sometimes he can be his own worst enemy." Molly finished Troy's sentence like she used to do. "It's a Carter male trait. My dad was the same but in this generation we're doing things differently. Zach and Beth, Cole and Melissa and now Bryce and Carrie, work as a team with my mom. This ranch is a real family effort and that includes Cole's stock contracting business."

Molly hugged herself again as the cold wind swirled around the yard and cut through her jacket. Nobody had asked if she wanted to be part of the family business officially, and she hadn't offered. She shouldn't feel left out because she'd always said ranch life wasn't for her. So where had that unexpected sense of loss come from?

"Auntie Molly." Paisley and her brother, Cam, ran around the side of the barn followed by their stepcousin Skylar. All three kids wore parkas, hats and mittens and reminded Molly of herself at that age. "Grandma said you were out here. I wanted to ask if… Oh, sorry, Mr. Troy." As Paisley skidded to a stop, she almost collided with Troy, and he held out a hand to stop her from falling.

"No problem, and you can forget the mister, it's Troy," he said as Molly hugged her nieces and nephew.

"The school bus just dropped you off?" Molly asked as the kids crowded around her talking about their day. Their excited chatter warmed her inside and out.

Cam tucked one mittened hand into hers. "Grandma's looking after us until Daddy, Carrie and Aunt Melissa finish work. Can you play cars with me?"

"And do wedding hairstyles with me and Skylar?" Paisley's expression was hopeful.

"But I want cars and—"

"I want to do hair *and* make cookies," Skylar interjected.

"That's a lot of things," Molly said to forestall an argument. "I love spending time with you guys, but you still have barn chores, remember? I'll pitch in so they'll go faster." She glanced toward the ranch house where her mom waved from the back deck.

"I have another idea." Troy grinned at the kids. "If I help with barn chores, Cam and I could play cars while you ladies do hair. I won't be able to stick around long enough to make cookies, but can you save me some? I love cookies." He made a funny face and rubbed his stomach.

"Yay!" the kids shouted, and raced into the barn.

"But I... You... You're busy." Molly stared at him open-mouthed.

"Yeah, but I like kids and I have to hang around until the contractor gets here." He checked his phone and then turned it off. "Deal?" He gestured to the kids, who were already putting on their barn boots, and then held out his hand.

"I guess." Before Molly knew it, her hand disappeared into his, the brief contact making her palm tingle.

"Are you coming? We hafta get started," Cam hollered.

"On our way," Molly hollered back, all of a sudden light-hearted.

With the children nearby, Molly could avoid an uncomfortable moment alone with the man who occupied her thoughts way too much. For now, she could relax, have fun and forget that he was only back in her life because he was her boss.

CHAPTER FOUR

TROY LOCKED HIS truck where he'd parked it in front of the bank on High Valley Avenue and crossed the town's wide main street decorated with pumpkins, hay bales, paper lanterns, black cats and smiling ghosts.

He must have temporarily lost his mind. That was the only reason he'd ducked out of work with hardly a second thought to spend an hour yesterday afternoon playing cars with a little kid. It had been fun, though, and he'd gotten a kick out of Cam, as well as Paisley and Skylar. And their auntie Molly who was so sweet and distracting any man would find her hard to resist.

At least that's what Troy had told himself as he'd tossed and turned most of the night alone in his big, almost empty house at the Bitterroot Ranch. For the first time in years, it had been thoughts of a woman instead of his job keeping him awake—something that couldn't continue since the woman was Molly.

Coffee. That's what he needed to jump-start his day. A café sign beckoned out of the early morning mist, and warm yellow light spilled onto the street along with the scent of fresh roasted coffee beans. He pushed open the door of the Bluebunch Café and a bell jingled overhead. The dark-haired woman behind the counter gestured in greeting as she spoke to another customer. It was only late October, not even winter, and already the weather was cool and crisp, so the café's warmth was welcome.

Troy rubbed his chilled hands together as he studied the chalkboard menu. He'd have to buy a few pairs of thick gloves and warmer clothes. Despite his years in California, he was Montana born and had always considered the state his true home. He'd cope with winter without complaining in exchange for the joy of being back in this land of big sky, fresh air and natural beauty everywhere he looked.

"What can I get for you?" The woman behind the counter turned to him with a friendly smile. "If I was to guess, I'd say you like an espresso but might occasionally be tempted by a foamy cappuccino." She tucked her hands into the pockets of a red apron with Bluebunch Café in white script across the bib. "You strike me as a muffin guy. Blueberry oat, maybe? Although I bet you wouldn't turn down chocolate." She laughed at his surprised expression. "I'm Kristi Russo. Café owner and barista with a sideline in matching coffee and muffins to my customer's personalities. You must be Troy Clayton."

"Yeah, I am, and an espresso with one of those blueberry oat muffins sounds good." In his local coffee place back in California, he'd never exchanged more than a few words with any of the baristas. None of them had ever presumed to guess his coffee and muffin preferences either. Even if they had, he couldn't imagine they'd be so scarily accurate.

"Coming right up. You'll soon get to know everyone. I knew who you were because the town's been buzzing about the Bitterroot's new owner." Kristi operated the gleaming silver espresso machine with ease. Then she popped a muffin from the glass display case onto a white plate. She seemed to be assessing him, and then she nodded. "Take any free table through there." She indicated the main part of the café. "If there isn't one available, go ahead and share."

"I… Okay." He took his tray, laden with his espresso cup, muffin plate, utensils and a pot of butter, by reflex. He'd planned to get a coffee to go but it wouldn't hurt to sit for a few minutes. He could catch up on email here as easily as at home.

"Good food and good coffee should be savored, not rushed." Kristi glanced over his shoulder. "Hey, Molly. I'll be with you in a minute. I just need to check on my sunflower bread."

Molly? Had Troy somehow conjured her up because in the past twenty-four hours she'd never been far from his thoughts? He turned and tightened his grip on the tray. She was real enough, and the hair on his arms rose. She was in jeans and a dark blue jacket, and her pretty blond hair was tucked up under a lighter blue knitted hat with only a few tendrils sticking out to frame her face.

"Hi." Her face was already pink from the cool morning, but as Troy returned her greeting, the pink deepened. "Small-town life. We can't escape each other."

Not that he wanted to. The realization shot through him, and jerked him into awareness before he'd taken even a sip of his espresso. Only a brief glimpse of Molly would brighten the gloomiest day. "You're in town early."

"I'm part of the volunteer crew getting things set up for this weekend's art fair, and there's a meeting at the craft center. The fair is showcasing some of my late brother Paul's paintings along with work by other local artists. The event's raising money for a disability charity. You might have seen the posters around town." As she spoke, Molly pointed to one on the café's wall.

Troy nodded and took a closer look at the poster. Paul, Molly's eldest brother, had died from complications of cystic fibrosis before Troy had worked at the ranch, but he remembered folks talking about him with respect and fondness. "I'll stop by." And make an anonymous donation to the charity in Paul's memory.

Kristi returned and glanced between them. "Your usual, Mol?" To Troy, she added, "Our Molly's an everyday black coffee fan. No nonsense, keep things simple, old school."

"That's me." Molly's laugh was light. "And a muffin of the day, please. I dream of Kristi's carrot muffins in Atlanta."

While Molly and Kristi exchanged teasing banter, Troy considered his espresso. What did it say about him? Maybe that he was busy, driven, valued efficiency and knew what he wanted? "I was about to find a table. You're welcome to join me, Molly, if you're staying."

"What did I say about savoring food and coffee? Adding good company makes it even better." Kristi's eyes twinkled. "A table for two just opened up by the front window. You'd better grab it before someone else does."

As others in the line that now snaked behind them to the café door murmured agreement, Molly's face went from pink to red. "Thanks, but I have to head straight over to the craft center. We're having a working breakfast."

"Another time then." Kristi's smile was knowing. "I expect you two have lots to catch up on."

"I...uh, sure." Her face still flaming, Molly grabbed her takeout coffee and muffin bag and made her way through the crowd to the outside door.

Kristi waved Troy toward the free table while simultaneously boxing up a dozen muffins for a white-haired man talking on his cell phone. "Along with you having worked at the Tall Grass, you and Molly are two country kids who made it in the big city. You must have lots in common."

"Of course." Troy made his expression neutral. Long ago, he'd learned to never let his face show what he was thinking, but something about Molly—and this close-knit town—made him perpetually second-guess himself.

Inviting her to share his table had been an impulse, something else he'd schooled himself never to do. Yet, as he made his way to that window table, which currently framed Molly's trim figure disappearing into a building across the street, unfamiliar regret prickled.

He wasn't used to neighbors taking an interest in his personal business, and if he'd sat here with Molly he might have gotten the town talking. But if yesterday with her and the kids had shown him anything, it was that the two of them *could* be friendly and collegial. Despite his ill-judged comment about being her boss.

Kristi was right about him and Molly having a lot in common, and maybe like him, Molly now felt somewhat out of place here. Although Troy was a country kid at heart, living in bigger places had changed him. It had likely changed Molly too. He'd never let what others might think or say bother him, and he wouldn't now. Maybe he and Molly could find a fresh start, or at least common ground to build on.

Troy sipped his coffee and ate the delicious muffin, ignoring his phone and the waiting messages and instead looking out the café window. As the sun burned away the mist, and the small town came to life, that sense of regret grew. Good coffee, good food and good companionship *were* important. Maybe, in keeping his life so closed and prioritizing work, he'd missed out on other things.

"Mind if I join you?" Mr. Kuntz hovered by Troy's table with a laden tray and a beaming smile.

"Go ahead." He could linger here a bit longer, and it would be useful to get Mr. Kuntz's input on different types of cattle feed.

However, as Mr. Kuntz set out his breakfast and chatted about the weather, Troy's regret increased yet again. The other man was a reminder of who Troy really wanted to sit here with.

Molly. And the unfinished business that still loomed large between them.

MOLLY SQUEEZED HER mom's hand as a boy and girl from the local elementary school cut the ribbon to proclaim the *Paul Carter Memorial Art Fair* open. Cheers and applause rang out from the crowd gathered outside the Medicine Wheel Craft

Center. While this event was wonderful, it was also emotional, and her mom had been on the verge of tears all morning.

"Thanks, honey." Her mom sniffed and patted her eyes with a tissue. "I truly feel your brother is here with us." She glanced at Zach, Cole and Bryce, who stood on her other side. "Your dad is too, so despite missing them both, my memories make it a happy day."

Even good memories could be bittersweet, and Molly had a lump in her throat as she and her family made their way into Rosa's craft center with its adjoining gallery space. While most of Paul's paintings were displayed here, some had also been hung at the Bluebunch Café, High Valley's community center and the town hall. They'd visit those venues later, following the map in the town's "art trail" leaflet that Carrie, Bryce's fiancée, had designed. There was even a children's corner where some of Cam's drawings were on show. Her nephew loved art as much as Paul had, and it comforted her to think of that talent continuing into the next generation.

"Welcome." Rosa hugged Molly's mom and the two friends stood close together for a moment. "I gave Paul his first real drawing pad, do you remember? The kind true artists use."

"It was for his sixth birthday because back then he drew on every scrap of paper he could find," Joy said.

Rosa's eyes were soft with emotion. "I knew then he had a special gift, and I'm thrilled his work is now on display for everyone to see and enjoy."

As Rosa led them through the exhibition, Molly was in awe of Paul's talent. Only in his early twenties when he died, she'd always thought her brother hadn't had a chance to live, but she'd been wrong. He'd left a legacy in their hearts and through his art that was bigger and more profound than some who lived many more years.

As locals and out-of-town visitors thronged the gallery space, Molly stood in a quiet corner to study a large, gold-framed oil Paul had titled *Montana Summer*. Between the vibrant green fields stretching to the distant Rocky Mountains and a herd of the Carter family's red cattle with their distinctive brand, she drank in details large and small. In the foreground, the state's bluebunch wheatgrass framed a curious brown rabbit, while above, a meadowlark soared high against a vivid blue sky.

It was a stunning piece of landscape art in its own right, but it was even more meaningful because it was home. Molly knew the exact hill from where Paul had captured the scene, and his painting took her there with him.

A memory surfaced of a long-ago summer day when their folks had gone to town and left Paul to babysit her. They'd been on the front porch and, still as statues, watched a butterfly that had landed on one of their mom's rosebushes in the garden below. Paul had told her all about butterflies, and their journey from caterpillar to cocoon and beyond. Now from Molly's adult perspective, she thought he might have been talking about himself and living life with resilience despite challenges. Now she was the one who needed a tissue, and she dug in her crossbody bag for one.

"Here." A strong hand passed her a travel-size tissue pack.

"Thanks." Troy had always had a knack of being there when she needed comfort, and it seemed he still did. She swallowed the tears and dried her eyes. "I didn't know Paul well as a person because he was so much older than me, but seeing his work here..." She gestured around the busy gallery and craft center. "It hits me, you know? Maybe in his art Paul recorded his life and everything he loved for all of us. I know he wouldn't want us to be sad, but I can't help it."

"I bet he'd understand." Troy's quiet voice soothed her. "I expect he'd tell you to go ahead and cry if you need to. Lots of others are." He gestured to Molly's mom being consoled by her fiancé, Shane, and even the usually unsentimental Cole had his face buried in his wife Melissa's shoulder. "There's no shame in honest, heartfelt emotion."

"I know but..." Molly found another tissue as her tears flowed again. "Paul's death so young was tragic, but since I can't change what happened to him, I've tried to learn from it." Maybe that's why she'd set goals and gone after them with such single-minded determination. More than many people, she understood how life could be cut short, so she'd crammed as much as possible into hers so far. However, in keeping herself so focused on work and school, had she missed out on other, maybe even more important, parts of living?

Troy patted Molly's arm, his touch tentative at first and then, as she didn't shrug it off or move away, his hand settled in the crook of her elbow like it once had. "Paul would be proud of you for working as a nurse with kids. It's a fine job, and you're making a big and important difference in lots of lives."

"Nowadays that's mostly through medical research rather than patient care." When Troy took his hand away, Molly felt a sense of loss as surprising as it was unsettling. "I like research, but I miss working closely with children and their families."

"Couldn't you do both?"

"Not at the moment. My new job is in a research institute, not a hospital ward." Molly fell into step with Troy as they moved through the gallery. "I'm working with one of the doctors I got to know through my master's project. She won grant money and put together a team for a project focused on cystic fibrosis in teenagers. It's a fantastic opportunity I'm excited to be a part of." For Molly, it was also personal. In her own small way, she could contribute to advancing knowledge so future families might not experience the heartache and loss that cystic fibrosis had brought to hers.

"Sounds impressive." Troy put out a hand so a group of teenagers absorbed in their phones wouldn't bump into her.

"To an outsider, maybe." Molly smiled her thanks. Troy had always looked out for her, and while she could take care of herself, she'd forgotten how good it felt to have him by her side. "Research is the kind of job where not a lot happens from day-to-day but then, if you're lucky, there's an exciting breakthrough that makes everything worthwhile." The hope of such a discovery was why she loved her job. Yet, did she really want to spend her whole life in a lab? There was a special and more immediate excitement in ward nursing when a sick child got better, and Molly shared in a worried parent's relief and gratitude.

"I get it. I want to make a difference in my work too. My business partner and I are working on a clean energy project where we're hoping for one of those 'exciting breakthroughs' of our own." Troy's voice held the passion Molly remembered, except, back then, he'd been talking about the life and future they wanted to make together.

"That also sounds impressive." Molly's fingers tingled with an urge to reach for his hand and clasp it in hers.

"It will be if we can pull it off, but more than a few people have said it's wishful thinking." Troy laughed. "I've learned to ignore the doubters, or at least not let them get to me."

"That's a good way to be." Molly wasn't there yet, but she'd grown in confidence since she'd left small-town Montana, and when it came to work, she wasn't afraid to stand up for herself and what she wanted. Now she had to figure out how to do that in her personal life—once she had one.

As they reached the children's art corner, Molly stopped in front of one of Cam's drawings. A horse, Daisy-May, according to the name he'd printed in green crayon, stuck her head over a barn stall in the middle of a group of stick figures Cam had labeled as his dad, soon-to-be stepmom Carrie, sister Paisley and Molly's mom.

"Do you like it?" Cam tugged Molly's hand. "Mrs. Rosa asked me and the other kids to tell visitors about our pictures. We're official tour guides." He showed her the "Junior Guide" badge pinned to his blue-and-white-checked flannel shirt.

"I love it." Molly studied the bright crayon drawing. It was simple, but Cam had captured the feeling of ranch life and family in a way some much older and technically skilled artists had never mastered.

"I'll draw a picture with you in it next." Cam looked at her trustingly. "Two pictures so you can take one with you, and I can keep one. I can make your hair the same color as Paisley's." He pointed to his sister's fluorescent-yellow tresses and looked between Molly and Troy. "Doesn't my aunt Molly have nice hair? She's really pretty, don't you think?"

"She sure is." Over Cam's head, Troy caught Molly's gaze. The attraction that was both familiar and new sparked between them once more.

Troy made a choked sound, and even Molly had to smile. Kids didn't have a filter, and it didn't mean anything important that Troy thought she was pretty.

"There you are, Molly! I've been looking for you everywhere. Isn't this wonderful?" Molly's mom appeared with Nina Shevchenko, one of the fair organizers, and several members of the Sunflower Sisterhood.

"She's been in Troy's capable hands almost the whole time. Not literally, of course." Nina laughed, and the others joined in with the joke while giving Molly and Troy interested, sideways glances.

"Troy's been kind in keeping me company." Molly sent Nina and the others a quelling look. She knew about small-town life. Two single people of a similar age could hardly spend more than a few minutes in each other's company before the gossip mill went into overdrive. "This fair's great. You've done a fantastic job. I've heard lots of people say they hope it becomes an annual show and sale for all local artists. Keep Paul's name, but make it into something bigger for both the town and the charity."

"Wouldn't that be amazing?" Joy's expression was tender. "Rosa said somebody made an anonymous five-thousand-dollar donation in Paul's memory. Can you imagine? I wish I knew who it was so I could thank them personally, but we're going to put a notice in the local newspaper and online. Hopefully they'll see it and know how grateful we and the charity are."

Molly glanced at Troy, who stood with his back to them, listening to Cam chatter about the different drawings. Troy hadn't known Paul personally, so he'd have had no reason to make such a big donation. It had to be someone else, but who? Perhaps a group of businesspeople had gotten together, but why stay anonymous?

"You and Troy look like you were enjoying yourselves. It seems you have a real connection," Nina said conspiratorially. "Werner and I both noticed it." She nodded at Mr. Kuntz, who'd joined them. "Your mother says you don't have anyone special in Atlanta. You never know, you might meet a special someone here."

"I'm going back to Atlanta in a few months." Molly liked Nina, but what was it about small-town life that made people who'd known you from infancy offer well-meaning advice like you were their own child? "Besides, I'm not looking to meet anyone right now. I'm too busy."

Nina laughed. "Love hits when you least expect and don't think you're ready or have time. That's the beauty of it, my dear."

"Look at Shane and me." Molly's mom spoke up, and a smile played at the corners of her mouth. "Never say never."

As the conversation moved on to the upcoming weddings, Molly took a glass of sparkling water from a passing server and made her escape.

Of course, she couldn't plan love, but she did have a life plan and it didn't include settling down in High Valley—or with Troy. And while today had been great, and maybe she and Troy could even be friends, this kind of small-town nosiness was one of the many reasons she loved the anonymity of Atlanta. There, nobody expected her to be paired up or made embarrassing personal comments.

But whether she liked it or not, Troy was back in her life,

and there was still something between them. As she pretended to study a pencil sketch of a flock of chickens, she eyed him, now drawing with Cam and several other kids at a low table.

Something she had to deal with.

CHAPTER FIVE

SEVERAL DAYS AFTER the art fair, Troy stepped outside onto the front porch of the Bitterroot Ranch house, *my house*, he reminded himself, and almost tripped over a red cooler sitting by the front door.

He bent to read the handwritten tag tied to the handle. *A few of my homemade Italian goodies to welcome you to High Valley. All good wishes, Angela Moretti.* In case Troy didn't know who she was, she'd also added: *Nina Shevchenko's friend, and Carrie Rizzo's aunt. You can leave the empty cooler at the Tall Grass Ranch next time you're passing.*

Last week Nina had delivered a blue cooler filled with food, and on Sunday afternoon various neighbors had dropped off chocolate chip cookies, an apple pie, three casseroles and a towering orange chiffon cake.

"More treats?" Cathy McCabe joined Troy at the door.

"Yep."

She gave him a teasing grin. Cathy's folks had been friends of his grandparents. She was older than him, in her forties now, but Troy remembered her from when he was a kid. The two extended families often met up for the Fourth of July weekend. She was what his folks called "good people," and when Troy heard she now lived in High Valley, he'd been happy to reconnect. He'd ended up hiring her to do general housekeeping for him at the Bitterroot. "In the freezer with the rest?"

"I guess so." Troy brought the cooler into the house and opened it. "I'm keeping a list so I can thank people, but I don't expect to be fed. I can cook, you know. My mom taught me."

Cathy exclaimed over the treats as they unpacked them. "I'm betting your mom didn't teach you to make Italian food like Angela Moretti. You haven't lived till you've tried her lasagna, risotto and gnocchi."

"No." Troy laughed. "You and your kids are welcome to join me in eating this stuff. Look at the size of this lasagna. It's for a family." A familiar hurt tugged at his heart. He wanted a family of his own, but even if he found the right woman, would he be able to trust in her—or love?

"My boys love Angela's lasagna so yes, please." Cathy was a single mom with teenagers at home, and her expression was both honest and grateful. "You're really generous to us. Thank you."

"You don't need to thank me. You guys are like family." Troy checked to make sure he had the keys to his pickup. "I appreciate everything you're doing around here." In less than a week, the house had gone from dusty to sparkling clean. From the fall wreath on the front door to the flowering indoor plants that now lined his sunny office window, the place felt more like a home. "Take some cookies for the boys too."

"You're becoming the uncle my kids have never had." Cathy's brown eyes shone. "I'll send Wyatt over later to take a look at that snowblower in the shed. You'll soon need it, and my son can fix anything mechanical. No need to buy new when something can be fixed."

That was the motto Troy had been raised with too. "Great. Call me if there's a problem. I'm heading to the Tall Grass so I should be in cell range most of the time." He didn't need to drop by the ranch this afternoon, but somehow he kept find-

ing reasons to be there. Today, it was the arrival of Cole's
rented bull.

"Sure. Tell Joy and Molly I say hi." Cathy grinned. "Molly's
going to look gorgeous at the double wedding. I sew for the
dress shop when Donna, the owner, gets busy, and I'm working on Molly's gown now. The guys will all be lining up to
dance with her at the reception. If you want to have a chance,
you'd better ask her early."

"I won't be at the reception. I mean, there's no reason for
me to be invited," he added. He was Cole's temporary business partner, not a family member or a close friend.

"The actual wedding ceremonies are small, and I heard
they're having a lunch afterward that's for family only, but
the reception's a potluck and most everyone in town's going.
Shane's hosting it at the Squirrel Tail Ranch—that's his spread.
It's a resort so there's a lot of event space."

"But I'm new here and—"

"It'll be a great way for you to meet folks," Cathy broke in,
and her eyes narrowed. She studied him from behind a stack
of foil-wrapped food parcels. "If you don't go, people might
get the idea you're too big for your boots."

Although Troy didn't want to let himself get any closer to
Molly, he couldn't tell Cathy the truth. "As long as I won't be
intruding, it sounds like fun." If most of the town was there,
he might not even see Molly except at a distance.

"Great. You can bring something for the potluck. Show off
your cooking skills. Women like men who are handy in the
kitchen." Cathy's laugh was easy. "If you haven't guessed, you
buying the Bitterroot has caused quite a stir. You sure won't
lack for dance partners. Molly had better ask *you* early." Without seeming to take a breath, she continued, "I'll email you
the potluck sign-up information. I'm on the organizing committee. Joy and Carrie wanted an old-time community fall
supper, so we're making it happen for them."

Muttering something about needing to get to his meeting,

Troy fled to his pickup. His thoughts whirled as he drove along the highway. He wanted to be part of the High Valley community, but he'd planned to get involved gradually. Maybe start by joining a running group or the woodworking club Werner had mentioned.

He'd also planned to avoid anything except a business relationship with the Carter family, at least while they were in business together. However, he'd only been back in town a week and so far he'd ended up in the middle of a Carter engagement party, he'd comforted Molly at an art fair where the Carter family was front and center, and now he was set to join the celebration for two Carter weddings. The line between business and personal wasn't just blurring, it had disappeared entirely.

Fifteen minutes later, and no closer to figuring out how he could get back to a business-only relationship, he turned into the long driveway that led to the Tall Grass Ranch, following what must be the livestock trailer with Cole's rented bull.

"Hey." Cole waved from the barnyard once Troy had parked by the fence.

Molly came out of the barn, bundled up against the cool October breeze in a pink fleece jacket, white knit hat, faded jeans and boots. From a distance, she looked eighteen again, and Troy's heart turned over. But he wasn't twenty and still wet behind the ears anymore. He was older, with enough life experience to be wary, no matter how pretty a woman's face. Yet, as Molly drew closer and he saw the woman she was now, not the girl she'd once been, it wasn't that old teenage attraction that had him churned up. Instead, it was a new and grown-up longing.

"Thanks for coming by." Cole approached Troy's truck and spoke to him through the half-open window. "You didn't need to be here when the bull arrived, but I appreciate it."

"No problem. Since I suggested you rent Cupid, I wanted to check him out."

"Cupid?" Molly joined her brother as Troy got out of his pickup.

"The owner's daughter named him." Troy laughed, and she and Cole joined in. "His mom's called Venus."

As Cole guided the driver to back the livestock trailer toward the barnyard gate to unload, the wind caught Molly's loose hair, and blond strands brushed against Troy's jacket. He tensed, and his pulse raced at the memory of how soft and silky her hair had been and how he'd liked to run his fingers through it.

"I talked to Cole and have started to tackle his paperwork." Molly tucked her flyaway hair under her jacket collar. "I've made an online schedule and contact list from the handwritten notes Cole had scattered across his desk." She rolled her eyes. "It's shareable so we can all access and update it as needed. Now Cole has to get into the habit of using it, so I set a reminder on his phone."

"That's great. I need to set myself one of those reminders." Despite having a virtual assistant, paperwork was still the bane of Troy's life. "Thanks for getting Cole on the right track."

Her expression turned impish. "I made him a deal."

"Yes?" He liked this new, more confident grown-up Molly.

"No more early barn chores for me until Christmas." Her smile was smug.

"Good for you." Heat radiated through his chest. With his employees, acquaintances and even people he considered friends, there was always an element of competition. However, with Molly things were comfortable and familiar. She wasn't trying to impress him, and it didn't seem like she wanted anything from him either.

"Cole says I drive a hard bargain." She bumped his arm, and he bumped hers back, lighthearted. "With four brothers, I learned from the best."

"It's a good skill to have." In business, as well as life. While Troy wasn't ruthless, he tried to make sure nobody took advantage of him. It worked both ways, though, and when it came to his team, Troy had confidence in them and hoped he'd earned their confidence in return.

While he and Molly had been talking, the livestock driver had gotten the trailer into position and now he and Cole unlocked the rear doors.

"Tell me more about this bull," she said. "Cole's excited about breeding him. It'll be tight, but there should be enough time this year before the truly cold weather sets in."

"We've talked about conditioning Cupid for breeding next spring too. He's a winner, and although it will take time, he'll get Cole where he wants to go in rodeo stock contracting."

As Troy told Molly about what made the bull special, she nodded and asked thoughtful questions, reminding him that unlike the women he usually met in California, she understood ranching and agricultural life. There was something reassuring and comforting about being able to be fully himself with her in a way he couldn't with friends and colleagues who hadn't grown up in this world.

Cole's voice interrupted them. "Come and see Cupid. You can stand on the other side of the fence."

"He's smart to use a bull staff." Troy indicated the pole with a fastening at one end that was clipped to Cupid's nose ring. It kept the animal at a safe distance as Cole led him into a separate paddock beyond the cow barn.

"Cole's calm and assertive so Cupid's already looking to him as the leader." Molly followed her brother's every move. "You don't mess with two thousand pounds of bull, but Cole knows how to work with them. You see how he doesn't hesitate? He might not have been the flashiest cowboy on the rodeo circuit, but Cole was one of the best. He's going to be one of the best stock contractors too."

Now in the paddock, the reddish-brown-and-white bull turned in a circle while Cole remained alert and aware without making eye contact.

Molly's loyalty to her brother was evident, and Troy respected her commitment to family. It mirrored his own. From what Troy had seen so far, Molly was as kind and natural as she'd been as a girl. Yet, she'd still broken his heart and he'd never reconciled how she'd ended things between them with the person he'd thought he knew and loved.

As Cole moved toward the paddock gate, never turning his back on Cupid, Molly offered the trailer driver a drink and snack from the small staff kitchen in the ranch's barn office. Like the rest of the Carter family, she was friendly and built relationships that were honest, genuine and lasting.

So why hadn't she been that way with him?

Troy met Cole as he slipped out through the gate and closed it behind him, leaving Cupid to explore his new surroundings. "Wow. Fantastic job."

"No problem." Cole grinned. "At least if you know what you're doing. Take it from me, a cowboy with the scars to prove it. Never trust even the mildest mannered bull because he can always surprise you."

Like Molly had surprised Troy, and why he had the emotional scars to prove it. That was why he'd been guarded ever since and only dated casually, not willing to risk getting his heart broken a second time. So no matter how honest and genuine Molly seemed, was it possible to ever trust her again?

"HAPPY HALLOWEEN, KIDS." At Healing Paws, the town's animal physical therapy clinic associated with its veterinarian's office, Molly put chocolate bars into four trick-or-treat bags.

As the pirate, ghost, princess and lion shouted their thanks and left for the next stop on High Valley's Halloween "No Tricks, Just Treats" tour, she went behind the reception counter to refill the pumpkin-shaped bowl. She'd worked at the vet clinic during the summers she was home from college. Now, whenever she was back in town, she filled in at Healing Paws if they needed extra staff. Her presence here today, however, was for fun, not work.

Carla, the receptionist, smiled at Molly from her seat at the computer. "If you see a bumble bee, cat and caterpillar, that'll be my three. Give me a shout, okay? My hubby texted they should be in soon."

"Sure." Molly poured treats into the bowl, ready for more children to appear. She still loved decorating her place and dressing up to greet trick-or-treaters. This year, with a bag, balloons and sign Cam made for her, she'd fashioned a jelly-bean costume to wear over a black T-shirt and leggings. With her hair in two ponytails and colorful makeup, it was simple but effective.

More important, it reminded Molly of her dad. She couldn't remember a time when he hadn't called her "Jellybean," the childhood nickname that had stuck when, as a premature baby, he said she was hardly bigger than a jellybean. He'd loved Halloween as much as she did, and even though they didn't get many trick-or-treaters out on the ranch, they'd always decorated the house together.

She swallowed a lump of emotion as the bell over entry door jingled. "Happy Halloween, I hope you like…" She came back around the desk with the treat bowl but stuttered to a stop as Troy appeared in front of her with a small brown dog on a leash.

"We keep running into each other." A smile tugged at the corner of Troy's mouth. "Meet Acorn. The vet sent us over to make an appointment."

"I didn't know you had a dog. I mean…there's no reason I should have known. It's your business." The more Molly said, the more flustered she got.

"Acorn's a recent addition. She's a senior dog the rescue was having trouble finding a home for. Her owner died a few months ago. When I saw the ad, I applied to adopt her." Troy's smile broadened as he took in Molly from head to toe, and her face heated. "Cute costume."

"Thanks." She took an instinctive step back, and her balloons bobbed between them. "I...uh...chocolate bar?" She thrust out the candy bowl. "We also have dog treats if Acorn would like one. Kristi at the Bluebunch made them."

"When it comes to chocolate, you don't have to ask me twice." He took a bar and then grabbed a dog treat from the container Molly indicated and knelt to Acorn's level. "Would you like a cookie, sweetheart?"

Acorn thumped her tail, and by her adoring expression, she was already head over heels in love with her rescuer.

Just when Molly thought she'd hardened her heart to Troy, he did something like adopting sweet Acorn that made him even more appealing. Sharing a rented condo and working shifts, she couldn't adopt a dog, and she wouldn't let herself long for something she couldn't have. While it wouldn't be the same, she could volunteer at an animal shelter in Atlanta. That would keep her busy outside of work, and if she was busy, she wouldn't have time to think.

After Acorn had crunched the treat and wagged her tail again, Troy scooped the little dog into his arms. "Here, girl, come say hi to Molly. Acorn's timid from being so long in the shelter, but she likes having her ears rubbed." He demonstrated as Acorn rested her head against his broad chest.

Molly moved closer and reached over her balloons to pat the dog's soft ears.

Acorn rewarded her with a gentle nose nudge.

"I think she's saying 'more, please.'" Troy chuckled. "I only picked her up last night, so we're still getting to know each other. The vet says she's healthy, and some canine physical therapy will get her more active."

"Yes, you wanted to make an appointment." Troy hadn't come here to see *her*. She knew that. He was just being friendly like he would be with any acquaintance. "All the therapists are great but Cole's wife, Melissa, works here and she specializes in older dogs. If she has an opening, she'd be great for Acorn."

The bell over the door rang again, and more costumed children came in with parents taking pictures on their phones.

"Happy Halloween." She turned to the kids and handed out candy. "Amazing costumes."

A toddler dressed as a green dinosaur let out a wail as a Great Dane bigger than he was came out of a treatment room with its owner.

Molly stood between the child and dog. "Zeus won't hurt you. I know him, and he's a softie. Are you scared because he's so big?"

The boy nodded, clung to his mom's leg and cried harder.

Molly untied an orange balloon from the end of the Halloween arch she'd made earlier. "There you go." The little boy took the balloon and a sob turned into a hiccup. "I know a song about a dog and a balloon. Would you like to hear it?"

The child gave her a solemn nod and sniffed.

Molly launched into the upbeat tune and then danced around the clinic's waiting area as she sang. "Come on." She waved at the boy, and he and his mom, followed by Troy, joined in.

As Molly's gaze caught Troy's, he shrugged, and his blue eyes twinkled before they sang the catchy chorus together. He had a good voice, but it was the expression on his face and in his eyes that make her legs tremble and heat surge through her body.

Acorn let out an excited bark, and the Great Dane sat on his haunches and watched them like the gentle giant he was.

Molly finished the song with a flourish, and the boy clapped and laughed. "All better now?"

Still clutching the balloon, he gave her a shy smile.

"You're fine, aren't you, William?" The mom ruffled his curly, dark hair, and the affectionate gesture made Molly's heart squeeze. "William hasn't been around dogs, any animals really, because his sister has allergies. Thanks for helping him feel comfortable. You're great with kids."

"Anyone would have done the same." Since the other children and parents had left, Molly gave William a few extra treats. "Have fun." She turned to William's mom. "Before he sees a dog again, the two of you could think about how to handle it. Planning always makes me feel better." It was also a way for her to feel like she had some control in an uncontrollable world.

"Great idea." The mom nodded. "My husband and I moved to High Valley last month, and everybody's been so kind and welcoming. I'm Brooke Kaplan."

Molly introduced herself, exchanged numbers with Brooke and invited her and William to visit the ranch. But the whole time, an awareness of Troy coursed through her.

She hadn't planned it, but the connection between them was stronger than ever.

After Brooke and William left, followed by Zeus and his owner, Troy and Acorn made their way to the clinic door.

"Bye." Molly's mouth got dry.

"I guess I'll see you at the ranch." Troy's deep voice reverberated above Molly's head and forced her to look at him. His eyes were so blue and framed by eyelashes she used to tease him were too long to be real.

"Yeah."

"Like Brooke said, you were great with William." Troy's warm breath brushed her cheek as they both reached for the door handle at the same time. "I remember my mom singing that song to me."

"My mom sang it to us too." Once, Molly had been certain she'd sing it to her own kids. However, to be a mom, she had to meet the right man and be in the right place in her life to settle down and have kids. "It was nice of you to join in. I never knew you liked to sing." He'd be a great dad to some lucky child. The thought intruded and she forced it away.

"As a hand, I used to sing to the cows." Troy's eyes teased her. "My dad said it kept them calm, but don't tell anybody." He put a finger to his lips. "Also promise me you won't tell anyone I was singing and dancing around." He winced and tugged at his jacket collar.

"I won't but I can't speak for Carla." She darted a glance at the receptionist who'd been clapping along and was now clearly eavesdropping on their conversation. "Or Brooke. She and William were pretty impressed with you."

Although Brooke was around Molly's age, like Carla she'd given Troy the kind of approving look usually reserved for a mom checking out their daughter's date. She'd mentioned having a daughter so maybe that was why, but it had reminded Molly that if she'd stayed here, she'd likely have been married or at least engaged by now. Most of her close friends in Atlanta were single, but here she was surrounded by couples and not only in her family. The majority of her high school friends had gotten paired up long ago. "William looked like you were his new hero."

"He's a cute kid." He hesitated as if he was going to say something more but instead looked at Carla and then opened the clinic door. "See you."

As he and Acorn disappeared into the street thronged with costumed kids and families enjoying both the event and sunny October afternoon, Molly hugged the treat bowl. That ER doctor she'd gone out with a few times would never have sung and danced with a scared little kid, maybe not even one of his own. For him, appearances were everything. Unlike Troy, who wasn't afraid to show his silly side.

And who was a good man to his core, something she'd sensed but hadn't been mature enough at eighteen to fully appreciate. From dogs to people, he'd be there for those who needed him without expecting any kind of return.

That was the kind of man she needed. Memories, loss and then regret mixed together inside her. But Troy was here in

High Valley, and she wasn't, at least not long-term. Like they'd always been, their lives were on different paths, and then as now, she couldn't...*wouldn't* let herself be distracted.

CHAPTER SIX

ONE OF THE things Troy prided himself on was never losing control either in business or his personal life. But there was something about Molly that made him forget himself and lose his usual inhibitions. That had to be the reason he'd sung and danced at Healing Paws like a goofy kid. Almost a week later, he still cringed at the memory.

However, he seemed to be the only one who was embarrassed or thought he'd done anything out of the ordinary. When he'd taken Acorn back to the clinic for her session with Melissa, Carla had greeted him warmly and invited Troy to join her and her family for a Sunday dinner. And when he'd bumped into Brooke and William at the grocery store, the little boy had hugged him right in the middle of the produce aisle.

As Troy rode out of his barn on Winnie, a Morgan horse the previous owners of the Bitterroot had sold with the ranch, he considered how much his life had changed since moving here. For a start, he couldn't remember when he'd last stopped work at midday on a Friday to do anything else, let alone go riding. However, on this first Friday in November, the sun was high in the clear blue sky, and with harvested fields stretching around him to the horizon, the weather was perfect to take a look at his new property. There was no better way than on horseback to get to truly know land, and just then, there was a part of Troy that felt like he was king of the world.

In California, he'd been crowded between the ocean, mountains and people, but here he could breathe in a way he'd almost forgotten. He waved to his foreman and two ranch hands working in the barnyard before taking a rutted path down a low rise that led alongside the fields closest to the house. He could already picture next summer's crop here with grain waving in a warm breeze. He planned to buy more cattle and build up the Bitterroot's herd. *So many plans, so little time.* He chuckled. It was a good problem to have, and out here he had both new energy and a fresh sense of optimism.

Half an hour later, he and Winnie rode along the fence line by pastureland that bordered the Carters' horse barn. He hadn't planned it, but thanks to an old path across the fields, Troy had ended up on Carter land. Since he was here anyway, he might as well check on Cupid. And if he happened to accidentally run into Molly, so much the better. His skin tingled and he caught his breath. Where had that thought come from? While it was both surprising and new, it somehow felt right. Although he didn't want to examine his feelings too closely, Molly was one of the reasons his life had changed for the better.

Dismounting in the barnyard, he introduced Winnie to one of the nearby hands. "I won't be long so no need to put her in a stall. She's a friendly girl and will be fine in the pasture with the others." He gestured to where several of the Carters' horses had gathered near the fence.

"Sure." The man nodded, and he and Troy began to untack her, both of them speaking in a reassuring tone.

Troy had always talked to horses. Now with Winnie, it was a way for them to get to know each other and build a trusting bond. He gave her a final pat and then went into the barn, blinking as his eyes adjusted from bright sunshine to the dimmer interior. Cole was usually here at this time of day, so he'd find him before going to see Cupid.

"Hey, girl." He greeted Cindy, Joy Carter's seal-brown mare, who was on stall rest due to a muscle injury. "I know being stuck in here is boring but it's only for a few more days."

Cindy nickered, and Troy reached across the stall door to rub her forehead. Pigeons cooed in the barn loft, and muted sunlight patterned the floor of the central aisle. As Troy stepped away from Cindy's stall, he whirled around at what sounded like a sob.

"I can't talk to anyone except you." Although Molly's voice was muffled, Troy would have known it anywhere. "I like Shane, but I miss Dad. You remember him, don't you?" There was a gulping noise like Molly was choking back tears. "Of course you do. He raised you from a foal. Everything is changing. Not for you, Daisy-May, but me. Mom's moving, and Zach and Beth will be living here and I... Home won't be the same."

Troy hesitated. He could leave the barn right now, and Molly would never know he'd heard her crying and sharing private thoughts with her horse. Except, he wasn't that kind of guy, and he'd have wanted to comfort *anyone* who was hurting or in trouble. Even though she'd hurt *him*, he still hated to think of Molly being upset and alone.

Cindy stomped her front feet and whinnied.

"It's okay." Troy spoke to her soothingly. "I'll go see what's wrong."

The crying stopped as if someone had turned off a water faucet. Troy walked along the aisle, but the other stalls were empty as was the tack room. "Hello?" His voice echoed, and wings fluttered as the pigeons flew overhead. "Molly? Cole?"

A horse nickered. Troy stopped in front of a towering stack of straw bales, which were new since the last time he'd visited. "Anyone here?" He poked his head around an end bale, and Daisy-May let out a loud whinny.

"Hi." From the horse's other side, he glimpsed Molly's tearstained face. "If you're looking for Cole, he had to go into town, but he should be back soon." She fiddled with one of Daisy-May's rear hooves.

"I wanted to check on Cupid but thought I'd say hi to Cole first. If you need—"

"I'm fine. I was riding on the creek path and after last night's rain, it was muddy."

She sniffed and returned to untacking the horse. "You can wait for Cole in the office."

"I could but…" Troy drew in a deep breath. Once, he'd felt so connected to Molly, like she was the other half of himself. And while he'd convinced himself he was over her, maybe he never truly would be. Seeing her now, all he wanted was to help and make things better in whatever way he could. "You're upset and I don't want to leave you alone."

"You heard that?" Her face, which had been a mottled red, paled.

"I wasn't eavesdropping, but when I came into the barn, well… I couldn't help overhearing. Maybe I should have left but I couldn't do that either." Troy drew closer to her. "Of course, with your mom marrying Shane things will change, but she'll still be nearby."

"I know but…" Molly gulped and rested her head against Daisy-May's neck, and Troy's heart squeezed at the memory of how she'd once laid her head against *his* neck. "I want Mom to be happy and although she's marrying Shane, she'll never forget my dad. I'm not a kid so Shane won't be my stepfather in that way. But even though I moved away and changed, home has always been here and the same, you know? Beth and Zach are talking about redecorating, and I thought I was okay with everything, but I guess I'm not."

Troy understood what she meant. He'd lost his own childhood home on the cusp of adolescence. "Your brothers all have their own places and families, but the Tall Grass Ranch and your mom being here, that's your anchor."

She nodded. "I miss my dad so much. Shane would never

think of trying to replace my dad, but this kind of change is hard. I guess I hadn't truly realized that even here, nothing can stay the same." She dug in the pocket of her jeans for a tissue. "I'm being foolish. Forget I said anything."

It was too late for Troy to forget because for the first time since they'd both returned to High Valley, he'd seen the real Molly. "You're not being foolish. I bet if you talked to your brothers, you'd find they're having some of the same feelings."

"I doubt it. Zach's excited about the baby, Cole's focused on his stock contracting business and Bryce is about to have his own new start with Carrie." More tears welled in her beautiful blue eyes. "I'm the only one who..." She gulped. "I have my own life, but it's not here. The next time I come back to High Valley, everything will be different."

"It will, but some differences can be good." Troy paused. She'd been vulnerable with him, so now he needed to take a risk and let himself be open with her. "When my folks lost our ranch, it took a long time for me to accept what had happened. I was angry and hurt and sure I'd never settle anywhere else, especially in a city. But I did." He'd had to. "My mom and dad kept a lot of our family traditions the same and that helped. But most of all, I came to realize that what makes a house a home is family, no matter where you are. You'll still have your family, only in different places."

She rubbed her eyes. "Zach says he won't change Dad's basement workshop, and they're keeping all our height measurements on the wall by the kitchen door. Beth's even talking about framing them. It's right they make the ranch house their own, and for now I'll still have my bedroom here but..." She shrugged and more tears fell. "I guess after losing Paul and my dad, I focus more on any changes here being bad rather than good."

"Come here, Mol." Troy closed the space between them and held out his arms.

She stepped into them, and he hugged her—as a friend who

wanted to offer comfort, he reminded himself as awareness of her warmth and closeness surged through him. He touched her cheek to wipe away a tear and then held her even closer.

Troy's knees went weak as he breathed in her recognizable fragrance, that delicate jasmine overlaid with a hint of vanilla. Holding Molly was like coming home to someplace familiar but also new. And as feelings Troy had tried to forget flamed into life, he never wanted to let her go.

MOLLY LET HERSELF relax into Troy's embrace. Although she prided herself on being independent, there was no shame in leaning on someone when you needed to. Especially when that someone was Troy, who'd always held her in the right way, not too tight but with a gentle firmness. Like he was taking her burdens and making them lighter simply by being there.

With her face buried in his shoulder, she savored his scent. The crisp cotton of his Western shirt beneath his unbuttoned jacket, and the warmth of his skin below were better than any aftershave. It was the familiar "I'm here for you no matter what" aroma that had once represented comfort, love and a sweet tenderness she'd never found with anyone else.

Molly didn't know how long they stood there together, only that hugging Troy was even better than she remembered. When Daisy-May nudged her shoulder, as if to remind Molly she'd left the horse half untacked, she had to force herself to take a step back.

"Thanks." She rubbed her face and tried to quell her panicked thoughts. She never let anyone see her inner turmoil, so why, out of all people, had she let down her guard with Troy? "I'm not usually so emotional."

"Forget about it." As if he sensed her embarrassment, he stared up into the barn loft instead of at her. "I'm glad I happened to be around."

She turned to Daisy-May and secured the stirrups and then

Troy unbuckled the girth, the two of them working together in silence like they used to.

Troy had never been a big talker, but after his care and concern, the next step was up to Molly. "I owe you an explanation." He'd broken down her protective walls, and she couldn't live with herself any longer if she didn't tell him at least part of the truth.

"About what?" His voice had a hint of a quiver as he put the girth on top of Daisy-May's saddle.

Maybe the hug had affected him as much as it had her, but she couldn't let herself think about the torrent of emotion it had unleashed—one that had shaken her to her core. They kept bumping into each other and for her, it was often when she was at her most vulnerable. Once and for all, she had to deal with the past and the pain she'd caused. Maybe that way they could both move on. Troy with his business, the ranch and making a life here. And her with her future in Atlanta. Not here and not with Troy.

"About why I broke up with you." She gripped the saddle by the pommel, and he took it by the back as they lifted it up and off Daisy-May.

"You were going to college. It was a summer romance." He took the saddle and put it on a nearby rack keeping his back to her.

"That's true, but…" Molly studied his stiff shoulders. "I also thought I was too young to be so serious about you—about anyone." And because her feelings for Troy had been so big and intense, she hadn't known how to handle them. She'd been afraid. The only option she'd seen then was breaking up with him, but she hadn't counted on the magnitude and intensity of those feelings either. "I didn't only *want* to go to college, I *needed* to." She took a steadying breath as Troy turned to face her. Had his eyes always been so blue?

"I knew how important college was for you. Did you really think I'd have tried to stop you from going? I thought what we had together was important too, and we could have lasted no matter what." Now those eyes held both disbelief and hurt. "We were both young, but that doesn't mean what we felt for each other wasn't real."

How could she make him understand something she'd never truly understood herself? Maybe those feelings had been too real. At eighteen, she had been confused, overwhelmed and still grieving her dad's death, and the only thing she had known with any certainty was that she had to leave the ranch. "I knew you wouldn't have stopped me from going to college, but I was scared of being like my mom. My mom *wanted* to go to college when she was my age, but she didn't. She married my dad instead, so she's only taking college classes now. I always wanted to go to college and become a nurse, but I also *needed* to follow my dreams. If I hadn't, I'd have regretted it. I might have ended up resenting you and us." She stared at her feet as her thoughts turned inward.

"But I planned on college too. We talked about how I'd already taken a few courses at night and was saving to go full-time." Troy leaned against the barn wall and crossed his arms in front of his chest. "I'd never have held you back. We could have both gotten our degrees and supported and encouraged each other." His mouth settled into a stubborn line that Molly remembered. "I asked, but you wouldn't even try to make a long-distance relationship work."

Because she'd thought it would be better to break things off before she got in even deeper. Yet, the hurt had lingered for years. "My mom and my brothers sacrificed a lot to give me a college education. I didn't want to disappoint them."

Even to her own ears, Molly sounded unconvincing, but it was the best she could do. Troy was astute and always went right to the heart of the matter. It was undoubtedly one of the qualities that had helped him succeed in business, but it was also a reminder she needed to be on guard with him.

"So, you disappointed me instead." Troy's voice was flat before he took Daisy-May's bit and wiped it with a clean cloth.

"I'm sorry." Her chest hurt, and the world seemed to spin around her.

"I'm sorry too." Troy exhaled. "But it's ancient history." He gave her a pained smile, and his eyes were dull. "We were kids. Despite what I thought back then, we probably wouldn't have lasted together anyway."

In any relationship, but especially a long-distance one, communication was key. Molly's stomach flipped. She'd done what she thought she had to and had saved both of them more hurt later on. "No hard feelings?"

"Of course not." He focused on the bit and avoided her gaze.

"Cole will be back soon." She had to change the subject. It wouldn't do any good to prolong this conversation. If she did, she risked saying something she couldn't take back. "From what I've seen, Cupid's settling in great. As bulls go, he's a sweetheart."

"Good to hear." Troy shrugged as if Cole and Cupid were the last things on his mind.

"I guess I'll see you at the weddings, if not before." Molly took the bit from him and gathered the rest of the tack. She'd let Daisy-May into the pasture once Troy was on his way.

"Sure." But as he turned and went down the barn aisle without looking back, his boots left a dull echo that stabbed her heart. Because of how he'd comforted her, Molly's emotions churned even more than before.

Except this time, they weren't about her mom's remarriage and the changes it would bring. They were about Troy and, despite the years and history between them, how he still made her feel.

CHAPTER SEVEN

"HEY, MOM." Putting his phone on speaker, Troy lifted the steak from the pan to a plate already loaded with a baked potato and green beans. The meal was basic but filling, perfect for one person. "What's up?"

"Nothing. I wanted to hear your voice." His mom's warm laugh bridged the distance between San Francisco and Montana. "Your dad's at the golf club, and I just came back from my tai chi class. We're going out to dinner and a movie later. It's been a busy week at work for both of us, so we've hardly seen each other."

Although neither of his folks had to work, they wanted to and said part-time hours kept them active. His mom was an office administrator, and his dad loved serving customers at a neighborhood hardware store. What did it say, though, that his folks, at almost sixty, had a more active social life than Troy?

"That sounds fun." He sat at one end of the rustic kitchen table the previous owners had sold with the house and put the phone beside it. Troy could picture his mom curled up on the living room sofa near the table with a display of framed family photos. No matter where they lived, those photos were a constant. A symbol of roots, family unity and cherished bonds.

"What about you? Any news? Even after all these years, I

still miss Montana." His mom's voice had the wistful quality it always got whenever she talked about her home state.

Troy stared out the kitchen window into the darkness interspersed by shadowy outlines of the leafless trees that encircled the rear of the house. "Everything's okay. The usual. The ranch foreman and hands are doing great." The Bitterroot ran as efficiently as he suspected it always had, and Troy sometimes felt superfluous. "Pete and I are ramping up for a new product launch. It's looking good to be on schedule and under budget."

But his business partner, Pete, was carrying more of the load while Troy found reasons to visit the Tall Grass Ranch. Although he'd tried to keep from thinking of Molly and how perfect it had felt to hug her in the barn, he couldn't stop himself. For a moment, he'd forgotten how things had ended between them, caught up in the power of a hug meant to comfort her but, for him, had become so much more. In the past few days, though, he'd only glimpsed her a couple of times around town. Once coming out of the Bluebunch Café with several other women, and then when she and her mom were heading into the craft center as Troy parked his truck nearby.

"As for Montana, we might have snow when you're here for Thanksgiving." Would his parents and sister, Sara, make the ranch house feel more like home? "You and Dad will like seeing snow."

"As long as we don't have to shovel it." There was a pause on his mom's end of the phone. "What's wrong, honey? Aren't you happy at the ranch?"

"It's great. Everybody in High Valley has been really welcoming." There was no reason for Troy to be so restless and unsettled.

"What about the Carter family? Is everything…okay there?" Troy's mom was the only person who knew about his heartache over Molly. He'd assured her that investing in Cole's stock contracting venture was only business, but now he wondered if he'd deceived himself and then her.

"It's fine. Molly's back in town because her mom's getting married again, but anything between us is water under the bridge." *Liar*. Troy's skin still tingled at the memory of holding Molly close and the way her head had nestled into his shoulder. "Joy's having a double wedding just before Thanksgiving. Her son Bryce—Molly's brother—is getting married too."

"That's so romantic." His mom's voice softened.

"I was about to have dinner so can I call you tomorrow?" The last thing he needed was for his mom to start talking about weddings.

"Don't mind me. We can chat while you eat." His mom laughed again. "When we visit, I'll bring a card and a small wedding gift to leave with you to give Joy. What about a basket of my homemade jams, jellies and pickles?"

"I'm sure she'd like that." What else could Troy say? His mom was kind and thoughtful—she and Molly's mom were a lot alike in that way.

"That summer you worked at the Tall Grass, Joy guessed how I worried about you. She'd email me every few weeks to say everything was okay. As a mother herself, she understood the pain of the empty nest."

Troy rolled his eyes, even though his mom wasn't there to see it. "I was twenty. You didn't need to worry." He cut a piece of steak, but his appetite had disappeared.

"No matter how old your child is, you worry about them and you miss them. We raised you to spread your wings, and your dad and I are so proud of everything you've achieved. But that summer was the first time you'd lived away from home. You'll know what I mean once you have children yourself." She didn't huff, but she might as well have.

"I'm not ready to become a parent yet." It had been fun spending time with Molly and her nieces and nephew, and with little William at Healing Paws. His heart constricted. He'd love to be a dad but right now it was an *if*, not *when* he had kids.

"Have you met anyone in High Valley?" His mom's tone was too casual.

"I've met lots of people here." There was hardly a day that someone didn't drop by, usually with food, and whenever he went into town, he stopped and chatted with folks.

"That isn't what I meant, and you know it." His mom's mock chiding made Troy chuckle.

"Subtle, Mom. When I meet a special woman, I'll let you know." A siren wailed in the background on his mom's end of the phone. After only a short time in High Valley, he'd adjusted to country life and didn't miss city sounds. "I have a work call soon and—"

"You're working in the evening?" His mom made a tsking sound. "You work far too much. You're only young once and—"

"It's fine, Mom. Nobody's telling me I have to work. It's my choice." But was that because he didn't have much else in his life? "Can you message me your recipe for snickerdoodles? I signed up to bring a dessert to the Carter wedding potluck and your recipe for those cookies is the best ever." It wasn't a lie, but he needed to divert his mom from his single status. "I'm also making that pumpkin chowder you and Dad like."

"Of course, but..." A pause and Troy could almost guess what his mom was thinking. "You're going to the weddings? Are you sure that's wise, honey?"

"I'm not going to the ceremony, but there's a community reception afterward. Everyone in town's invited. It would look strange if I didn't go."

"I suppose, and with a crowd, it's not like you'll have much to do with the family, will you?"

His heart pounded. He was a grown man, but he still valued and respected his parents and their opinions. "If you need to say something to me, go ahead." His meal forgotten, he rubbed at his temples where a headache had started.

"I'm glad you're being sensible about Molly. You never forget your first love nor should you, but you've both moved on. The two of you are different people now. You might be able to be friends, but you have to think of the future, not the past."

"You know me, Mom. I'm all about the future." He gave a hollow laugh. "Talk to you soon. Say hi to Dad for me."

As they said their goodbyes, Troy's stomach knotted. His mom was right. He and Molly *were* different people now, and she no longer even lived in High Valley. But each time he saw her, it was like he went back to who he'd been—where that future he thought of was with her. Even if they were able to somehow be friends, would he always yearn for more?

MOLLY WAS USED to city traffic, which was the reason she'd left the ranch half an hour earlier than necessary for the short drive into High Valley. When she wasn't in medical scrubs, she was used to city clothes too. After parking her SUV near the Bluebunch, she again glanced at her tailored jeans, chunky gray sweater, black heeled boots and black puffer jacket. Did she look too dressy for a Sunflower Sisterhood meeting to make wedding favors? Even if she did, it was too late to change.

She left her vehicle and locked it with the key fob, though it was unlikely anyone would try breaking in here.

Minutes later, she entered the café and greeted the women seated in a big circle behind tables arranged in the center of the room. "Hi, everyone. I thought I'd be early but you're all here!"

Kristi, the café owner, welcomed Molly with a smile while others waved or called out friendly hellos. "You *are* early. Everyone else is even earlier. We like chatting, that's all."

Molly's mom patted the empty chair at her side. "Sit by me, honey."

As Molly sat, there was a ripple of whispering around them. The other women seemed to be conspiring for a moment. Before Molly could ask what was going on, everyone shouted, "Surprise," and she and her mom stared at each other, wide-eyed.

"What's… I thought we were making the honey jar wedding favors." Her mom laughed and put a hand to her face as Nina and Angela unrolled Bridal Shower and Bride-to-Be banners, and Rosa appeared from the café's kitchen with a yellow and white balloon arch decorated with artificial sunflowers.

"I didn't know about this shower, I swear." Molly shook her head and laughed with the rest.

"We didn't tell you because Joy would have gotten it out of you." Rosa set up the balloons behind Joy's chair.

"It's all good." Kristi set out plates of party snacks and the other women carried more decorations out of the back.

"But you already had an engagement party for me at the community center." Molly's mom looked near tears. "It's too much. I don't know what to say."

"That party was for everyone. This shower is only for the Sunflower Sisterhood. And you don't have to say anything except shout surprise when Carrie, Paisley and Skylar get here. Double wedding, double bridal shower." At Molly's other side, Melissa tied more balloons to the café walls. "I asked Carrie to pick up the girls from gymnastics to delay her. Bryce just texted me they should be here any minute. Right on time." Melissa gave Joy a mock glare.

Taking a sparkly princess-style crown from Nina, Molly set it on her mom's head. "I didn't think anything of it when you called and said you were staying in town, and you'd see me at this meeting. If I'd known about the shower, I'd have come up with a reason to get you to come home instead."

"Don't worry," Melissa reassured her. "Joy has a sixth sense when anybody's keeping a secret. That's why we couldn't risk telling you. Living in the same house, she'd have had it out of you in no time."

A chill crept up Molly's spine. The only big secret she'd

ever kept from her mom was that summer romance with Troy. Had her mom known all along?

"So that's why everyone but me is dressed up." Her mom glanced around the group. "Even you, Molly. You must have suspected something was up."

"I didn't, truly. I'd have found a way to get you to come home and convince you to dress up, I swear." In her city clothes, although still casual for her, she didn't look out of place. However, clothes or not, for the first time since coming back to High Valley, she felt like she belonged in a way she'd never done in Atlanta.

"Carrie's truck just went by," Angela said. She was keeping watch by the café door. "Now she's parking down the street. Everybody ready?"

An excited murmur went around the group, and Molly squeezed her mom's hand. Although she'd been to wedding showers in Atlanta for friends from school and the hospital, this event was personal and extra special.

"I'm glad you're here." Her mom squeezed Molly's hand back, and tears shimmered in the depths of her blue eyes.

"Me too." Molly's heart was full. She'd come home lots of times during her years away, but until now she'd never felt the tug of home so strongly. It must be prewedding emotion, but as she glanced around the circle of faces—family and friends old and new—fresh longing rose inside her.

As Beth and Melissa chatted, their expressions animated as they talked about Beth's pregnancy, Molly's heart tugged in a different way. Like Carrie, who'd soon become a stepmother to Paisley and Cam, all three of her sisters-in-law were mothers *and* independent career women right here in High Valley.

Before she could get too caught up in her own thoughts, the bell above the door jangled again. Everyone, including Molly, shouted, "Surprise!" as Carrie, Skylar and Paisley came into the café.

Kristi flipped the sign over to read Closed, though she didn't lock the door, saying something about a delivery. As the party got started and plates of food began to circulate, Nina nudged Molly's arm.

"Want one of Kristi's mini quiches?" She held out a plate.

"Thanks." Molly took one of the delicious savory pastries, as good or even better than anything she'd had in Atlanta.

"Be sure to save room for Kristi's huckleberry cheesecake," Nina said. "It's well on its way to putting High Valley on the culinary map."

"Oh?" Molly asked politely.

"Mmm-hmm. When Kristi won the cooking competition in High Valley's Spring Food Festival, the Bluebunch was featured in a state tourism campaign. An East Coast food journalist saw it and came here on vacation. She wrote a magazine article about the café and that cheesecake and included lots of pictures. As soon as it came out, the phone started ringing with people wanting to order food and café hats, mugs and aprons online. Carrie got her set up with the technology side of things, so Kristi hired me for several extra hours a week and now Angela as well to fulfill orders. Last Monday alone we sent out fifty packages. We even shipped three dozen Montana blueberry muffins to Alaska."

"I'll have to place a regular order once I'm back in Atlanta."

As Molly passed the plate of mini quiches around the circle, she discovered that since this was a second wedding for Joy, and Carrie was moving into the home Bryce had shared with his late wife, none of them needed a lot of household items. As a result, the Sunflower Sisterhood had decided to make the shower a charity fundraiser with the theme of Shower High Valley with Compassion. However, the women had still gone in together to buy two group gifts.

"Wow!" Carrie exclaimed over a coffee maker and selection of gourmet coffee. "Thanks, everyone. You know I need coffee to get started on those early mornings. Actually, every morning." She stuck a gift bow on Paisley's head while Mol-

ly's mom did the same with Skylar, and both girls laughed.
"Now Bryce's old coffee maker can go in the barn, and we'll
use this new fancy one in the house."

"You know me well." Joy had unwrapped a wicker basket
holding a teapot, "Mr. and Mrs." mugs, and a range of tea ac-
cessories and specialty teas.

While Molly admired the gifts with the others, her thoughts
swirled. High Valley was still the small town she'd grown up
in, and as interconnected as it had always been, but it was
more outward looking now. Or maybe the town had always
been that way, but Molly was seeing it—and the people who
lived here—through new eyes.

"Hey, guys. You can leave the chairs in my new workroom
behind the kitchen." Kristi's voice rose above the conversation
as the café door opened to let in several men.

One of them, Nina explained to Molly as she pointed him
out, was Kristi's fiancé, Alex Greenwood, the chef at Ruby's
Place, a restaurant across town.

"Help yourself to food from the platters on the kitchen counters," Kristi added. "I made a batch of mini pizzas for you
guys. There's also BBQ chicken bites and pretzel dogs." She
kissed Alex's cheek, and he smiled as the women greeted him
and the others.

"What about the table? You want it in the workroom too?"
Werner leaned on the open door. "Sorry to disturb you, ladies.
We won't be a minute." His smile broadened as Nina joined
him and held the door. "I'll take the other end, Troy. That's
right. Hold it steady and lift sideways."

Molly couldn't help it as her gaze connected with Troy's.
He nodded in greeting, and she waved back.

Molly's mom put her tea gift basket by her purse at Molly's side. "Kristi's offering cooking classes for team building
events. There's one for the town council tomorrow, but there
was a mix-up and the rented chairs and table were delivered
to the hardware store instead of here. Werner got a group of

fellows together to move them over. It's nice how Troy's becoming part of the community."

"Yes." But Molly barely heard her mom's words. Troy was only moving a table, but she couldn't take her eyes off him. No other guy ever wore a pair of faded jeans so well. And when his winter jacket fell open to expose a blue T-shirt that hugged his toned chest, her mouth went dry.

As she took a slice of huckleberry cheesecake from Beth, she had to make herself focus on the luscious dessert rather than Troy's voice coming from Kristi's kitchen.

She could get used to life here, but admitting it to herself would turn everything about who she'd always thought she was upside down. And while that would be hard enough, how could she ever admit to anyone that for the girl in her high school graduating class voted most likely to succeed, true success might be entirely different from what she'd always thought and said?

CHAPTER EIGHT

"GO DO YOUR THING, CUPID," Troy said, as Cole opened the livestock trailer and let the bull into the pasture with the cows.

Beside him, Molly grinned, and she quirked an eyebrow. "His 'thing'? I grew up on a ranch. There's not much about cow breeding season I don't know."

Troy's face heated but he didn't reply.

Cole shut the pasture gate behind Cupid and joined them by the fence. "Molly used to pitch in with us for calving season. Good practice for delivering human babies, right, sis? Same idea."

Molly gave her brother's shoulder a playful swat. "In theory, yes, but don't talk about calf birthing around Beth. She's nervous about labor and delivery."

"I won't." Cole made a zipping motion across his mouth. "Zach's sure a bundle of nerves. He's got a stack of books about pregnancy and birth in the barn office, and different route maps on his phone to get Beth to the hospital depending on the time of day and weather. I've never seen him so worked up."

"Sometimes the dads are more anxious than the moms," Molly said. "I've seen all kinds."

As Molly rested her elbows on the fence, and the wind caught her ponytail, Troy's heartbeat sped up. In jeans, a barn jacket, cowboy boots and a white cowboy hat, she looked as much a part of this vast landscape as the tall pasture grass, distant mountains and grazing animals. Out here, it was easy for him to picture Molly always being at his side, and the two of them working their own ranch together. Having a couple of kids one day as well.

Troy shook himself and turned back to Cole. He needed to focus on work, not dreams that could never come true. "If you're all set, I'll get going." Back to the Bitterroot, his home office and whatever crises had come up while he'd been out of cell phone coverage.

"Sure. Do you mind giving Molly a ride back? Bryce asked me to take some soil samples for him."

"I expect Troy's busy. I don't mind waiting for you. I could even help with the samples," Molly replied before Troy could say anything.

"I'll be a few hours. I also need to check the fence line. Don't you have to help Mom with the last of the wedding baking?" Cole looked at his sister with a bemused expression.

"Yes, but—"

"What's the issue?" Cole's gaze went to Troy, and his eyes narrowed. Despite his easygoing, laidback manner, Cole was sharp, especially when it came to people he cared about. "Is there something going on with you two I don't know about?"

"There's nothing going on," Troy interjected. "And it's no problem for me to take Molly back to the Tall Grass." He kept his voice and expression neutral, found his keys and gestured to his truck parked beyond the livestock trailer. The drive would only last fifteen minutes or so. He could make small talk that long.

"Okay." Molly's voice was small, and she hugged herself. "Let's go."

Ten minutes later, Troy drove his pickup along a rutted, dirt track that edged the hilly pastureland. They'd already talked about the weather. Sunny and unseasonably warm for

Montana in November. How Acorn was settling in. Fine, and the dog was at the Bitterroot with Cathy. The chance of the hometown hockey team making it to the league finals. Excellent, they both agreed.

Now, hunched in the passenger seat, Molly stared out the window. Clearly, she'd rather be anywhere else but trapped in the truck's cab with him. However, if she wasn't going to address the awkwardness between them, Troy had to.

"When we talked in the barn about why you broke up with me, and we spoke about your mom remarrying, and your dad...how you're feeling..." The truck jolted into a rut, and he floored the accelerator until they'd cleared the next rise of land. "I want to make sure you know that conversation is only between us."

"Thanks." Her voice hitched.

"It's okay, truly." He couldn't see inside her head, but it made sense that even without everything else, her mom's wedding would be emotional. "I know I said before we couldn't be friends, but now..." He took a deep breath. "Why don't we give it a try? What have we got to lose?"

Maybe everything. And possibly his heart most of all. Troy had to ignore his doubts. He and Molly couldn't go on this way, edging around each other like polite strangers or the alternative, a closeness too reminiscent of the intimacy they'd once shared. He hadn't missed the curious looks they'd attracted at the art show, and back there with Cupid and the cows even Cole had been suspicious.

"You're right." Molly tugged on her jacket. "If Cole gets the idea there's something between us, he won't let it rest. He'll talk to Zach and Bryce and my mom, and they'll all make something out of nothing. Along with being the only girl, I'm so much younger than my brothers. They've always been protective." She chewed her lower lip. "When we talked we sort of cleared the air and dealt with the past, so okay, friends."

Although a statement, her voice rose at the end making it more of a question.

"Friends," Troy echoed as he turned into the gravel lane leading to the Tall Grass Ranch.

"We both want Cole's stock contracting business to be a success," Molly added. "After Melissa and Skylar and the rest of the family, it's the most important thing in his life." She looked out the truck window again as if, like Troy, she didn't know how to navigate this new "friendship" between them. What to say, what to do and, most of all, how to pretend their past had indeed been dealt with.

"Cole's lucky to have you. All of you." Like Troy was lucky to have his parents and sister. "Family first and—oh no."

"What?" Molly turned to look where he pointed and gasped. "What are Bryce's pigs doing on Mom's lawn? Mom and Shane want to have wedding pictures taken there."

As soon as Troy stopped and parked the truck in front of the ranch house, Molly jumped out of the vehicle and ran toward the four red-and-white pigs that rooted in the lawn amid scattered fall decorations.

He followed her, shutting both truck doors. "Hang on." The biggest pig must weigh around seven hundred pounds, and although Molly was strong, she was slight. Herefords were docile and usually quiet, but who knew how they'd act when cornered.

"They either broke through the fence or someone left the gate open." Molly stopped at the edge of the lawn strewn with half-eaten pumpkins and squash, several flattened floral wreaths, an upside-down scarecrow, three broken porch chairs and various ripped cushions. "Look at the mess they've made. Stop that…go away…you bad boy." She waved her arms at a piglet, albeit at least a two-hundred pounder, digging in a patch of lawn beside an overturned white garden trellis. "Mom's still in town. We're the only ones here except for the dogs." She indicated Joy's collie, Jess, and her beagle mix, Gus, who barked from inside a front window.

Molly's face was red, her chest heaved, and she looked like she was about to burst into tears. In the entire time he'd known her, Troy had never seen her so worked up. "I'm here, I'll help. It'll be okay."

"How? Even once the pigs are penned, we'll need a land-scaper and carpenter." She gestured to several broken porch rails, the wrecked trellis and mud-churned lawn. "Today's Friday. The wedding's next Saturday just over a week away."

"First things first." Troy touched Molly's arm. "Take a deep breath and get a bucket of feed from the barn. While you're doing that, call Bryce. We can make a food trail and lead the pigs to a fenced area. In the meantime, I have some grain in my truck. I'll make a start and try to divert them."

"Thanks." Molly put a hand to her face. "I don't know what's wrong with me. I'm usually good in a crisis. As a nurse I have to be."

"There's a big difference between a medical crisis and pigs running rampant where you're about to have wedding pic-tures. What these guys have done is personal." He patted her arm one last time before taking his hand away. He wanted to comfort and hold her close like he once would have, but he didn't have that right.

"My dad built that trellis and I… It's special to Mom and all of us." Her voice wobbled as she darted to the barn. She took off her cowboy hat as she ran, and her blond hair tumbled around her shoulders.

Troy's mouth went dry, but he turned away and grabbed the almost-empty feed container from his truck bed. *Focus.* He had to get the pigs penned, and then he'd figure out the rest.

Pigs or no pigs, Joy Carter would have the wedding photo setting she wanted. As Troy scattered grain in a trail, he pulled his phone out of his jacket pocket and scrolled to Wer-ner's number.

Folks in High Valley pulled together. When Werner had called Troy to help move that furniture to Kristi's café, Troy had been happy to lend a hand. Now he'd ask Werner to get the word out that Joy needed the town to pitch in to rescue an important part of her wedding.

Troy glanced at the piglet who'd abandoned digging the lawn to snuffle the grain Troy had sprinkled. "That's it, boy. Bring the others with you." He grinned as the mama pig followed her piglet and, as a group, they snuffled and ambled away from the lawn.

He left a message on Werner's voicemail and emptied the dregs of grain from the feed container along the path the pigs had decided to follow.

Joy had always been kind to him, and now Troy would return that kindness in whatever way he could.

"I filled a feed bucket and got hold of Bryce. He's nearby so he'll be here in a few minutes." Molly handed Troy the bucket, and as her hand brushed his, he drew in a breath as longing rushed through him.

"Great." Troy clutched the feed bucket handle, and his fingers tingled.

Molly put her hands on her knees and gasped for breath. "You distracted them." A slow smile spread across her face. "Good job."

"For now anyway. I appealed to their natural herd instinct." Unlike Molly, Troy hadn't been running, but he was still short of breath. He dug a scoop into the feed bucket and scattered more grain.

"Here, piggies. See what we've got for you? Yum, yum." She cajoled the animals, and there was a flutter in Troy's chest.

"Nice, pigs. Come on, baby." Troy held out more treats and made a soft, cooing noise at the smallest piglet.

"You should sing to them."

"Sing?" He raised his eyebrows.

"If it worked for those cows you milked back in the day,

maybe it will work for these pigs. But choose something upbeat. We need to keep them moving."

"I guess." Troy looked around but they were alone. "Okay, here goes." He launched into "Dancing Queen" by ABBA. It was the first catchy song he could think of, likely because his mom had it on what she called her "happy" playlist.

"Yeah. Good one. My mom's a huge ABBA fan." Molly joined in, her soprano blending with his deeper voice.

The mama pig's curly tail wagged and then the whole group picked up the pace, hoovering up scattered grain as they followed where Troy and Molly led.

"Teamwork." As Molly glanced at him, her smile became softer, more intimate and for an instant, she linked her fingers with his.

That smile and brief touch, her windblown hair and the sweetness of her voice all pulled Troy to her in a way that was both familiar and new. A way that if he was any kind of friend he couldn't—wouldn't—act on.

THE NEXT MORNING, the Tall Grass Ranch bustled with activity. "Ready?" Molly lifted one end of the broken garden trellis.

"Yep." Her mom took the other end and they headed toward a sawhorse Zach had set up in front of the house.

"What are you two doing?" Shane took the trellis from Joy and called a ranch hand to help Molly. "You're the bride, Joy. You should be relaxing and getting ready for our big day. Put your feet up or go to the spa in town." He glanced at Molly. "Can't you get your mom to stop working?"

She grinned at her soon-to-be-stepfather. "Nope. She likes to keep busy. We're alike that way." But here at home, for the first time in years, Molly's life wasn't taken up by school or a job and she was unexpectedly aimless. She also had too much free time to think about Troy, and the job in Atlanta waiting for her in January.

"Looking at this mess, how can I relax?" Wearing a barn

jacket that had belonged to Molly's dad and with her hair covered by a blue bandanna, Joy gestured to the wrecked lawn and battered porch. "It's worse than when the tornado went through ten years ago. It only took off the shed roof and went in a straight line through the pasture. Whereas those pigs..." She huffed out a breath and shook her head.

"It is what it is, isn't that what you usually say?" As Cole and Bryce assessed the damaged trellis, Molly wrapped an arm around her mom's hunched shoulders. "Who'd have thought those Herefords would have dug under a supposedly pig-proof fence? Or that their snouts would be strong enough to lift the fence posts clear out of the ground? It's part of ranch life, I guess. We're always learning something new." The pigs were only being true to their nature, and she had to admire their determination and ingenuity, if not the chaos they'd caused.

"It is." Her mom gave a short laugh. "But among other things, my porch chair cushions are beyond saving. I only bought them this spring. I didn't intend them to be used for pig bedding."

"With everyone pitching in, we're saving the most important things." Molly gestured to the volunteer work crew who'd given up their Saturday to tidy the lawn and repair the porch and trellis. "Like Dad's trellis." Her voice cracked.

"We are, and I'm not usually so on edge." Her mom fiddled with a button on her jacket.

"You're allowed. It's wedding nerves." Molly clasped one of her mom's cold hands. She'd been so focused on her own feelings about the wedding she hadn't considered her mom might be struggling. "If you're having seconds thoughts about getting married, you—"

"It's not that. Of course I want to marry Shane," her mom broke in. "But I'm too old to be so nervous."

"You're not old and anyone would be nervous, but you and Shane are going to have a wonderful life together." The more Molly got to know the older man, the more she liked him.

Maybe in time, he could be a friend and someone she could turn to for the kind of wise advice her father would have given. "Look at how he stepped up yesterday and again today? Some people wouldn't understand how important it is for you to have photos here, but Shane does and along with everyone else, he's making that happen."

"I know." Her mom's voice wobbled. "We could have had pictures taken at Squirrel Tail. Shane's ranch is already set up for weddings, but here he is, getting his hands dirty with the rest of us because it's important to me."

"There you go." Since becoming an adult, Molly hadn't spent enough time with her mom for them to become friends, as well as mother and daughter, but in the past few weeks their relationship had shifted, and she was grateful.

"Will this cushion work for you?" Rosa stopped beside them, along with Nina, Angela and the rest of the Sunflower Sisterhood. Except for Rosa, who held out a sunflower-patterned throw pillow, the others carried garment bags and their faces held suppressed excitement.

"It's beautiful but what did you do?" Joy looked at her friends.

Rosa hugged Joy. "I had enough fabric and foam in my workroom, so last night we got together and made you replacement porch cushions. They're a gift from all of us."

"You must have worked all night. You... Thank you." Joy swiped away a tear.

"It was a pleasure." Angela's voice was gruff. "You're always there for us and anyone in town who needs anything, so these cushions are the least we could do. Here." She handed Joy a pink gift bag tied with white ribbon. "This one is an extra from me. I had material left over from a baby quilt I made for the church's holiday bazaar. It seemed fitting."

As Molly looked around the group of women, her heart squeezed. They all had busy lives, but they hadn't hesitated to drop everything to support a friend in need. While Molly had friends in Atlanta, were they *true* friends like the Sunflower Sisterhood was to her mom? Or were they only friends for a reason and season in her life, linked to each other by work or school and little else?

"Oh, my goodness." Her mom's laughter drew Molly back to the conversation. "It's perfect." Joy held a rectangular pillow patterned with pink pigs aloft for everyone to see.

As Molly joined with the laughter and joking, she knew she'd remember today for the rest of her life. Although ranching was hard, there was a sense of community here she'd never found anywhere else. And, as the saying went, little things could indeed make the difference between hope and despair.

Leaving her mom to exclaim over the cushions, Molly went to a folding table Kristi had set up by the fence. "Can I do anything?"

"Yes, you're a lifesaver." Kristi paused in setting out a tray of oatmeal cookies. "If you can look after drinks and snacks, I'll head back to town. With the weddings and then Thanksgiving, it's extra busy at the Bluebunch. I love my job and my life, but right now I need an extra pair of hands."

"Sure. Tell me what you need."

"Just keep folks fed." Kristi collected her purse and several empty baking trays. "There's more food in the green cooler, and juice and water in the white one. Zach ran an extension cord from here to the house for the coffee maker. Rosa said she'd bring everything back to town for me."

"Wait." Molly gestured to the table filled with several kinds of sandwiches, cookies, muffins and a streusel-topped Bundt cake. "What about a price list and making change?"

"A price list?" Kristi's mouth fell open, and then she patted Molly's arm. "You've been away too long. Your mom needs us, so we're lending a hand. I can't sew, and I'm a hazard to myself and others using power tools, but I can show I care with food."

"Yes, of course." Molly's face heated. She'd spoken without thinking. Had she tried so hard to make herself into someone else, sophisticated city Molly instead of a country girl from an isolated Montana ranch, that she'd forgotten who and what she truly was?

Kristi's expression softened. "It's okay to love city life, but you're home now, at least for a while. And you don't have to choose city or country, but…" She stopped.

"You can't take the country out of the girl, right?" Molly had heard that expression too often, and each time it had made her either defensive or embarrassed. Now, though, it was different. She was proud of coming from a place like High Valley.

"No, that wasn't what I was going to say." Kristi studied her with a serious expression. "All I meant is when you go back to the city, you can take some of High Valley and us with you." She spread her arms wide, taking in the surrounding landscape and the friends and neighbors busy with various tasks.

As Kristi dug out her keys and walked toward the Bluebunch delivery van parked outside the fence, Molly stared after her. She'd always thought her two lives were separate and Montana was the one she wanted to leave behind, but now, she wasn't so certain.

"Can I get a coffee and slice of cake, please? Kristi's pumpkin Bundt cake is my new favorite."

Molly turned at Troy's voice. "Sure." Her hand trembled as she picked up the coffeepot and filled his mug with one of the delicious local roasts Kristi served in the café.

"Are you okay?" When Molly raised her head, Troy looked at her with a concerned expression.

"I'm fine." She cut a generous slice of cake and put it on a paper plate for him.

"It's different being back in Montana, isn't it?" Troy's tone was kind.

Out of everyone, he was perhaps the most likely to understand how Molly truly felt. "It's good but I feel torn, you know?"

He nodded. "I'm a small-town, country boy who made good

in the city but sometimes…" He took a sip of coffee and looked beyond Molly. "It's like I don't really belong anywhere."

"Me too." A weight lifted from her chest as she acknowledged a truth she'd never shared with anyone. "What do you do when you feel that way?"

"What can any of us do?" Troy laughed before sobering. "Be yourself, find folks who 'get' you and make it work. Like Beth." He gestured to Molly's sister-in-law who sat in a lawn chair and handed Zach and Bryce the tools they needed to fix the trellis. "She must miss things about Chicago."

"She does, but she says she now misses Montana when she visits Illinois." Molly had been so wrapped up in her own life, she hadn't thought about what it was like for Beth to move from Chicago to High Valley to marry Zach. However, she'd never seemed to regret that choice and went between both worlds with ease.

"It'll work out, Molly." He gave her a teasing grin. "But I have to say, it's hard to escape the place you grew up. Or the sound." He jerked his chin toward the speakers Cole had set up on the porch, which blasted country music. "The only advice I can give is for you to be you, the whole you. Why can't you be as at home here in cowboy boots and jeans as you are in Atlanta in medical scrubs?"

Yet, as Troy returned to helping Zach and Bryce with the trellis, and Molly served coffee to Nina and Werner, all she wished was that it could be that simple.

CHAPTER NINE

CROUCHED IN THE choir loft at the church near downtown High Valley, Troy double-checked the internet connection and gave a thumbs-up to Mitch, the camera operator. "It's working now." While Troy hadn't planned on attending the Carter double wedding, the team Carrie had hired to livestream the ceremony had all gone down with food poisoning. In the ensuing panic, Troy and anyone else with technical expertise had been drafted to help.

Mitch, a college freshman who was home for the Thanksgiving break, darted an anxious glance at Carrie's dad behind Troy. "We're ready to start the wedding livestreaming, Mr. Rizzo. Your family in Italy will feel almost like they're here."

"Good." Frank Rizzo, who Troy had met a quarter of an hour earlier, clapped Mitch's shoulder before turning to Troy. "You'll stay here to make sure there aren't any more problems?" He gave Mitch a sideways glance as if he doubted the teenager's capabilities.

"Sure, but Mitch is experienced. We've also got the high school film production teacher and his students on the main floor recording from there, along with a camera technician and backup equipment." Troy made his tone reassuring. "Try to relax. Although it's not exactly what Carrie and Bryce planned, we'll manage."

Mr. Rizzo patted his face with a white handkerchief. "I'll be more relaxed once this whole shebang is over. What kind of place doesn't have consistent internet?"

"That's rural Montana for you, but see?" Troy indicated the computer he'd set up at one end of a pew. "Looks like they're all here now. Carrie wanted them to have their cameras on and not be muted so they can join in." On the screen, people waved and clapped.

Mr. Rizzo waved back.

The organist, who'd introduced herself earlier as Kim, began to play "Ave Maria," one of Troy's mom's favorite songs.

"Um, sir, it's time." Mitch gestured to the grooms, Bryce and Shane, at the front of the church with the other Carter brothers and Shane's son.

"Oh, right." Mr. Rizzo thanked Mitch, and then spoke in an undertone to Troy. "You keep an eye on him, you hear?" He rolled his eyes in Mitch's direction. "I don't want anything to spoil my daughter's wedding day."

"It won't." Out of Frank's view, Troy crossed his fingers. "Now go walk Carrie down the aisle."

With a final dubious look at Mitch, Frank disappeared down the stairs to rejoin the rest of the wedding party.

"Here goes." Mitch spoke to Rob, the high school teacher, through his headset, and Troy did a final check of the internet connection, including the backup network he'd set up just in case.

Kim shuffled her music and began playing another classical piece, this time joined by a male soloist, Carrie's cousin from Kalispell, who sang an Italian aria.

Keeping one eye on the computer, Troy watched from above as the brides, Joy and Carrie, and their attendants moved down the aisle to the front. He drew in a harsh breath when the overhead lights caught Molly's blond hair as she preceded her mom.

Troy barely noticed the brides, the other bridesmaids or Skylar and Paisley, the adorable flower girls. Instead, his gaze followed Molly. She wore a silver-gray dress, and while most of her hair was loose, the back part was caught up in a delicate floral headpiece. As she reached the front of the church, she took Paisley's hand, and her smile made Troy's mouth go dry. From here, they could have been mother and daughter, and the sweet scene made him imagine how Molly might care for her own child one day.

"Troy. We're losing signal." Mitch's frantic whisper pulled Troy back to what he was supposed to be doing, and he turned to the computer to switch over to the backup network.

As the ceremony went on, there was more music, several readings, oohs and aahs from the Italian family on the livestream and those in the church and a burst of applause as both newly married couples kissed. Then Joy with Shane, and Carrie with Bryce came back up the aisle, beaming. Carrie's cousin, as comfortable with country as opera, sang a Rascal Flatts hit, this time accompanied by Kim on guitar, and two of Joy's nephews on banjo and ukulele.

Troy tapped one foot in time to the music and laughed along with the congregation as Bryce gave Carrie a twirl at the end of the aisle.

When Frank escorted Carrie's mom from their front pew, he glanced up at the choir loft and gave Troy and Mitch an approving nod, and Troy exhaled with relief. It had been last-minute, but they'd pulled it off. In Italy, Carrie's family clapped and cheered, and Mitch darted downstairs to film a message from Carrie and Bryce to their virtual guests.

"Troy?" At Molly's voice, he whirled around.

"Hey." At a distance, she'd taken his breath away, but up close she was a vision. Her face was flushed, and her blue eyes sparkled. "Aren't you supposed to be down there doing maid of honor stuff?" He tried to joke as her nearness made him lightheaded.

"Mom won't miss me for a few minutes. I wanted to thank you for pitching in. I…all of us…we really appreciate it."

Her lips parted and as she smiled and moved closer, Troy inhaled her sweet jasmine fragrance. "Not a problem." His breathing quickened, and his heart pounded.

"Well, thank you…for everything. With the pigs and now today, you've been a real friend." She wet her lower lip with her tongue, and Troy noticed, not for the first time, how appealing her mouth looked. "I should go." She glanced at the musicians who chatted as they gathered up their music. "There's photos and then a lunch for family and close friends, but see you at the town reception at Squirrel Tail later?"

"Of course." He fiddled with a computer cable. Molly had been pretty as a teenager and maturity had simply added to her beauty. It wasn't only her looks, though. She was gorgeous inside and out. "It's a long day for you."

"Yes, it had to be a morning wedding because of the time difference between here and Italy." Her gaze dropped to her bouquet of pink roses mixed with some kind of white flower and greenery. Did she also feel the unspoken attraction that hummed between them and was she as uncertain as Troy about what to do about it?

"Right." Although Molly had called him a "real friend," his feelings for her were more than friendship. And, if he was honest with himself, he'd never gotten over her the first time and maybe he never would.

When she looked at him again, her expression took away whatever breath Troy still had left. Tenderness, and maybe something even deeper, flickered in her eyes and across her face, and they both stepped forward to close the remaining distance between them.

"Mol? We're waiting for you to take pictures on the church steps." Cole's voice echoed up the stairs, and Molly jumped away from Troy as if someone had poured a bucket of ice-cold water over her. "See you."

"Yeah." As she darted away, followed more slowly by the soloist and banjo and ukulele players, Troy's chest was heavy, and his stomach knotted. He packed up the rest of the computer equipment, and his thoughts turned inward, ruminating on the past. He'd loved Molly with all his heart and a foolish part of him still did.

"You finished up here?" Kim, who was around Troy's mom's age, gave him a curious look as she put on her coat.

"Almost. I'll turn off the lights when I leave." He made a show of winding up the last electrical cord.

"Thanks." Kim hesitated. "I've known Molly her whole life. I'm not saying there *is* something between the two of you, but if you'd like there to be, why not take a risk and tell her?"

"It's not that simple." Troy put the cord in his backpack and added a laptop.

"Or maybe you're making it too complicated?" Kim's laugh was light, her smile warm. "Beneath that city gloss, Molly is still a country girl. Look at the weddings today. They mixed city, country and even Italy just fine. When it comes down to it, people are people and much the same no matter where they live."

They were, and maybe Troy *was* overthinking everything. He took risks all the time in business, and that was part of the reason for his success. Was it a mistake to be so guarded in his personal life?

As Kim left, he considered what she'd said. He couldn't ignore his feelings for Molly any longer, and maybe he shouldn't. He was beginning to realize that he'd idealized Molly back then, but she was as human as any other woman. Some light flirtation might be exactly what he needed to put his feelings for her behind him once and for all. Now, he only had to convince his heart to follow his head and not want anything more.

MOLLY HAD WANTED to kiss Troy right there in the church choir loft, in full view of the musicians and anyone else who might have seen them. In the wood-beamed barn at Squirrel Tail that Shane had converted into a reception venue, Molly put a hand to her face as embarrassment rolled over her again. So far, she'd managed to avoid Troy at the party, and with most of the town around, it should be easy to continue to keep her distance.

Carrying a plate of food from the buffet, Molly glanced around trying to find a spot to sit. Since this reception was informal, there wasn't assigned seating, and she'd lost sight of her brothers in the crowd. She moved toward a round table with several empty chairs. If she texted Cole, they could find each other and—

"Hey, Molly." Troy patted the chair beside his. "I'm on my own. Want to join me?"

She looked around again but anybody she knew was already with a group. "Okay." She smiled at a couple engrossed in conversation on the other side of the table. She recognized the woman as one of Carrie's cousins. As Molly sat next to Troy, two gray-haired couples took the remaining empty seats and introduced themselves as ranching friends of Shane's from Wyoming.

"It's a fantastic spread." Troy indicated his plate piled high with food.

"Yes." It was like every Montana "fall supper" Molly could remember, and a true community gathering with good food, friends and cheer. "Although there's a caterer for the meat and other big dishes, it's a typical High Valley potluck like Mom and Carrie wanted."

It was also the kind of event Molly hadn't realized she'd missed, but now, looking at her own plate where one of Angela's mini barbecue chicken calzones nestled beside Nina's traditional Ukrainian cabbage rolls, along with other treats she remembered from childhood, her mouth watered.

Troy grinned as he dug into his meal. "After the ceremony,

I went home and chopped wood. Werner told me I'd need to work up an appetite for tonight."

"Smart." Molly pushed away the image of Troy lifting an axe and bringing it down on a block of wood. Since it had been a warm day, he might have taken off his jacket and in short sleeves, his forearms would... *No.* She took a bite of the savory calzone and chewed with determination. Carrie's cousin and her boyfriend were still absorbed in each other, and the couples from Wyoming talked about corn and barley prices, so she and Troy were on their own. "Nobody goes home hungry after *any* High Valley party."

Troy laughed and as they ate their meals, Molly relaxed. He was good company and as easy to talk to as he'd been long ago. Until tonight, they'd talked mostly about ranch business, but as their conversation ranged from movies to books and travel, she found they had more in common than she'd expected.

"You ate what?" She stared at him wide-eyed as he recounted a business trip to Hong Kong.

"Duck's tongue and goose feet. They're both delicacies." He showed her a picture on his phone. "Pete's, my friend and business partner, family is from China. Thanks to him, I didn't embarrass myself or our hosts."

"I'd like to travel." She admired a picture of Troy and Pete on the deck of a ferry with the impressive Hong Kong skyline behind them. "I've only been outside the US once, and that was to Canada." But once Molly started her new job, along with saving for a place of her own, she wanted to plan some vacations.

"Where do you want to go?"

"I've been thinking about Costa Rica. All the wildlife. The rainforest. I'd also like to visit England. The Carter family came from there way back. There's all that history and old buildings and fish and chips."

By how he listened to her and asked attentive questions, Troy seemed truly interested in what she had to say. Unlike some guys she'd dated, he was focused on her rather than looking around for someone else or trying to take over the conversation. *Hang on.* She wasn't dating him. They were only chatting because they'd ended up sitting together.

As she mentioned other destinations, she realized she was babbling, but how Troy looked at her threw her off center. Although surrounded by other people, there was an intimacy between them that made her nerve endings quiver. And although he looked great in ranch clothes, in his navy suit, crisp white shirt and perfectly knotted striped tie, he oozed a different but similarly appealing masculinity.

"London's a fantastic city." As Troy talked about visiting a customer there, his words washed over Molly. *Big Ben. Westminster Abbey. Buckingham Palace. The Tower of London.* All places she'd read about or seen in movies and longed to experience in real life. "Sorry, what did you say?" Caught up in a daydream about walking by the River Thames with Troy, she realized he'd stopped talking and was looking at her with his eyebrows raised, having evidently asked a question.

"I said it looks like there will be a lot of leftovers." He nodded toward the buffet table.

"There always are, everything gets donated to the local food bank." It was part of the ethos of "giving back" that Molly had grown up with and one she now tried to live in her own life.

"That food bank helped my folks once. It was the Christmas they lost the ranch and before we moved to Bozeman. They didn't want to go to the one closer to home where people knew them, so they came here. I'm glad it's still going. I'll have to drop by and thank them." A faint flush crept across Troy's cheeks as if he was embarrassed to have shared something so personal.

"The team would appreciate that." Molly paused with her last piece of cabbage roll partway to her mouth. "Lots of people need a helping hand at one point or another. The food bank's discreet and…" Her face heated and she stumbled over her words. Troy was such a success now she'd almost forgotten how his family had struggled.

Troy focused on the remains of his meal as if Rosa's delicious bannock bread held the meaning of life.

Molly decided to redirect their focus away from the awkward moment. "So, what are you doing for Thanksgiving?"

"My parents and sister are coming here." Troy's anxious expression eased as if he was grateful for the change of topic. "I told my mom I'd make Thanksgiving dinner, but my stove conked out yesterday. Since I can't get a replacement delivered until after the holiday, we may end up microwaving something." His laugh was forced. "I found a few questionable recipes online for microwaved holiday meals, but maybe we should go to Billings and have Thanksgiving at a hotel there instead."

"What's this about Thanksgiving at a hotel?" Cole stopped behind Molly's chair.

"Troy's parents and sister are joining him for the holiday, but his stove's not working so he's—"

"You can't go to a hotel." Cole's eyes widened, and he shook his head. "Join me and Melissa at our place. We're hosting everyone this year since Mom and Shane will be on their honeymoon."

Molly's heart squeezed. She'd already been preparing herself for her first Thanksgiving apart from her mom. But spending it with Troy on top of that? She couldn't. "I'm sure the—"

"Thanks for the invitation, but we couldn't." Troy spoke at the same time as Molly. "Thanksgiving's for family and—"

"The more the merrier. When I was riding rodeo, I spent too many Thanksgivings and other holidays away from home eating overcooked turkey in some soulless hotel or diner. Melissa won't mind me inviting you and your family." He patted Molly's shoulder. "Like Mom says, Thanksgiving's about bringing people together and sharing food and friendship. It wouldn't be the holiday without a few extra, would it?"

As she nodded, Molly's stomach lurched and she put her

cutlery back on her plate, her appetite gone. She'd kept her previous relationship with Troy secret from her family, so she had only herself to blame that Cole and the others had welcomed him like a long-lost relative. Another awkward moment.

"If you're sure it's okay, we'd love to join you. I'll let my folks know." Troy's voice was strained, suggesting he was as uncomfortable with forced holiday proximity as Molly.

She gave Cole and Troy a bright smile. It was only a day, but between now and Thursday, she'd do her own online research. Starting with tips about spending Thanksgiving with your ex.

As Troy turned to speak to one of the Wyoming ranchers, Molly shivered as coldness swirled from her stomach up her windpipe.

Troy *was* her ex, and though she'd spent years trying to convince herself he was only a teenage crush, she could admit now that he had been much more. They shared common interests and values, and if he lived in Atlanta, he was the kind of guy she could get serious about.

But he didn't, so she couldn't let herself think about anything long term—no matter how much she might want to.

CHAPTER TEN

ON THE MONDAY morning of Thanksgiving week, Troy sat behind the desk in his home office, held his phone to one ear and stared out the window at the harvested fields etched in silver frost. "It's not a good time for me to come to Texas. Why don't you come here instead?"

"Why would I come to Montana?" On the other end of the phone, Pete's voice was astonished. "I thought we agreed that when we needed to meet in person, you'd either travel to me in Austin or we'd meet in San Francisco."

"We did but…" Troy paused and rubbed his free hand across his forehead where the start of a headache throbbed. He hadn't lived here long and didn't want to leave the ranch, even for a few days. Or leave Cole on his own with the stock contracting business. Sure, he'd be within easy contact by phone, text and email, but it wasn't the same as being here and available for anything that might come up. And not that he could say so to Pete, but if were honest with himself, he also didn't want to miss any opportunities to spend time with Molly. "Think about it, will you? You can see my ranch. I could even get you on horseback."

Pete laughed so hard he snorted. "Ranch, okay, as long as it's not too rustic, but riding a horse? I live in Texas. If I wanted to, I could ride horses at home. But I'm a city guy, remember? Being too far from the bright lights could be fun for a few days in summer but not that far north between October and April." He made shivering noises.

"Sure, but…" Troy looked at the fields again. He'd met Pete in college and although the guy was his best friend, Troy had never talked to him about where and how he'd grown up. "It's important to me."

"What's going on? Truly?" Pete's voice softened, and children's laughter echoed in the background. Pete and Tina had married soon after they'd both graduated from college and now had two young kids. While Troy liked spending time with them, their family togetherness also made him feel lonely.

"Nothing's going on. I want to show you my new place, that's all." A pickup truck drove along the highway that bordered his ranch, and Troy craned his neck to take a closer look. Was that the Tall Grass Ranch logo on the door?

He hadn't seen Molly since the wedding reception at Squirrel Tail, and although she'd tactfully changed the subject, he still cringed at how he'd opened his big mouth and let her see his vulnerability. He'd never spoken with anyone about those lean years when his folks had struggled.

"Okay." Pete gave in. "I'll do it, but only because you're family to me. But I'm not getting anywhere near a horse except for looking through a window at one, or if it's safely on the other side of a stall door or fence from me."

"Deal. Thanks, buddy." Troy let out a breath he hadn't realized he was holding. Outside, an engine rumbled and then stopped and what sounded like a truck door slammed. "I have to go."

"Hang on, it's a woman, isn't it? That's really why you want me to come to the back of beyond." Pete's voice sharpened with interest and curiosity.

"Of course not." The front doorbell rang and, still holding the phone, Troy left his office to go to the top of the stairs.

"But—"

"Let me know when you've booked flights." Troy looked out the stairwell window. That truck, now parked in front of his house, did belong to the Tall Grass Ranch, but from here he couldn't see who was at the door.

"You've got it bad, buddy." Pete laughed as Troy disconnected, went to the bottom of the stairs and checked his hair in the mirror by the front door.

Maybe he did have it bad. Since the wedding, he hadn't been able to stop thinking about Molly, but it was too new and confusing for him to talk to Pete or anyone else about.

He opened the door and made himself give a neutral smile. "Hey, Molly." She'd looked elegant in that dress at the wedding and now, in jeans and a cozy blue jacket the same color as her eyes, she looked cute. Either way, she was gorgeous and turned him inside out and upside down.

"Hi." She held a soft-sided cooler bag, and her smile was tentative. "We're on our way to town." From the truck, Cole waved at him. A dog's head bobbed excitedly in the back window. "We, um…here." She thrust the bag at him. Her cheeks turned a pretty shade of pink. "With your stove not working, and Cathy away visiting her sister, I…we wanted to make things easier for you."

"Thank you." The tension in Troy's shoulders eased, and he put his free hand to his chest. "That's really kind and thoughtful."

Molly waved away his appreciation. "I should have thought to save some food from the reception for you but—"

"It's fine." The food bank needed it a lot more than he did. "I…uh… I guess I'll see you at Thanksgiving at Cole and Melissa's."

"Yes." She fiddled with the tassels of her blue-and-white scarf.

Cole beeped the truck's horn, and his beagle, Blue, stuck his head out the half-open rear window and barked.

"I should go." Molly half turned.

"Wait." Troy took a deep breath. "I saw posters in town about a holiday tree lighting ceremony the Friday after Thanksgiving. I wondered if you'd like to go with me. As a friend, of course."

"I... As a friend. Sure."

She smiled, then nodded in the direction of the truck and jogged down the porch steps to rejoin her brother.

As the Tall Grass truck disappeared at the end of his lane, Troy closed his front door and went to pat Acorn. Either because of her age or history, the dog never came to greet visitors, instead preferring to stay in what was now "her" chair by the living room window.

Some light flirtation. There had been too many people around for Troy to flirt with Molly at the wedding. However, and although his invitation to the holiday tree lighting had been a spur of the moment impulse, maybe it was what he needed. Even if she was still a country girl at heart, anything between them didn't have a future with him here and her in Atlanta. Once Molly was past history, Troy could move on and stop comparing every woman he met with her.

He scratched Acorn's ears, and after stowing the food in the kitchen, as he went back upstairs to his office, the dog followed. Thanksgiving with Molly and her family would be fine. The tree lighting ceremony would be as well. They were the kinds of things friends did together.

But as Acorn hopped onto Troy's lap, blocked his view of his laptop screen and nudged his hand so he'd scratch her ears again, Troy couldn't shake a persistent sense of unease.

What if his plan didn't work? And what if flirtation made him fall further into whatever "this" was with Molly? Something that made him think about a future with her rather than their past.

"HAPPY THANKSGIVING." Molly handed Melissa the tin of pecan pie brownies she'd made, took off her coat and smoothed her cozy, cream-colored sweater dress. Paired with brown Western boots, it was casual enough for a Carter family gathering but a step up from the jeans and T-shirts she usually wore around the ranch.

Melissa thanked her as she led the way to the back of the cozy, two-story frame house. The place, a few miles from the main ranch house, had been built by Molly's great-grandparents. In their day, what was now the family room had been a summer kitchen.

"It's my first time hosting a holiday celebration for a crowd. I'm nervous, especially because we only moved in here two weeks ago." Melissa's laugh was quick and high-pitched. "I'm still getting used to the kitchen."

"Don't worry." Cole joined them as they reached the comfortable den, and he wrapped an arm around his wife's shoulders. "We're all family here. Well, almost." He indicated Troy and a couple who must be his parents, who sat on the sofa at the far end of the room near Carrie's folks and her aunt Angela. "The Claytons are so happy to have been saved from microwaved turkey burgers, they're sure not going to complain if anything goes wrong. Come on, Mol. I'll introduce you."

"That's okay, I'll—" Molly looked around, but having driven herself, rather than coming with Zach, Beth and Ellie, she was the last to arrive and everyone else had already gathered in groups. She made herself smile as if the Claytons meant nothing more to her than any of the other guests her family invited each year.

Cole made the introductions, and Molly smiled harder, hyperaware of Troy, who'd nailed Thanksgiving casual with style in black jeans, a pale blue button-down shirt, navy blue pullover sweater and boots.

"Please call us Val and Jeff." Mrs. Clayton, whose light brown hair fell around her shoulders, gave Molly a warm smile. Her smile and her eyes were like her son's.

Molly swallowed and turned to Jeff, a balding man with

a silver beard, who shook her hand and said, "Good to meet you. Troy's talked a lot about you."

"Jeff." Val shook her head and gave her husband a mock glare. "Here's our daughter, Sara." She turned to a young woman with long, dark red hair who, except for her striking blue eyes, didn't look like Troy or either of their parents. "Sara's a college senior in Oregon, but I expect Troy already told you that."

Molly nodded and kept her smile in place as she greeted Sara. Troy hadn't told her anything about his sister or his parents, at least not recently. She wondered what he'd told his folks about her, then or now.

"Since everyone's here, let's eat." Cole clapped his hands and began directing people into the dining room much like Molly had seen him herd cows. As she started toward her usual spot at the kids' table, Cole added, "No, Mol, you don't need to stay here with the kids. They'll be fine with Ellie looking out for them." He gave their niece a fond pat on one shoulder.

She followed his lead and found herself seated—of course— next to Troy, with his family across the table from them.

"The place still looks the same," Zach said as he held out a chair for Beth. "But I guess we only moved out a few weeks ago."

"How are you settling into the main ranch house?" Bryce waited for his new bride, Carrie, to take her seat. They'd postponed their honeymoon to spend Thanksgiving with Paisley and Cam but were heading to Jamaica for a week in December in a gap between Carrie's rodeo competitions.

"Apart from the boxes still piled everywhere?" Zach chuckled as he took his own seat beside Beth. "We've left a lot of stuff still packed up because we're going to do some painting to make the house our own. Starting with the baby's room, of course."

To Molly, he said, "And you'll always have your room to come home to. Don't worry about that, sis."

"We'll keep a space for you here too, Mol." Cole sat at the head of the table decorated with turkey art made by the kids, mini orange pumpkins and red, yellow and brown paper leaves. In only a few months, her brother had taken to domestic life like the proverbial duck to water.

"Our guest room is yours whenever you want it," Bryce added.

Molly nodded and tried not to grimace. She didn't have a place of her own right now, but she would again soon. And although her brothers meant well, she wouldn't spend every vacation in Montana. Besides, when she did visit, she could stay with her mom and Shane.

As Melissa carried a golden-brown turkey in on a platter from the kitchen and set it in front of Cole, her brother bowed his head to say grace, and the familiar words her dad used to say rolled over Molly. Thanksgiving was about family, and although her dad was gone, and her mom was now married to Shane, traditions continued and were added. Nothing stayed the same, least of all Molly herself. She needed to embrace change instead of resisting it.

"Has anybody heard from Mom?" Cole started to carve the turkey, and Melissa passed around serving dishes with mashed potatoes, roasted vegetables, corn bread and, new this year, Carrie's mom's Italian charcuterie board and Angela's home-made Asiago bread.

"Not apart from a text saying they'd arrived safely in Sedona." A small smile played around Zach's lips. "You'd better not be messaging her either. Let Mom have a honeymoon without thinking or worrying about us."

Since Zach and Beth's baby was due so soon, Molly's mom had wanted to stay in the United States for a honeymoon trip, but she and Shane planned to go to Europe in the spring. After so many years of sticking close to home, her life was changing in big ways and travel was likely only the start.

"All of us except for Molly are settled," Cole said. "And

unlike me, Mol's never caused Mom any grief, so what does she have to worry about?"

"Mothers always worry, no matter how old their kids are." Val gave Troy and then Sara a loving smile. "So, Molly, tell us about your job. Troy says you're a nurse."

As Molly answered Val's questions about the hospital and her master's research, she was conscious of Troy next to her, his chair so close that his knee bumped her leg when he passed a bowl of green beans to his dad.

"Sorry." Troy moved his leg away, but then bumped Molly's knee again when Sara asked for the corn bread.

Molly's whole body tingled and, as Troy's folks and Sara chatted with Beth and Zach about the baby, she tried to focus on her food instead of his nearness. The table was crowded with so many people around it. Under the circumstances, he'd have bumped anyone. And Cole had placed them beside each other, so it wasn't as if Troy had sought her out. As she lifted her eyes from her plate, they exchanged a brief glance, and his slow smile made the hair on her arms rise.

"It was nice of Cole and Melissa to invite my family to join yours for Thanksgiving." Troy spoke in an undertone, although since Cole was telling a funny rodeo story with Skylar perched on his lap making horse sounds, nobody else was paying attention to him.

"It's good to have you here. I…we…my family's always welcoming," Molly stammered. They weren't touching, but it was as if the two of them were connected at an emotional level that superseded any physical contact. Flustered, she set her cutlery down on her plate and rested her hands on her lap.

He leaned closer. "I have a lot to be thankful for, but I've always been grateful for that time we shared. We were young, but what we had together was important."

"It was." No matter where Molly went, she'd always carry the memory of Troy in her heart.

One of Troy's hands clasped hers beneath the table. She

froze. This touch wasn't an accidental knee bump. It was purposeful, and as his fingers curled around hers, she let her hand relax in his.

Molly's stomach fluttered and then, with a quick squeeze, it was over, Troy let go and he turned away to speak to his sister.

He'd only held her hand for a brief moment, but it was intimate, intense and opened Molly's heart to his in a way she'd never experienced with anyone else.

It also meant she, and her heart, were in big trouble.

CHAPTER ELEVEN

LATER THAT NIGHT, Troy flipped on his kitchen light and made his way to the cupboard next to the sink. Since the antacids weren't in the medicine cabinet in the upstairs bathroom or the powder room, the only other place they might be was here.

He pressed a hand to his rolling stomach and opened the cupboard door. On a Montana ranch, there wasn't a 24/7 pharmacy or grocery store on the corner so he should have remembered to stock up.

"Troy?" Footsteps padded from the living room, and he turned to see his mom in a pink housecoat, fluffy pink slippers and a sleepy Acorn nestled in her arms. "I thought you'd gone to bed. I hope you're not up working."

"No." He'd tried to work, but after fifteen minutes of sitting and staring at the computer without seeing the document he'd opened he'd given up and headed to bed. "I can't sleep." He grabbed the bottle of antacids, found a glass and filled it with water from the sink faucet. "Too much rich food or maybe I'm coming down with something." He didn't feel sick, though, only unsettled. Joining Molly's family for a special holiday like Thanksgiving could have been awkward. Instead, it had felt right and comfortable, like he belonged. And when, on impulse, he'd taken her hand, the two of them had fit together in a way he'd never felt with anyone else. "Where are Dad and Sara?"

"Your sister's talking to a friend, and your dad's watching football." Still cuddling Acorn, his mom pulled out a stool and sat behind the kitchen island. "It's a clear night. I opened the living room curtains and looked out at the fields. With the lights off, and in the moonlight, I remembered the Thanksgivings we had on our ranch. You were little and Sara hadn't been born yet. Your dad's folks and mine were still alive, and all the aunts, uncles and cousins would travel to be with us." Her voice was tinged with sadness. "Still, life goes on."

Troy swallowed one of the tablets and sat across from her. "If our old ranch ever comes up for sale, I'll buy it for you."

She shook her head. "That's sweet but no. That ranch is the past, and I don't want to revisit it. You have a wonderful place here, and it's your future. If you ever need help, your dad's itching to get back in a cattle pen or behind the wheel of a tractor."

"I'd be happy to have you both come out and work with me." He loved having his folks and Sara here, but there was still an emptiness in his house—or maybe his heart—that not even his closest family could fill.

"Molly's a beautiful young woman. She's smart and clearly devoted to her family, but…" His mom shifted on the stool and fiddled with Acorn's collar. "Be careful, that's all."

"What are you talking about? Molly's a friend, nothing more." He tried to make the words casual, but his mom knew him too well to be fooled.

"Do you usually hold hands with your friends at the dinner table?" His mom's eyes twinkled.

"I… No…but…" Troy headed up a multimillion-dollar business, but his mom could still make him feel like a kid caught raiding the cookie jar. "You saw?"

"Not at the time but Skylar told me. She asked if you were going to be her new uncle." His mom chuckled. "Not much gets by kids, and she was on Cole's lap. I guess she had a good view."

Troy dropped his head into his hands. "Do you know who else Skylar told?" He might have some questions to answer the next time he was around Molly's family.

"My guess is Paisley because those two girls are best friends, but I also told Skylar that whatever was going on between you and Molly was private and not anyone's business." His mom's expression softened. "Like I said when Cole talked about Joy, mothers worry about their kids even when they're grown up. Molly hurt you, and I don't want you to get hurt again."

"I won't get hurt because I *am* grown up." He shrugged. "It was a bit of flirting, that's all." Flirting that had been a lot more intense than he'd expected and, for a moment, he'd forgotten they had an audience.

"You've never been one to flirt unless you were serious about a girl." His mom studied him, and Troy's face heated. "And from what I've seen Molly's the only girl, or woman, you've ever been truly serious about."

"I've dated other women. Like Kelly."

"Kelly was wonderful, but you broke things off with her and now she's married to someone else. I know because I bumped into her mom at the yoga studio a few weeks ago. So, what's going on?"

"I don't know." And that was the truth. Troy had cared about Kelly, but he hadn't loved her in the way he knew he should. The way he'd once loved Molly. "I'm not in a rush to settle down."

"If you met the right woman you would be, and Molly... can you trust her?"

That was the issue. Troy prided himself on being a good judge of people, but with Molly he'd been wrong. And with Kelly and the few other women he'd dated, he'd always held part of himself back.

"I *want* to trust Molly. She knew me before…everything."
He raised his arm in a sweeping gesture that took in the ranch
house and surrounding land. "These days, I never know if
people like me for me, or what they think I can do or buy for
them." It was the first time he'd voiced the fear that ate him
up inside. "Apart from you guys and Pete, I keep to myself."

"Oh, honey." His mom got up, set Acorn on the floor and
came around the kitchen island to wrap Troy in a hug. "Your
dad and I are so proud of your success, but none of the money
or what it buys matters if you aren't happy."

"I *am* happy." As Troy returned his mom's hug, the backs
of his eyes burned. "I have you and dad and Sara. Pete and
his family. This ranch. Interesting work that more than pays
the bills. Compared to lots of folks, I'm lucky."

"You are but…" His mom squeezed his shoulders before she
stepped back. "You remember after we lost our ranch? Your
dad worked the night shift at that factory. I was doing days at
the grocery store, and you worked part-time at the gas station
while you were still in high school, and you babysat Sara. The
four of us were crammed into our small apartment that always
smelled of greasy food from the restaurant below."

Troy nodded. How could he forget? It had been one of the
hardest times of his life.

"Looking back, I often wonder how we survived it, but we
did. And that Thanksgiving, I remember sitting at our kitchen
table and feeling thankful. I didn't have much, but I had a
loving husband and two wonderful children. We all had our
health, and I had hope and faith that things would get better.
They did, eventually, and thanks to you, as far as material
things go, I've been blessed beyond my wildest imaginings."
She hesitated and a frown creased her forehead. "All I'm saying is I could lose everything tomorrow and as long as I still
had your dad, you and Sara, I'd be thankful. That's what I
want for you. A loving partner and a family who'll be there
for you no matter what."

Troy wanted that too, but he didn't know how to get it. And even if he did, could he trust it would be the kind of forever relationship his folks had?

"The right woman won't care about what you can buy for her." It was like she could read his thoughts. His mom gave him another hug. "She'll love you for who you are. 'For richer, for poorer,' like in the wedding vows."

Troy admired her optimism, but he couldn't be so certain. Life hadn't made him cynical but it, and the rough-and-tumble of the business world, had made him wary.

"I want the best for you, honey, and if that's Molly, well, the two of you were so young before. Now, you've both done a lot of growing up. Any child of Joy Carter's is bound to have a sensible head on their shoulders. And you're right. Molly did know you before, so she's not likely to be dazzled by riches."

"No." Troy had to chuckle. Molly was the least pretentious woman he knew.

"I won't interfere, but I'm always here for you. Your dad is too." His mom moved toward the fridge, and Acorn followed. "As for your tummy upset, ginger tea will fix you up better than any of those store-bought pills. I brought fresh ginger with me." She opened the fridge door and rummaged in the crisper drawer. "I expect you drink too much coffee. Along with all that screen time, it's no wonder your digestion and sleep are upside down."

"Mom." Troy huffed in frustration.

"Or I could make you warm milk?" She sent him a teasing glance. "Remember when you were little? A cup of warm milk sent you right off to sleep."

"I'm fine but okay, ginger tea." He rolled his eyes like he'd done as a teenager. He'd admitted enough embarrassing stuff to his mom tonight. He wasn't about to acknowledge she was right about his coffee drinking and what his doctor called "bad sleep hygiene."

Still, shutting off screens several hours before bed and

homespun remedies like ginger tea and warm milk wouldn't cure what truly ailed him.

Once again, Molly had gotten under his skin. And rather than running away from what was happening between them, the only cure, if he could call it that, was facing those feelings head-on.

ON FRIDAY NIGHT the week after Thanksgiving, Molly tucked her fuzzy blue scarf into the neck of a parka she'd last worn in high school and pulled the hat that matched the scarf and gloves farther down over her ears. Waking up this morning to a light dusting of snow on the fields and a thin skim of ice on a half-filled water bucket she'd left outside the barn made her feel like a kid again, excited with the changing seasons.

Or was her excitement more about going with Troy to tonight's town tree lighting? She stole a glance at his profile as he stood by her side in Meadowlark Park. He'd picked her up at the Tall Grass half an hour ago, and although neither of them had said much on the way into town or while strolling past bustling and brightly decorated stores as Christmas music played, the silence between them was comfortable.

Despite that hand-holding at Thanksgiving, which she was pretty sure no one had spotted since none of her family had mentioned it, they were here as friends. Nothing more. Yet, no matter how many times she reminded herself of that, it still felt like a date.

"Are you warm enough?" Troy took Molly's arm to shield her from several kids who darted through the crowd with glow sticks that lit up the night like winter fireflies. In jeans, and bundled up in a parka, hat and gloves, he looked like most of the other men here, but there was something about him. No matter what he wore, he made Molly's stomach flip.

"I'm fine." If anything, she might be too hot, but that was because of him. Even though the kids were gone, Troy still held her arm and despite her parka and sweater beneath it, her skin tingled with awareness.

"Would you like a hot chocolate?" With his free hand, Troy indicated the nearby stand trimmed with red and white holiday lights.

"Sure, but I can—" She reached for her purse, but he stopped her.

"My treat." He grinned. "I invited you so you're my guest. It's the least I can do after your family hosted mine for Thanksgiving."

"Did your folks and Sara get home okay?" Molly liked Troy's family, but she hadn't missed his mom's assessing looks.

"Yeah, and my new stove was finally delivered this morning. Out here, I'm learning I have to order stuff early and stock up on food and other supplies in case of emergency." He shrugged and shook his head. "I'm going to San Francisco for Christmas so it will be a while before I get to try the stove out to cook a big meal."

"Oh." Of course he'd want to spend Christmas with his family. She was surprised at how much she'd gotten used to having Troy nearby. As he ordered and paid for their drinks, he took his arm from hers, and Molly hugged herself, unexpectedly bereft.

"Hey, Molly." Hannah, an old friend from high school, came over. "I heard you're back in town for a while. You should come to one of our group dinners. The guys watch the kids so we women can have a night out and enjoy ourselves." She darted a curious glance at Troy while also helping a dark-haired toddler with his mittens.

"Thanks, I'll keep it in mind. So far, I've been busy with family things." Molly smiled at the little boy, who happily told her that his name was Noah. He looked to be about two, and judging from the bulge under the front of her coat, Hannah was pregnant again.

"It's the third Thursday evening of the month at Ruby's

Place, the Western-themed restaurant off High Valley Avenue. Most of the old crowd turns up. We meet at six." Hannah grinned at her husband, Mike, who'd been a few years ahead of Molly in school.

"Sounds good." Molly took the paper cup of cocoa from Troy and introduced him to Hannah and her family. She smiled at Noah again and pushed away a surprising tug of longing.

"Noah, no. That's Ben's, not yours." Hannah removed a glow stick from her son's mittened hand, which he'd apparently taken from another boy.

"But I want to be a superhero." Noah's small face screwed up, and he started to wail.

"Sorry. We'll have to catch up another time." She gave Molly an apologetic glance.

"Hey, buddy." Troy crouched to Noah's level and said something to him. The boy stopped crying, nodded and then grinned.

As they said their goodbyes, Molly told herself she should enjoy this time of being on her own. She had her path, and she was happy with it. Yet, in Atlanta, far away from her nieces and nephew and working in a research institute, she missed the joy of children in her life.

"What next?" Troy looped his arm through Molly's again as they moved away from Hannah and her family and rejoined the crowd.

"The tree lighting will start soon." She sipped the sweet cocoa, enjoying the feel of Troy's arm in hers. She hadn't heard what he'd said to Noah, but it had charmed the little boy and diverted his attention, which was the point. She suppressed the way-too-appealing thought of Troy with kids of his own, and the less-welcome one of whatever woman he'd become a parent with. "The town's also collecting money and gifts for a toy drive over by the pavilion." With the weddings and Thanksgiving, Molly hadn't had time to shop, so she'd given a check to one of the organizers when she'd been in town getting groceries.

"Already taken care of. I dropped some things off this afternoon."

"He sure did." Nina appeared on Troy's other side, accompanied by Werner. "The bed of his pickup truck was full to overflowing. You were much too generous, and we sure appreciate it. Some lucky kids on Christmas morning will as well."

"It was nothing." Even in the growing darkness, Molly spotted the faint flush on Troy's cheeks.

"If that's nothing, I can't imagine what 'something' is," Werner said. "Don't be so modest. Between that and your check for the food bank, you gave us over—"

"Great to see you both but we need to get going," Troy interrupted. "We have to get a good spot to see the holiday lights go on, don't we, Molly?"

"Yes, but..." As Troy steered her away from Nina and Werner, she shook her head at him. "What did you do?"

"Nothing important, but it was also supposed to be private." Troy tossed his empty cocoa cup in a nearby recycling container and then did the same with Molly's.

"Haven't you learned nothing much in High Valley is private?" Yet, although people here liked to talk about their neighbors, they were kind and caring to anyone in need. "If you keep on this way, the town will name something after you. You're too young for a statue and besides, you're still alive..." She stopped at Troy's expression, which showed not only embarrassment but verged on annoyance. "Sorry, I was teasing."

"I know, but it bugs me when people make a big deal about me giving to charity. I got lucky in my life so I want to give back. I shouldn't be celebrated for that."

As a ranch hand, Troy had had no reason to be arrogant or pretentious, so Molly hadn't thought his kindness and humble nature were anything special. Now, she knew differently. "I shouldn't have joked. You were always private, and I respect that." She respected him too and, if she wasn't careful, it would be easy for her to fall in love with him again.

"*We* were private." His face was troubled.

As it turned out, that privacy had been for the best because when Molly had left for college, nobody, Troy most of all, had known the heartbreak she'd taken with her.

"What about here?" He stopped near a tall tree. "We have a good view but it's not as crowded."

"Fine with me." Along both sides of High Valley's main street and here in the park, trees and lampposts were strung with holiday lights and decorations. In a few minutes, the town's mayor would say a few words and then Santa would flip a switch to light up the town at this dark time of year. "I came to this event with my parents and brothers when I was small. My dad carried me on his shoulders so I could see everything. Then after Paul passed, we stopped coming. Paul loved holiday lights so being here hurt. Mom and Dad didn't even decorate much at home for a few years."

Troy squeezed her gloved hand. "It must have been so hard for all of you."

"It was and still is in a lot of ways. There are gaps in my family that will never be filled, but we make new memories, right?" She made herself give Troy a bright smile.

"We do but—"

Static crackled and cut off whatever Troy had intended to say. Then the mayor's voice came over a loudspeaker as she welcomed everyone and made a few announcements. Then it was time for the main event. "Now it's my pleasure to invite Santa to turn on the holiday lights for us." She gestured to the jolly man in a red suit and white beard that Molly had spotted strolling along High Valley's main street earlier giving out candy and having photos taken with kids.

"Ho, ho, ho." Santa hopped onto a temporary wooden platform beside the mayor.

"That's... No, it can't be." Molly glanced around. She'd seen

Melissa and Skylar over by the pavilion, but come to think of it Cole hadn't been with them.

"What? Who?" Troy looked around as well.

Molly lowered her voice. "I think that's Cole up there. Rosa's husband usually plays Santa, he's the deputy mayor, but that's not him. And look at how Santa is walking over to the light switch. That's Cole's cowboy gait for sure." She put a hand to her mouth, covering a laugh as Santa bantered with the mayor.

"Wow. Cole's disguised his voice but it's him all right." Troy and Molly chuckled together.

"Shush. We don't want to spoil anything for the kids."

Santa flipped the switch and the park was illuminated with multicolored lights. Then, as Luke Bryan's rendition of "Run Run Rudolph" blasted from the sound system, everyone began to dance. Melissa even jumped up to join Santa while Rosa's husband, who'd stayed behind the other town councillors, extended a hand to the mayor.

"I'm not much of a dancer but shall we?" Troy gave Molly his hand.

"Sure, everyone else is." From couples to families spanning multiple generations, High Valley was in a party mood. Yet, as Molly's hand slipped into Troy's like it belonged there, and he drew her close to him, her laughter stopped. And as they swayed together, her heart caught in her throat.

"Look." Troy gestured with his chin toward the sky.

Molly glanced up. "It's snowing." Fluffy flakes drifted lazily around them, landing on their faces and parkas. The colored lights and smiles in the crowd swirled together as the song changed to Thomas Rhett's "Christmas in the Country."

"Magical, isn't it?" Troy's voice was husky in her ear, and then Molly's head was on his shoulder as she nodded. She loved this song, although when she'd had to work last Christmas and hadn't been able to come home, it had made her cry.

Without her noticing, they'd danced away from the crowd

into what in summer was a small ornamental garden shielded by a high and bushy cedar hedge.

"Troy, I…" The music and crowd noise faded until it was only the two of them.

"May I kiss you?" The softness in his eyes and gentle smile almost undid her, unlocking feelings she'd thought were gone forever.

"This is probably a mistake but…yes," she whispered in response to his question as his lips drew closer.

"You and me were never a mistake."

Then he kissed her, or she kissed him because she didn't know which of them moved first.

"Okay?" He drew back and studied her face.

She nodded, unable to speak. For the first time in years, she was complete and felt like she was where and with the person she was meant to be. Her legs shook, and she held him tight so she wouldn't fall over.

"I tried, Molly. I really did, but I still have feelings for you. I can't help it."

"I can't either. I still have feelings for you too." The intensity of that kiss didn't lie. And after years of being cautious in her dating relationships and never meeting the right guy, maybe now she needed to take a chance.

"Good." He gave her a half smile and then another kiss mixed with a snowflake landed on the end of her nose. "We're adults. We can enjoy each other's company for the next few weeks and see what happens."

"Yes." Molly didn't have any long-term expectations. She was still going back to Atlanta, although right now it might have been Mars for how remote it seemed, but she couldn't plan her whole life. And being an adult meant she knew how to keep herself and her heart safe.

She tilted her head for one more kiss and didn't let herself think about the future or the past. All that mattered was now.

CHAPTER TWELVE

TROY GLANCED AT Molly in the passenger seat of his truck where her blond hair shone in the muted light from the dash. Outside, snow still fell and now covered the two-lane highway that led back to the Tall Grass Ranch.

"The road's getting slippery. Otherwise, I'd hold your hand." Kissing her had been the best and now she seemed too far away. He hadn't planned to kiss her, but when the right moment had presented itself, why not? It was only a kiss. Still, that one kiss had turned into a few more, and when they'd stepped away from each other and returned to the main area of the park, he couldn't pretend that something momentous and maybe even life-changing hadn't happened.

"I'd rather you keep both hands on the wheel than we end up in the ditch." At the warmth and teasing in Molly's voice, Troy's spirits lightened. He'd been afraid she regretted those kisses, but she'd only gotten quiet like she used to.

He chuckled. "Does High Valley still have a towing service?" Forget about the road conditions, he might be on a slipperier slope with Molly than in the truck.

"Yes, Mike's older brother runs it now, but he and his crew will likely be busy in town. Lots of tourists were at the tree lighting, and some of them won't have winter tires on yet.

You'd have better luck calling someone with a tractor." Gazing out the truck window, her eyebrows drew together, and she fidgeted in her seat. "The weather's getting bad. Will you be okay to drive home after dropping me off? I'm sure Zach and Beth would make up a spare bed for you or, if not, there's always space in the bunkhouse."

"That's a good idea. I could ask one of the hands to look after Acorn." Troy peered out the window as well. Even with the truck's high beams, he could hardly see more than a few feet in front of them. "The last time I checked, a storm was forecast but it wasn't supposed to hit until three or four hours after midnight. I'd forgotten how fast winter can blow in out here."

"Me too." When he stole another glance at her, Molly bit her lip. "We had a dusting of snow last night, but this storm's the real deal. What can I do?"

"Look for any landmarks." Maybe they should have stayed in town, but the snow and wind hadn't been bad then. And he'd been so caught up in Molly, Troy hadn't paid attention to anyone, or anything, else or thought to check for an updated weather report. "Do you still have cell service?"

She pulled her phone out of her bag. "A weak signal. I'll text my brothers in our group chat. We—"

The truck veered across the road, and Troy gripped the wheel and steered into the skid. "Hang on." After a few endless seconds, he righted the vehicle.

"Ice?"

He nodded, slowed the vehicle even more and put on the hazard lights. He and Molly were both Montana born. No other words were needed. Ice was dangerous enough on its own, but mixed with heavy snow and high winds, the weather conditions were like driving blind.

Molly pointed her phone's flashlight toward the swirling snow. "We should be close to the ranch by now, but my text didn't go through. Wait, is that a light?"

"Where?"

"There's Bryce's driveway on the right. He's got the porch lights on."

Troy drew in a breath and turned the truck to where he thought the driveway should be.

"Whoa." Molly's voice rang out as the vehicle lurched forward and there was a prolonged crunching and cracking noise before they slid to a stop in a snowdrift.

"Are you okay?" Adrenaline surged through Troy as he hit the emergency brake and then reached for her.

"I'm fine. What about you?"

"Fine." Except for feeling like a fool. He squeezed her gloved hand. "I'm so sorry. I'd never do anything to put you in danger and—"

"In this weather, it could have happened to anyone." Although her words were reassuring, was that laughter in Molly's voice? "You missed the ditch, but I think you hit the mailbox and the shelter Bryce built for Paisley and Cam to wait for the school bus."

Way to go, Clayton. This situation was embarrassing enough without him having destroyed Carter property. Troy released the brake, shifted gears and pumped the accelerator to try to reverse the truck, but they were stuck. He leaned his head on the steering wheel and accidentally hit the horn.

"Troy, it's…" Molly's voice shook.

Was she laughing or crying? He raised his head. She was laughing, but was it because she was in shock? "Molly, I swear this was an accident. I'll talk to Bryce and pay for the damage I've caused and—"

"I know. It's okay." She gulped. "Only in Montana. The two of us should have known better."

Answering laughter rose up in Troy's chest. "You're sure you're okay?"

"Absolutely."

"We'll have a funny story to tell one day." He took her hand again and tenderness washed over him. He wanted it to be a story they told to their family and friends, children and then grandchildren. Laughing at themselves, but laughing together as they were now. No matter what happened, Molly put Troy at ease and made everything better. What would it be like to go through his life with her by his side? "Molly, I—"

Someone banged on the outside of the truck, and a beam of light shone through Molly's window. She yanked her hand away.

"It's Bryce," she said shakily.

Although Troy appreciated the help, he wished it hadn't been one of Molly's brothers. "Can you get your door open?"

"I think so." Molly pushed on her door until it opened part-way and then swung her legs out of the truck's cab.

"I've got you, Mol." In a parka and snow pants and with his face almost obscured by a hat and scarf, Bryce half carried his sister to what must be the laneway before returning to the truck.

As Troy shut off the vehicle and slid across the bench seat to exit the truck in his turn, another beam of light almost blinded him. "I'm sorry. Before I knew it, we were sliding and—"

"Molly told me." Bryce lowered the flashlight, and Troy blinked. "All that matters is the two of you are safe." He gave Troy a hand to help him over a snowdrift and shut the truck door. A small smile played around his mouth. "We needed a new mailbox anyway. As for the school bus shelter?" The smile broadened, and Troy breathed easier. "I should warn you my daughter will try to negotiate for a fancier replacement than that wooden shed I knocked together."

"No problem." Troy followed the path cast by Bryce's flash-light as they rejoined Molly and waded through snow to the house. "Whatever you all want, I'll cover it."

"Good. You're off the road so we can get the tractor and pull your truck out in the morning." Bryce sobered. "As for the rest of it..." He paused as they reached his front porch.

"What do you say we keep whatever's going on with you two between ourselves?"

"There's nothing going on." Molly stopped, and her gaze caught Troy's.

Bryce chuckled as he looked between them. "I wasn't born yesterday. It's your business, but I hope you know what you're doing." Then he opened his front door, and Carrie greeted them with blankets, hot cocoa and insisted they stay the night—Molly in the guest room and Troy on a pullout sofa in the family room.

An hour later, after he'd called one of his ranch hands to see to Acorn and once the house was quiet, Troy stretched out on the sofa, warm and cozy as snow still fell heavily outside. Yet, Bryce's warning echoed in his head. He didn't know what he was doing and maybe Molly didn't either, but it sure felt good.

Perhaps, and for now, that was enough.

AT CARRIE'S FARMHOUSE the next day, where Joy and Shane were living while their own house was being built, Joy stored her empty suitcase in the bedroom closet.

"I think that's everything unpacked. I appreciate you coming to help, honey." She glanced at Molly, who sat on the dressing table bench by the window. "I'm sure it won't take long for me to feel at home here, but right now, it's all new and strange."

Joy had lived at the Tall Grass Ranch for more than forty years. In the past few weeks, everything in her life had changed, from a different view beyond her bedroom window to a kitchen she was still finding her way around to getting used to being married to Shane.

"You're happy, right?" Molly set out toiletries on top of the dressing table with her back to Joy.

"Yes." So happy Joy was almost afraid to say so out loud, afraid she'd jinx this unexpected later-in-life love that had blessed her beyond her greatest imaginings. "I'm getting used to Shane's habits as he is to mine. Our honeymoon was wonderful, but I must say I'm glad to be home." Not that Carrie's farm was home yet, but as soon as the plane's wheels had touched down in Montana, Joy had been home in the way that counted the most.

"That's great, Mom." Molly put Joy's jewelry roll in one of the dressing table's drawers, the only piece of furniture Joy had kept from her old bedroom because it had been her mother's.

"So, what's going on here? Tell me all the news." Joy patted the cushioned window seat that overlooked a snow-covered pasture.

"Nothing much. You've probably already heard most of it from Rosa." Molly padded across the carpeted floor in her sock feet, joined Joy on the window seat and sat cross-legged.

"I sure heard about Cole stepping in to play Santa at the tree lighting. Rosa said her husband thought it was time for someone new to take over, but who would have thought it would be Cole? Certainly not me." Which showed Joy that no matter how old they were, her kids could still surprise her. "How are you doing, Jellybean?" Something was different about Molly and although Joy didn't have proof, from what Rosa had said, she suspected it had something to do with Troy.

"I'm fine." Her daughter's smile was innocent, but a faint pink tinted her cheeks.

"I bumped into Troy at the Bluebunch earlier. I thanked him for looking out for you the night of the storm." Joy gazed out the window at the snowy fields and the ridge of low hills behind Carrie's house. She wouldn't ask a direct question, but it didn't do any harm to lead the conversation in a way that might get her daughter to open up.

"Mom, you didn't have to. I'm a grown woman. Troy and I looked out for each other." Molly fiddled with a curtain tie, and the pink in her face deepened.

"That's what he said, although he seemed keen to emphasize it was him, not you, who'd hit Bryce and Carrie's mailbox and bus shelter." Joy suppressed a smile. Troy had been so embarrassed it was both awkward and sweet and that, more than anything, told her he had feelings for Molly. "I won't interfere but from what I've seen, you and Troy might have something more than a working relationship. He's a good man and—"

"Oh, Mom." Molly dropped her head into her hands. "I don't know what to do. I never told you, but Troy and I were involved before, the summer after I finished high school. We broke up before I left for college but now... I guess you never forget your first love." Her laugh had a hollow sound.

Joy's heart pinched. "You don't, but..." Her words trailed off as she studied Molly's bent head. Joy had married her own first love, Dennis, so who was she to advise? However, now she loved Shane too, so she knew you could have more than one love in a lifetime. "Back then, I suspected you and Troy had feelings for each other. But because of how things were between you and me, I didn't want to say anything. It was hard." How hard, Joy had never told anyone, not even Rosa. "And when you came home for Thanksgiving and Christmas, it seemed like you were avoiding me."

"I wasn't, not really, but those things were hard for me too."

"It's okay, I understand." Finally, she and Molly were talking honestly with each other, and Joy didn't want to mess anything up. "I knew you needed to become your own person, and separating from me was part of growing up." However, in the intervening years, Joy had wondered if she'd ever get her daughter back and have the closeness they'd once shared.

"I thought if I told you about Troy, you'd be upset. You wanted me to go to college and do all the things you never had a chance to. I also wanted to go to college for myself. So, with Troy, it was only a summer thing. I never forgot him, though, and when I came back here in October, seeing him again stirred up all sorts of feelings." Molly finally raised her head and tears pooled in her eyes.

"Oh, honey." Joy hugged her daughter, and Molly snuggled close like she'd done as a little girl. "All I want for you, all I ever wanted, was for you to be happy. I'll be okay with whatever that happiness means to you. It's wonderful having you home and—"

"You'd like me to stay." Molly's voice was flat.

"Of course, but I know it's not that simple. From the time you were in grade school, you wanted to live in a city. Your dad and I had a lot of time to accept you'd be leaving the ranch. We never tried to stop you either and now you're thriving. You did so well in college and grad school and you have a great career waiting for you. You've only gotten started on that journey." Joy hesitated. "When you tell me about going to shows and parties with friends, I'm glad. You deserve to have fun and get all dressed up to go to fancy events in style." There had been times when Joy had imagined that kind of life and now, with Shane, she'd have it. Still, she'd loved her years on the ranch with Dennis and their family. "I see why you're torn. I like Troy, but when you go back to Atlanta one or both of you could be hurt."

"We're realistic so nobody will get hurt. Whatever's between us isn't serious." Molly stuck her chin out.

So they did have a relationship now, one that was new and fragile. Joy stopped herself from saying something that might push Molly away again. "Even so, there's Troy's investment in Cole's business to consider. I have to look out for all my children. If Troy were to pull out of that deal, Cole would be devastated. He's finally happy and settled and his stock contracting venture has only just begun to turn a profit." Joy patted Molly's back before her daughter straightened and brushed away the tears.

"I'd never do anything to put Cole's business at risk. Besides, Troy's smart. He knows he's made a good investment, and the money he loaned Cole is separate from anything to do with us. Not that there is an *us*, not really. You don't have anything to worry about." Molly's smile was forced.

"I hope you're right, but I'm always here if you need to talk or…anything." Joy stuttered to a stop and clasped her hands together. There wasn't a map for this stage of the parenting journey, but the one thing Joy knew, had learned with Zach, Cole and Bryce, was that she had to respect her adult kids' boundaries. Although she still wanted to protect them like when they were small, she couldn't. So, somehow she had to find the right balance, which was different for each of them.

"Thanks, Mom." Molly stood and smoothed her pretty hair. "I'd appreciate it if this conversation could stay between us. I don't want my brothers to get involved. Well, Bryce already suspects, but it's private."

"Of course." Joy stood and followed Molly to the bedroom door as her daughter's cell phone chirped.

"Oh, that's Troy. I need to call him. I'll meet you in the kitchen in a few minutes. We can unpack your last boxes, at least the ones you moved here and aren't storing until the new house is ready. I'm glad you brought Grandma's dishes. They'll look great in that glass-fronted cupboard." Molly took her phone out of the back pocket of her jeans and went to the open area at the end of the upstairs hall where Joy planned to set up her sewing machine and craft table.

As she went down the stairs to the kitchen, Molly's soft voice reached her, the words inaudible, but their warmth and affection unmistakable.

Despite her daughter's reassurances, Joy *did* have something to worry about. But like with all her kids, she had to trust Molly to figure things out for herself—and only give a nudge when, or if, it was needed.

Joy had her own new life to focus on. The back door swung open, and Shane came in stamping fluffy snow off his boots. He hung his parka on a hook in the mudroom, then stepped into the kitchen with a grin. He opened his arms to her, and Joy went into them.

And as she wrapped her arms around her husband, she willed herself to focus on the happiness she had rather than worry about a future that might never happen.

CHAPTER THIRTEEN

"SHE'S GORGEOUS." From across the paddock fence at the horse rescue, Molly patted Cara, the fourteen-year-old bay mare Troy had brought her to visit. "You've seen her vet records?"

"Yes, and everything health-wise looks good. The staff here hasn't seen any behavioral problems with her either." Troy stood across the fence from Molly, next to Cara. He gave Molly a lopsided grin. "It's my fourth visit here. Cara started off as a show horse and then became a companion animal. When her owner had medical and financial issues and couldn't keep her any longer, Cara came to live here. The staff promised they'd find her a loving home."

"She seems like a sweetheart. Friendly and easy to catch and lead. Have you tried grooming her yet?" From what Molly had seen, Cara would make a wonderful family horse. She listened well, appeared eager to please and as a Morgan she'd be versatile, as good with beginners as with more experienced riders. If Molly was setting up her own barn, Cara would be a perfect choice.

"No grooming yet. Since she's already tacked up, why don't you come into the paddock and see how she handles?" Troy's expression was boyish and here, twenty miles north of High Valley, he was more like the ranch hand Molly remembered.

"Okay." Molly had stayed on the other side of the fence to keep her distance from Troy, not Cara. Her lips still tingled at the memory of those life-changing, earth-shattering kisses the night of the tree lighting ceremony. While she wanted to kiss him again, her mom's gentle warning brought some of Molly's own doubts to the fore. Yet, when Troy had texted and asked her to come and see Cara, it had been impossible to resist spending more time with him.

She climbed the paddock fence and hopped to the ground on the other side like she'd done as a kid. She rode sometimes at a horse barn in Atlanta. There, she'd have used the gate, but the place had antique chandeliers hanging from skylights and custom leather seats in the tack room. The only time most of its clientele scaled fences was atop eye-wateringly expensive horses on a show jumping course. "Hey, Cara. You're so pretty. Are you going to show me what you can do?"

The horse studied her and then, as if deciding Molly was someone she could trust, nudged her hand. "She's between fifteen and sixteen hands?" Molly dug in her pocket for one of the treats she'd stashed there earlier. She assessed Cara from all angles, giving the mare a chance to get to know and feel comfortable with her.

"You still have a good eye. According to her vet records, she's fifteen two." Troy's expression was approving. "Do you want to ride her? She was fine with me on my last visit, but I'd like to see how she responds to a woman."

"Sure." Before Molly returned to Montana, it had been at least six months since she'd made it out to that equestrian center in Atlanta. But even on the rare times she'd ridden there, it hadn't been the same. She might have adjusted to an English instead of a Western saddle, but it wasn't home so she hadn't felt comfortable.

She donned the riding helmet Troy handed her, and then he gave her a boost onto Cara's back. She settled and rubbed the horse's sleek neck.

"You okay up there?" Troy shaded his eyes against the bright sunshine that reflected off the white snow. Fine lines that hadn't been there before gave his face both maturity and character.

It was a face Molly could still let herself love and, as she eased Cara into a walk, she drew in a shaky breath. "I'm great." With Cara's reins between her hands, a saddle beneath her seat and Troy walking alongside, happiness surged through Molly. Despite the frosty weather, she was warm and cozy and, if she hadn't been on horseback, she might have jumped for sheer joy. No matter her conflicted feelings for Troy, she loved Montana and she'd missed both the place and times like this one.

"You sure look great." Troy's voice was husky.

"So do you." His hair, which had grown a bit longer, stuck out from under his cowboy hat. And in his worn jeans and winter barn jacket, against the backdrop of this big and rugged landscape, he looked like he belonged here.

Maybe she did too. As she settled into the saddle, they smiled at each other, and Troy raised one of his hands to hers. For a moment, as their gloved palms connected, a different kind of warmth, electric rather than cozy, surged through Molly and left her breathless. When he took his hand away, she fumbled with Cara's reins. "Want to see her trot?"

"I'd like to see both of you trot." While Troy's eyes and expression teased her, the faint flush on his cheeks wasn't only from the cold weather, suggesting he was as attracted to her as Molly was to him.

Molly laughed and, as Cara turned her head as if to ask what was funny, she encouraged the horse from a walk to a trot. Cara made the transition seamlessly, and Molly patted the horse's neck before waving at Troy who now stood by the fence to watch.

Molly didn't only feel happy. She also felt content, as if life had brought her almost full circle back to Montana and this man, where she'd always been meant to be.

"WHAT DO YOU think of this dark red one?" In the middle of a display of sofas at a furniture store in the nearest big town to High Valley, Troy turned to Molly. He'd taken a rare day off work and didn't want his time with her to end. After visiting the horse rescue, he'd asked her to check out living room furniture with him.

"I like it. Since it's modular it will be more versatile." With her hands on her hips, Molly considered the one they'd both looked at first and had then come back to.

Troy dragged his attention away from the rosy curve of Molly's lips and back to the sofa. "What do you mean?"

He'd never been big on shopping, preferring to either buy online or get in and out of a store as fast as possible. Being here with Molly, though, was different, and he saw the sense of taking the time to pick out something that would suit both his house and his life. It was also fun to watch her consider the different pieces of furniture, wave away the sales guy and instead guide Troy through what was to him a bewildering maze of styles, upholstery choices, arm height and trim.

"Modular means it comes in different pieces, and you can arrange them in different ways or even add parts later. You could use this sofa all together in your living room or have a smaller piece in another room. This one doesn't have a pull-out bed, but it's a lot like the sofa you slept on at Bryce and Carrie's the night of the snowstorm, remember?"

How could Troy forget? He couldn't stop thinking about that night. Kissing Molly, enjoying each other's company like they used to and then laughing together when he'd missed Bryce's driveway and driven into a snowbank. Some women would have mocked him, but Molly had seen the funny side and her good humor had lessened Troy's embarrassment. Then, as now, he wanted to throw caution to the wind and ask her to stay here so they could be with each other forever.

"This smaller piece would fit in what used to be the parlor. Acorn and I like to watch movies in there." Since Cathy had repainted the room for him, it was snug and inviting. Troy could imagine Molly curled up next to him on this sofa with a bowl of popcorn and mugs of cocoa.

"Nice. This piece has been pretreated with an upholstery protector so if you spill anything, the stain will come out." Molly grinned as she pointed to a label attached to one of the sofa's arms.

"How do you know all this stuff?" Troy understood complex computer coding, but this world was alien.

"I worked in a hardware store part-time in college. It also had a furniture and appliance department, and I sometimes had to cover that area."

"You must have been their top salesperson." Troy sat on one end of the sofa and patted the space next to him. "Come on. Try it out with me."

Molly hesitated and then sat where he'd indicated. "Working in the hardware part of the store reminded me of the ranch. After my brothers left home, I worked with my dad. He taught me how to shingle a roof, build a chicken coop and do rudimentary plumbing. If your toilet ever backs up, I'm your woman. I've saved lots of money over the years doing repairs myself."

"I used to work alongside my dad as well. Those were good times." Nowadays, Troy missed working with his hands and although he'd hired Cathy to paint several rooms, part of him wanted to grab a brush and join her. "Coincidentally, my dad has a part-time job in a hardware store in San Francisco. He loves it."

"He told me about that job." As Molly shifted on the sofa, her thigh brushed against Troy's and even that brief touch made his breath catch. "Your folks and Sara are great."

"Like you are with your family we've always been close."
Although Troy loved High Valley, he missed having his folks
nearby.

Molly's smile faded and she stood, putting more space between them. "So, are you going to buy this sofa?" She inclined
her head toward the middle-aged sales guy who hovered at
a distance. "If you want, I'll negotiate to try to get you free
delivery and maybe even one of these small end tables." She
rubbed the scratch on a table displayed by the sofa. "A bit of
sandpaper and stain would fix up this beauty in no time, but
they can't sell it as is, at least not for full price."

"I could use you on my team. I mean my work sales team,
not at the ranch, although you'd be terrific there." His tongue
tripped over the words. The more he said, the worse it sounded.

"It's okay. I know what you meant." Molly's eyes twinkled.
"Not having money has taught me to be financially savvy. I
guess it's become a way of life."

"Even when you have money, it's still good to pay attention
to what things cost." Troy had worked hard for his success, and
he'd never spend recklessly or risk losing the security money
gave him. "I like the sofa so go for it."

As Molly spoke to the sales guy, who introduced himself as
Mark, Troy watched with both amusement and awe. Like most
people, he wanted to get a good deal, but since the sofa was
already on sale, it wouldn't have occurred to him to bargain.
Along with free delivery and the damaged table, Molly also
got him a coupon for a discount on any future purchase over
two hundred dollars—which he'd use because Troy's house
was still half empty.

Troy thanked Mark as he rang up the purchase.

"Don't thank me. Thank your wife." Mark smiled before
glancing at Molly, who'd wandered over to the recliner section
and was now chatting with a white-haired woman.

"She's not my wife. Just a friend." Troy rushed to clarify.

"Too bad, buddy, she's a keeper." Mark shook his head. "A

woman like her is one in a million. I should know. I've been married to one of my own for almost twenty-five years."

As he put his credit card and the store coupon in his wallet, Troy's good mood evaporated. "I'll be back here for sure. I moved onto a ranch near High Valley in October."

"Nice area. My mom grew up around there."

"Definitely a nice area. Thanks again!" Troy waved at Molly, hoping she'd understand the urgency of his gesture. In small-town and rural Montana, the usual "six degrees of separation" was more like one or two. Mark's mother was undoubtedly related to someone who knew Troy or Molly, and news the two of them had been furniture shopping would make it back to town before they did. And with each retelling, the story would be embellished until they hadn't only bought a sofa but an entire primary bedroom suite because they were planning a Christmas wedding.

"All set?" Molly rejoined them. "Mrs. Klein over there is looking for an ottoman to match her recliner. Since you were busy, I made a few suggestions." She grinned at Mark. "She's from High Valley and knows your mom and mine."

Mark grinned back while also giving Troy a sideways glance. "A keeper, remember?"

"Yeah." As Troy shepherded Molly out of the store, he was torn between laughter and embarrassment.

"What did he mean about a keeper?" Molly's expression was curious.

"He was talking about the sofa. That it would last me a long time." Troy improvised before laughter won out. "Folks in High Valley will likely find out we've been shopping for furniture together."

"I guess I've lived away too long." As they reached Troy's truck, the embarrassment Troy had felt was mirrored on Molly's face. "Roots still run deep here. We may have some explaining to do, but I'll set anyone straight who asks." Her smile was rueful.

Which was what Troy would do too so why did he have a brief pang of regret? "As long as we're on a roll, why don't we give people something to really talk about?" They both knew it was a bit of fun, so the excitement coursing through Troy was only because he liked a good joke.

"Meaning?" Her eyes twinkled, and when Troy opened the passenger door for her, Molly hopped in. "Troy?"

Her jeans seemed to make her legs longer, and she looked good up there in his truck. "Oh, right." He went around and climbed into his own seat and started the vehicle. "I could either take you right back to the Tall Grass, or since Zach mentioned the youth hockey team he coaches is playing an early game, we could stop by the arena. Get something to eat at the concession stand and cheer on the team." His breath quickened as he waited for her to answer. It wouldn't be fancy, but unlike the tree lighting and going to look at a horse and then furniture, it was definitely a date.

He knew it and, by the way she tilted her head and smoothed her hair, Molly did as well.

"Sure, that sounds fun. Zach will be happy to have us there supporting him and the kids." Her voice was light but as Troy let the truck idle, she reached out and covered his free hand with one of hers. "I know we can't get serious, but I want to spend time with you. Let's make whatever moments we have together count."

Troy nodded and a lump rose in his throat. Those moments were going by too fast. What would he do when none of them were left?

CHAPTER FOURTEEN

"GO, GRIZZLY BEARS!" At Molly's side in High Valley's ice arena, Troy jumped to his feet and cheered as one of the players on Zach's team scored a goal. "Great shot! Way to go, Wyatt!"

"I didn't know you were such a big hockey fan." Molly finished her burger, which tasted just like she remembered.

"I wanted to play when I was a kid, but with all the equipment, registration fees and travel to away games, youth hockey's expensive. I had one season where I learned the basics of the game and worked on skating, but after that my folks couldn't afford to keep me in the program. I played soccer instead and ran track in high school." He shrugged as if it didn't matter, but in his expression Molly saw the disappointed boy he'd once been. "Wyatt is Cathy's older son. I've hired him to do odd jobs around the ranch when Cathy's working at the house. He's a good kid. I talked to Zach about him and well… I wanted to do what I could so Wyatt could play with the other guys his age." Troy's face reddened. "Let's keep that between us, okay?"

"Sure." Molly's heart squeezed.

Troy gathered up their empty food containers. "Chance, Cathy's younger boy, is more into music and academics than sports. He's a math whiz and made it into the state round of a middle school competition in Billings in March. Wyatt's going to hang out with me when his mom and Chance are away for those two days."

Without Troy saying a word, Molly knew that along with Wyatt's hockey equipment, he had something to do with covering Cathy and Chance's travel costs. "You're a good man, Troy Clayton, and those boys and their mom are lucky to have you in their lives."

"It's me who's the lucky one. The three of them are my family here." He put a paper bag with their garbage and recyclables under his seat. "Speaking of family, I mentioned Pete to you before, right? He's my business partner and closest friend, and he's going to be here for a couple days this week. We'll be working nonstop, but you might see us around town." The pink on Troy's face intensified. "If he was going to be here longer, I'd invite you over to meet him. And Cole, of course."

"Of course." If they were a real couple, Troy would want her to meet his friends, but since they weren't, and even if he and Pete had time, it would be a business instead of personal get-together.

"Pete lives in Texas, so you'd think he'd know about ranching and cowboys, but he doesn't. He grew up in Florida and since moving to Austin, unless he's flying somewhere else, I don't think he ever ventures much beyond the city limits." Troy gave Molly a teasing grin. "He's a city guy like you're a city girl."

"I'm..." Molly stopped as Troy jumped to his feet again when the Grizzly Bears scored another goal. "That's it, guys!" Despite a pang of sympathy for the opposing team's goalie, who sprawled in the crease with his head in his hands, Molly clapped and cheered with the rest of the hometown crowd, most of whom she recognized at least by sight.

She'd almost told Troy she wasn't sure if she was truly a city girl, but she wasn't entirely a ranch and country girl either. So, what did that make her? Confused and torn between two places that in different ways were both her home.

The buzzer rang to signal the end of the game, and they began to gather their things. Molly folded the blanket they'd brought from Troy's truck to keep warm. It was so cold in the arena she hadn't even unzipped her parka and had only removed her gloves to eat. That was small-town hockey and once, when she hadn't known any different, she'd assumed all arenas were like the one here.

"Hey, Molly. You didn't say you'd be at tonight's game." Cole stopped by their seats. Bryce appeared behind him with Paisley, Cam and Skylar in tow. "If we'd known, you and Troy could have sat with us."

"Coming here was sort of...spur of the moment."

"Carrie's away for a rodeo, and Melissa had a work dinner, so we brought the whole crew." Bryce glanced between Troy and Molly, and a small smile tugged at his mouth. "Mom and Shane were supposed to be here, but they stayed with Beth. She wasn't feeling so good, and Ellie had a sleepover at a friend's. Zach didn't want to leave Beth alone when he had to coach." Bryce waved at Zach, who was still behind the home team's bench talking to his assistant coach and several players.

"I told Beth to call me if she ever needs anything. For a mom-to-be, no question or concern is too small." Molly wrapped her scarf around her neck. "That goes for the rest of you too."

"It's fantastic to have a nurse in the family." Cole fell into step with Molly as they made their way as a group to the arena exit. "I'm having this twinge in my right knee. I wondered if—"

"You've had that 'twinge' since your last rodeo accident, and your excellent physical therapist is already taking care of it." Molly gave him a playful swat. "Unless it's an emergency, I don't treat family members, I only answer questions."

"Don't the new accessible seats look good?" Since Zach

wasn't with them, Bryce assumed the role of family peace-maker and diverted the conversation. He pointed to a reserved row on the arena's main level. "The Sunflower Sisterhood worked hard to raise money for them, and Mom says they've only gotten started. The next time you're home, I bet you'll see even more changes here, Mol."

"By this spring, my business will have really taken off," Cole added. "I've got a bunch of new rodeo contacts lined up, Cupid did his job and everything's looking good."

"Skylar and me are gonna compete in more horse shows after Christmas," Paisley said. "We want to win lots of rib-bons."

Cam slipped one of his hands into Molly's. "You'll miss seeing us in the spring school play. I'm a villager. My teacher says that's someone who lives in a place even smaller than High Valley. Paisley and Skylar are stars in the sky, and they get to sing a song."

"That sounds great." Molly squeezed Cam's hand. "I'm sorry to miss it, but I'll see all of you in the Sunday school Christmas Eve pageant."

"We'll send Molly lots of pictures from the play and Car-rie will video tape it," Bryce said with a quick look at Troy, who'd so far stayed silent.

Molly wasn't leaving until after the new year, but her fam-ily was already anticipating when she'd be gone. "And we can have video calls all the time." Except they weren't like being in the same place as people you loved. She manufactured a smile before Cam went ahead with his sister and Skylar. "Maybe you guys can visit me in Atlanta."

"Maybe." Bryce's smile was wistful. "It's a long trip, though, and with Carrie's rodeo schedule and the kids and the ranch, it's not easy to get away. Our honeymoon will be our biggest trip for quite a while."

They exited the arena into the parking lot, Molly said good-bye to her family, shivered and pulled her hat farther down over her ears. One thing she didn't miss about Montana was the winters.

"Are you cold?"

Molly nodded and tried to keep her teeth from chattering.

As they rounded the corner of the arena building, Troy held her close, his big body sheltering her from the worst of the blustery wind. "It was fun to see your family. Did you hear Paisley and Skylar telling me knock-knock jokes? Those girls are hilarious."

Molly hadn't because she'd been talking to her brothers and then Cam, but Troy was good with children, and they responded to his interest and attention. "Until I went to college, it used to bug me I couldn't go anywhere around here without bumping into someone I'm related to. Now I realize how lucky I am." She stopped by Troy's truck and looked at the clear, starlit sky.

"Are you making a wish?" Troy opened the truck door for her.

"I should. There's sure enough stars up there to wish on." Her pulse raced, and she had a new appreciation for this wonderful world and everything in it.

"Do you remember when we wished on a star?" His voice was low, and his warm breath brushed her cheeks.

Tongue-tied, she nodded and then clambered into the truck. As he closed her door and came around the vehicle to his side, memories flooded through her. That July night by the creek behind the ranch, they'd each wished on the brightest star they could find and then kissed and said they'd love each other forever.

"What did you wish for?" Troy started the truck to warm up the vehicle.

"I don't remember." She did, but she wouldn't tell him then or now.

"Well, I hope your wish came true." This part of the parking lot was mostly empty, and with the darkness outside, the truck's cab was like cocoon. "Mine didn't, at least not yet, but I can still hope."

At the warmth and yearning in his eyes, and gentle smile that had always turned her insides to mush, Molly's breath caught. Had he wished for what she had?

"Aww, Mol." He leaned close and his lips brushed hers in a kiss that was slow, sweet and soft. A reminder of their past and, if she still believed in wishes, maybe even a promise for the future.

She'd told her mom there was nothing to worry about, but as Molly returned Troy's kiss, she knew she'd been wrong. Spending time with Troy, and these achingly gentle but oh-so-meaningful kisses, didn't only risk Molly's heart but also her soul.

With each passing day, she was more torn between wanting to stay here and give her relationship with Troy a real chance or going back to Atlanta like she'd planned. And no amount of wishing on stars would give her the answer she needed.

"SO THAT'S DOWNTOWN High Valley." On Wednesday, Troy stepped out of the Bluebunch Café with Pete and gestured to the town's wide main street.

"It's picturesque. I'd like to bring my family back in the summer, but I still don't understand how you can live here." Bundled up in a scarf, hat and too big parka he'd borrowed from Troy, only Pete's eyes and a narrow strip of his face showed.

"It's home." Those two simple words meant so much. No matter where Troy went in the world, this corner of Montana would always call him back.

"Where's that craft place you mentioned?" Pete looked toward the distant mountain range and then back to the windswept street. "I'd like to buy a few presents for Tina and the kids. Get a start on my holiday shopping."

"The Medicine Wheel Craft Center is just across the street,

but when have you ever started holiday shopping before December 23?" Troy led them to Rosa's store.

"Since I married Tina, and she showed me the benefits of thinking—and shopping—ahead." On the other side of the street, Pete turned in a slow circle. "Wow. This town sure goes all out for the holidays." He gestured to what had to be a seven-foot-high candy cane hanging from one of the Victorian-style lampposts that lined both sides of High Valley Avenue.

"The town council likes to aim high. Halloween, Thanksgiving and Christmas are all a big deal here. It's a fun way of bringing people together. Tourists enjoy it as well. Or so I've heard," he added since Pete stared at him with raised eyebrows.

"I don't know what it is, bro, but something about you is different. You're more..." He paused as Troy opened the craft center door and they went inside into the warmth. "Chill maybe." Pete took of his gloves and rubbed his hands together. "Whatever it is, it suits you."

"Thanks, I think." Troy tried to joke but except for his family, Pete knew him better than anyone. While Troy didn't think he was different, maybe High Valley had changed him. "What do you want to look at first? I remember Tina likes pottery so there's a big display—"

"Troy?" Molly's voice stopped him.

"Hey. I'm... This is..." In dark jeans, trendy boots and a fuzzy white sweater patterned with cheerful reindeer, Molly was both cute and beautiful, and for a moment he was lost for words.

"You must be Troy's business partner. I'm Molly Carter. Troy invested in my brother's stock contracting operation." She held out a hand to Pete with a friendly smile.

"Yeah, I'm Pete Wong. Nice to meet you. Troy mentioned your brother. We're both diversifying our individual portfolios by investing in smaller businesses." After smiling back at Molly, Pete glanced at Troy and along with a knowing look, his dark brown eyes twinkled.

Troy knew that twinkle. It was the "there's something going on here you haven't told me about, but I'll find out later" expression. However, unlike in business, this time it was personal.

"Welcome to the Medicine Wheel Craft Center." Rosa appeared at Molly's side and introduced herself. "How can we help?"

We? Troy looked from Molly to Rosa.

Molly grinned. "I'm helping Rosa today because she's got some big holiday orders to finish, and her usual part-timer is sick." She turned the full beam of her gorgeous smile on Pete. "Troy said something about pottery. If you're interested, we have a range of items from mugs to larger serving bowls, all made locally."

As Pete followed Molly to the display, Rosa touched Troy's arm. "If Molly hadn't gone into nursing, she could have made a fortune in sales." She clamped her lips together briefly as if holding back a laugh. "I wanted to pay her for her time today, but she said she was happy to volunteer. She always was a kind girl. Can I show you anything? I've got some new silver and moonstone jewelry in. Molly admired a bear paw necklace earlier. Come, I'll show it to you."

"But…" Troy stuttered. He had to get control of himself. As Rosa led him over to the jewelry near the cash register, he tried to explain himself. "I'm not looking for a gift for Molly, but maybe for my sister or my mom for Christmas."

"Of course." Rosa opened the glass display case.

At the other side of the craft center, Molly had moved on from pottery to telling Pete about dream catchers and children's beading kits.

"Here's the necklace Molly likes." Rosa lowered her voice. "The blue matches her eyes, don't you think?"

It did, but Troy wasn't about to admit that to Rosa. A small blue stone sat in the center of a miniature silver bear paw, and while Rosa told him about the artist who'd made it, Troy's thoughts wandered. He'd never given jewelry to a woman he wasn't related to. But Molly wasn't just any woman. She was his friend, and this pendant would be a memory of going to the hockey game to see the Grizzly Bears play.

"I'll take it." He glanced over his shoulder to make sure Molly was out of earshot. "Could you wrap it for me as well?"

"Of course." Rosa leaned across the counter and her voice dropped to a whisper. "If you want it to be a surprise, I can set it aside for you to pick up later."

"That's great. I'd also like those green beaded earrings for my sister, and the white-and-blue bracelet for my mom." He pointed.

"I made those pieces myself. If the bracelet doesn't fit, tell your mom to bring it in the next time she's here and I'll alter it." Rosa tucked the earrings and bracelet beneath the counter with Molly's necklace. "It's like old times having Molly in town. She was a lovely girl and she's grown up to be a fine woman. I often wonder if she'd decide to settle here…if she met the right person."

"She seems happy in Atlanta." Troy spoke around what felt like a marble at the back of his throat.

"There are different kinds of happiness. What makes you happy at one point in your life might change. No, I can take your payment later." Rosa waved away Troy's credit card. "You came back here. Molly could do the same."

"I doubt it." He shook his head.

"But the two of you are good together."

Troy liked and respected Rosa. He might have told someone else it was none of their business, but Rosa was different. Along with Joy, she was like a town mom. "You shouldn't listen to gossip." He gave her a rueful smile.

"I don't." Rosa's voice was tart. "But I can't help seeing what's in front of me. You should do the same."

Pete trotted up to them, saving him from having to answer

Rosa. Molly followed with one of the craft center's wicker shopping baskets piled high.

"Thanks to Molly, I've done most of my holiday shopping. They can also ship a box to me, so I don't have to carry a bunch of things on the plane." Pete beamed. "I even got a baby blanket for my cousin, and she's not due until February. Molly's amazing."

"She sure is." Troy made himself join in the easy banter. Molly *was* amazing, and the more time he spent with her, the more he knew that she was everything he wanted in a woman now and forever. However, he couldn't let himself fall in love with her again, and not only because she was leaving High Valley soon.

She'd broken his trust, and his heart, once. Now, despite all his good intentions, he was giving her a chance to do it again.

CHAPTER FIFTEEN

"SINCE ZACH CAN'T be here, I appreciate you coming with me to this checkup." As they entered the lobby of the county hospital, Beth's face above her burgundy maternity parka was pale.

"I'm happy to be here." Waiting in front of the bank of elevators, Molly gave her sister-in-law's arm an encouraging squeeze. "It's nice to be in a hospital again."

"Nice isn't the word I'd use." Beth's voice was small. "I'd rather see my ob-gyn in her regular office. Being here reminds me of visiting Ellie's mom before she passed. She was so sick and I… Let's say hospitals aren't my favorite place."

"I understand and I'm sorry. I didn't think." Molly's voice softened in sympathy. She'd never want to hurt or upset Beth. They moved into an elevator, and Molly pressed one of the floor buttons. "All I meant is I miss nursing, and since I've spent a lot of time working in hospitals this one feels familiar." It had been built after she left for college, replacing an older hospital in town. Although smaller, it was as modern as those in Atlanta and, judging from the range of clinics listed on the main floor noticeboard, was a medical hub for the area. "Try to relax. You haven't had any unusual or concerning symptoms, have you?"

"To me, everything about pregnancy is unusual and concerning," Beth said as they left the elevator and walked toward the maternity assessment clinic where her doctor worked two days a week. "Maybe if I'd gotten pregnant for the first time in my twenties, it would be different but I'm in my late thirties. Whenever anyone describes me as at an 'advanced maternal age' I worry."

"I get that, but you're doing all the right things and you've had a normal pregnancy so far." Molly paused to give Beth a quick hug. "I also hear you have a great doctor, so you and the baby are in good hands. And Zach—"

"Is more worried than me. I'm the one trying to calm him down. He's upset about not being able to come with me today, but maybe it's for the best. Last time, he started talking about stages of calving and asked if it would be the same for me."

Molly laughed. "That's a ranch husband for you."

"I know and I wouldn't change him. He loves me and wants to help but sometimes…" Beth rolled her eyes and laughed too.

Beth checked in with the receptionist and was ushered into the exam area right away. Molly took a seat in the spacious and welcoming waiting room. The off-white walls and soft lighting were soothing, and combined with comfortable furniture in blues and greens, a basket of toys and a large fish tank, it appealed to her as both a nurse and a patient, if she were ever to…

She stopped herself. Although she wanted children, and thanks to testing knew she didn't carry the cystic fibrosis gene, she wouldn't be having them at this hospital. Besides, she was traditional and wanted to have a husband first.

A family came in—a heavily pregnant woman, a man and a toddler who ran around the room in circles with his arms outstretched like an airplane.

"Hang on, Thomas." The man chased after the boy and gave Molly an apologetic look. "He's full of energy."

"It's fine." Molly grinned and made airplane noises for the little guy.

"Hey, you look familiar." The man scooped Thomas up and studied Molly more closely.

"So do you." Her mind scrolled through various possibilities. "High Valley High School, maybe?" She introduced herself and gave her graduation year.

"That's it. I'm Cal Young. My wife was Kendra Jacobsen." He jerked his chin toward the pregnant woman at the desk. "We were five years ahead of you. Closer in age to your brother Bryce. That's why you look familiar. I came out to the Tall Grass a few times when Bryce tutored me in chemistry."

"Small world."

"That's Montana." Cal and Molly spoke together as Kendra joined them.

"What are you up to these days?" Cal sat beside Molly with Thomas on his lap while Kendra took a chair with a footrest across from them.

"I'm here with my sister-in-law, my brother Zach's wife." Best to get that detail in as soon as possible in case Cal and Kendra assumed *she* was pregnant. Even an innocent mention to someone else that they'd seen her here could take on a life of its own. "I'm home for an extended vacation. I'm a nurse in Atlanta."

"Small world, I'm a nurse here!" Cal said. "We both work at this hospital, in fact." He gave Kendra a fond look.

"I'm a physician assistant." Kendra beamed back at her husband. "We knew each other in high school but only started dating when we moved back here after college. Now neither of us can imagine living or working anywhere else."

As Molly passed the toy basket to Cal and Thomas, her heart twisted. It must be comforting to be so certain of yourself and your place in life.

Cal nodded agreement as he took out red, yellow and green blocks for Thomas to play with. "I worked in Los Angeles for a year and although I learned a lot, it was impersonal, you know? Here, I really get to know patients and their families. It's also a great place to raise kids."

"It sure is." Kendra rested a hand on her pregnant belly. "Between my family and Cal's, we have lots of willing baby-sitters."

"Too many, sometimes," Cal joked. "Still, it means we can have date nights."

"If you're interested, the hospital's hiring. I could put in a good word for you." Kendra studied Molly and, under her probing gaze, Molly's cheeks warmed. "Apart from the whole family and community thing, for me the best part about working here is that I feel needed. We're rural, and while I once thought that was a disadvantage, I like knowing I'm helping people who really need my skills."

"I'm not looking for another job right now, but thanks." Even as her stomach churned, Molly kept her voice light.

"Well, if you ever change your mind, give me a call. Here's my number." Kendra held out her phone and they exchanged details. "Before this place was built, you likely remember folks having to leave the area if they needed specialist treatment. My dad's fine now, but he had cancer two years ago. It meant the world to him, my mom and our family that he could be cared for here in a place that's familiar. If he'd had to go to Billings in the winter, he and Mom would have had to live there. Here, they both had family and friends for support." Kendra snagged her son as he darted toward the fish tank. "If you want to look at the fish, you need to ask Mommy or Daddy to go with you so we can lift you up."

"Molly?" The receptionist came from behind the desk. "Beth wants you to come in for a minute."

Molly got to her feet. "Great to see you guys. Good luck with everything." She grinned at Thomas.

"I'm going to be a big brother," he said. "I get to listen to the baby's heartbeat in Mommy's tummy."

"You'll be a super big brother." Molly knelt to Thomas's

level. "When I was your age, I had four big brothers. They helped my mom and dad look after me." As far back as Molly could remember, Paul, Zach, Cole and Bryce had been there for her. Protectors, teachers, role models and her very own cheering section when she'd played sports or took part in activities at school or church. Zach, Cole and Bryce still looked out for her, even when she no longer needed them to.

"I like you." Thomas flung his arms around Molly and gave her an exuberant hug. "Can you come to my house?"

"Thanks for the invitation. Maybe another time, okay? I have to go see someone." Molly stood.

"Are you going to be a big sister?" As Cal picked up Thomas, the boy spoke over his dad's shoulder.

"No, an aunt. It's kind of like a big sister." Except, Molly would only see Beth and Zach's baby infrequently. Just like her other nieces and nephew. She'd be the faraway aunt who sent gifts for birthdays and Christmas but who, when she visited, would be almost a stranger.

As she waved goodbye to Thomas and followed the receptionist, Molly couldn't hold back a sigh. She couldn't be in two places at once, so she had to make the best of it.

"Hey, Beth. What's up?" Her sister-in-law lay on an exam table with an ultrasound technician on one side.

"I thought you'd like to see the baby. Zach and I don't want to know whether it's a boy or girl, so if you spot anything don't tell me, okay?" She gestured to the screen.

"Wow." Molly leaned closer. Although she'd accompanied lots of pregnant women to sonograms, Beth was family, and that baby on the screen was her... Molly's throat tightened, and she reached for Beth's hand.

The sonographer, a middle-aged woman whose name badge said Lynn, smiled. "Mom and baby are doing fine."

"It's amazing, isn't it?" Beth's eyes shone.

"It sure is." Any new life was a miracle, but having a personal connection made it extra special. "Thanks for letting me come in. You, the baby…" With her free hand, Molly rubbed at her eyes.

Although she loved medical research, she missed working with patients. Yet, she'd been so focused on one path she hadn't let herself consider other options. Could she work somewhere else and develop her career in a different way? Ideas flooded through her like the spring melt from the mountains that filled the creeks and rivers here.

"I'll give you two a minute." Lynn stepped away.

"Sorry." Molly sniffed and grabbed a tissue from a nearby box.

"No need to apologize. From TV commercials with cute baby animals to when Kristi gave me a free chocolate chip cookie, I cry at almost everything these days. I can only imagine what I'll be like when I see our baby for the first time." Beth paused. "I wanted to ask you… I already talked to Zach and he's okay with it. Would you be with us for my labor and delivery? We'd both be more relaxed having you there."

"I'd be honored." Molly reached for Beth and hugged her. She could think about those new and surprising career ideas later. Right now, she wanted to soak in this special moment she was privileged to share.

"Before Zach and I got married, I didn't have a sister, but now with you I have the one I always wanted." Beth's voice was choked. "Thank you."

"I should be the one thanking you." Molly's voice cracked. "I never had a sister either but now I do."

Out of all the moments in Molly's life so far, this one was among the happiest. And she'd keep it in her heart to treasure forever.

"TAKE CARE OF YOURSELF, BRO." As Pete finished packing his computer bag in the Bitterroot ranch house's living room later the same day, he patted Troy's shoulder.

"You as well." Troy returned the gesture. "Say hi to Tina and the kids for me."

"Sure. The kids will love the board game you bought them. We'll play it as a family over the holidays." Pete stuffed a charge cord into the top of the bag.

"Send me some pictures."

Pete seemed like he wanted to say something else, but busied himself with his bag. Except for when they'd gone into town for lunch at the Bluebunch and shopping at the craft center, Troy and Pete had spent their time together working. However, after bumping into Molly, Troy hadn't missed his friend's barely suppressed curiosity and sideways looks. "Okay, spit it out. I know you want to."

"What?" Pete knelt to put the board game into his overnight bag.

"You know exactly what." Troy sat on the edge of his new sofa still covered in plastic since being delivered two days before.

"Okay." Pete drew out the word. "I figured it was your business."

"It is, but you're my oldest friend." And Troy needed somebody to talk to who wasn't from High Valley and could be objective. "What do you think?"

"About Molly?"

"No, the cattle out there in the pasture. Of course Molly."

"She seems great." Pete took his luggage into the hall, grabbed his jacket from the hook by the front door and slipped into his boots. "She's smart, kind and beautiful. The whole deal."

"But?" Troy followed his friend and shrugged into his own coat and boots. "There's a 'but' there."

"Maybe." Pete opened the front door and cold air rushed in. "She lives in Atlanta for a start. Fantastic city but you haven't mentioned moving there."

No, but what if he did? Troy could rent out the ranch or use it as a vacation property. Let Cathy and her boys live here. Her house in town was too small for the three of them. Or he could offer her the bungalow if his folks didn't want it. He stepped onto the porch and inhaled a lungful of fresh, crisp winter air.

"As long as there's an internet connection, I can work from anywhere." His gaze took in the gracious two-story white clapboard ranch house with its wraparound porch, surrounded by snow-covered fields that stretched into a blue haze. *His* house. *His* fields. And *his* cattle grazing in them. Land he didn't work himself right now but planned to one day and pass it on to children, grandchildren and great-grandchildren. A legacy like the Carter family had. Which took him back to Molly, the only Carter who'd made a life somewhere else.

"But do you want to work anywhere?" Pete gestured to the ranch. "That only makes sense if you like the place you're working from. You haven't lived here long, but the Bitterroot is home, right?"

"Yeah." Troy wanted to grow old here with a family around him. He followed Pete down the porch steps to his friend's rental car parked in front of Cathy's vehicle.

"Back in college, you mentioned a girl from Montana a few times. It sounded like she was important to you. Was that Molly?" Pete put his bags in the trunk of the car.

"It was." Troy wanted to leave that history behind, but it kept rearing up to intrude into the present. "We dated when Molly was eighteen and I was twenty. But we're adults now, and we've both changed."

"I'm also guessing she dumped you back then which is why you never said much about her to me." Pete snorted like Troy's dad did when he thought one of his kids had done something unwise.

"Yes, but—"

"When it comes down to it, you're still the same guy I met in college. Hardworking, devoted to your family, supersmart and loyal. And if somebody breaks your trust, you might give them another chance but I'm not certain you ever fully forgive them."

"Of course I do." Unease itched at Troy like a mosquito bite in summer. Was Pete right?

"What about when Dean shared that idea of yours with a competitor? Did you forgive him?" Pete shut the trunk and turned back to Troy.

"Professional misconduct's different, but I didn't fire him." Still, had he truly accepted his employee had made an honest mistake?

"No, but you watched over him so closely Dean left anyway." Pete shook his head. "All I'm saying is whatever went down between you and Molly, you need to be sure you're being honest with each other."

Troy *had* been honest with her, but had she been honest with him? He scooped up a handful of snow and made a snowball. With the temperature around freezing, it was perfect snowball-making weather. "How do you and Tina make it work? It takes a special kind of woman to be with guys like us."

"You mean a guy like you." Pete scooped up some snow as well. "Thanks to Tina, I have a life beyond work."

"So do I." Troy had spent more time with Molly recently and less on work. They were behind on a couple of projects and a new business pitch was also delayed, but those things would likely have happened anyway.

Pete tossed the snowball in Troy's direction. "Go with the flow for a change. As for Molly, I like her but make sure she likes you for you. With Tina, I know she does because we met in college. Back then, a fancy date was takeout food and a picnic blanket under the stars. Actually, that's still a great date."

Troy had simple tastes, and from what he'd seen Molly still did too, but how could he be sure? "Hey." Snow cascaded over him.

He threw his snowball at Pete, who returned another snow volley, the two of them pelting each other like kids.

"Hang on." Pete roared with laughter. "Do you remember the snowball fight—"

"That work term we spent in Boston. I sure do." Troy gathered more snow as a truck rumbled up the lane. Probably the fuel delivery he expected. "Do you give up?"

"No way." Pete stopped laughing and lobbed another snowball as Troy darted behind Cathy's car.

"Missed me." Crouched by the vehicle, Troy took aim at Pete as several cows in the nearby pasture came closer to investigate.

"Uh, Troy?" Pete's voice was muffled.

"What?" He sent another snowball over and this time, instead of Pete's deeper voice, there was a feminine shriek followed by a dog barking.

He scrambled to his feet and put a gloved hand to his mouth as heat rushed to his face. "I'm so sorry. Molly...are you okay?"

She stood beside Pete and brushed snow off her hat and coat as Cole's dog, Blue, let out a cacophony of howls from a Tall Grass ranch pickup.

"I'm fine." Her eyes narrowed. "But it's two against one, Clayton, and as a pitcher, I led the High Valley senior girls' softball team to the divisional championships two years in a row."

"I... You..." Pete glanced between them. "I have to get to the airport."

"Stand back. This won't take long." Molly's gaze didn't waver as she shaped snow into a ball and launched it toward Troy.

He ducked but the snowball still hit him face on. He sputtered and then laughed as a cow mooed and a ranch hand came out of the barn to see what was going on.

"Truce?" Molly joined Troy and brushed wet snow off his face with one end of her scarf.

"Yeah." At the tenderness in her eyes, his laughter stopped.

And as they stared at each other, it was as if the past had been wiped out, like fresh snow had covered the muddy pasture and made everything new again.

He was as vulnerable as he'd ever been with anyone, and in that instant, Troy knew he'd truly forgiven her. The past was the past, and all he wanted was to think about the future—with her.

CHAPTER SIXTEEN

"I LOVE YOU, Daisy-May." Molly patted the Appaloosa's neck. As they came over a rise and into open pastureland alongside the highway, she urged the horse into a trot. Two days after she'd dropped by the Bitterroot to deliver paperwork for Cole and ended up in a snowball fight with Troy, warmer weather and wind had cleared the snow away and today winter seemed like a distant memory.

The breeze whistled past Molly's ears beneath her riding helmet, and she urged Daisy-May to go faster. "Atta girl." She laughed, at one with the horse and the big landscape like she'd been that day with Troy and Cara. Here, though, she was on a familiar horse and riding across land she'd known from birth. Land that was part of her family's heritage, and she hoped would continue to be worked by Carters and their descendants beyond her own lifetime.

"Do you want to slow down? I keep forgetting you're a senior lady now." Daisy-May had been born at the ranch, back when Molly's whole world had been her family and this place.

Daisy-May tossed her head and kept up the pace as if she, like Molly, relished the rare chance to run free.

"Okay, let's go." Before she gave the horse her head, she waved at a van passing on the highway, the logo on the side panel telling her it belonged to the Bluebunch Café. If Kristi wasn't driving, it would be one of her staff, all of whom Molly had gotten to know. In some ways, she'd slipped back into life here as if she'd never been away, but she'd also met new people who could become friends.

"Easy, girl." As they approached hillier, more uneven ground, she slowed Daisy-May to a trot, then a walk and to a stop while she checked her phone. There was a text from Hannah rescheduling that monthly dinner with high school friends, and another from Brooke, William's mom, organizing a time to visit the ranch and asking if Molly would like to meet up for coffee sometime.

As she typed quick replies, horse's hooves thundered, and a bay horse appeared at the top of another rise.

Molly shaded her eyes against the sun to take a closer look. Was it Cara? The rider waved, and Molly waved back. In town and out here, she greeted people she might not know personally but who would undoubtedly have people in common with her. Montana was largely rural and dotted with tight-knit towns like High Valley, so friendliness was a way of life. While as a woman riding by herself she'd stayed near the road and within cell phone coverage, she'd never had a reason to be afraid anywhere.

Horse and rider galloped toward her as several more vehicles passed on the highway, and Molly waved again, this time at Shane who, given the direction he was heading, was undoubtedly on his way to Squirrel Tail. It hadn't taken long for her to be immersed in her neighbors' lives again. However, that interest in other people, which at first she'd tried to dismiss as nosiness, was genuine caring and concern.

"Hey, Molly." Troy drew Cara to a stop beside her.

"Hey." Since that snowball fight, something had changed between them, and as they'd said goodbye to Pete, for a moment it had felt as if she and Troy were a couple. Had he sensed that new closeness too? "You decided to buy Cara, then?"

"Yep. Picked her up from the rescue yesterday."

As Troy rubbed Cara's ears, Molly's stomach flipped. Beneath his gloves, his hands were strong but gentle and when he held her close, she... *Stop it*. She mentally berated herself. "How's she settling in?"

"Making herself at home like she's always been at the Bitterroot." He shook his head and he put a hand to his chest. "I give her a week until she's ruling the roost, or should I say the barn."

"Only if you let her. Remind her who's the boss. You don't want a diva," she teased him, and gathered up Daisy-May's reins.

"You're right." Troy's smile was wide as he patted Cara. "I've had enough divas in my life. I don't need another one, even if she's a horse."

Past girlfriends? Troy had never talked about any of his other relationships and neither had Molly, but maybe it was time. "A guy I dated for a about a month last year was sure a diva. Everything was a big drama, and he always had to be the center of attention no matter what."

"So why did you go out with him?" Without needing to exchange any words, they walked Cara and Daisy-May side by side, as comfortable together as if their years apart didn't matter.

"A friend at work set us up. Joel seemed fun at first." And she'd been dazzled by his good looks, fancy car and what had seemed to her to be his urban sophistication. "It wasn't serious, and when I found out what he was really like I ended it."

"Did he take it badly?" There was an edge to Troy's voice that might have been jealousy.

"No, I think he was relieved." She chuckled. "We had completely different ideas about family, money, food preferences, pretty much everything. He also said horses smelled, although he'd never been closer to one than watching a parade."

"Big mistake." Troy's laughter rang out. Then his tone became more careful. "Have you dated a lot?"

"No and only one guy seriously. I went out with him my junior year of college. We're still friends but it didn't work out. I guess I haven't met the right guy." Maybe because nobody could ever match Molly's memories of Troy. "What about you?" She studied the distant mountain range as if absorbed in the scenery.

"Like you, I've dated, but the relationships never seemed right. I'm still friends with one of them. She's married now." Troy also gazed into the distance. "Along with my mom, Pete and his wife used to try to set me up with women, but I asked them to stop. Work keeps me busy, and maybe I'm one of those lone wolves who's better on his own." He shrugged, but his stiff posture atop Cara and the tightness in his jaw belied his attempt at casual indifference.

Molly opened and closed her mouth as she struggled to find the right words. "I always pictured you with a family. From what I remember from a school project about wolves, most of them live in packs." The careful crayon drawing she'd made of a mom, dad and several wolf pups popped into her mind.

"You don't always get what you want, do you?" A cloud drifted across the sun, shadowing Troy's face.

"No, but you could still have a family." She could have one as well, and if she applied for a job at the county hospital or another local health clinic, maybe that family could even be with Troy. Her heart thudded. They could start over, and if they were honest about what was going on between them, they could have another chance.

As Troy turned Cara around, the sun came out again and bathed him in light. "I should get going but..." He hesitated and then drew the horse closer to Molly and Daisy-May. "I'm going to Calgary for two days later this week. There's a livestock auction there I want to check out. I'll keep my eyes open for any cattle Cole might be interested in."

"Great, yes." Molly blinked at the change of subject. "Have a good trip."

"Thanks. When I'm back, the town's holiday parade sounds like it could be fun. If you don't have any other plans, I wondered if you'd like to go with me?"

"Sure. It would be fun. That parade has always been a big event. The ranch usually has a float, but not this year because of the weddings."

"Great." Troy's smile lit up his face.

"It's a date then." Molly's high voice didn't sound like hers.

Daisy-May pawed the ground and nickered, and Cara joined in.

"I think our horses are saying I need to kiss you."

"Yes." Molly leaned toward him, and as his lips met hers, a soul-deep rightness washed over and through her.

She wanted to stay here and be close to her family and old friends. And most of all, to be near this man who completed her in ways she hadn't known she needed—and the only guy she'd ever been truly serious about.

And one day soon, she'd find the courage to swallow her pride and admit to her family she wanted to change her life.

OVER BREAKFAST IN the hotel's restaurant in downtown Calgary, Troy glanced from the snow-covered street back to his phone to check his email. There were two messages from Pete, several from customers, a couple from Cole and one from Molly.

Ignoring the others, he opened Molly's first. While he hadn't admitted it to himself until afterward, he'd ridden in the direction of the Tall Grass Ranch the other day in case Molly might be out riding at the same time. And when he'd spotted her, his heart had filled with something that felt a whole lot like love.

He chuckled at the joke she'd sent him and typed a quick reply telling her about the livestock auction and heifers he'd bought. While he could have bid over the phone, he'd wanted to see the animals in person and talk to some of the stock contractors.

What about having dinner at Ruby's Place after the parade?

He added to his text. He'd give her the bear paw pendant then and think of something else for a Christmas gift. Maybe one of those hot chocolate gift boxes Kristi had at the café, along with a candle in one of the pottery holders she'd helped Pete choose for Tina.

"Troy?"

He looked up from his phone. "Cassidy?" He stood out of courtesy and before he realized what she intended, she'd pulled him into an embrace and kissed him on both cheeks.

"I thought it was you." Without waiting for an invitation, she sat across from him. "It's been years. What are you doing here?"

Under the guise of checking for toast crumbs, Troy used a napkin to brush at his face and remove any lipstick marks she might have left behind. It was only eight in the morning, but she was immaculately put together in a tailored charcoal business suit and cream blouse, subtle eye makeup and red lipstick, her dark hair pulled into a sleek bun.

"I'm here on business, heading home today. How about you?"

He'd gone out with Cassidy several times soon after he finished college and moved to California. He remembered her as smart, ambitious and pretty. He also remembered that over dinner at a cute and cozy diner he'd hoped she'd like as much as he did, she'd said he wasn't her type.

"It's too bad you won't be in Calgary longer." She waved down a server. "A coffee, and get me whatever your fruit bowl special is. And make it quick." Her eyes narrowed, and she pursed her lips.

Troy blinked. If one of his employees had spoken to anyone like Cassidy had done, Troy would have had a word with them. In life, as well as business, he didn't have time for rude people.

"Thanks." He gave the server a sympathetic smile as the teenager filled Cassidy's mug and then topped up Troy's coffee.

"I heard you're doing well." The server forgotten, Cassidy gave Troy a sunny smile and reached for his hand.

He drew away to pick up his cutlery. Although the food was good, breakfast was all of a sudden a lot less appealing. "I'm getting by."

"Don't be so modest. That's not what Darius says." That was odd. Darius was the friend of a friend who'd introduced them, and Troy was no longer in touch with him. "I also read that article about you." She mentioned a business magazine that had featured Troy and Pete on the cover about a year ago. Cassidy eyed him over the rim of her coffee cup. Had her brown eyes always been so cold? "How did they describe you? An entrepreneur who makes money and an impact, wasn't it? And those photos." She leaned across the table toward him, and Troy leaned back. "You should wear a suit more often, but there's also something about a cowboy." Her gaze dropped to his checked Western shirt.

"I want to give back. Lots of people are the same."

Troy focused on his omelet. He still felt uncomfortable whenever he thought of that article and the photoshoot. The magazine had sent a big city stylist to work with him and Pete, and while the guy on the cover might look like him, it was in no way the "real" him. It was only after the shoot was over and he'd gotten out of the borrowed designer suit and shoes that he truly felt like himself again.

"What are you up to these days?" He could make polite conversation for a few more minutes.

"I'm still in technical sales." Several heavy bracelets clanked against her coffee cup as Cassidy set it on the table. "I'm here on business. My company has a couple of clients in Calgary. Can't you stay longer? We could—"

"No, I can't." Troy picked at his savory home fries without tasting them. Just then, the server returned with Cassidy's order.

"I said a fruit bowl. I didn't mean with yogurt," she barked at the server, whose face reddened to his ears.

"Don't worry about it. I'll take that fruit and yogurt in a container to go. I can have it later. I planned to grab some from the buffet anyway on my way out." He tried to reassure the poor kid. He'd leave him an excellent tip and speak to the restaurant manager before leaving the hotel. Cassidy was the problem, not the server.

She reached for his hand again, but Troy kept a firm grip on his cutlery. "Why did you decide to bury yourself in rural Montana?"

"How do you know I live in Montana?" When he'd been interviewed for that article, he still lived in San Francisco. He'd never told the journalist he was looking at Montana ranches either. Bumping into Cassidy here was undoubtedly a coincidence, but had she kept tabs on him all these years? His muscles quivered, and he pushed the remaining food around his plate.

"I don't remember." She made a vague gesture and avoided his gaze.

"Oh, really?" Troy kept his private life private and his friend group small. He raised his eyebrows.

"Someone must have mentioned it to me." Her laugh tinkled. "How much land do you have?" Her brown eyes glittered, and this time there was no mistake. She wasn't interested in him. She was only interested in his money. "I imagine you're redoing your house. If you need an interior decorator, I could hire someone for you and oversee their work."

"I have enough land to keep me busy. As for the house, it's a work in progress, but I've already hired someone." Cathy wasn't an interior decorator, but she was handy with a paint-brush and that was all he needed right now.

The server reappeared and slid Cassidy's replacement fruit bowl in front of her like a rabbit trying to avoid a fox. Then he handed a take-out container to Troy for the fruit and yogurt bowl. Troy took it as his cue to leave. "I need to check out and—"

She made a moue with her lips. "But you haven't finished your meal." She pointed to his plate.

He ate the last of his home fries and drained his coffee mug. "There, done." He tried not to grimace.

"I'm still in San Francisco. The next time you're in town we'll have to get together. There's a wonderful new restaurant near Fisherman's Wharf. The chef's from France and is getting lots of publicity for his unusual food combinations and dramatic presentation. You could take me there." She toyed with a piece of melon and gazed at him from under her eyelashes.

Troy cleared his throat. "I'm not into fancy restaurants, remember? Good, home-style food is more my style." Like Kristi served at the Bluebunch. Although Kristi's fiancé, Alex, the chef at Ruby's Place, had also worked in France, he relied on simplicity instead of drama or the unusual to create a special meal.

"You're missing out." Cassidy flicked her gaze upward and let out a heavy sigh. Some men would likely find her appealing, but to him she seemed both manipulative and deceitful.

Unlike Molly. Her windblown hair and rosy cheeks flashed into his mind, along with the memory of kissing her. And when she hugged him, it felt right, honest and good. Everything the embrace Cassidy had forced on him didn't.

"I seem to remember you saying I wasn't your type." He couldn't keep amusement out of his voice.

"We didn't really have a chance to get to know each other." When her smug smile appeared, he knew their conversation was well and truly over.

"As I also remember, that was because of you, not me." Troy got to his feet and picked up the take-out container. Breakfast was included with his room, so he didn't have to wait for the check, and the food Cassidy had rejected was included in the buffet that was free for all guests. "Enjoy your stay. Take care." He wouldn't lie and say it was great to see her again or offer any other meaningless platitude.

"But..." Her mouth gaped open, and if she'd been one of his cows, she'd have bellowed in anger.

Troy grinned and held back a laugh as he made his way to the front of the restaurant to find the server and then the restaurant manager.

Cassidy might have fooled him once, but he wouldn't be taken in by someone like her again.

He wondered what he'd ever seen in her, although he supposed that back then she'd seemed friendly and sincere. Ambitious, sure, but there was nothing wrong with being career-oriented. He'd liked that she had goals and was driven like him.

But had she dropped him because he wasn't successful enough for her? As he stopped at the end of the line for the host stand, the aftertaste of the excellent coffee was acrid in his mouth. Had Cassidy changed or had his judgment been flawed?

Deep down, in a place he usually kept hidden even from himself, he was still the kid whose family had lost their ranch and had to depend on the food bank. And an adult who, despite his outward success, still carried the self-doubt he'd had as a kid.

The first time, he'd rushed into a relationship with Molly. They both had, and when they were together, anything had seemed possible. It still did. Molly wasn't anything like Cassidy, but how could he be certain she truly liked him—all of him—and not only the man he'd let her see?

CHAPTER SEVENTEEN

SLEIGH BELLS JINGLED, and Molly waved at her mom and Shane where they perched atop the light wagon that was usually stored in one of the Tall Grass Ranch barns. She stood on tiptoe to speak into Troy's ear, so he'd hear her over the excited crowd. "They weren't going to enter a float this year, but the kids were so disappointed not to be in the holiday parade, Zach and Cole put something together at the last minute. Isn't it a fun surprise? Both horses are so calm and don't get distracted. They've taken part in lots of town events."

Pulled by Daisy-May and Zach's horse, Scout, the vintage wagon had wheels decorated with white lights, while the bed featured red-and-white fabric candy canes, an inflatable snowman and a green plywood Christmas tree. Paisley, Cam and Skylar each kept hold of one of the family dogs, kids and canines both wearing Santa hats. With the softly falling snow, it was simple but magical, like a holiday card come to life.

Troy nodded, but his smile didn't reach his eyes. He'd been distant when she'd picked him up at the Bitterroot to come to the parade, but he was likely tired from his trip.

"Daisy-May's well trained and she's still fit enough to pull that wagon, especially with another horse helping. It's special for me to see her do it. My mom made those candy canes and the tree years ago." Molly gave the kids a thumbs-up. "The red fabric came from a dress I had in second grade. I remember Zach helping her to make the tree, and we all painted it with some of Paul's leftover paint."

"My mom does stuff like that." This time, Troy's smile was warmer and more natural.

Molly let out a relieved breath as the next float, decorated like a gingerbread house, came into view. "Oh, wow. That's amazing, isn't it?" She nudged Troy's elbow and pointed. "The O'Reillys own a construction company. If you're looking for someone to work on your place, you should call them."

"Is there something wrong with my house?" Troy's voice had an unexpected sharp edge.

"I haven't been inside so how would I know?" Molly stared at him trying to work out what was wrong. Troy would invite her to see his place when he was ready. He'd mentioned Cathy was doing some painting. Maybe he wanted everything to be finished before he had visitors apart from his family and Pete. "All I meant is houses often need things done to them and you work hard. You might not have time to take care of certain things yourself." She hesitated but Troy looked at the float, not her. "Like if there's a storm and you need to have shingles replaced, or you want to put in a new bathroom or kitchen. The O'Reillys are working on my mom and Shane's new house."

Troy's tense expression eased. "My mom did say the kitchen needed an upgrade. Sorry, I have a lot on my mind." He squeezed her mittened hand. "As for seeing my house, I want to give you a tour, but it's been a mess and I still have stuff everywhere." He bit his lip. "I want it to look nice for you."

"It's fine." But was it? If they were in a real relationship, wouldn't he talk to her about what was on his mind? Even if she couldn't help, she could listen. And why would he think she'd care about the state of his house? He'd only moved in recently, so it wasn't surprising he was still settling in. "Why don't I get us some hot chocolate and a bag of Kristi's mini sugar cookies?" She gestured to the pop-up food stand down the block from them at the Bluebunch Café. "That wind feels like it's coming from the North Pole, and the snow's getting heavier—"

"Molly?" Zach tugged at her parka sleeve. "Come quick. It's Beth. She…she can't be having the baby now, right? But she says she might be, and Ellie's calling an ambulance, and I don't know what to do." He rubbed his face and his voice shook.

"Beth's not due for two weeks yet but let me take a look." She turned to Troy. "Take my keys and get the first-aid kit from my trunk."

"Sure." Troy took the keys and left at a jog as Molly and Zach ran along the block to the corner near Rosa's craft center.

"Hey, Beth." Molly sat beside her sister-in-law who huddled on the curb and clutched her belly. "What's going on?"

"I don't know." Beth's face was pale, and her eyes were wide and frightened. "I'm having these pains, and the ambulance can't…" She jerked her chin at Ellie and then doubled over, letting out a low moan.

"There's construction so the bridge is out between here and the county hospital and ambulance service." Ellie's voice was steady, but her lips trembled as she glanced at Beth. "The dispatcher said they'll go around the other way, but it will take longer and with the snow…" She gulped.

"Why don't you come with us, Ellie?" Nina and Werner appeared out of the crowd. "We'll get you a snack while Molly talks to Beth."

"Good idea." From what Molly had seen so far, Beth indeed looked like she was in real labor. "Let's get you indoors and warmed up. The craft center's open." She got Beth to her feet. "Zach?"

"Is she… It'll be fine, Beth. Hang on until the ambulance gets here." Zach took his wife's other arm and between the two of them they guided Beth into the building.

"Hang on?" Beth's voice came out in a shriek, and she doubled over again.

"Sorry, I didn't mean…" Zach's gaze met Molly's over Beth's head. "Should I boil water or something?"

"Boil water?" Beth gritted her teeth. "I'm supposed to be in a nice, clean hospital where everything's already sterilized. My hospital bag's at home, and I can't…" She moaned and leaned against Molly.

"People boil water in movies." Zach's face was ashen, the tendons in his neck stood out and his usually measured voice was shrill. "Should I get Mom?"

"Yeah." Molly rubbed Beth's back. "Let's go into Rosa's workroom, honey. It's more private and I need to examine you." Her always stoic and calm and controlled big brother was an incoherent and panicky mess, but right now Zach was the least of her worries.

"Yes, and go get your mom." Beth waved in her husband's general direction. "Oh." Her voice echoed in a long-drawn out wail. "My water hasn't even broken."

"That doesn't necessarily mean anything." Molly glanced at Rosa, who'd followed them in. "Do you have any old sheets and something Beth could lie on?"

"In my studio office. I'll find clean towels as well." Rosa patted Beth's arm. "We're here for you. Between the two of us, Joy and I have had ten kids of our own, and Molly's a great nurse who's delivered lots of babies."

As Beth gasped for breath, she tried to give them a shaky smile.

Molly didn't consider several rotations on a maternity ward as delivering lots of babies, especially because she'd always assisted an experienced ob-gyn, but she'd do the best she could. Beth and the baby were depending on her. As Rosa returned with sheets, towels and a yoga mat, Molly helped Beth lie down and lowered her voice. "Is there anyone on call at the town's medical clinic?"

"No, we rely on the county hospital for after-hours care."
Rosa glanced at Beth and then back at Molly with a worried
frown. "The only doctor I can think of who lives nearby is on
the other side of that bridge."

"I'm sure the ambulance will be here soon." Molly spoke in
her normal voice as Beth gripped her hand tight. She wasn't
actually sure of anything except that it looked like she'd be
on her own with Rosa and Joy. Melissa was at a conference
this weekend, and Carrie, who'd taken an advanced first-aid
course, was on her honeymoon with Bryce.

Between them, Molly and Rosa got Beth out of her parka,
boots and maternity jeans.

Rosa grabbed a blanket from the workroom table, a multicolored pictorial tree design, and covered Beth.

"That's beautiful and things might get, you know, messy."
Again, Molly spoke in an undertone.

"It doesn't matter." Rosa tucked the blanket around Beth.
"If ever one of my 'Tree of Life' designs was appropriate, it's
now."

"Give me a minute to wash my hands, and then I'll examine you. I know it's hard but try to relax." Molly had to think
of Beth as any other patient. If she let this situation feel personal, she'd be in the same state as Zach.

After using the sink in the corner of the workroom, she did
a quick exam and then scooted up to crouch by Beth's face.
"You're definitely in labor. Even if the bridge wasn't out, I
doubt you'd make it to the hospital. You're going to have your
baby here. Everything will be fine." She made her voice sound
strong and confident. "It's fast, but everything's progressing
normally."

There was a rustle at the workroom door and Zach poked
his head inside. "I'm back with Mom and your first-aid kit.
Troy's outside if you need anything else. He put the Closed
sign on the craft center door."

"Come in." From the yoga mat Rosa and Molly had covered with sheets, Beth gave Zach a pained smile. "This baby obviously has a mind of its own. Not surprising, given what the two of us are like. I didn't plan on this kind of birth, but I guess I don't have a choice."

She didn't, and if Molly's instincts were right, this baby was coming within the next half hour, maybe sooner. "Zach, sit by Beth's head, hold her hand and coach her with her breathing like you practiced in your class. Rosa, I need you to time Beth's contractions. Use my phone." Molly unlocked it and passed it to her. "Beth, is it okay with you if Mom helps me?"

"Of course." Beth's initial terror had passed, and now her face held both determination and bravery. "Is Ellie staying with Nina and Werner? I need to—"

"You don't need to do anything except focus on yourself and the baby." Although Zach's face was still gray, he now seemed, if not calmer, at least like he'd gotten himself and his emotions more under control. "Cole took Ellie and the other kids back to the ranch with him. I just spoke to Ellie. She's worried for you but she's safe."

"Good." Beth panted and sweat trickled down her face.

"Tell me what you need." Her mom's voice shook but she straightened her shoulders, took off her winter coat and rolled up her sleeves. As Molly rummaged in the first-aid kit for surgical gloves and other supplies, her mom leaned closer and to Molly alone whispered, "You've got this, Jellybean."

Molly gave her mom a wobbly smile. She and the others were here for her, Beth and this newest Carter baby.

Beth screamed as another contraction hit, and Molly focused on what she had to do. Nothing had ever been more important.

"IT'S BEEN HOURS. What's taking so long?" Outside the craft center, Troy paced. The holiday parade had ended, and somehow the news had made its way around town that Beth was in labor. A small group had now gathered on High Valley Avenue.

"It's only been about twenty minutes." Nina patted Troy's back. "With my first baby, I was in labor for almost a day."

Troy shuddered. He wasn't the baby's dad, and he was barely keeping himself together. How had his parents gone through this experience twice? From outside the closed workroom door, where he lingered in case anything else was needed, he heard Beth's anguished cries. He also heard Molly's calm expertise in what, although he had no medical knowledge, was clearly a crisis situation.

"Why don't you come over to the Bluebunch with us, son?" Werner's voice was fatherly. "Kristi's opened the café so we can wait in the warmth and have a hot drink and something to eat. All today's baking is gone, but she's got a pot of chicken soup on the stove, and Alex brought leftover chili from Ruby's Place."

Troy shook his head. "You two go on." Nina and Werner held hands, and Nina looked almost girlish while Werner had a protective, loving air that was new. "I'm fine."

He wanted to stick around for the Carter family like they'd been there for him that summer when he'd been desperate for a job. He wanted to be there for Molly. Not that he could do anything practical, but he wanted to be here, as close to her as possible and not across the street in the café.

"Call or text us as soon as you hear any news." Nina hugged him before she, Werner and several others headed to the café. Both that building, and the other side of the town's wide main street were almost obscured by snow which now, fueled by a gusty wind, fell like a thick, white curtain.

Troy stamped his booted feet to get the circulation going again and shook snow off his parka hood. He wasn't used to standing around doing nothing. "Come on." He gestured to the few who remained, including a guy he recognized. "Mike, right? Hannah's husband? We met at the tree lighting."

"Yeah." Mike nodded and drew closer. "My dad owns the hardware store. If the ambulance has trouble getting through,

Dad has snow chains and other stuff so we're sticking around in case we're needed." He introduced his friends. "We all played football together back in the day so we can offer muscle."

"If your dad has extra shovels, we can start clearing a path." The snow was so heavy that any path might have drifted in as soon as they'd cleared it, but Troy had to do something.

"Good idea. Dad's gone on his snowmobile to pick up a bag of baby and hospital things Hannah's putting together for Beth, but I've got a key."

At Mike's friendly smile, some of Troy's tension eased. When the two of them went into the hardware store to find and distribute snow shovels to the impromptu work crew, he reminded himself that unlike Cassidy, people here *were* genuine. As soon as the words were out of his mouth, he'd regretted speaking so sharply to Molly earlier when she mentioned making repairs to his house. He'd apologize to her as soon as he could, but right now he'd support her in the only way he could think of.

"Ready, guys?" He held up a shiny aluminum shovel before scooping it full of snow. "I'm guessing the ambulance will need to park here." He indicated a partially drifted space in front of the craft center.

"Ready." Mike and the guys were in a football huddle, and he gestured to Troy to join them.

Although he'd never played football, as part of that huddle Troy had a new sense of belonging, not only in himself but High Valley. These people didn't care about how much money he had. He was just one of the guys lending a hand to support a friend and neighbor in need.

And as he cleared wet snow and bantered with the other men, and Kristi, Nina and a few others came from the café with takeout cups of soup, hot cocoa and coffee, a sense of warmth enveloped Troy. It didn't only come from the hearty nourishment and backbreaking physical work but also from his heart, soul and this place.

"Anybody else hear that?" Half an hour later, Mike raised a hand, and an ambulance siren wailed in the distance.

A cheer went up, and Troy and the others leaned on their shovels, watching as a plow mounted on the front of a pickup truck cleared the western length of High Valley Avenue for the ambulance to follow.

"Good job." Mike exchanged a high five with Troy. "You'll have to join us for burgers on our next guys' night out. I owe you a beer."

"Sounds like a plan, but we all need a beer." Troy texted Werner and stood with the others as the ambulance pulled up and parked, and two paramedics got out and went inside the craft center carrying a stretcher.

Less than a minute later, Mike's dad arrived on a snowmobile with a small suitcase strapped to the back.

"I keep thinking about Beth and Zach." Mike wiped his ice-encrusted brow with a gloved hand. "I can only imagine what they're going through. It was hard enough for us when Hannah had our first and that was in the hospital."

"Yeah." Clearing snow had momentarily distracted Troy, but now worry flooded back. "Look. Is that Zach?" He peered through the window.

"He's with Rosa and Joy." Mike joined Troy at the window. The crowd around them grew as people in the café, including Nina and Werner, returned to wait outside. "The paramedics must be taking over. No, here one of them comes."

Although Troy now had his nose flattened against the window, he couldn't see Molly, Beth or a baby. But Zach wouldn't be standing there talking to Rosa and Joy if things weren't okay.

The crowd fell silent as one of the paramedics returned. "Clear a space, folks. We're bringing mom and baby out.

They're both doing fine, but we're taking them to the hospital to be checked there."

"A baby." The words echoed around the snowy street as everyone moved back, and the paramedic went back inside, this time carrying the suitcase from Mike's dad.

Troy's legs went weak with relief, and he gripped the handle of his snow shovel to stay upright.

"Beth did amazing, and our baby's a girl." Zach stepped out of the craft center and spoke to the crowd. "As for my sister? I don't know how to tell you everything Molly did for us."

A cheer went up, and as Zach stood in the open doorway, he brushed tears from his cheeks.

"Here they come. Hip, hip, hooray." Werner's voice rang out, and then everyone joined in as the two paramedics carried Beth out to the ambulance on the stretcher as Zach walked by her side and held her hand.

"There's Molly." Mike nudged Troy's ribs and gave him a knowing smile. "Looks like she's got the baby."

Following behind Zach and Beth, Molly carried the small, precious bundle wrapped in a blanket. Troy's heart punched against his chest, and for a moment he struggled to breathe.

"Zach and Beth must have asked her to carry their girl. If I'd gone through what Zach has, I'd be afraid of dropping my kid. It's one of those times you're grateful there's an expert around to take charge." Mike shook his head and led another cheer for Molly.

As Molly waited outside the ambulance while Beth got settled inside, she scanned the crowd. Was she looking for him?

Troy made his shaky feet move toward her, and then she spotted him and smiled.

He tried to smile back, but tears burned at the backs of his eyes. *You're incredible.* He mouthed the words, and she scrunched up her face like she didn't understand.

He'd tell her later, but as he held her gaze for an instant that felt like a lifetime, he knew that what he felt for her wasn't fleeting or superficial but rather a deep and forever love.

She cradled her newborn niece and adjusted the blanket around the baby's tiny face with tenderness and maternal care. What would it be like seeing her hold their own newborn baby one day?

"You okay?" At his side, Mike took Troy's elbow.

"Yeah. It's a miracle." Troy didn't have any words beyond that.

To him, Molly was as big a miracle as the baby. But even as love and awe enveloped him, stronger than anything he'd ever experienced, he forced himself to be logical.

He loved Molly, but how could he ask her to stay in High Valley? Even if she was sincere, and he finally knew in his heart that she was and he could trust her with everything he had, today had also shown him she was destined for bigger and better things.

Troy would never hold her back or want her to give up her big city life and career for him.

CHAPTER EIGHTEEN

"THERE YOU GO, GIRL." Back at the Tall Grass Ranch, Molly latched Daisy-May's stall after stabling the horse for the night. "It was a big day for us."

Daisy-May gave a soft nicker, and Molly rubbed her nose.

With Beth giving birth in Rosa's craft center, it had been a bigger day for Molly than Daisy-May, but the horse had done her bit in the parade and represented the Carter family well. "I'm proud of you, girl. 'Night, 'night, sleep tight." She chuckled as she repeated the bedtime rhyme her dad used to say to her.

As she left the barn, her boots sank deep into fresh snow, but the storm had passed to leave a crisp and clear December night. Montana weather often changed fast and never more so than today. She leaned her elbows atop the pasture fence and stared at the starlit sky.

Beth and her new baby were staying at the hospital overnight, so Zach was with them, and Ellie was having a sleepover at Cole and Melissa's. While Cole had taken Ellie, Skylar, Paisley and Cam home with him, her mom would head back to Carrie's farmhouse after she finished checking on the chickens in their coop. So apart from the hands, Molly would be alone at the ranch. She wasn't lonely, though. Instead, and for the first time in months, she felt at peace.

Her thoughts drifted back to holding her new, still unnamed niece by the ambulance. As she'd lifted her gaze from the baby's sweet face, it was as if she saw everything, and everyone, anew. And then, when she'd spotted Troy, it was like it was only the two of them. In that moment, and despite how she'd tried to deny her feelings, she'd known she loved him with every part of herself, now and forever.

She scanned the sky, trying to pick out constellations she remembered from her dad's astronomy book, which still sat on the shelf in the family room. There was so much artificial light where she lived in Atlanta she rarely saw stars, or even thought to look for them. Here, she drank in the overhead vista.

There was something about the winter silence, and that big familiar sky, that quieted and unsnarled her tangled thinking.

Footsteps crunched on the snow, and she turned. "Hey, Mom. Are you heading home?"

"Nope." Her mom's smile was wistful. "I called Shane and told him I wanted to stay here tonight with you. Carrie's house is great, but in a lot of ways, this ranch house is still home for me." Her mom stood beside Molly at the fence, her dogs Jess and Gus sniffing around their feet. "It's such a pretty night, but I'm restless."

"I always thought you were the most settled and steady person I know." Molly stared at her mom.

"Maybe on the surface but not always underneath." Her mom chuckled. "Inside, I often feel about sixteen, but here I am a grandma once again."

"And an inspiration to us all." Molly patted one of her mom's mittened hands.

"Thanks, honey, but today you were the inspiration. The way you delivered the baby." She sucked in a quick breath and shook her head slowly. "It seems like yesterday you were a baby yourself. Your dad would be so proud of you. I sure am."

"At first, I was scared." Her heart had raced, and for a few minutes she'd hardly been able to control her shaky limbs. But then she'd moved beyond the fear and found a sense of purpose, made a plan and had mentally talked herself through what she had to do to keep Beth and the baby safe.

"We were all scared, Zach most of all, but you were a pro. Today will go down in the history of High Valley and you were a big part of it." Her mom wrapped her hand around Molly's. "Folks are calling you a hero."

"I hope that doesn't last long." Molly gave a mock shudder. "You know me, I don't like being the center of attention."

"True, but sometimes I don't know if I *do* know you." Her mom's blue eyes were troubled.

"For the last while, I haven't known myself either." She bent to pat the dogs, and Jess leaned against Molly's leg.

"And now?"

"I'm still figuring parts out, but I..." Molly took a deep breath. "I've been lost for months, maybe even a few years, but I need a place to belong, and I want it to be here in High Valley."

"You'll always belong here, no matter where you live, but I—"

"Wait, I need to tell you the truth. All of it." If she didn't, Molly might lose her courage. "I want to be here to see my new niece and the other kids grow up. I want to be a real part of their lives and someone they can count on."

"What about your job? Nursing is what you always wanted."

"It still is, but today showed me I want to be a nurse here. I want to care for local children and their families and be part of this community. Someone like me is needed, and I hear the county hospital's hiring." After she talked to Troy, she'd call Kendra and ask her to put in that "good word" the other woman had offered. "If I'm a local hero, that should help me get a job, don't you think?" She tried to joke but her voice quavered.

"Oh, my dear." Her mom's arms came around Molly in a hug both loving and fierce.

"You aren't disappointed in me?"

"Why would I be?" Her mom cupped Molly's chin and looked into her eyes.

"Because you...my brothers, the whole family, you sacrificed a lot for me to go to college. I don't want you to think I'm a failure if I choose a career as a rural nurse over a city research job." She pushed the words out, afraid of what she'd see in her mom's face.

"All I ever wanted, all me and any of us still want, is for you to be happy." Her mom kissed Molly's cheek. "Changing your mind doesn't mean you're a 'failure.' It means you've grown and changed like we all do."

Molly had been so afraid and embarrassed to admit the truth to anyone, let alone herself, but now, with only a few words, her mom had made everything okay.

"The only failure would be living a life that no longer fits, and the rest of the family will feel the same." Her mom's voice was firm. "If anyone else asks nosy questions or judges you, who cares? That's their problem, and whatever they think isn't important."

"I guess so." Molly had been focused on one way of thinking for so long, it was hard to all of a sudden see herself and her choices through someone else's eyes. "I know I can be happy here."

"And we'll be happy to have you, me most of all." Her mom rested her hands on Molly's shoulders. "Maybe it's because you've been away that you know where you want to be. If you hadn't spread your wings, your roots wouldn't have called you home."

"You always did have a way of putting things." Molly laughed and then sobered as her mom tilted her head to one side and gazed at her with an expectant air. "What?"

"You can tell me it's none of my business, but I have to ask. Does Troy have anything to do with you being happy here?"

She could deflect her mom's question, but what was the point? Unlike her change of career direction, she wasn't embarrassed about her feelings for Troy. "I love him, Mom. I thought what we had was casual but it's not. It's serious, at least for me. But I'm not staying in High Valley because of him." She rushed on. "I don't know if he feels like I do, but if he does, I want to give our relationship a real chance."

However, there had been something in Troy's expression as their eyes met while she waited by the ambulance that had given Molly hope he might love her like she loved him.

"And if he doesn't share your feelings?"

In the distance, a coyote howled, and Molly shivered. "It'll hurt, but I'll pick myself up and move on. I won't run away because of Troy or any man." Yet, as Molly had cradled Zach and Beth's baby, she'd imagined her and Troy raising their own children here one day.

"All of us will be here for you, no matter what. We're your family." Her mom hugged Molly again, and in that embrace she knew she'd finally found her way home to stay.

They walked back to the ranch house with the dogs, the home that had sheltered Molly's family for several generations. She also knew that after being honest with herself and her mom, she now needed to be honest with Troy.

AT SEVEN IN the morning, the day after High Valley's holiday parade, Troy checked the email from Pete again, hoping the problem wasn't as bad as it had seemed the night before. Studying the attached document, he zeroed in on a column of figures.

The mistake was obvious, and he should have caught and corrected it a few weeks ago. Now it was too late and would cost them. Not only money, which was bad enough, but this kind of situation could also damage their professional reputation. They'd built their business on honesty, trust and care. If someone messed up, the responsibility ultimately rested with the guys at the top—in this case, him.

He stared out his home office window at the snowy fields and cattle grazing in a winter pasture. His heartbeat sped up, and a tingling sensation flooded the back of his neck and across his face. He couldn't avoid the truth any longer. He'd paid less attention to work because of Molly, and this problem was the result. Cause and effect, like he'd learned from his folks long before any school classroom.

I'm sorry, son. You can't play hockey because we can't afford the equipment this year.

That microscope kit's expensive. What about putting this mini kit on your Christmas wish list instead?

We'll manage somehow. Don't worry. Go out and play.

The voices of his mom and dad came back to him across the years. They'd sacrificed for Troy and his sister, likely more than he knew. And sacrifice had become a way of life he hadn't questioned. His folks had done the best they could, and so Troy did his best as well. He still did.

He rubbed a hand across his neck before picking up his phone to call Pete.

"I'm sorry." His hands were clammy, and a headache pounded behind his temples. "This is my fault."

"How could it be your fault?" Pete's voice cut through Troy's whirling thoughts. "Tim and his team made the mistake, not you."

"Tim reports to me. When he sent the draft document, I should have spotted there was a problem." Troy kept his voice low and controlled, and he turned away from the computer so he didn't have to face the evidence. "You and I also know Tim's not as meticulous as he could be."

"So? Mistakes happen. As for Tim, he's a good guy, and nobody's as meticulous as you."

"I took my eyes off the ball." And Troy couldn't forgive himself.

"You're human." Pete exhaled. "But knowing you, nothing I say is going to make you see things differently."

"I wasn't doing my job." Troy resisted the temptation to put his head on the desk and close his eyes, hoping that when he woke up all his problems would have magically disappeared.

He'd tossed and turned the whole night thinking about work, Molly and what he needed to do. The problem was that he was unsettled, unsure of where he and Molly stood, what they wanted, what kind of future they could have. He could focus on work if they were both committed to their relationship and all that that entailed. But he wanted to be here, in High Valley, and that had never been Molly's dream. If she didn't resent him now for asking her to stay here and give up her exciting city job, she would in a few years. He couldn't do that to her—or himself. If they built a life together and she left again, he might not survive the pain.

You can run your business from anywhere. The insistent voice in his head grew louder with the words he'd said to others and himself. But the issue was bigger than geography. With Molly by his side, he could find a way to be happy in Atlanta. But he'd begun to find the roots here he'd longed for. Just as he worried she'd resent him if she stayed, would he resent her if he left High Valley? Perhaps the truth was that he couldn't let a personal relationship distract him from work at all. He'd committed to that idea for years and it had served him well. This crisis could be contained. The next time, he might not be so lucky, and he couldn't risk losing the financial security he'd worked so hard to achieve.

Pete was still trying to convince him that this wasn't the end of the world. "We'll fix the problem and absorb the financial loss. It'll be fine. We have enough free cash."

True, but losing these funds could also impact Troy's personal investment in Cole's business. "I'm on it. I'll send you a new proposal later today."

As he ended the call, he dropped his face into his hands.

First, he had to make sure Cole and his business would be okay. Then he had to see Molly. His stomach rolled as he considered what he had to say and how to say it. Even if it didn't feel so now, it was for the best for both of them.

He focused on the computer screen, opened a new document and input different combinations of numbers, trying to lose himself and his heartache in financial projections. He'd always liked math because numbers didn't lie. He also knew where he stood with a spreadsheet. And once he made a plan, he stuck with it until he reached his goal. He tapped the computer keys and didn't let himself think about Molly.

Several hours later, he let out a long breath as he found a solution. It wasn't perfect, but he'd handled it as best he could without hurting their employees or investors. He'd also absorb the personal financial loss so there was no risk to Cole's business.

At his side in her bed, Acorn whined as if she sensed Troy's distress.

"It's okay, sweetheart." He picked the dog up and rested his face against her soft head. "I know what I'm doing."

Acorn nosed his cheek, and Troy swallowed the tsunami of emotions that threatened to overwhelm him.

The sooner he saw and spoke to Molly the better. Before he lost his nerve, he grabbed his phone and sent her a brief text.

She replied in seconds.

I'm at the Tall Grass. Not leaving for the hospital until around two this afternoon. See you in twenty minutes.

She ended the message with smiley face and heart emojis.

Troy's chest hurt, and he made himself take several deep breaths. As he gathered up his keys and put Acorn back in her bed, his gaze caught the small box from the Medicine Wheel Craft Center covered in shiny green paper and tied with a curly silver bow. It held the bear paw pendant with the blue stone he'd intended to give Molly over dinner after the parade.

For an agonizing instant he stared at it and remembered what it represented—the fun, the laughter and the love. Then he opened the bottom desk drawer, took the box and put it at the back behind old project files.

What he was doing was for the best for both he and Molly. Before he left the house, he also messaged Pete.

Found a solution. All good.

It would be good, if not right now, then in the future. All he had to do was convince Molly. And then himself.

CHAPTER NINETEEN

"I WASN'T EXPECTING to see you today. What's up?" As they walked away from the Tall Grass ranch house along the snow-covered path to the creek, Molly slid her arm through Troy's. "I'm always happy to see you, but you look rough. Bad night?"

He looked worse than rough. He looked haggard, as if he'd aged years overnight. He was still handsome, though, and she imagined what he'd look like as they grew older. Was now the right time to tell him she loved him and wanted to make a future together? No, she'd better wait to hear what he had to say first.

"I didn't sleep well. Work stuff." His arm beneath hers was stiff and although they stood close, there was nevertheless a distance between them that so far Molly hadn't been able to bridge.

"Would it help to talk to me about it? I could listen, and as an outsider I might have a new perspective." Unease curled from Molly's stomach to lodge in her throat. Her instinct told her whatever was bothering Troy was more than something to do with work. Yesterday at the parade he hadn't been himself, and before Beth had gone into labor Molly had wanted to talk to him about it.

"There was a problem that bothered me all night, but I found a solution this morning." Troy took his arm away to dig in his jacket pocket for a pair of sunglasses.

"Oh, well, that's good, then." Molly found her own glasses. The sunlight against the snow was bright and made her squint, but not being able to see Troy's eyes also made her wary.

"Molly, I…" Troy stopped by the edge of the creek. "There's no easy way to tell you this."

"Tell me what?" Her stomach lurched.

"It's not you. It's me." Despite the dark glasses, his anguished expression was clear.

"What do you mean?" Except, she already knew. He was breaking up with her. They'd never even made their relationship official, so how could it be over?

"Getting involved with each other, even though we kept it casual, was a mistake. I can't give you what you need and deserve. The kind of lifetime love your brothers and their wives have. Like your folks had and now your mom has with Shane."

"I don't understand." Tears stung behind her eyes, but by sheer force of will she held them back. "We're good together and—"

"We were but it won't work." Troy paced along the bank of the half-frozen creek where water still trickled in the middle. "I have a lot going on with my business and I don't have time for a relationship, especially a long-distance one."

"What if I disagree? You haven't given us a chance, not really. And…" Molly gulped. "I only decided for sure last night, but I'm going to stay in High Valley. I'm applying for a job at the county hospital. If I'm here, we can—"

"No, we can't. And you shouldn't stay here because of me or because you think we have a future together."

Molly took several steps back. "I'm not choosing to stay here just because of you." Although, given the pain she felt now, she'd underestimated how hard it would be to see Troy around town. And how, in only a short time, his life and hers had gotten intertwined.

Troy turned to face her. "I care about you, Molly, but it's over." His voice cracked. "It's for the best. You'll see. Nothing will change with my investment in Cole's stock contracting business, and we can still be friends."

"*Friends?* I don't think so. I don't understand. I thought we had something special."

"We did and…" He continued pacing and dug a narrow path in the snow with his boots. "You have a great job in Atlanta. I won't let you give it up for me."

"Shouldn't it be *me* who makes that decision?" Anger mixed with hurt made her voice shrill. "Is this because I ended our relationship before, and you want to get back at me?" She'd never thought Troy was mean or vindictive, but had she misjudged him? The night before she'd been so sure he loved her, but this man was a stranger.

"Of course not. The past is done. I'm talking about now. The Atlanta job is what you've been working toward for years. Apart from family, what's here for you?"

"How can you say *apart* from family? I love my family, I always have, but the past while has shown me how important that bond is. I need to be part of their lives in a way I can't on occasional visits. I need them to be part of my life as well." She sucked in a breath as Troy stared at her, his lips pressed tight together. "I also have a community here and sense of belonging I've never found anywhere else. I can get a job here that would make me an even bigger part of High Valley. Yes, I'd be giving up a job in Atlanta, but I'd gain a lot more. Things I can't put a price on." Molly put her trembling hands into her jacket pockets and clenched her fists. "Maybe for you, life's about work and money, but it's not for me."

"My work's important to me and the money gives me security but…" Troy's face went red. "I want you to be happy. I'm doing this for you."

"If you truly wanted me to be happy, you'd listen to what I'm saying, and you wouldn't throw away what we could have together. You're making excuses. And you're breaking up with me because you think it's somehow better for me, but I think it's really for you because you're too afraid to take a chance in life." Her voice rose higher. "You're right, Cole's business is between the two of you, and this shouldn't affect it. As for the rest? I'm staying here and if that's a problem, sell the Bitterroot and go live somewhere else. If all you think about is work, it shouldn't matter where you live." She whirled around and started back along the path to the ranch house.

"Molly, wait I..."

"What?" She turned and pressed one hand to her heaving chest.

"These past weeks have meant a lot to me."

"If that were true, you wouldn't say we were a mistake." She hesitated for a few seconds in case he realized what he was giving up, but he stared at his boots. "Have a good life, Troy. I hope money gives you enough of that security."

With one last look at his bent head and hunched shoulders, she turned around again and started for home, walking as fast as she could before breaking into a run. When she reached the barnyard fence, she veered toward the house and stumbled in snowy tractor ruts. Half-blinded by tears, she took off her sunglasses and shoved them in her pocket. If she could only make it inside the house and upstairs to her bedroom before—

"Molly? If you have a second, I... Hey, what's wrong?" A pair of strong arms came around her, and then she was pressed against Cole's broad chest. "Are you hurt? Did someone hurt you?"

"I'm not hurt." At least not physically. "But..." She buried her face in her brother's jacket and choked back sobs. "I thought you went into town."

"I started to, but I came back because... It doesn't matter. Is it Troy?"

Molly nodded and cried harder as Cole half carried her the rest of the way.

"I'll return the money he invested. I can pay him back over time. I won't be beholden to anyone who's hurt you." He guided Molly up the stairs to the back deck and then into the ranch house kitchen.

"What on earth?" Her mom's voice penetrated Molly's sobs.

"You need that money. Besides, Troy said…" Molly hiccupped. "He said it wouldn't make a difference to his investment. I said the stock contracting business was between the two of you. It's okay. I'm okay."

"You're not okay, and I'm not okay taking money from Troy. It's tainted." Cole pulled out one of the kitchen chairs and Molly almost fell into it. "Besides, I'm going to be a successful stock contractor, and why should a guy like him benefit?"

Her mom knelt to take off Molly's boots and then unzipped her parka. "You're freezing, honey. Let's get you a blanket and a mug of tea. I just made a pot for myself."

"Here's a blanket." Shane hovered in front of Molly between her mom and Cole. "I'll be in the barn office if anyone needs me."

"What did Troy do?" Cole thumped around the kitchen in his sock feet.

"Nothing." *Everything.* "I thought there was something special between us, but he…whatever it is…was, it's over." She huddled in the chair and curled her hands around the mug of tea her mom gave her. Despite the warmth of both it and the blanket, she shivered so hard her teeth chattered.

"I want to stay here but how can I? I'll always be worrying about bumping into Troy around town." She pulled a handful of tissues from the box her mom had set on the kitchen table and mopped her eyes. "I'm so embarrassed."

"It's Troy who should be embarrassed, not you." Cole stopped by Molly's chair and crouched in front of her. "Do you want me to talk to him?"

"No." Molly gave him a wobbly smile. "I'm too old to have my brothers fighting my battles."

"But you're never too old to have your family in your corner." Molly's mom pulled out another chair, sat and tucked the ends of the blanket around Molly's trembling shoulders. "There's no reason for you to leave because of Troy. How about this—why not go back to Atlanta for a few months and take the time you need to find a suitable job here? It doesn't have to be right in High Valley."

Molly nodded and sipped the hot tea. Her mom's suggestion was good, and it would give her time and space away from Troy and this heartbreak to clear her head and be ready for job interviews. "I do want to be in Montana. That hasn't changed. And I want to be in or close to High Valley so I can visit you often."

"Maybe Troy will leave. Once folks find out how he treated you, it won't be comfortable around here for him." There was a determination in Cole's voice that told Molly he was keen to be the source of that discomfort.

"No." Molly put a hand on her brother's arm. "This thing is between Troy, me and our family, nobody else. I won't be the subject of town gossip." If people talked about her or she became an object of pity, she couldn't live here, ever. And although she'd told Troy he could sell the Bitterroot and move somewhere else, would he? Owning that ranch was his dream come true.

"Okay, but if I ever bump into the guy behind a barn, I'll have a thing or two to say to him." Cole stood and paced around the kitchen again.

"You won't do any such thing." Molly's mom's voice was soft but firm. "It isn't your fight to take on. If you want to give Troy his investment back, fine, but that's it. Understood?" She eyed her son with an expression Molly remembered from childhood.

"Yeah." Cole gave a short laugh. "It doesn't mean I can't think about what I'd like to say and do to him, though."

"Make sure you stick to thinking. That goes for Zach and

Bryce as well." Molly's mom was almost a foot shorter than Cole, but she didn't stand for any nonsense. She never had. "Don't you have something to do outside or in one of the barns?"

"I can take a hint, Mom." Cole gave her a curt nod.

"Good." She turned to Molly again as Cole put his outdoor clothing back on. "I have my homemade chicken noodle soup and your favorite ice cream in the freezer, and there are chips and cookies in the pantry. We can snack and binge-watch old movies."

Those were her mom's feel-better remedies for everything from a head cold to heartbreak. "Don't you and Shane need to go home?" Molly blew her nose and tried to pull herself together. "I was planning to go to the hospital to visit Beth and the baby, but I…" She couldn't face Zach and Beth's happiness right now.

"Zach texted. Beth and the baby are being kept in for another day or two, but he's on his way back here to pick up some things for them." Her mom stroked Molly's hair. "If you want, I can make up a care package, and you can come stay with Shane and me for a few days. It'll be quiet, and you can take the time you need to figure out next steps."

"I'd like that." Molly straightened. She'd gotten over Troy once before so she could do it again.

And in the meantime, no matter where she was, she'd find happiness in the life she had and would build, and not let herself imagine what might have been.

"YOU GUYS HAVE worked a bunch of extra hours lately." In the barnyard at the Bitterroot, Troy spoke to his foreman and ranch hands. "Leave early and go spend time with your families or do holiday shopping. You too, Wyatt." Cathy's son was smart, ambitious and reminded Troy a lot of himself at that age. "I'll finish up here."

"Thanks, boss." Wyatt grinned. "I can go home with my mom now instead of her having to come back for me."

"How many times have I told you not to call me boss? It's Troy, remember?" If he ever had a son, he'd like one like Wyatt.

"Yeah... Troy." Wyatt's grin widened, and he ran to the house to find Cathy as the others murmured their thanks and left.

Although it was only midafternoon, daylight was already fading. Day or night didn't matter, though. Troy felt like he'd been living life in a permanent state of gloom ever since he'd ended things with Molly. That would pass. He had to give it time. In the meantime, there was no better remedy for his misery than keeping busy.

He waved at Cathy and Wyatt as they came out of the ranch house and got into Cathy's car, and then he went into the barn. "You'd like to spend time outside, wouldn't you, girl?" He unlatched Cara's stall and led her out, setting his phone on a nearby shelf so it wouldn't fall out of his pocket while he did chores. Then he led Winnie out as well. "You two can keep each other company."

He tried not to think about the irony of them being more sociable than him. He had friends in San Francisco, but apart from Pete, how many true friends did Troy really have? Werner and Mike had the potential to be friends, but building a lasting friendship meant spending time together. In the past week, he'd turned down a dinner invitation from Werner and Nina, and Mike and the guys for beer and pizza while watching hockey and playing pool. He'd had work calls both nights, but could he have rescheduled those to do something fun instead?

Outside the barn, he opened the pasture gate and removed the lead ropes and halters from both horses. "There you go. I won't be long, but you can enjoy some fresh air."

After patting Winnie, who was as friendly as Cara, he let the gate swing shut behind him as his thoughts swirled. He'd spotted Cole in town earlier, but although he'd waved, Cole hadn't returned his greeting. And last night, Troy had found an envelope from Cole in the mailbox at the end of the lane. It had contained a check for part of the money Troy had invested in Cole's stock contracting business, along with a note outlining a repayment schedule for the rest. So far, Cole hadn't replied to Troy's voicemail messages and texts.

On his way back to the barn, he saw a ladder propped against the outside wall to the left of the barn door. It reminded him that he'd asked one of the hands to fix the roof where water had leaked into the tack room. He hadn't followed up on whether the job had been done, and it would only take a minute for him to check it now. He moved the ladder into position by the corner, made sure it was steady and then climbed its metal rungs.

If not for the situation with Molly, Cole could have been a friend as well. And Bryce and Zach. For a while there, Troy had almost felt like part of the Carter family.

Reaching the top of the ladder, he checked the seal. The hand had done a good job. Was that another hole farther along the roof as well?

He missed Molly and her family but...

As he leaned forward, the ladder wobbled, Troy's right foot slipped, and when he grabbed for the ladder, it flew backward through the air, taking him with it.

Troy waved his arms and shouted before he hit the snowy ground with a thud. Pain shot through him, and when he tried to sit up, he gasped and fell back.

"Molly." Something wet trickled along Troy's cheek, and then there was only darkness.

CHAPTER TWENTY

MOLLY AND COLE drove along the highway from High Valley to the ranch. Molly turned off the radio. Her life was hard enough right now without a sappy song about loving and losing reminding her of her troubles.

In only a few days, it seemed as if she'd eaten almost her body weight in ice cream, cookies, chips and chicken noodle soup. She didn't know how she'd make it through Christmas without falling apart.

"I appreciate you coming with me." When Cole glanced at Molly, his face wore the same perpetually worried expression as everyone else in their family. "Thanks to you, for the first time ever I'm finished my holiday shopping before Christmas Eve."

"No problem." She'd wanted to get out of the house, and when Cole had gone to his physical therapy appointment, she'd hung out with Kristi in the kitchen at the Bluebunch. Since Kristi didn't know what had happened with Troy, she'd treated Molly like she always did. More than anything, that "ordinariness" had soothed the ache in Molly's heart. "Mom's going to love that spa gift card and framed family picture you got for her."

"I hope so." Cole's anxious expression eased. "Like you

said, she doesn't need 'stuff.' When Melissa suggested we all wear holiday sweaters and have our picture taken, I thought it sounded fun."

"It's adorable." After she'd helped Cole choose a frame, Molly's eyes had filled with tears as she looked at the sweet photo of the smiling family of three and their dog. She was happy for her brother, but seeing his contentment with Melissa and Skylar was a reminder of what she'd let herself imagine having with Troy.

She looked out the passenger window, afraid Cole would try to comfort her. Although her family was kind, if they kept fussing over her, she'd never be able to move on. Outside the truck, the rolling snow-covered landscape stretched out in an endless vista, and gray clouds scudded close to the horizon. "Looks like another storm coming in."

"Yeah." Cole slowed the vehicle. "Hang on, what are those horses doing running loose?"

"Where? Oh, no." Molly swiveled to see. "That's Cara, Troy's new horse. The other Morgan must be his as well."

Cole pulled over onto the shoulder. "No halters or lead ropes. They must have gotten out. I have a couple of rope halters in back."

"Pull into the laneway," Molly said, gesturing to a wider area with space to park. "While you try to get the horses to trust you, I'll look for a grain bucket and hay or feed." When it came to catching horses, there was nobody better than Cole. "The place looks deserted." Although worried about the animals, Molly let out a sigh of relief at that. She didn't want to bump into their owner.

"I saw Troy in town on my way back to meet you at the Bluebunch." As he drove the truck halfway up the lane, a flush crept across Cole's face. "He waved but I pretended I didn't see him. I couldn't face talking to him and not saying something, since I promised you and Mom I wouldn't."

"I'm glad you avoided him. I'd have done the same." Hopefully by the time Molly had to see Troy again, she could be if not friendly, at least civil. She wrapped her scarf more firmly around her neck, pulled on her hat and mittens and was out of the truck as soon as Cole parked it. "I'll be back in a few minutes."

As she ran up the rest of the lane, she glanced at the horses again. Catching them and getting them to shelter before the storm broke was all that mattered. Most ranchers kept extra buckets near the barn, and there would likely be a feed trough in a nearby pasture.

In her haste, Molly skidded on a patch of ice, staggered but kept her balance. The barn was to her left and the house to her right. No lights shone from any windows, but Troy's truck was parked near the front porch.

"Troy?" Molly shouted into the howling wind, but even if he'd been around it was doubtful he'd have heard her.

In the growing darkness, she walked around the pasture fence where an open gate caught in a snowdrift showed her how Cara and the other horse had escaped.

As she moved forward, an automatic light outside the barn came on to illuminate the barnyard, and Molly gasped. Why was the barn door open? While it would make her job easier because she'd find an ample supply of grain and buckets inside, no rancher or hand would leave without closing up.

"Troy?" she called again, and glanced around. Inside her mittens, she curled her fingers into her clammy palms. Cole was only in the lane. If horse thieves or cattle rustlers were around, she or her brother would have seen people and at least one other vehicle.

Molly took out her phone and found the emergency call key. Maybe she was being paranoid and there was nothing to be afraid of, but it was better to be prepared. She reached the barn door in a few strides but before going inside scanned her surroundings once more.

In the overhead light, something silver gleamed on the

ground around the corner, and the snow was dotted with bright reddish patches. Her heart raced as she hurried to the side of the barn to investigate further.

"Oh, no," she gasped, and with shaking hands used her phone to call an ambulance. She managed to give her location.

Six feet or more beyond the ladder, Troy lay sprawled in deep snow. His right foot was twisted beneath him, and blood trickled from a cut on his head.

"Troy." She touched his cheek, and his eyes flickered open.

"Molly?" His gaze was unfocused, and when he tried to reach out a hand to her, he winced.

"Don't move. An ambulance is on the way." She pulled off her scarf and pressed it to his head while also checking for other injuries. From the angle of his foot, she suspected his ankle was broken and that was only what she could see.

"Oh, Molly." Troy rested his head against her knee. "The ladder...the last thing I remember is slipping. Flying."

"Cole's rounding up the horses." And she was supposed to help him. With the hand that wasn't holding her scarf against Troy's head, she called her brother to tell him what had happened. "He's bringing blankets from his truck." She took off her parka and covered Troy with it, all the while murmuring reassuring words.

He was conscious but only barely, and while she focused on basic, makeshift first aid, she tried not to let herself think about any other possibilities.

"What horses?" Troy's voice was slurred. "I put Cara and Winnie in the pasture. I let everyone go home early." He moaned as she touched his chest around his ribs. "You're my angel."

"No, I'm not. I'm a nurse and you're going to be fine." He likely had some broken ribs, along with his ankle, but right now she was most concerned about what was going on internally and any injuries she couldn't see.

"It was a mistake. A big mistake." He tried to raise himself up and then fell back with a groan. "Tim. I fixed it. Cole can't know. That I love… Don't tell…my mom."

He was clearly mixing up his words. "You can call your mom later. I know you love her and your dad and Sara. Right now you have to stay still."

"But I love…oh, Molly. It was bad."

Troy wasn't making any sense. Had he only cut his head, or did he have a traumatic brain injury? She patted his hand, and it convulsed beneath hers before he muttered something else unintelligible.

"Here." Cole appeared at her side with several blankets and leading Cara and the other horse.

"How did you get them both?" Molly stared at him open-mouthed as she tucked the blankets around Troy, and Cole gave her his own parka.

"Piece of cake. I was a rodeo cowboy, remember? Rounding up horses is all in a day's work." His feeble attempt at joking couldn't mask his clenched fists, tight jaw or the sallowness of his skin. "How bad is it?"

"He'll be okay." *Bad enough.* A person couldn't fall off a ladder and expect to come through unscathed.

"I was there when Dad…" Cole's voice was choked. "He was fine one minute and then the next…the tractor rolled and…"

"I remember." Over the intervening years, Molly had managed to think about her dad without bringing to mind how he'd died, but even before Cole had mentioned the accident, it had come flooding back as she knelt over Troy.

An emergency siren echoed, and she let out a breath. Lights flashing, an ambulance came up the lane and parked, and two paramedics raced toward them.

"I'll see to the horses. If you hadn't…" Cole's face worked as if he held back tears.

"If *we* hadn't." Molly stood and squeezed her brother's arm before greeting the EMTs and giving them a brief rundown of what she thought had happened.

Yet, as she watched them load Troy into the ambulance, she felt stomach-churning fear along with her love for him.

He'd done her a favor by ending their relationship. This kind of accident was why she'd vowed long ago never to marry a rancher, cowboy or any other man who made his living on the land. It was dangerous work, and she didn't need to look any further than her dad to know you could lose someone you loved in an instant.

She'd get over Troy in time. It was for the best that he didn't love her back.

"THERE YOU GO." Two days after his accident, Cathy set a tray with Troy's lunch on the table by the recliner Werner had insisted he borrow. "Are you sure you don't need anything else before I come back at dinner? I still think you'd be better having someone around overnight. The boys and I would be happy to stay here as long as you need us to." She shook her head and frowned. "You look bad."

He *felt* bad, but he could manage the physical injuries and they'd heal in time. The ache in his heart was the bigger problem. "I'll be fine." He tried to smile but even that hurt.

"It's okay to ask for help, you know." Cathy rearranged a quilt that Rosa had made and sent to him over Troy's legs. "Everybody's worried and wants to pitch in to help you. And your mom called me again last night. Your folks want to come here now."

"The ranch hands are looking out for me and Acorn." He didn't want his mom and dad to see him like this. Since he couldn't travel to San Francisco, it would be hard enough having them here for Christmas—and asking about Molly. He patted the dog curled up on his lap. Since he'd gotten home from the hospital, Acorn had hardly left his side. "If I need you or anyone else, I can call." He indicated his phone on the table.

"From now on, keep your phone with you." Cathy gave him a mock glare. "If Molly and Cole hadn't happened along, you'd have frozen to death out there. When the hospital called me, at first I couldn't make sense of what that doctor was saying."

Troy hadn't wanted to worry his folks or Pete, but what did it say about him that the only person he could think of to ask the doctor to call was someone who worked for him? "You've been great, Cathy. Truly. I don't know what I'd do without you. Now go get your boys and take them to their dental appointments."

Cathy picked up her purse and car keys from a table near the living room door. "If you can't reach me, call Werner or Nina. They make such a sweet couple. We're all thrilled for them."

The older couple *were* sweet, but seeing their later-in-life happiness was a poignant reminder of Troy's solitary state.

"I'm surprised Molly hasn't been by. None of the Carters have called either. Joy's usually one of the first to rally around whenever someone's in need." Cathy's eyes narrowed. "Is there something going on I should know about?"

"Molly and I...it's a business relationship. Like with Cole." Troy rubbed Acorn's ears.

"Right." Cathy's laugh was short. "If that's what you want to call it, fine. You can lie to yourself but don't lie to me."

"I don't want to talk about it." Helpless in the snow, fearing he was going to die, he'd faced more than a few hard truths. He loved Molly and he always would, but he'd made a mess of everything. And when she'd appeared at his side, like the angel he needed, he'd been desperate to tell her how he felt but hadn't been able to find the words.

"You don't need to talk to me about it." Cathy put on her winter coat and boots. "You need to talk to her."

"I do, but how?" Abandoning any pretense of hiding his real feelings, Troy picked at the foil cover on the food he had no interest in eating.

"Since you can't go to her, ask her to come here." Cathy's

tone was soothing. "I expect one of those brothers of hers would give you a hand. From what I hear, all three of them made their own mistakes with the women they love."

"I do love Molly." There, he'd said it out loud and it felt good. And somehow he had to win her back.

"I thought so." Cathy nodded. "You're a smart guy, but in love, that can be a disadvantage."

"How so?"

"You're making decisions with your brain instead of your heart. In business you also pay attention to your intuition, right?" She pulled on her fleece hat and mittens.

"Yes, but..." Troy had analyzed the situation from every angle. He'd assembled evidence and made the most logical decision based on the facts. He put a hand to his head as the pieces of a puzzle clicked into place. "You're right." And he was wrong, so wrong, and now he had to fix it.

"If I were you, I'd call Bryce. Cole can be hotheaded. He speaks and acts before he thinks. And since Beth and the baby have only come home from the hospital, Zach's naturally caught up in their new family. But Bryce is levelheaded. Besides, he's just back from his honeymoon. He'll likely be sympathetic to a lovelorn guy in need." Cathy's smile was teasing. "And it's almost Christmas, and that's the season of miracles."

He needed a miracle, that was for sure. "Thanks, Cathy. I owe you." For things no amount of money could repay her for.

She waved a dismissive hand. "What else are friends for? You'd do the same for me."

"Yeah." He'd been so sure making money was the key to security that he hadn't understood what real security meant. It was everything Molly had talked about. Family, friends and a community you could count on. "Go on, I'll be okay."

"You will. Good luck."

As Cathy opened the front door, a gust of cold air came in but instead of making him cold, and despite his bandaged head, it seemed to blow away the last of the cobwebs that had muddled Troy's thinking for weeks.

His lunch could wait. Instead, he picked up his phone and scrolled to Bryce's number.

"Troy? What's up?" When he answered, Bryce's voice was cool.

Molly's brother had only said a few words, and Troy was already sweating. "It's…" He'd learned in business that with certain people it was best to be direct. Bryce seemed like one of them, and Troy sensed the guy didn't like having his time wasted. "It's about Molly. I need to talk to her and—"

"Why do you think my sister will want to talk to you?" Although Bryce was polite, he cut straight to the point too.

"She probably won't but… I love her, and I made a big mistake. I need to explain but I'm stuck at my house. I have a fractured ankle and a couple of broken ribs, stitches in my head and bruises all over. I can't drive." He could barely make it to the bathroom without help. But he didn't have a brain injury or paralysis and he was still alive. All things considered, he had to look on the bright side. "I won't hurt her again, I promise." His voice cracked, and Troy tried to cover it with a cough. Which was a mistake because it hurt his ribs.

Bryce exhaled and silence hung between them for several seconds. "I want Molly to be happy and despite everything, you seem like a good guy. So, okay. What do you need?"

"If you can get Molly to my place, I'll do the rest."

It wouldn't be fancy, but it would be honest and heartfelt. Troy could only hope that would be enough.

CHAPTER TWENTY-ONE

"I'LL BE BACK in ten minutes. Promise you won't leave? And if I don't come back, you'll come in and get me?" Standing outside Troy's front door, Molly glanced at her brother who'd parked his truck at the foot of the porch steps. "This whole thing also stays between the two of us, right?" She'd gotten herself somewhat back together and didn't need the rest of the family chipping in to console her or even worse, offer advice.

"I promise, and of course I won't tell anyone. Not even Carrie." Bryce leaned across the truck to speak to Molly through the half-open window. "For what it's worth, Troy sounded really sincere."

He'd sounded sincere before he'd broken up with her. He was also a business whiz. He must be used to telling people what they wanted to hear. Molly took a deep breath and went into the house through the unlocked door.

"Molly? Is that you?" Troy's voice reached her from a room off the main hall.

"Yes." She took off her winter boots but left her coat on so she could make a quick getaway. "Why did you want to see me? And why couldn't you say whatever you need to over the phone?" Molly hovered inside what turned out to be the living room door, keeping a good fifteen feet between her and

Troy, who sat in one corner in a dark brown recliner with Acorn on his lap.

His face was pale and from the cast that covered most of his right foot to the surgical dressing on his head, he must be battered, bruised and in pain. But he was still the man she'd foolishly fallen in love with. The nurse in her wanted to assess his condition and comfort and care. The woman, however, tried to harden her heart.

"You could hang up on me on the phone." His smile was awkward, and he flinched as if even that minor movement hurt. "As for wanting to see you? I've missed you, Molly, and I had to apologize in person."

"Apologize?" Her stomach rolled and her breath quivered.

"Yes. Won't you sit down?" He gestured to a cozy armchair upholstered in a cheerful red plaid near the fireplace. "Or take the sofa. You picked it out with me. I guess we should have bought a recliner too. Since I can't make it upstairs to my bedroom, this chair is on loan from Werner."

Molly sat on the edge of the chair. If she'd had a real relationship with Troy, she'd have visited his house before. Instead, she was seeing it as a stranger. The living room was welcoming, though, and from the basket of red and white flowers on a shelf by the window to the comfortable furniture and Western-themed art, it felt homey.

From Troy's lap, Acorn's soft, brown eyes were solemn as she stared at Molly.

"As you can see, I'm not very mobile."

"Yes." She clasped her hands so he wouldn't see them shake.

"Before I say anything else, I want to thank you. You and Cole saved my life." Troy's voice was low and husky with an intimacy that made her pulse race.

"Anyone would have done the same." The trembling in her hands increased. Even if she and Troy weren't together, Molly didn't want to think about a world without him in it.

"Maybe, but when you showed up, at first I assumed I'd

imagined you. I thought you were an angel." He pulled at the collar of his shirt, which was a dark blue flannel one Molly hadn't seen before.

"So you said." She kept her voice neutral. He'd said a lot of other things lying in the snow by the barn as well, but since none of them had made sense, she hadn't let herself dwell on them.

"You see, the thing is…" He hesitated and patted Acorn who snuggled closer into the curve of his arm. "Even before I fell off that ladder, I wasn't happy, but I couldn't figure out why. Now I know it's because I sent you away. I tossed away what we had like it didn't matter when it mattered more than anything, at least to me. I'm sorry for that and a bunch of other things."

Molly stilled and pressed her lips together.

He shifted on the recliner, and she resisted the urge to go over to him and rearrange the pillows that propped up his hurt ankle. "Because of how I grew up, I've always needed to feel secure. Making money gave me that security so that's why I focused on it. But in the last few days, what with the accident, and now being stuck here hardly able to do anything for myself, it's shown me that real security isn't found in making money at all."

"Oh?" Her heart raced, and her insides felt like a washing machine on the spin cycle.

"No, what's truly important is everything you said by the creek that day I…we… Anyway, it's being part of a close-knit community. Being supported by family and friends who are there for you because they care and don't expect to be paid. And…" He hesitated again, and in the depths of his eyes Molly saw something she thought she'd lost forever. "It's love. I love you, Molly. I did before and I do now. Even when we were apart, I tried to move on, but my heart never forgot you. The love and security I really need are with you."

"I... You..." She brushed away unexpected tears. "I need that with you. I love you too, but—"

"Wait. I have more to say, and I...you might not love me after I tell you." His mouth twisted.

"Go on." Molly waited and time slowed, making her hyper-aware of the warmth that flooded through her body. All she wanted was to go to Troy, wrap her arms around him and say nothing else mattered. Whatever was troubling him, they'd figure it out together. However, a sixth sense told her he needed to be on his own right now.

"I made another mistake. Not with you but it could have hurt you, or rather Cole and his business. I fixed it, and I didn't want to tell you, but you need to know." A red flush spread across Troy's cheeks. "A project Pete and I are currently backing... I didn't check something as thoroughly as I should have and so Pete and I lost money I'd counted on earning for Cole's investment. I took responsibility and the financial hit personally. Pete wasn't mad at me, but I was sure mad at myself." He gulped. "I hadn't been paying as much attention to work as I should have been, and at the time I thought it was because of my relationship with you. That's why I said we couldn't be together. I thought I couldn't let myself be distracted by you or anyone else or I'd lose that security money gave me." He bent his head, and his voice shook. "I was wrong, Molly, and I hope you can forgive me."

"Of course, I can. You made a mistake. That makes you human." She couldn't sit on the other side of the room any longer, so she went to his side and knelt by his chair. "I love you and part of loving someone is being there for them in good times and bad. It's loving every part of them and recognizing we're all imperfect."

"I don't deserve you." He reached for her, and Molly eased carefully into his open arms. For the first time ever, she saw the real Troy, faults and all, and it only made her love him more.

"Well, that could be a problem because I'm not going anywhere." She laughed through her tears. "I doubted you and I was wrong. You're a good man and sincere." The kind she needed in her life for always.

"But your job...you can't sacrifice your career for me. I won't let you." He moved back and winced. "My ribs, I..."

"You poor thing." Molly gave his arm a gentle pat as she extricated herself from his embrace. "You've been honest with me, so now I need to be honest with you." As she looked into Troy's eyes, she saw all the love and trust she'd ever need but, as he'd done, she had to take this last step alone—before what she hoped would be a lifetime together.

"Okay." He patted Acorn, and she put one hand over his. "I love you and that won't ever change but...." She took a deep breath.

This was it. No more secrets between them, ever.

TROY STUDIED MOLLY'S bent head. He'd never known or even imagined having a love like the one he had for her, and he wanted to spend the rest of his life showing her how much she meant to him. She'd accepted him, all of him, and in her he'd found a partner who'd be with him for himself, not what he could buy her.

"It's okay, whatever you want to tell me." He clasped her cold hand, giving the unspoken acceptance and reassurance she'd given him.

She finally raised her head, and he wanted to see those loving blue eyes looking at him until he took his last breath. As if he was the most important person in her world, and she trusted him with her heart and soul. In that moment, he promised himself he'd never take that trust for granted or do anything to make this woman who was his world ever think any less of him.

"I'll start with my job." She sat on a nearby footstool and gave him the ghost of a smile. "I love nursing, and I always thought my goal was a research position in a big city. But the

Subscribe and fall in love with a Mills & Boon series today!

You'll be among the first to read stories delivered to your door monthly and enjoy great savings.

MILLS & BOON